Gunboat and Gun-runner

Also from Westphalia Press
westphaliapress.org

Gunboat and Gun-runner

by T.T. Jeans

with a new introduction
by Paul Rich

WESTPHALIA PRESS
An imprint of Policy Studies Organization

Gunboat and Gun-runner

Westphalia Press
An imprint of Policy Studies Organization
1527 New Hampshire Ave., NW
Washington, D.C. 20036
dgutierrezs@ipsonet.org

ISBN-13: 978-1935907404
ISBN-10: 1935907409

Cover design by Taillefer Long at Illuminated Stories:
www.illuminatedstories.com

Updated material and comments on this edition
can be found at the Westphalia Press website:
www.westphaliapress.org

This edition is dedicated to
William Morris of the Next Century Foundation,
remarkable scholar of the Arab world,
its history, and its nuances.

Still Smuggling in Turbulent Seas

Unlike some books, this one is by someone who had ample experience with the adventures it relates. Surgeon Rear-Admiral Thomas Tendron Jeans RN (1871-1938) entered the Royal Navy in 1894 and retired in 1926. He was in the South African war of 1899-1900, and World War I serving in the Dardanelles and Suez Canal actions. He was made Commander of the Order of St. Michael and St. George by King George V in 1919.

His first book was as co-author of Naval Brigades in the South African War, 1899-1900. He was also a writer of sea life in the Navy, the last being published in 1913. He discovered he had a facility for writing adventure stories and produced *Midshipman Glover* (1905, 1909), *John Graham* (1913), *A Naval Venture* (1917), and *On Foreign Service, or The Santa Cruz Revolution* (1920). In 1927 he authored what I consider his most interesting work and certainly astoundingly still pertinent, *Gunboat and Gun-runner.*

G

In that same year, he complains in his autobiography, *Reminiscences Of A Naval Surgeon*, that boys' books were largely lacking in real naval background. This he can be said to have remedied. In *Midshipman*, the British subdue pirates in the South China Sea. In *On Foreign Service* the Royal Navy puts an end to South American despots (shades of the later Falkland War!). In *Gunboat and Gun-runner,* Iran is smuggling to troublemakers who are trying to upset Middle Eastern regimes. *Gunboat* ends with the promise of an invasion of Afghanistan, to teach the brutes a lesson!

So here we are, getting along in the 21st century, and Admiral Jeans is still right, as he notes in his own preface, that the volume is free of improbabilities. Where we might part company is over whether given modern technology these incursions are still a "ripping show."

Paul Rich
Garfield House, Washington

H

Gunboat and Gun-runner

A Tale of the Persian Gulf

BY

SURGEON REAR-ADMIRAL T. T. JEANS,
C.M.G., R.N.

Author of " John Graham, Sub-Lieutenant R.N."
"On Foreign Service" " Ford of H.M.S. *Vigilant*"
&c.

Illustrated by C. M. Padday

BLACKIE & SON LIMITED
LONDON AND GLASGOW

C.697

THE *BUNDER ABBAS* COMES UPON A LARGE ARAB DHOW IN THE
VERY ACT OF LANDING GUNS

Page 105   *Frontispiece*

Preface

For many years the fierce, unruly tribes beyond the north-west frontier of India have only been able to obtain rifles from the Arabian coast. Arab dhows bring them across the Persian Gulf and adjacent waters, and caravans of camels convey them to their destination through the mountain passes of Baluchistan.

Ships of the Royal Navy and the Royal Indian Marine, armed launches manned by officers and men lent from the Royal Navy, and ships' armed cutters cruise and patrol these waters from one year's end to another, overhauling dhows, landing men to search villages suspected of concealing arms, and ceaselessly striving to put a stop to this trade.

My story describes the conditions of service in one of these armed launches, and is based on actual occurrences which took place some ten years ago. Most of the incidents have been described to me by participators in them. The proof-sheets have also been revised by officers who have themselves taken part, during more recent years, in the suppression of "gun-running".

As a result, the story is, I trust, free from errors and improbabilities.

T. T. JEANS,

Surgeon Rear-Admiral, Royal Navy.

Contents

Illustrations

GUNBOAT AND GUN-RUNNER

CHAPTER I

A Splendid Appointment

At the time this yarn commences I was a lieutenant of four years' seniority, a "watchkeeper" aboard H.M.S. *Russell*, longing earnestly to see the world, but with no probable prospect of my desires being realized.

I had been serving in the Channel and Atlantic Fleets, continuously, for seven years—appointed from one ship to another, from a battleship to a destroyer, from a destroyer to an armoured cruiser, and from her to the *Russell*. In fact, I began to wonder whether my whole naval career was to be spent plodding round the British Islands, and the limits of my world were to be bounded by an occasional view of the coast of France, and a still more infrequent sight of the rugged headlands of Spain.

Then, by a lucky stroke of good fortune, my chance did at last come.

I happened to be on forty-eight hours' leave in

London, and at my club, the "Junior", met a captain under whom I had served a year or two previously.

We talked about our former ship, and I told him how tired I was of sticking at home, and how anxious I was to see some foreign service. He jerked out, in the abrupt way he had: "Why, man, clear out! —get along to the Admiralty!—full speed!—off you go! I was talking to the Second Sea Lord not half an hour ago, and he'd just heard that a lieutenant was wanted for the Persian Gulf. Give him my card. Why, bless my rags, I haven't one!" and he scribbled his name on the back of a club envelope and hustled me out.

I found myself jumping into a hansom (there were no taxis available then as now) and driving to the Admiralty before I fully realized what I was about to do.

"No, the Second Sea Lord won't see nobody," a porter at the Admiralty told me; adding, mysteriously: "The First Lord 'as just a-been an' sent for him. You 'ad better see Mr. Copeland, 'is sec-re-tary."

I always feel overawed at the Admiralty—merely being in the same building with their "Lordships" is enough to overawe any humble lieutenant—so I meekly followed the porter into a waiting-room, pacing up and down restlessly till he came back again, beckoning me with a confidential air. "'E'll see you, if you step this way. 'E is in a middling good temper this morning—ain't 'ad many to worry 'im."

A Splendid Appointment

My interview with Mr. Copeland was short and sharp.

"What do you want?" he said curtly, more or less as if I was a pickpocket or a beggar asking for a penny.

"I hear there's a vacancy for a lieutenant in the Persian Gulf. I'm Martin—Paul Reginald Martin of the *Russell*, four years' seniority next May—and I want to go there. My late captain gave me this for the Second Sea Lord;" and I handed him the envelope with the pencil note: "Give this chap the job if you can", and his signature.

The secretary glanced at it, threw it on his desk, and looked at me suspiciously. "Yes, yes! I don't know how he came to hear of it. Collingwood, of the *Bunder Abbas*, has died of sunstroke. Quite right! quite right! I'll put your name down for her —if you wish."

"Please!" I said.

"Do you know what the job is?" he asked, as if, did I know, I should not be so keen to go.

"Not in the least," I answered; "and I don't mind, so long as I can get abroad and out of the Channel Fleet."

He smiled unpleasantly. "It's a patrolling job, and a lonely one."

He said this as though—officially—he ought to warn me, though—individually—he didn't care a button whether I went or not.

That gave me some idea of the job.

"The gunner's gone mad too. We'll have to send another out, I suppose—confound him!"

I could not help smiling at the idea of a mad gunner being left there.

He cut my smile short with a sharp: "I'll put your name down.   Good morning!"

I backed clumsily out of the door.

"What's the *Bunder Abbas*?" I asked the porter outside.

"The *Bunder Habbas*!" he corrected me, repeating the name to give himself time to think.

"Something in the Persian Gulf?" I said, to aid his memory.

But he didn't know—none of the other porters knew; so he rang up some mysterious individual on the telephone.

"There's a gen'l'man 'ere wants to know what the *Bunder Habbas* his.   *Habbas—Bunder Habbas*—hout in the Persian Gulf."

He had a slight argument about pronunciation and spelling, and then turned to me triumphantly.   "She's a harmed launch, sir, that's what she his, a-looking out to stop them Arabs a-gun-running," and hastened to answer a bell, pocketing the half-crown I gave him.

I hurried away down the corridor, and was so excited that I did not notice my former captain until he tapped me on the shoulder.

"I've just come round," he said; "will see the Second Sea Lord myself—put in a word for you—thought I might fix it up at once—good luck to you if you get it."

"Thank you very much, sir," I said gratefully, and hurried out into Whitehall.

"Armed launch!   Skipper of an armed launch—

Collingwood dead of sunstroke—gunner gone mad," and I grinned to myself and walked along like a bird.

"Fancy getting away from all this!" I thought, and looked round at the babel of traffic and the throngs of people. Fancy getting away from the Channel Fleet for a time! I thought of my ship, the *Russell*, lying under Portland Bill, with other huge grey monsters; and thought of the tense readiness for war aboard them, and the strain of it, month after month. In a few weeks, with luck, I might be three thousand miles away, patrolling the Persian Gulf— free as air — with a good launch under me, and probably a 4.7-inch gun in her bows, ready to tackle any gun-running Arab dhow which came along. Prize money, too—there'd be a chance of that as well.

It was grand.

Collingwood, poor old Collingwood — I'd known him in the *Britannia*—dead of sunstroke, and the gunner gone mad! That didn't sound as if the job was exactly a bed of roses. But Copeland had put my name down—the die was cast; I didn't mind if the whole crew had died of sunstroke and plague combined. I rather hoped that they had, and that any other chap who applied for the *Bunder Abbas* would —well—feel a little less keen about her when he heard.

I didn't notice the rain or the mud splashed on my trousers from the roadway. I could have whooped with joy.

All these silly clothes my tailor bothered to make tight here or loose there, to show more or show less of the waistcoat, as silly fashion changed—why, with luck, in a month's time, a pair of flannel trousers and a cricket shirt would be all the wardrobe I should want. I'd be my own skipper, with a dozen blue-jackets, and a stout launch under us; that 4.7-inch gun — or perhaps it would be a twelve-pounder—shining in the bows under the awning. Wouldn't it shine, too! There'd be nothing much else to do but burnish it, and burnished it should be till I could shave by it.

All that afternoon I waited patiently at the club for the evening paper, and directly the waiter brought it into the smoking-room I pounced on it.

Sure enough, under "Naval Appointments" was my name—"Paul R. Martin appointed *Intrepid*" (she was one of the cruisers on the East Indies Station) "for armed launch *Bunder Abbas*".

I gave a shout of delight, which rather startled some old fogies there; and a man sitting near—a naval doctor whom I knew slightly—laughed at me, wanting to know what was the matter.

I pointed out the appointment.

"Look at that! Isn't that grand?"

"*Bunder Abbas*," he said, as we lay back in the luxurious chairs—they really did feel comfortable now that I was going out to the waste parts of the world. "That was Collingwood's launch. What's become of him?"

"Died of sunstroke," I told him.

"Really, now?" the doctor went on; "he's only been there three months. I knew him slightly; he relieved a chap who had beri-beri, or one of those

funny tropical diseases—sometimes you swell, sometimes you do the other thing. I forget now which he
did before he was invalided home. I did hear; it was
quite interesting. So you're off there? Well, good
luck! Are the 'footer' results in that paper?

"D'you want any tips for the Persian Gulf?" he
asked presently, when he had finished reading the
football news. "Whatever you like to eat, don't
eat it. (You can't get it, so you needn't bother to
remember that tip.) And if you want gin or whisky,
or any comforts like that, chuck them over the side:
they may kill the sharks; they won't kill you. In
fact, my dear chap, whatever you like doing and
want to do, there's only one tip to remember if you
want to keep fit—don't do it!

"If you get beri-beri," he called after me as I fled,
"you might let me know whether you swell or do the
other thing."

I packed my bag, not in the least disturbed by anyone's gloomy remarks, and went back to my ship at
Portland.

My orders came next day.

I was to take passage in a P. & O. mail steamer,
sailing in twelve days' time (a luxury I never expected), and join the *Intrepid* at Aden, where further
orders would be given me.

A fortnight later I was tumbling and churning
through the "Bay" in the P. & O. *Java*, as happy
as a king, without a care in the world.

A lieutenant named Anderson shared my cabin.
He was going out to join the *Intrepid* as one of her
watchkeepers. As, but for him, I should probably

never have survived to write the account of what happened to us later on, I will give an idea of what kind of chap he was. First of all, he was known to his chums as " The Baron " or as " Baron Popple Opstein ", though why these nicknames ever stuck to him I don't know.

He was a great lumbering, clumsy giant, with a long red face, a big hooked nose, and a large mouth, always smiling, and showing the whitest set of teeth I have ever seen. He had laughing blue eyes, which saw everything except people's faults, and a mop of yellow, silk-coloured hair which grew down his great red forehead in a quaint triangular patch pointing to his nose. His whole face beamed good humour and kindliness; he was the simplest, happiest soul alive—one of those men with whom it is good to live. He never did much talking, and never wanted anyone to talk much to him; but would sit smoking his old, disgracefully charred pipe, and beam by the hour, just happy to have the dancing sea under his feet and the fresh salt air in his lungs. He really was a splendid-looking fellow, but by some odd twist in his mind imagined he was ugly. This made him rather retiring and bashful. He would sooner try to stop a mad dog than be introduced to a lady. " " My dear old chap," he would say, if I wanted to introduce him to one of the lady passengers, " what on earth can I talk to her about? She doesn't want to hear about scrubbing hammocks, or the gunnery manual. I can't think of anything else to talk about."

The result was that we both kept pretty much to ourselves, and amused ourselves watching the others.

There was a major on board going out to India—a fussy, conceited individual who imagined that all the ladies must be head over heels in love with him. He tried to patronize us, but we gave him the cold shoulder, and so did a little pale-faced, rather nice-looking girl about twenty-two, with hair the very same shade as the Baron's. She was not English—I could tell that by the way she talked—and she kept almost entirely to herself. I never spoke to her during the voyage, but once I overheard her snub the major in broken English, in the most deliberate, delightful manner, and as he went away, with a silly expression on his face, our eyes met. There was such an irresistibly humorous twinkle in hers that I smiled too—I really could not help it. At that her smile died away, as if ashamed of itself, her pale face flushed, and I followed the major, feeling like a naughty boy who had been caught prying.

At Port Said we picked up Mr. Thomas Scarlett—Gunner, R.N.—serving in the *Jason*, which was doing guardship there.

I had seen his appointment to the *Bunder Abbas* in the newspapers, and, as we should have to live together for the next two years, I was anxious to know what manner of man he was.

He certainly looked a queer chap, tall and thin, with stooping shoulders, bushy black eyebrows meeting across his forehead, two piercing black eyes deeply sunk beneath them, a beaked nose over very thin tight lips, and the blackest of hair, moustache, and pointed beard. He looked very much like a vulture, with his long thin neck stretching out from a low collar, much too large for him. When he talked, the words tumbled out, one after the other, so quickly that, until one became used to him, it was difficult to understand what he said.

We soon found out that he had been in the Persian Gulf many times in the course of the last few years, so Baron Popple Opstein and I used to take him along to our special corner on deck, and ask him questions. He gave us the impression that he did not wish to go out there again, and whenever he talked of the Persian Gulf and of his former experiences there he seemed nervous and very ill at ease. But, once we made him talk, his stories of pirates, pearl-fishers, slavers, and gun-runners were as absorbing as one could wish. Old Popple Opstein's face would grow purple with excitement. Mr. Scarlett, too, would often work himself into a great pitch of vehemence as he told some especially thrilling yarn.

"You might be an Arab yourself," I said one night, when he had brought a story to a climax, leaving us breathless and fascinated with his glowing, fiery description.

"I am almost, sir," he said. "My father was the constable of the Residency at Bushire, and my mother was half-Arab."

That explained his dark complexion, and why, in the middle of a yarn, he would often slide off his chair and sit Moorish fashion—cross-legged. He could always talk more easily in that attitude.

Ever since he had joined the Navy he had served, off and on, in the East, his knowledge of all the languages and different dialects of those parts, picked up when he was a boy, being so useful.

One night, four days out from Suez, we were making him tell us all he knew about gun-running. It was very warm, damp, and unpleasant, so he took off his coat. In doing so he happened to pull the shirt sleeve of his left arm above his elbow. By the light of a lantern overhead we saw something glittering round his arm. My chum peered forward to look at it, but the gunner hastily pulled his sleeve down.

"What the dickens is that?" we both asked.

First glancing fore and aft, to see that no one was near, he very reluctantly pulled up his sleeve.

He held his arm so that the lantern light fell upon it, and we saw that the thing round his arm was a small snake, marvellously enamelled—a cobra it was. The joints, even each separate scale, seemed flexible, and as he worked his muscles underneath it the snake seemed to cling more tightly to his skin, in the most horribly realistic fashion. Two greenish-tinged opal eyes blinked at us as the light overhead flickered in them.

The Baron leant forward to touch it, but Mr. Scarlett, with a sudden look of horror, shot out his right hand and clutched the Baron's hand so violently that he cried out.

"Don't touch it, sir! For God's sake, don't touch it. There's poison enough in that thing to kill a dozen men!" he gasped fiercely.

"What is it—what do you mean? Tell us!" we cried.

Some passengers coming along the deck, he instantly covered it with his sleeve.

"I generally wear a bandage over it," he said nervously. "The night was so hot that I took it off."

"Well, tell us about it," we urged him. "Where did you get it?"

"Jassim gave it to me," Mr. Scarlett answered, his black eyes burning strangely as he looked round to see that no one could overhear him. "I'll tell you when and how that snake came here. It's a long story—and a sad one. When you have heard it you will know why I do not want to go back to the Persian Gulf. But, for God's sake, sirs, don't ever mention it to a soul!"

We promised—we would have promised anything to learn its story.

CHAPTER II

The Story of the " Twin Death "

" It was nearly thirty years ago when I first saw that bracelet," Mr. Scarlett began in a strained voice. "I was only a boy then. It was brought to my father's house, at Bushire, by a Banyan jeweller—a friend of his—who showed it to him as one of the most marvellous and curious pieces of workmanship in the East. I remember how frightened I was to hear the stories he told of it, and to see them examining it.

"When the jeweller had gone, my father, who knew its history, told me that, when it was pulled off the arm which wore it, it would writhe and strike with the poisoned fangs in its head, and kill both the wearer and the person who tore it off.

"There is an Arab song, nearly two hundred years old, which sings of it. The song is about the woman who first wore it. She was the favourite wife of a murdered Sultan of Khamia, and fell alive into the hands of his Persian conqueror. He wanted to marry her because she was so beautiful, and she dared him, if he would win her, to tear the bracelet off her arm—dared him in front of his Court—and he was so mad with love that he did so, although he knew what would happen. The snake struck them both, and they died. In that Arab song she is supposed to sing several verses after the fangs struck her, but," Mr. Scarlett's voice trembled hoarsely, " I know that she had not time."

"You don't mean to tell us that this is the same one?" the Baron asked breathlessly.

" It is, sir. I wish it wasn't."

" But how did you get it?" he asked again.

" Let the gunner spin his yarn," I told him impatiently.

" Well," he went on, " it has always been worn by the chief wife of the Sultan of Khamia. It is her privilege to be the only wife who follows her husband at his death. She had to kill herself by tearing it off her own arm, and if her courage failed her a slave stood by to do it, and the two would die. The slave was not likely to fail her, for to die by 'the twin death' was supposed to be a sure way of attaining Paradise, and not many slaves ever thought that they would have the chance to get there.

"Some of this my father told me, and the rest, and many other things besides, I learnt afterwards from the Arabs up and down the coast.

" I saw it next eight or nine years afterwards. I was an ordinary seaman in a gunboat lying off Muscat, and, happening to be ashore one afternoon, with nothing to do, I noticed that there was quite a crowd of natives gathered on the shore.

" They told me that the Sultan of Khamia was just going to embark on his way to Mecca, so I stopped to see him, knowing that he was the worst brigand

and pirate in the whole of the Gulf, and wishing to see what kind of chap he was.

"Presently he came down with a crowd of attendants to guard him—a fine-looking fellow he was—and after him followed some hooded cages or palanquins. Inside these, hidden from view, were, I knew, his favourite wives, accompanying him as far as Jeddah. Out of the first stretched a beautiful arm, and on it was that snake bracelet.

"I half expected to see it, and recognized it at once. You should have seen that crowd of natives give way and fall back. Everyone knew what it was, and what it meant. They edged away as if it was the devil himself.

"The closed cages were taken on board a lighter; the lighter was towed out to a little steamer rolling in the mouth of the harbour between the two old Portuguese forts, and I soon forgot all about the bracelet.

"Five years afterwards fate brought me to the Gulf again. I was a petty officer in the gunboat *Pigeon* then, and everywhere we went we heard the name of Jassim, the now Khan of Khamia—the absolute despot of the south-western part of the Persian Gulf, the head of the Jowassim tribes of slavers and pirates, and the terror of the seas. Not a dhow dared leave any port without first paying tribute to him, and the tales of his atrocities made our blood boil with rage; because he was not satisfied with being master of the Gulf, but he'd swoop down on coast towns, demand tribute from them, and, if there was any resistance—even hesitation in paying—he would kill every man, woman, and child in ways so callously brutal that you could not imagine a human being capable of inventing them.

" His latest exploit had been to capture the whole fleet of pearl-fishing dhows and trading baggalows[1] inside Muscat harbour.   He filled them with his rascally followers — Bedouins chiefly — and thought himself strong enough to tackle the English.

" We soon heard that he was preparing to seize the pearl-fishing dhows which were then fitting out at Bahroin—under the English flag and the English guns of the fort there—to sail for the pearl banks, down south.

" The *Pigeon* and the old *Sphinx* were therefore ordered to search for Mr. Jassim and teach him a lesson.

" Well, after dodging in and out of the bays in that rocky coast, shoving our nose in, finding nothing, and shunting out again, we found him, one morning, anchored at the head of a shallow bay with all his fleet.

" Four hundred and twenty-two dhows we counted, their sloping masts and yards showing up like a forest against the shore.   Every one of them was flaunting the red flag with a white border, the flag of the Jowassims.   The whole place was a-flutter with them.

" At the top of the bay Jassim had built himself a fort, and lived there, we found out afterwards, in great style, with his harem, sheikhs' sons to wait on him, gold plates to eat off, and everything simply tiptop.

" Four hundred odd dhows were there, manned for

---

[1] Baggalow=large ocean-going dhow.

the most part by dare-devil Bedouins, with a fair sprinkling of Beni Ghazril, Ballash, and Ahmed tribes—all low-caste tribes not too keen on fighting. Armed they were with old smooth bores—nine-pounders, there or thereabouts—and the little *Pigeon* was equal to taking on the lot if she could only have fetched in close enough; which she couldn't, as she drew too much water.   We had to anchor five miles away from these dhows—five miles if a yard.

"Out came a sheikh or a khan—some big swell—to say that Jassim was only waiting for a change of wind to come out and eat us up.   As it was blowing a steady shamel (you two gentlemen will know what that is before you've been out here long), blowing right into the bay, and not likely to ease down for two or three days, we didn't trouble about them try-ing to escape.   Well, the skipper sent that sheikh chap back with a flea in his ear, and presently Jassim himself came along in a grand barge, flying the Turkish flag—like his cheek!—and as cool as any-thing comes up the side and gives our skipper two hours to clear out of it.

"The cheek of the man amused the skipper, who merely took him aft into his cabin, kept him there for two hours, talking and drinking coffee, showed him his watch and that the two hours had gone by, told him he would have hanged him had he not been flying the Turkish flag, and sent him back to his fleet.

"The tide rising presently, we chanced our luck and moved in a bit closer.   Directly we moved, those dhows, hundreds of them, let rip at us with their old pop-guns, the shot plunking into the water half-way, and not even the 'ricos' reaching us.

"That was just what the skipper was waiting for. He opened fire with our four-inch guns, keeping it up from four o'clock that afternoon till six, and setting a good many of the dhows on fire. Just before the sun went down, along came the old *Sphinx*, paddling furiously, and chipped in with her old-fashioned guns, till neither of us could see a thing to aim at, except flames occasionally. The whole bay was a mass of smoke from the dhows we had set on fire with our shells.

"It was a fine sight as the sun set behind the great mountains inshore, and the dark shadows of them came racing across the plain and the harbour, showing up the flames still more brightly.

"If you ever cruise along that coast don't miss that sight—the sight of those shadows as the sun sinks behind the mountains," Mr. Scarlett interrupted his yarn to tell us.

"Well, all that night we and the *Sphinx* fired occasionally to keep the Arabs' nerves on edge, and made all ready to send in every boat we possessed, at daybreak, to see what we could do.

"That was the longest day's work I ever did, and the worst—the worst," Mr. Scarlett hissed out, apparently waking up and altering his voice, as if he had been somebody else telling the yarn before, or as if he had suddenly turned over a fresh page in a book he was reading, remembered the terrible ending, and wanted to shut it up.

The Baron and I almost jumped out of our chairs.

" Yes, the worst. My God! it was the worst."
He jumped to his feet, looked ashamed of himself, sat
down, and went on to tell us in a strained voice, as
though the ending was too terrible, how the crews of
the *Pigeon* and *Sphinx* had pulled ashore in their
boats, like midges round a horde of elephants. He
said that two of the bigger dhows, placed end on end,
would be nearly as big as the *Victory*.

We did not believe him.

He told us how, as one boat would clap alongside
a huge towering dhow, her demoralized crew would
clamber down the other side to their boats or jump
overboard. The bluejackets had brought tins of
paraffin, with which they set on fire each dhow they
boarded, adding still further to the terror and disorder,
until the crews of all those four hundred odd junks
abandoned them and clustered at the edge of the
shore, behind the walls of Jassim's fort, shouting
bravely and shooting off their crazy rifles in de-
fiance.

So the bluejackets left off their work of destruction,
the boats pulled ashore together, the men wading
as soon as their keels grated on the beach, whilst the
Nordenfeldts and Gardner guns in their bows fired
point-blank into the demoralized crowd of Arab scum.
There must have been fifteen thousand of them on the
beach; but panic broke out among them, and they
melted away from the shore and from the fort, scurrying away inland in front of that handful of bluejackets
until they had taken refuge in the defiles and crevasses
of those barren mountains, where (as Mr. Scarlett told
us) you could hardly believe it possible for a goat to

live, but where they sought shelter like frightened sheep.

When he had come to this point Mr. Scarlett paused a little, as if he was reluctant to go on. Then he started again hurriedly:

"And we came back, very slowly back, panting, our feet red-hot and our tongues swollen with thirst, the blazing sun on our backs. And we found Jassim squatting on his prayer mat on the sloping shore, his back turned to the sea and his burning ships, his face turned to the sun.

"A woman crouched at his feet.

"These two were alone, the only living things there; no other human being had stayed with him; she alone of all his harem and his people remained to share his fate. I was sent for to act as interpreter; and our skipper—a tender-hearted man—had pity on Jassim now that his power was absolutely broken, and gave him the choice of coming on board or staying where he was. Jassim chose to stay, answering proudly and defiantly, as though he was still lord of a powerful fleet, or as though his spirit was not broken. Then it was that I saw this hateful snake for the third time—it was on that woman's arm."

Mr. Scarlett's voice began to tremble, and as he coiled cross-legged on the deck, and put his hands to his forehead, we could see his dark, burning eyes gazing outboard, across the deck and the deck rails, to where the sea and the blackness of the night sky met each other, a dark rim beyond the moonlit sea surrounding the ship. His face was haggard and drawn, as if he saw what he was about to tell us.

"Yes, he was there! Jassim was there, his head bowed beneath a coarse burnous[1]; and whilst the rest of us went away to loot the fort and destroy the guns, a seaman and myself were left as guard on those two.

"I spoke to him in his own tongue, told him to cheer up, that his luck was 'out' now, but that it was fate, and a better time would come. He seemed not to hear; he just sat gazing at the sun as it sank lower and lower towards the rim of the mountains, where all his men had disappeared; and his wife crouched moaning before him, putting a hand out now and again to touch him, just to remind him that she was there and suffering too. Presently she bared her left arm, and moaned to him not to allow himself to fall into the hands of the infidel, but to seek Paradise and take her with him, holding out her arm with the snake coiled round it, imploring him to pull it off and set them both free.

"Jassim never answered her, never looked down at her, never moved a muscle of his face, and never looked at that bracelet.

"But the sight of it was too much for the seaman left on guard. Poor fool! he thought it would be a fine curio, and before I could stop him he strode forward, bent down, and seized it.

"The woman gave one shriek of agony as he pulled it from her arm, and with an oath I saw him throw it down in the white sand, where it coiled and writhed, whilst he looked at the back of his hand and wiped away two tiny spots of blood.

[1] Burnous = loose Arab cloak.

"'Suck them, for God's sake, suck them! The thing's poisoned!' I yelled, and, springing to the woman, bent down and sucked two little marks on her arm just below the shoulder.

"Jassim never moved an eyelash.

"The woman jerked herself from me as if the touch of an infidel defiled her, and as if she courted death. She had scarcely dragged herself again to her knees before she began to writhe with pain, and her arm became a dusky swollen purple, spreading upwards over her shoulder as I watched.

"The seaman, cursing, was staggering down to the sea, but swayed and fell half-way, rolling convulsively, clawing at the sand and jerking himself towards the edge of the water.

"I could do nothing for either, and I could not take my eyes from that woman. She was appealing to Jassim to make the snake kill him, so that they should not be separated, and she implored him to hold her, so that she could die in his arms. Never a muscle did he move; and she cried piteously for him to look at her, just one look. But Jassim would not look at her. Her face was dusky now, her swollen tongue came out of her mouth, and in her agony her pride was broken, and she asked me for water. It was the last word she spoke, poor soul! I had some in my water bottle, so knelt down and held it to her lips. But she could not drink, so I poured a little into her mouth and over her face. Her dark eyes, dark as velvet they were, gave me one dumb look of gratitude; then the life went out of them and she was dead.

"As I knelt, Jassim must have stooped down and picked up the gold snake, for he suddenly flicked it round my arm, saying in a deep guttural voice: 'Blessed is the giver of water — above all men. Allah, the great, the compassionate, gave water to those that burned in Hell, even as thou gavest! Thy reward shall be great; only become a true believer, for this is the key of Paradise.'

"I jumped to my feet, half-dazed, and dared not touch the thing as it clung to me, snuggling tightly round my arm.

"The woman was dead. I ran to the sea; the bluejacket's body was moving gently as the tiny waves rolled in. I knew that he was dead, and I turned to implore Jassim to take it off if he knew how to do so without killing me.

"As I turned, the lower edge of the sun touched the top of those awful mountains, and Jassim, crouching on his prayer carpet, a little patch of red on the sloping white beach, with the dead woman in front of him, suddenly raised himself to his knees, held wide his hands, and called: 'Allah ho Akhbar', as though summoning the faithful to prayer and his contemptible followers back to him.

"Then he prostrated himself, and, raising himself again, commenced: 'Bismillahi! Rahmanni! Raheem!' whilst I stood awed as he recited the prayer, till the upper rim of the sun disappeared, and those dark shadows came again down the sides of the mountains and along the waste of sands, rushing like evil spirits towards us. . . .

"The first lieutenant was at my side shaking

me. He had his hand on the snake, as if to take it.

" ' What the devil do you mean by looting?' he said; but I gave a shriek, and sprang away, striking up his hand.

" As I retreated backwards, step by step, I told him what had happened. He did not believe me; he thought me mad—that I had a 'touch of the sun'. But he let me be, presently, and I covered that thing up with the sleeve of my flannel as best I could—and found myself back again on board the *Pigeon*. Perhaps I was mad, for I could never remember how I did get aboard, and I was on the sick list for many days, lying in a cot, covering the snake with my free hand, and moaning for people to let it be—so they told me afterwards."

The gunner stopped talking, breathed heavily, and wiped his forehead.

He began speaking in his ordinary composed way:

" Since then, thirteen years ago—aye, thirteen years it is next June—an unlucky year—that thing has coiled round my arm and never left it."

My chum's eye had been gradually starting more and more out of his head.

Now he gasped out:

" Never! Do you really mean it?"

" No, never," Mr. Scarlett groaned.

" But, man, a pair of long pincers seizing the head and neck and sliding a sleeve of thin tin or something like that underneath—next your skin—why, there are heaps of ways you could get it off—safe ways—if you really wanted to do so."

" Don't you think I've been tempted, sir; dozens of different ways have been suggested. All seemed safe, but there was just the chance that the thing would strike somewhere—and—and—I'd seen those two die, and put off trying for another day, till now I'm almost used to it.

" Look," the gunner said, pulling up his shirt sleeve and holding out his arm so that the moonlight showed the snake. " Watch its head!" and he very softly began to push one finger underneath a coil. As he did so, the head began to raise itself from his skin, and a tiny dark line, not visible before, showed across the end where the mouth was.

" Stop!" we both cried, perspiration pouring from me and running down my back, the Baron's mouth wide open with fear. "Take your finger away." And he uttered a hoarse, gasping laugh as he knew that at last we were convinced. He drew back his finger, and the head lay back again.

" Now you can guess why I don't want to come back to the Gulf. This bracelet is known to every Arab there. The Sultan of Khamia is certain to find out, sooner or later, that I have it, and then there will be an end to me. Why, sirs, he would give half his wealth to get it back, and once it becomes known that I have it he will get it somehow or other. Getting it, I must die."

" Man alive," the Baron cried, "why don't you try? A thin sheet of tin or something pushed under it, then seize the head with pincers! Why, man, it simply couldn't bite you! There'd be no risk whatso-ever."

"But I can't," Mr. Scarlett almost moaned. "I can't face it. If anything did happen—I've seen those two die—remember that. It seems part of me now—thirteen years it has been there—and I've been brought up amongst Arabs—my mother was half an Arab, and there's something in my blood which won't let me try. It's fate—Kismet—and I dare not fly in face of that."

The Baron fell back in his chair hopelessly.

"Then why didn't you back out of coming here? Why didn't you explain?" I asked.

Then his manner changed again. He had come out of his dreams, and began talking hurriedly as if his lips were shaking.

"Truth is, gentlemen, I'm a born coward. I was too frightened to let on that I was frightened of coming out this way again. It's the same thing with many things I do. I'm too frightened to let on as how I'm frightened, and up to now things have gone all right. I'm a coward, sir, and I don't mind telling you," he said, turning to me. "We have to live together for the next two years—if I'm spared—and you'll find that out before you've known me many weeks, so you may as well know now. Feel my hand, sir!"

I felt it. It was cold and clammy and trembling. His dark face looked a ghastly mud colour.

"That's simply because I've been talking about it, and it reminds me of things which have been—and might be again."

"Come down below and have a brandy-and-soda," I said, and we took him down below, rather glad to get into the noisy glare of the smoking saloon, even though it was so hot.

We always slept on deck, the Baron and I, but that night, whether it was the heat or the effects of the gunner's story, precious little sleep did we get; so, after tossing about restlessly for an hour, we gave up trying, and leant over the deck rails and talked.

" I'm sure it would be as easy as winking," my chum said. " One could lash wire or even string round its head, so that the mouth could not open. The fangs couldn't come out then.

" I wonder what became of that man Jassim," he broke in presently. " He's probably dead, so no one could possibly know that the gunner has it. If he keeps it covered up he will be as safe as anything."

He gazed out over the sea, thinking.

" And probably what poison is left in it wouldn't kill a canary now," he burst out again—neither of us could take our minds off the snake. " Thirteen years ago! It must have lost its power by now."

We went to our beds after a time and tried to sleep. Baron Popple Opstein was soon snoring, but presently jumped up, shrieking, and I saw him trying to pull something off his arm.

I shook him until he woke up, very much ashamed of himself. He was perspiring like a drowned rat, and it made me feel queer and shaky. I did not like the mystery of the beastly thing. I had to live with the gunner and it. If he was going to fill me up with many more such stories, I should soon be frightened of my own shadow.

CHAPTER III

Skipper of the "Bunder Abbas"

Two days later we arrived at Aden, and found the *Intrepid* anchored close to Steamer Point, looking cool and comfortable under her white awnings and white paint. The officer of the "guard", coming across for her mails, took the Baron and myself back with him.

As skipper of the *Bunder Abbas* I felt a somewhat important personage, but Commander Duckworth, the captain of the *Intrepid*, a short, red-faced, wiry man, full of energy, soon disabused me about that.

It was terrifically hot in his cabin, and he was not in any mood for talking.

"Eh, yes, Martin—you are Martin, are you?—so you've come to take poor Collingwood's job. I won't shake hands—too hot. Well, passages have been booked for you and your gunner in that steamer," pointing to a disreputable little steamer I could see through the gun port. "She leaves to-morrow morning at daylight. You will go aboard her to-night. We lent Wilson, one of our fellows, to the *Bunder Abbas*, until you came. You'll find him at Jask—only too anxious to see you, I expect. You'll take her over from him, and the boss at the telegraph station—a kind of political agent—will pass on any orders to you. You are, more or less, lent to the Indian Government, you know."

I did not know, but that was nothing.

His letters were brought in then, and he nodded for me to leave. However, I was so fearfully keen to learn more that I blurted out:

"Any chance of picking up a dhow or anything like that, sir?"

"Of course there is always a chance," he said energetically. "Wilson will tell you all about everything: good morning!"

I went away to the ward-room, hoping to get more information there; but the place was a litter of newspapers, and everybody was busy reading letters and paid little attention to me.

"*Bunder Abbas.* What size is she?"

"Oh, about as big as that table!" was all that I could get out of them.

The Baron and I parted company that afternoon, when I went aboard the little steamer—the *Ras-al-Musat*. I found the gunner already there, and also that solitary little lady, with the yellow hair and humorous grey eyes—the little lady who had snubbed the fussy major—and me. She also was bound for Jask, of all places in the world, and, as at meal times she sat on the captain's right and I on his left hand, we had to talk. However, she was much more interested in Mr. Scarlett and his stories of Arabian life than in me.

At daybreak of the fifth morning we dropped anchor two miles off Jask, and I strained my eyes to catch a first glimpse of the *Bunder Abbas*, though in the hazy light I could not distinguish her amongst a cluster of dhows, anchored close inshore. All I could see was a wide sweep of yellow sand and a low-lying peninsula, jutting out into the sea, with some glaring white square buildings at its end.

The place—if it really was an inhabited place—seemed absolutely asleep, until, presently, some small, crazy lighters, full of jabbering natives, came slowly off to unload whatever cargo we had for them.

Half an hour later I spied a tiny little tub of a dinghy pulling our way. As she drew closer I saw that Wilson was in it. I had known him when he was a sub-lieutenant, and I met him at the gangway.

"Jolly glad to see you," he burst out. "Everything's all right aboard the *B.A.* I've ordered a chunk of goat for your breakfast—couldn't get anything else. I told the political chap, up at the telegraph station, that you'll be coming to see him. He will tell you anything you want to know. Here's the 'signal book' and the 'cruising order book'. Sign your 'tally' there. There are no more confidential books to hand over."

I signed the receipt for them.

"Now you're the skipper of the *B.A.* I've finished with her, thank Heaven! Griffiths, in the dinghy, can take you back now."

Having so satisfactorily (?) concluded the formalities of handing over command, Wilson took some letters which I had brought for him, and went off to read them. I presumed that he was going to Karachi to catch a steamer back to Aden, but did not take the trouble to ask him before the gunner and myself left the *Ras-al-Musat*.

If you had seen us being pulled inshore in that tiny dinghy to join my first command you would have laughed. The dinghy's stern was nearly level with the water, and her bows so cocked up in the air that Mr. Scarlett had to creep for'ard to "trim the dish".

As we gradually drew nearer the shore, I noticed a weird odour in the air.

" What's that?" I asked the bluejacket, sniffing it in.

" All them Arab or Persh'un places smell like that, sir," he said. " You'll not notice it in a week's time."

I sucked it in through my nose. At last I had come to the edge of things, and cut myself adrift from civilization. It was grand, and I felt as happy as a bird—and looked like one, too, I expect, perched as I was on the top of my two cases.

" That's 'er, sir," the bluejacket said presently, jerking his chin over his shoulder. Then I saw the *Bunder Abbas* for the first time. She and I were to have many exciting experiences together during the next few months.

As I saw her then she looked draggled to a degree. Her sides were a positive disgrace—paint off in large patches; her awnings were dirty and badly spread on bent, crazy-looking stanchions; and her rusty un-painted cable hung drearily out of a most disreputable hawse-pipe.

In her bows, under the awning, there was a gun, in

a dirty canvas cover—a six-pounder I guessed—and aft two Maxims were cocked up at different angles, in the most slovenly manner. Their water-jackets, which should have been so bright, were painted a beastly mud colour, and from the muzzle of one dangled a bunch of green bananas.

"Your own mother won't know you in a week's time, my sweetheart," I chuckled to myself, as the bluejacket tugged at one oar and twisted the dinghy alongside.

I swung myself aboard, to be met by a bearded petty officer with a shifty, crafty face, who saluted me about a dozen times in the first two minutes. Five or six disreputable-looking sailors peered round the corner of the engine-room casings to take stock of me, and some lascars sitting jabbering round a stew-pot took no notice whatever.

I looked round. The deck was littered with rubbish; men's clothes were stretched on it every-where—to dry; burnt matches and cigarette ends lay in every corner.

"We ain't scrubbed decks yet," the petty officer said, following my eye, his hand bobbing up and down to his forehead all the time. "Wouldn't you like to see the orficer's cabin, sir?" he added hastily, to distract my anger, and led me up a ladder, through an opening in the fore awning, to a platform round the mast and funnel. On this platform deck, for'ard of the mast, were the steering-wheel, compass, and engine-room telegraphs, also a tiny little signal-locker; aft of the funnel was a diminutive deck-house, about half the size of a railway compartment. It had a low bunk on each side, with scarcely room to stand between them, a few shelves, lockers under the bunks, and a cracked looking-glass. Overhead the paint-work was blackened by an oil lamp which swung from the roof and looked as if it had not been cleaned or trimmed for years.

Outside the cabin there was just enough deck space for a small folding table and a couple of canvas fold-ing chairs.

" Them chairs belonged to Mr. Collingwood, what died of sunstroke, and the gunner, what went off 'un 'is 'ead," the petty officer explained.

I made a grimace.

" You'll 'ave a cup of corfee?" he asked, rubbing his hands together and smiling ingratiatingly as a dirty unkempt Indian boy (a Tamil I found out after-wards) brought two cups of horrid-looking coffee and a tin of condensed milk with milk congealed down one side of it. " Mr. Wilson 'as ordered your break-fast, and this 'ere boy—Percy we calls 'im—looks arter you two orficers."

Nothing seemed to stop his talking machine.

I snorted—it was the only way I could express my feelings—and looked round to see what had become of Mr. Scarlett, who had disappeared.

" What's your routine on board?" I asked, going down the ladder again to that six-pounder in the bows.

" We ain't exactly got none," the petty officer answered. " Mr. Collingwood, 'im what died of sun-stroke, 'e didn't 'ave no regular routine—an' Mr. Wilson didn't alter nothing."

He said this in a half-fawning, half-defiant manner, as much as to say: "Don't you come making trouble."

Mr. Scarlett joined us, his black eyes gleaming, stepping through the little crowd of lascars and scattering them.

"They won't hang any more bananas on my guns," he chuckled.

I had heard a splash, so guessed what had happened, and smiled until that petty officer, hanging round to join in the conversation, explained that "They were a bunch Mr. Wilson bought yesterday, off a Karachi dhow, and 'ung 'em up there to get a bit ripe for you two orficers." He looked so cunningly pleased that I told him sharply to clear out of it and I'd send for him when I wanted him.

I smothered my anger, went up to the little cabin, and began to stow away as much of my belongings as I could cram into the two shallow drawers under the bunk, kicking out "Percy", who wanted to help. He did not seem to mind, and was back again in a minute. If he was dirty, he had a cheerful little face and a pair of big dog-like eyes. He pleaded with them so hard to be allowed to stay and help that I had not the heart to kick him out again.

That "chunk" of goat soon disappeared, once Mr. Scarlett and I settled down to breakfast. Whilst we were busy with it a European-built boat pulled past us from the steamer, with our little yellow-haired friend under the awnings. I almost felt inclined to wave to her, but, not wanting another snub, did not do so.

"I expect she's going to live at the telegraph station. She won't find many comforts in this place," Mr. Scarlett said grimly, pointing to the various square, white-faced buildings at the end of Jask peninsula.

Down on the low ground, where the peninsula joined the coast line, there was a neglected-looking red - brick building among some palm trees (Mr. Scarlett said it was a fort), and another, larger and more imposing, some little way inshore. With the exception of these there was precious little to see except sand-hills, a few scattered palm trees, and perhaps a hundred native huts dotted among them. We could see the track which led inland to the town of old Jask, though the town itself was not visible. On the horizon the misty outlines of barren mountains rose high into the burning sky. Even at this hour the sun was very fierce.

Presently that European boat came pulling off to the *Bunder Abbas* with a note for me from the Englishman in charge of the telegraph station—the acting political agent—asking me to breakfast with him and not to bother with formalities.

"Off you skip, sir," Mr. Scarlett advised me. "They calls their lunch 'breakfast'. I'd like to have a few kind words with the men whilst you are away." So on shore I went, landing on a broad, sandy beach, where crowds of Arabs or Persians, and niggers of sorts—every sort, I should fancy— were unloading those wretched lighters and some large dhows lying half out of water. Donkeys, as patient as donkeys are all the world over, and camels, as supercilious and discontented as they, too, always are, were being laden with bales of merchandise.

One of the boat's crew—a Zanzibar nigger he was —led me through them, away from the shore and the native huts, through a small grove of palm trees, where that old fort stood, and across an open culti- vated space, sloping gently upwards towards the tele- graph station. At the top of this was a double line of wire entanglements extending from side to side.

I opened my eyes as I saw these, and still more when he led me through some roughly-designed earthworks, evidently meant for protection. Then we came to the big barrack-like telegraph buildings them- selves, with a line of iron telegraph posts running from them down the peninsula and then along the edge of the shore to the east'ard as far as my eye could see. My guide led me to a building surrounded by a strong stone wall, with loopholes through it, and at the entrance a short cheery man with a round red face and a scrubby, yellow moustache was waiting to wel- come me.

He was the political agent—Fisher by name. He introduced me to his wife, who came out to join us— a tired-looking little woman—and on the veranda, in the shade, which we hurriedly sought, was my little lady friend from the steamer, talking to a tall, good- looking chap. The political agent explained that this was Borsen, his right-hand man, the only other European there, and that she, his sister, had come out to keep house for him and be some company for Mrs. Fisher.

" They are the only two women here, and it is very noble of them to come to such a place as this," he said, speaking as though it might be jolly unselfish of them but that he wished they were not there.

" What do you think of your new ship?" he asked, smiling.

" You won't know her in a month's time," I smiled back.

" Shan't have the chance," he answered. " I have a very pretty job for you along the coast—keep you busy for the next three months."

I brightened up and wanted to hear more; but the head " boy"—a " perfect" old chap in a yellow silk turban — announced breakfast, and until we had finished there was no chance of my learning.

Then Mr. Fisher took me into his work-room, brought out charts, and explained things to me.

" Look," he said, pointing to the Arabian coast at a place called Jeb, some forty miles to the north'ard of Muscat. " I have information that several thousand rifles have been brought down there. The Arabs will be bringing them across at the first opportunity, and it was only yesterday that I heard that camels are being collected in two villages not far from here. It is fairly certain that somewhere between those two villages they mean to land them. You see that head-land jutting out—look—close to Kuh-i-Mubarak—thirty miles to the west'ard. There are two creeks; one just to the south'ard of it, the other about eleven miles to the north'ard. They are favourite places for landing arms, and those camels—a hundred or more —are somewhere close by.

"The chart does not show it properly. I'll draw you a rough sketch-map."

He drew a sketch and explained it. A hill named Sheikh Hill (there was a sheikh's house or fort on its summit) and the cliffs opposite it made an anchorage safe from any wind, but the creek leading from a little inlet past the village of Bungi (where half those camels had been collected) was very shallow indeed.

South of Sheikh Hill—eleven miles south—there was deep water right up to the shore under Kuh-i-Mubarak, and the creek there was deep, winding among sand-hills until it opened out into a "khor" or basin, with the village of Sudab on its edge. Here was the remainder of the camels.

The two creeks—the shallow one to the north and the deep one to the south—were connected up at the back of the sand-hills and behind the two villages by a channel some thirty yards broad, but so shallow that only at high water could even the native boats use it.

Behind all, some eleven miles inland, the Persian mountains towered up, and passes between them led to the desert table-lands behind.

"The track to Baluchistan and the north-west frontier of India lies across those table-lands," Mr. Fisher said, making a groove with his finger nail. "I want you to patrol from one creek to another, examining every dhow which comes along. I hope you will have luck. Remember that if a 'shamel' blows, the dhows will probably be driven south and make for the deep creek at the base of Mubarak.

"Gun-running has been very brisk lately. A

caravan of rifles actually passed last month within
sight of the old town of Jask, on its way to the Indian
frontier."

Then he told me more about this trade: how the
restless tribes on the north-west frontier of India will
give almost any price for a military rifle; that they
live by brigandage, looting peaceful villages on the
British side of the frontier, or, when not so employed,
fighting among themselves. They cannot get rifles
from India except by creeping up to a British picket—
natives or white men—shooting or stabbing, and stealing rifles in that way; so the Arabs ship them across
the Gulf, and take them up on camels through the
Baluchistan deserts. So many rifles are now captured
by our cruisers, gunboats, and steam-launches that
the demand is always greater than the supply; and as,
directly they have been run safely into Baluchistan,
rifles which originally cost three pounds are worth
thirty to thirty-five each, the temptation to deal in
arms is enormous.

" But who sells the Arabs these rifles?" I asked.
The business was quite a mystery to me.

The political agent shrugged his shoulders.

" You'd better not ask. We both of us have to
obey orders, and neither of us had better ask questions.
Get away as soon as you like. The *Intrepid* is coming
from Aden in a week's time, and will meet you off the
coast, but I want you there as soon as possible."

" I'll go back at once," I said eagerly.

He nodded approvingly, and took me to wish the
ladies good-bye.

" Do be careful," his wife said earnestly. " It was

terrible about poor Mr. Collingwood and his gunner; everyone was so upset."

"I nearly waved to you when you passed the *Bunder Abbas* this morning," I told Miss Borsen, "but was afraid you'd think me forward—think me like that fussy major."

She laughed merrily.

"You were quite right. You never wished me good-bye when you left the steamer, so I should not have waved back."

The political agent accompanied me part of the way.

"That looks as if you expected to be attacked," I remarked, pointing to the earthworks, breastworks, and lines of wire entanglement.

"That's all over for the present. Some wandering brigand tribe did make it unpleasant for us once, but that's ancient history now. Good-bye! Look! my wife and Miss Borsen are waving good-bye."

I waved my helmet, and strode down the path feeling quite a hero, my head full of my new job.

As my boat ran alongside the *Bunder Abbas* Mr. Scarlett, with a grim smile, received me, whilst Moore (the petty officer), looking as sulky as a bear, "piped" me over the side, and the crew, lascars as well, stood to attention.

"I've had a few words with 'em. Told 'em the *Bunder Abbas* wasn't a Plymouth ash-boat but a man-of-war, and they'd behave as such," Mr. Scarlett chuckled.

"We have to get up steam and start hunting dhows as soon as ever we can," I burst out enthusiastically, telling him what were my orders.

I expected him to be as pleased as I was; but his face fell and he would not look me in the eyes. I did not understand him yet—not in the least. However, there were many difficulties in the way of sailing immediately — chiefly due to the shortage of fresh water for the tanks and boilers. Moore did not know where to get any on shore. He said sullenly that it wasn't any use trying during the hot hours of the day, that everyone on shore slept then, and that the crew, too, generally slept. "It was a-working in the 'eat of the day what killed Mr. Collingwood, 'im what died of sunstroke," he muttered, reminding me of the latter's fate for about the tenth time since coming on board.

I told him to "Get out of it and go to Jericho!"

Fortunately there was a splendid fellow on board, Webster, the corporal of marines, who knew how to get water on shore. He, the Persian interpreter (a stolid, aristocratic individual in spotless white clothes and a black fez), and myself went ashore in the dinghy and made ourselves extremely unpopular, disturbing an Arab contractor and waking half the village (if you could call it a village). But we got our water alongside in a couple of hours and on board half an hour later. Oh, my head was hot! On shore the sun seemed to strike right through my helmet, glaring at me from the dusty, sandy ground and hitting me from every white mud wall. I had never been so hot in my life.

At last everything was ready. We hove up our rusty cable and slipped out through the cluster of dhows anchored near us. The sun was low, and as I set my course from a tall signal-mast at one corner of the telegraph buildings, the white walls were tinged a rosy red. At the foot of the flagstaff I thought I saw the figures of two women. Risking another snub from the little lady with the yellow hair and grey eyes, I waved my helmet. Sure enough, two white handkerchiefs fluttered for a moment. I smiled, pleased that she had forgiven me.

Then the sun sank in a glory of red gold, and off we steamed, whilst I smoked my pipe and watched the lonely telegraph buildings and the sand-hills behind them gradually sink below the horizon.

I was so happy that I would not have changed places with all the kings of England from William I —1066—that I could remember.

For the first few hours, as we jogged along, a half-moon gave plenty of light; but it set by midnight, and the night was dark, with hardly a breath of wind.

Several times dhows glided by noiselessly and mysteriously, with a phosphorescent glow along their water-lines, and each time one passed I felt as excited as a child. I was much too excited to sleep; kept Mr. Scarlett's watch, and gradually edged to the eastward so as to be about halfway between those two creeks, and five miles or so off the land, at sunrise.

That first sunrise—the flood of marvellously changing shades of delicate colours, spreading upwards from behind the Persian mountains—was magical. Even though my thoughts were full of other things, I almost held my breath as I watched it. Away inshore, to the south-east, was the little headland of Ruh-i-Mubarak, with a peculiar-shaped rock (marked on the chart) on its top; and to the north-east was

Sheikh Hill and the cliffs which the political agent had sketched for me. Between them the shore and the low sand-hills were, as yet, invisible, and not a sail was in sight.

"Well, here we are, Mr. Scarlett," I said with satisfaction, as he came to relieve me after a sound night's sleep. "We're just where I wanted to be. We'll go and have a look at that creek leading to Bungi."

In half an hour we had shoved the *Bunder Abbas* within a few hundred yards of the foot of Sheikh Hill, with its old dilapidated fort perched on top, and some white-robed figures squatting on the rocks outside it. I went right in, almost under the high cliffs on the opposite side of the little bay, until the mouth of the creek came in view, with a number of native boats drawn up on the sand, and, far inland, the tops of a few palm trees.

Mr. Scarlett, looking nervous and anxious, spotted a dirty-looking chap looking down at us from the tops of those cliffs. "He has a rifle," I said, handing him my glasses, and had hardly spoken before a spurt of water jumped up under our bows with a "flop", and a bullet, smacking against the anchor, squealed past us. I saw Mr. Scarlett's face turn grey, and his hand shook as he hurriedly gave back the glasses.

"He's an Afghan," he said; "an Arab would not fire without some excuse. We'd better get out of it, sir."

The man had flung himself down among the rocks at the top of those cliffs, almost over our heads. We could not have hit him with rifle, Maxim, or six-pounder; so, as I had seen all that was to be seen, I turned the *Bunder Abbas* round and went to sea again. The Afghan, or whoever he was, fired once or twice after us, but he was a wretchedly bad shot.

"Queer beggars, them Afghans," Mr. Scarlett said, recovering his equanimity when we were out of rifle range. "It don't matter where they are, but they'll take a pot-shot at a white man, even if they know they'll be scuppered the very next moment. You may bet your life, sir, that as there are some of them hanging round here, here they mean to land them rifles."

There was not a breath of wind to be felt, and no dhow could possibly run in for the next few hours, so I sauntered down to look at the creek near Kuh-i-Mubarak, eleven miles to the south. Here the water was very deep right up to the shore, and in the creek. I steamed up it for a mile and a half, winding between bare sand-hills, which concealed any view behind them, until it widened suddenly into a great basin or "khor" that shoaled rapidly.

"There won't be any water for us," Mr. Scarlett said, fidgeting.

Bother the water! I wanted to see all I could, so pushed on. I had not seen a single living thing or sign of habitation, so crept along, sounding as I went, until the sand-hills opened out and showed a wide plain dotted with palm trees, a few huts close to the water, and many boats drawn up in front of them.

"Look!" I shouted. "Look! Look at all those

things under the trees — camels, as sure as nine-pence!" Through my telescope I could see fifty or sixty yellowish-brown things kneeling, like lumps of mud, under the shade of those palms, moving their long necks, and some human beings were walking about among them. At any rate I had seen one lot of camels. I was quite satisfied, backed the *Bunder Abbas* out until there was room to turn her round, and put to sea.

All the rest of that day, the next night, and for three more days and nights we patrolled up and down from one creek to another, and not a sign of dhow did we see.

Those days were busy enough. Mr. Scarlett and I between us had "shaken up" the crew with a vengeance. Moore wished he'd never been born. I had the whole crew "fallen in" and said a few words to them, letting them know that I was going to stand no nonsense, and that until the *Bunder Abbas* was clean above and below, inside and out, bright work polished and paintwork clean, nobody would have any afternoon sleep whatever.

The trouble of it all was that there were so few of them that either they were on watch or standing off.

The whole crew consisted of only ten white men, besides myself and the gunner: Moore, the petty officer; Dobson, a quiet, determined-looking leading seaman; four able seamen—Andrews, Jackson, Wiggins, and Griffiths; a signalman named Hartley—the laziest man on board; and three marines—Webster, the corporal, and Jones and Gamble, privates. Picked men they were, I knew, though they had been allowed to get "out of hand". Webster, the corporal, was, as far as I could judge, the best man among them. He did the duties of ship's corporal, steward, sick-berth steward, and writer—and did them well too.

In addition to these there was Jaffa, the Persian interpreter, silent and dignified, always spotlessly clean — a good-looking fellow if he had not had a cataract in one eye. Jaffa was far and away ahead of all the other natives. He gave you the impression that he was the descendant of Persian emperors, brooding over the deserted grandeur and humbled state of his country at the present time. In fact, I treated him with the greatest respect from the very first day.

There were three lascar drivers and nine lascar firemen to look after the boilers and engine, their own lascar "bundari" or cook, another cook of some unknown nationality, and his boy, to cook for the rest of the crew. These two were the most depressed, dirty-looking objects I had ever seen. One or the other, generally both, could be seen at any hour of the day—or night, I believe—crouched on the deck, outside the little galley, swishing a dirty cloth round the middle of a saucepan or dish, gazing dejectedly across the sea, and looking as if they longed to jump into it and finish all their worries. Last but one was a snuff-coloured Goanese carpenter; and, last of all, Sinamuran, our Tamil boy from Trincomalee, who "did" for Mr. Scarlett and myself, and soon began to look quite respectable. We never had to call "Percy" a second time, day or night, before he had glided, silent as a ghost, to our elbows, looking with solemn black eyes to see what was wanted.

This was the strangely-assorted crew collected in the little *Bunder Abbas*—thirty in all, and speaking half a dozen languages. The white crew lived aft and the coloured men for'ard.

The bluejackets' uniform consisted of white, mushroom-shaped helmets or topees, white-coloured singlets, and duck "shorts". At night they wore their ordinary ship's caps, flannel jumpers, and duck trousers. I don't believe there was a yard of blue serge in the launch; so the "bluejackets" were not anything like the bluejackets one sees in England.

The armament of the *Bunder Abbas* consisted of that six-pounder in the bows, the two Maxims in the stern, ten rifles and sword-bayonets, ten cutlasses, and twelve revolvers. We had plenty of ammunition.

So now, perhaps, it is possible for anyone to picture us as we patrolled slowly up and down that coast, keeping well away from shore in the sweltering daytime and creeping closer during the comparatively cool nights.

For four days and nights there was scarcely a puff of wind to ruffle the surface of the sea—certainly not enough to move a dhow; so we saw nothing. But on the evening of that fourth day a fair breeze sprang up, only to die down again before midnight. Just before daybreak Mr. Scarlett woke me. As I jumped to my feet he pointed seawards, and there, sure enough, even in the indistinct light, was a dhow, about four miles off, crawling inshore with a fitful breeze behind her.

"That's no proper trader," Mr. Scarlett whispered hoarsely, his voice shaking a little. "Look what a wretched thing she is! The Arabs never run arms in a new or big dhow: the risk of capture is too great. See that signal?"

I looked ashore to where he was pointing. We were abreast Sheikh Hill, and on it we could see a red light being moved about.

"It's a warning signal," Mr. Scarlett said, "and she hasn't seen it yet."

"Off we go!" I chuckled, my heart thumping with excitement. "Get the guns cleared away."

"Aye, aye, sir," Mr. Scarlett answered bravely, but his voice trembled and his face turned that muddy colour again. He would not catch my eye, and went down on deck. I bit my lip with vexation. If I could not depend upon him at a pinch, what was I to do?

Percy brought me a cup of coffee, smiling, and looking at the dhow. I drank it at a gulp. Extraordinarily thirsty I was, and the air had a peculiar "dry feeling".

Griffiths happened to be at the wheel. I nodded, and he turned the launch towards the dhow, whilst I called down the voice-pipe to the engine-room and ordered more steam.

CHAPTER IV

Adrift in a Dhow

THE crew of that dhow sighted us long before the puffs of black smoke from our funnel showed that the lascars down in the stokehold were pitching on more coal. The queer-looking craft turned up into the breeze, hung there for a moment, as if hesitating what to do, and then paid off, turning to the south'ard.

Off we went after her, gathering speed—Griffiths at the helm, I standing by him, and the others down below, under the awnings, round their guns. I noticed that there was no dew on the awnings or decks—usually it was very heavy; the air, too, was extraordinarily dry, and a splash of water which fell on the deck as Percy brought my shaving water to the cabin dried in no time.

Griffiths was sniffing to wind'ard. "A 'shamel's' coming, sir, that's what it is—a big one, I fancy; the air's allus like this a 'our or two before they comes."

A "shamel"! I had read about a shamel—the Sailing Directions for the station was full of it: a changeable, boisterous gale from the north-west, coming when least expected, sometimes blowing with terrific force, and often lasting for five or six days;

but I was too excited just then to worry about it, even when Mr. Scarlett, putting his head up through the gap in the awning, called out huskily: "Bad weather from the north-west, I fear, sir."

The sun shot up from behind the Persian mountains, its face blurred and hazy.

"Aye, it's a shamel all right, afore long!" I heard Griffiths mutter.

Well, if it came, it came; I did not care what happened, so long as I got alongside that dhow.

In half an hour we were close enough to see that she was of about eighty tons, high in the poop, low in the bows, and very ill found. She had her big sail drawing full, and was streaking through the water. Presently she began to haul it farther and father aft, still keeping on her course.

"Ah! the breeze is backing," Griffiths muttered; "that's another sign we're in for it all right, sir. It's going to be a tidy one too."

We were now about a thousand yards from the dhow, and were rapidly closing. I ordered Mr. Scarlett to fire a six-pounder shell ahead of her.

The little cloud of smoke spurted out from beneath the awning, and the shell burst fifty or sixty yards in front of her bows. She took not the least notice, except to ease away the big sail again, still keeping on her course to the south'ard.

"The shamel's coming, sure enough; she's reckoning on that," Griffiths muttered under his breath. "When it comes, those chaps will carry on till they lose their mast. They have rifles, or they'd have lowered their sail. If they're caught, it means six months' 'chokey' for them, besides losing the dhow, so they're going to have a run for their money. That's what they're going to do."

I was so excited that I could hear my heart drumming in my ears.

The hardly ruffled surface of the sea now began to lose its clearness, and a little spray sprinkled the fo'c'sle, drying almost as it fell.

I called down to the fo'c'sle, and Mr. Scarlett fired a second gun, whereupon the crew evidently thought it wiser to haul down their big sail. Down it came, and, as we ran alongside, a little cur of a dog, running backwards and forwards, kept jumping up on the gunwale and barking at us. We could not help laughing at its absurd fury.

"Any fight in them?" I asked Griffiths.

"Not by a jugful, sir. They'll be as quiet as lambs. You'll 'ave to be mighty 'nippy' a-searching of 'er, sir; the shamel's coming."

As our sides grated together I clambered on board her, Jaffa, the interpreter, Dobson, the leading seaman, Jackson and Wiggins following me. The little dog snapped at us, then went howling aft to where the crew of the dhow—nine or ten of them—were squatting, glaring at us. There were two big hatches, one for'ard and the other aft of the mast, both covered with several layers of timber planks, securely lashed down. Beneath them were my rifles. I felt sure that she must be full of rifles, and that they were mine already. As Jaffa followed me aft, the others began to make the launch fast alongside with ropes thrown to them.

"Tell the nakhoda[1] to show his papers; tell him
to get his hatches uncovered," I told Jaffa; and he,
perfectly accustomed to this job, began jabbering to
a saturnine, bearded old villain who sat on the raised
poop-deck between the tiller ropes.

The dog snarled and barked from beneath the poop,
but the nakhoda and the rest of the crew sat there
absolutely silent, not moving a muscle, just looking
steadily at us.

I cursed them, but the only effect was to make the
old villain smile—a curious smile, which I could not
understand.

"Send everyone you can spare to clear away the
hatches," I shouted to Mr. Scarlett. "They won't
show their papers, and won't do anything."

Three lascars and the Goanese carpenter (yellow
with fright) climbed on board with axes, and all
my people began hacking at the ropes and hauling
away the balks of timber on top of the main-hatch
cover.

I yelled myself hoarse to make the Arabs come and
lend a hand; Jaffa, too, was trying to persuade them.
I pulled out my revolver and flourished it. Still no
one budged an inch, except the nakhoda, who kept
turning his head to the north-west.

It was half an hour's work to clear the main-hatch
cover of all that timber, and we were about to start
knocking out the securing wedges when I looked
towards the land. Sheikh Hill was now six miles to
the north; its outline was indistinct, and the water
under it had a peculiar greyish, muddy appearance.

[1] Nakhoda = captain.

I caught the nakhoda's eye, and saw that triumphant smile again.

"Hurry up, men! it's coming on to blow," I shouted.

Mr. Scarlett's voice, very shaky, called:

"I shouldn't open those hatches, sir. We're a long way to leeward."

Little I cared how hard it blew. Little you would have cared if you had been in my place, on board my first capture, feeling certain that there were hundreds of rifles and thousands of cartridges under those hatches.

"Dig out, men, dig out for blazes!" I shouted, and then saw Mr. Scarlett lean over the side of the launch and be violently sick—with fright, I presumed—and was madly angry with him.

That line of muddy-grey water was rushing towards us now; Sheikh Hill was shut out in a blurred haze, and as the lascars were hammering at those wedges the "shamel" struck us. It was like a wall of solid wind. With a rush and a roar it swept down upon us, and I should have been blown overboard if I had not been holding on to a shroud. It struck the high poop of the dhow, and swung her and the *Bunder Abbas* round like a top. Spray whirled in front of the "shamel", and drenched us to the skin. The big sail began lashing furiously from side to side, but not a move did the Arab crew make; the little dog had fled back under the poop, and the nakhoda was laughing in his beard.

Mr. Scarlett shouted for me to cover up the hatch.

Luckily we had not yet opened it.

I yelled to my men to get hold of the sail, to lash it to the yard and to haul taut the main sheets, the big block of which was banging about in the most dangerous manner.

Whilst we were doing this another squall struck us. The dhow's bows paid off before it; the sail partially filled and bore her over until the lee gunwale was awash, then bore her down against the *Bunder Abbas*, the yard of the big sail tearing away the after awning and crumpling the stanchions. The lascars and the Goanese carpenter, frightened out of their lives, jumped into the *Bunder Abbas* or were knocked overboard into her. Jackson fell into the sea between the two. I expected him to be crushed, but saw them drag him safely into the launch—waiting their chance. Mr. Scarlett and a couple of "hands" were lowering the hatches over the engine-room and stokehold; others on board her were battening down for'ard, as the seas poured over the bows.

It was marvellous what a sea had risen in such a short time. Waves, striking the side of the dhow, surged up and topped aboard the launch; she was half-buried in them. The Arabs, crouching nearer together under the weather gunwale, pulled their cloaks over their heads to protect themselves, chattering volubly and peering to wind'ard; the nakhoda, clinging to one of the tiller ropes, chuckled to himself.

The dhow fell off again broadside to the wind, seas began washing right over her waist, and one by one those balks of timber were hurled overboard. The launch was to wind'ard, now, banging against her side. I did not know what to do. I could not bring myself to abandon the dhow.

Whilst I was trying to make up my mind, the dhow gave a tremendous lurch, and the strain on the for'ard rope to the launch was too much for it. It rendered, and before another could be secured the dhow had swung away from her. Another wave fell aboard her; the *Bunder Abbas* was almost hidden in water; the damaged awning stripped and thundered to leeward, and she heeled over so much that for a moment I thought she would capsize. Then the stern rope parted and we drifted away from each other.

I yelled to Mr. Scarlett to come alongside again (my voice hardly reached my own ears), but a cloud of steam rushed hurriedly up from the boiler-room, and I knew what that meant—her fires had been put out, and she was perfectly helpless.

For a moment I wondered whether she could live in that sea. It flashed across my brain that I'd made a fool of myself and lost her; then a wave soaked me to the skin and half-smothered me.

By this time we were a quarter of a mile apart, the dhow with her tall sides and mast drifting to leeward much more rapidly than the *Bunder Abbas*. As I watched her, wallowing deeply, the after awning tore away completely, whirling and twisting. It was carried up in the air like a dry leaf, and was actually borne right over the dhow before it fell into the sea. I saw the nakhoda still smiling from under his burnous—he knew perfectly well that neither the *Bunder Abbas* nor her guns mattered now—and I realized that Dobson, Wiggins, and myself were alone with those Arabs in a crazy dhow, with a gale blowing harder every moment, and no possible means of leaving her. I did not count Jaffa, the interpreter; it was not his job to fight, and if it came to a scrap he certainly did not look as if he would be of any use.

"We'll have to take her into Jask, sir," Dobson roared in my ears. "Right to lee'ard it is, sir. This breeze will take us there in next to no time."

What a chap! This "breeze"! Call this tearing, roaring fury of a gale a breeze!

My aunt; so we would! I'd never thought of that. We'd take her into Jask. Yes, we would! But there were those Arabs to be reckoned with, and they might have something to say about that. We should have to master them first and make them help us or the dhow might not weather the gale. We could do that, Dobson, Wiggins and I; we had our revolvers, whilst they seemed to be unarmed.

With something definite to do, and with the relief of not having yet lost my captured rifles, I really minded but little what happened. Those rifles were mine, and sooner than lose them—I'd go down with them. Take her into Jask! Of course we would. But first I must stand by the *Bunder Abbas* until she had raised steam again and was in safety. She was all right so far—a thousand yards to wind'ard, rolling horribly. Someone began semaphoring, and I read, "Fires washed out—am getting out sea anchor—will follow as soon as possible;" so Mr. Scarlett, or Moore, or somebody, was keeping his head.

"We must try and work her up to wind'ard," I bawled in Dobson's ear, but he shook his head and bawled something back which I could not hear. I meant to try, and the first thing to do was to get control of the helm, though how to do that with all those Arabs squatting there, glaring at us, I didn't know.

"Tell them to get for'ard," I yelled to Jaffa, and saw him crawl aft and shout something at them, gesticulating in a commanding way, though those infernal fellows only smiled and sat still, half a dozen of them holding on to the tiller ropes.

Dobson looked at me and bawled in my ear:

"I'll get hold of the helm tackles—just you shoot if any of them tries any of their tricks."

"No! I'll go," I yelled, ashamed to funk the job.

I waited till the dhow was steady for a moment, worked my way along the weather gunwale, dodging those balks of timber which were being washed about the deck, until I was right in the middle of them. That beastly little dog snapped at my bare feet as I grabbed one of the tiller ropes to steady myself, and I kicked him back under the poop.

I yelled and waved to the crew to get for'ard, staying among them and kicking two of them in the ribs to make them let go of the ropes. They took not the slightest notice. The nakhoda was just behind me, and I feared, every moment, that I should feel a knife in my back.

Jaffa came scrambling to join me—I never thought that he would have the pluck to do so.

"Tell the nakhoda that if the crew don't go for'ard in two minutes I'll shoot him," I roared.

The nakhoda looked impassively to wind'ard whilst

I pointed my revolver at his head and held up my wrist watch, so that he could see it, and waited.

A minute went past—Jaffa looked nervously round; the nakhoda folded his burnous more closely round his head. Two minutes went by—not a single one in all that stolid group moved; they still clung to the tiller ropes. I gave him three minutes. Three minutes went by, and that Arab nakhoda knew per· fectly well that I would not shoot him in cold blood.

Nor could I. I let go the tiller rope and crawled for'ard again, absolutely not knowing what to do next.

We were driving and twisting, screwing and yawing before the gale like a bit of driftwood, seas toppling over the bows and the waist and washing right across the decks.   And that crowd refused to budge—would not have done anything to save their own lives, I believe.

If they had only taken the offensive and attacked us I should have whooped with the joy of fighting—that cargo of rifles down below was worth fighting for—but they would not.

Dobson it was who settled the question.

With a "Look out, sir, I'm going for 'em", he took the opportunity of a moment when the dhow was on a level keel and rushed into the middle of them.   He seized the burnous over the nakhoda's head, and before that malignant brute could get his hands free he had hauled the loose folds across his throat, choked him, pulled him off the poop on to the deck, and began hauling him for'ard.

In a trice those Arabs were on their feet, throwing

off their upper clothes, and snarling like a lot of dogs. Two of them caught Dobson's foot, and tried to throw him. Wiggins and I were among them in a moment, hitting right and left, until my knuckles were bleeding. In a jumbling, struggling crowd, with that dog barking and biting round us, we were thrown from port to starboard, as the dhow rolled; but somehow or other we managed to get between the Arabs and Dobson, who had never let go of the old man's neck.

A wave washed over us, and for a moment we had a breathing spell, and in that moment I saw the nakhoda free one of his hands. He had a knife in it, so I grabbed his arm, forced his wrist back, and gave him a blow on the back of his head with the butt end of my revolver which knocked him as limp as a rag.

As he fell, the crew, like one man, bent down to the folds round their waists, drawing knives. Two of them had pistols, and before either Wiggins, Dobson, or myself could use our revolvers they had fired, and a bullet had whizzed past my head.

A pistol went off behind me; one of the Arabs—one of the two with pistols—threw up his hands and fell. The others yelled and rushed for us; but we were ready now. I chose the second man with a pistol, fired, and missed him; another shot from behind knocked him over. I saw two more fall. I got a slice over the head, the man who did it being knocked down by Dobson before I knew he had touched me, and the rest had had enough of it, and scrambled for'ard. The dog tried to follow them,

but made the mistake of attempting a last snap at
Dobson's leg. Before you could wink, that little cur
was whirling through the air overboard. In two
minutes after Dobson had garrotted their nakhoda,
we were masters of that dhow.

I felt rather rocky, and sat down, holding on to
a rope, with blood simply pouring over my ear and
shoulder.

Then it was that I saw Jaffa. I had forgotten him.
He was standing behind me, calmly re-charging a
Mauser pistol in the most matter-of-fact way possible, and I realized that it was his shots that had
killed the two pistol men. I tried to show that I was
grateful. "Well shot, Jaffa!" I shouted. "Tell
them to take their dead and wounded for'ard."

Presently the six Arabs still on their legs crawled
and slunk aft, and dragged the two dead bodies away,
helping the wounded man along the deck, and then
sitting in a ring round the foot of the mast, motionless and mute as bats, drawing their cloaks round
them to protect them from the seas.

The nakhoda was still unconscious, so we secured
him to a ring to prevent him being washed overboard.

Someone lashed a handkerchief round my head and
stopped the bleeding. That made me more comfortable, and I was able to take stock of our position.

Kuh-i-Mubarak, that hill near the southern creek,
was now abreast us, just visible through the gale.
The shamel roared down on us more fiercely than
ever, driving in front of it a wild, jumping, short sea,
twenty feet high, with boiling crests. That such

waves could have been whipped up in such a short time seemed incredible.

Every now and then the launch's white side and her yellow funnel and mast showed up against the dark sky to wind'ard; so she was still safe. But we were more than two thousand yards to leeward of her, and how I was going to beat up against that wind and sea in this crazy dhow I didn't know.

However, I was not going to leave the launch helpless; I knew that she could not raise steam for a long time, and determined to make the attempt.

"I'm going to hoist that sail—part way up—see if we can work to wind'ard," I bawled to Dobson.

He shouted back: "She'll never do it, sir; not in this sea."

We should have to try anyway; so we rolled up and lashed the foot of that huge sail as firmly as we could, and, having done that, all four of us clapped on to the main-halyard purchase and slowly raised the big yard about three feet. What canvas was now free lashed about ferociously, giving us stern way.

"Stand by your main sheets," I yelled. "Stand by to ease and haul your tiller hard a-starboard."

Dobson and Wiggins dashed aft to obey, and, as the rudder was put over, our bows began to pay off from the gale, and, doing so, the full force of it broke on the beam; that scrap of sail filled, and bore us over until our bows were buried in the sea.

"Midships the helm!" I shouted, and watched to see how the dhow would behave. A squall struck her, and a wave of great height, leaping over us, surged on board—solid water. The dhow heeled

over till we could not stand, and those lashings round
the foot of the sail gave way like pistol shots, one
after the other; the whole of that huge sail shot out
like a balloon, and we gave a tremendous lurch.

Where the bows had been was now a churning
mass of water; the lee gunwale and the foot of the
lee shrouds were out of sight; I was up to my waist
in water; one of the Arabs was washed overboard,
and the nakhoda would have been had he not been
lashed to that ringbolt.

I struggled to the main sheet, yelling to Dobson
to ease it, but it was under water and had jammed;
no one could get at it.

I thought that unless the mast carried away we
must capsize.

"Cut it, for God's sake, cut it!" I roared, and
Dobson hacked away at one of the thick ropes.
Whilst he was sawing away—his knife was blunt
and would not cut—Jaffa, quick as lightning, pulled
out his Mauser pistol, put the muzzle up against the
rope, and fired in quick succession.

With a leap and a shriek the rope gave way, the
running parts lashed through the sheaves of the
"purchase", the sail flew out to leeward, and the
dhow began to right herself, shaking the water from
her like a dog.

Thank God we had not opened the hatch cover!   If
we had done so we should have sunk like a stone.

As it was, we were in a bad enough plight.   The
huge sail was beating madly, one second half-buried
in the sea, the next whirled as high as the masthead, and cracking with a noise like thunder, the

big block on the standing part of the main sheet attached to the sail being hurled about like a stone on the end of a rope. This block kept on sweeping over the stern, where we were taking shelter, splintering the railings like matchwood, and it was all we could do to dodge it. If it had struck anyone, that would have been the last of him.

Perhaps, for most of the time, the sail, or the lower part, was in the water, and the dhow could not lift it out or herself on an even keel; like a huge bird, with one wing broken, we went rolling and reeling to leeward, waiting for the mast to carry away.

To have attempted to drag the sail on board and smother it would have been sheer lunacy, even if we had twenty men to do it. It would have been as easy to try to stop a wounded elephant tearing up trees round him by lassoing his trunk with twine.

To add to our troubles, the seas were beating against the rudder, which was wrestling with the tiller ropes and trying to shake itself free.

Jask! I wasn't thinking of Jask then, or of Mr. Scarlett and the *Bunder Abbas*. What was to happen in the next half-minute was quite enough for me. We could not stand without clinging to something, the dhow was lurching too much, and sea after sea, four or five feet deep, in foaming cataracts, poured over the dhow's waist.

We had to do something: we tried to lower the big yard, struggling waist-deep in the sea to reach the foot of the mast, where those poor wretches of Arabs, in the last stage of fright, were clinging for dear life. We could not move it or its clumsy rope "sleeve", securing it to the mast, and Wiggins was banged against the mast by a wave—flattened against it like a fly on a wall. It was all we could do to prevent his being washed overboard. He broke two ribs, though we did not know that until afterwards.

As we scrambled back to the poop we saw the rudder head wrench itself free from the tiller ropes, and to the noise of the gale and the thundering of that mad sail now came the grinding noise of the rudder breaking itself to pieces under the stern. Thank goodness, it broke away before it had knocked a hole in our bottom, floating up and threatening to come inboard on the top of the next wave. However, we drifted away from it like a feather from a piece of seaweed, and had soon left it out of sight.

Why that mast did not go over the side I cannot think. The strain on it and the weather shrouds must have been enormous.

If it had broken we should have been perfectly help-less, and the end—well, as I said before, we were too busy with each succeeding half-minute to worry about anything beyond that.

We were drifting to leeward at a tremendous rate; Ruh-i-Mubarak was below the horizon, and the gale showed no signs of lessening.

"If this goes on much longer we'll find ourselves blown a hundred miles out to sea," Dobson roared in my ear. "We'd best cut away the mast. She'll ride more easy and won't drift so quick."

I looked to wind'ard. Even though the gale howled as fiercely as ever, the sky showed signs of clearing; the line of the horizon was certainly clearer than it

had been the last time I looked. I knew that these
gales often died down as quickly as they rose; the
fiercer they were the quicker over, and I still hoped
to sail into Jask. I even began to think how best
to rig a "jury" rudder.

So I shook my head at Dobson, and determined to
keep the mast unless things became worse, and we
hung on, dodging the waves and the block on that
main sheet.

Presently the sail began to give way, great rents
showing in it when it lifted, spreading and ripping,
and flying to leeward in long streamers, which one by
one tore themselves clear and spun madly down wind.

As each strip parted it eased the strain, until, after
a time, the dhow came on a more even keel, and in
the hollows of the seas wallowed less deeply.

Somehow or other we felt that the worst was over,
and began to look round us and shift into more comfortable positions. The old nakhoda—half-drowned
he was — began to recover consciousness, and the
Arabs ventured a little farther aft, crouching for
shelter under the weather gunwale.

There was now no sign whatever of the *Bunder
Abbas*—we had drifted out of sight of her long ago—
but the sky overhead was clearing; large blue patches
showed between the clouds, and though the gale still
shrieked down on us with unabated violence, our
spirits rose considerably.

The edge of civilization! Yes, I was there, with
a vengeance! What an extraordinary change seven
weeks had made, after my long seven years in home
waters! I could not help picturing the Channel

Squadron anchored, as I last saw it, under Portland Bill, and wondered whether it was still there, thanking Heaven that I was not keeping a monotonous day "on".

To make things still more comfortable for us, that big wooden block, in a last furious endeavour to dash our brains out, banged itself to pieces against a big wooden bollard on the poop, so we had no longer to dodge it. But to level up things we began to realize how horribly thirsty we were. We found some water, or rather Jaffa found some, under the poop, in an old kerosene tin. It tasted horrid, and was so brackish that it did little to quench our thirst. My head, too, now that I had not so much to think about, began to throb and ache. Wiggins began to complain of his side.

"We've got to stick it out, that's all," I called to them; and Dobson smiled cheerily, shouting back that he thought "this 'ere shamel wouldn't last long; it was too blooming strong at the start."

He talked about a shamel as if it was an old acquaintance—sometimes in a good, but now in a very bad temper.

I began to feel that the wind was not so strong; waves were certainly not breaking over the dhow so frequently nor with so much force. The lee gunwale was well clear of the sea.

I thought that now it might be possible to capture the remnants of that sail, so, making a rope fast round my waist, and telling Dobson to come with me, I scrambled to the foot of the mast. Whilst he stood by to "pay out" I chose a moment when the big yard over my head was still, climbed on to it, swung myself across it, and, holding on with arms and legs, worked my way along it slowly. It tried to shake me off every half-minute. Once it managed to get rid of my knees, whilst I clung like grim death, my legs dangling almost in the water. Then it tossed me like a feather, and I caught it again with my knees, waiting a moment till it was possible to wriggle along still farther. I managed to crawl almost twenty feet from the mast. That was far enough for my purpose. I wanted to secure my rope to it there—the rope round my waist—but that was the trouble; directly I let go with one hand, off I was jerked, just as if the beastly sail and yard were waiting their opportunity.

For a second I hung by one arm, my body actually in the water, then the sail, billowing up, lifted me with it, and I clung to that yard like a fly. There was a gap just below me, beneath the yard, where the sail had torn itself away from its lashing. I wriggled through it and over the yard again, the rope of course coming along after me, and by waiting my opportunity I managed another wriggle round the yard. There I was, with a turn of the rope round it and myself, secured to it like a pig lashed to a pole. However, I could not be jerked off and could use one hand.

Looking down I saw Dobson yelling encouragement; the Arabs were looking at me with frightened faces.

Dobson paid out the rope very handsomely, and in a couple of minutes I managed to take another turn round the yard, secure it, and unlash myself. Then, shinning and clinging like a limpet as the yard waved about, wriggling backwards when it was quiet, I managed to reach the mast and clambered down on deck.

"That's done 'im in the eye right enough!" Dobson shouted enthusiastically, as he grabbed me by the feet. "'Im" was the shamel.

Together we led that rope aft, passed it through a block under the lee gunwale, took a turn round a cleat, and the four of us tried to haul the yard on board, hauling for all we were worth.

We won a few inches at a time, between squalls, and another turn round the cleat would prevent the yard dragging them out again. Slowly, inch by inch, the end of it came closer to us, and at every inch the dhow would heel over a little more. However, I knew how much she would stand by now, so cared not a jot.

However, at last the yard and sail beat us. It was all we could do to hold in what we had won; not another inch could we gain. Then, to our intense delight, the six Arabs came aft and clapped on too.

"Go it, lads!" I yelled, and, working like one man, we pulled the yard towards us until the peak of it was close to the railings round the stern.

Dobson scrambled up with a coil of rope, lassoed it, and captured it for good and all.

It was grand.

"Now lower it!" I yelled, and we scrambled for'ard to the mast, Arabs and all, slacked off the main halyards, and down it slid.

The remnant of the sail made a last attempt to

escape, then draggled over the lee side, hanging down in the water—beaten.

No one wanted an order; Dobson, Wiggins, Jaffa, and myself, and every one of those Arabs, flung ourselves on to it to prevent it filling again, clutching and pulling till, in a minute or two, it was all on board, lashed to the yard, and as harmless as a handkerchief.

The dhow now came on a level keel, and, her stern paying off before the wind, our bows pointed into the sea. You can imagine what a relief this was after we had been rolling over on our beam-ends for so long.

However, she could not face the seas, and we were soon being spun round and round again.

"A sea-anchor; that's what she wants!" Dobson shouted. "That'll steady her, sir; she'll be like a cradle when she's got one."

There was plenty of timber on the fore hatch, so we unlashed it, and, making half a dozen long balks fast to a big grass hawser we found in the bows, we tipped them overboard, or allowed the seas to wash them overboard—whichever happened first—one after the other. As the dhow drifted to leeward so much faster than they did, the hawser soon tautened out, and brought our bows round into the wind.

Jolly proud we all were of that sea-anchor. It sounds easy enough to make, but if you had seen us trying to prevent those planks and balks of timber taking "charge" whilst we were passing the grass hawser round each one singly, leaping away as they tore themselves out of our hands and tried to break our legs, you would realize that it was not the simple matter it sounds.

We must have been struggling with it for at least an hour, up to our waists in water most of that time, and were thoroughly exhausted by the time we had paid out the whole of the hawser.

But we were now riding head to sea, our decks were not washed by the waves, and when we gathered on the poop to rest after our exhausting work we were as comfortable, as Dobson said, "as fleas in a blanket".

CHAPTER V

My First Capture

WITH that sea-anchor keeping our bows up to wind'ard, the worst of our troubles seemed to be over. My wrist watch had been broken in that first mêlée, so we did not know what time it was. From the height of the sun we guessed it to be nearly noon.

I climbed to the mast head. Not a sign of the *Bunder Abbas* could I see; in fact, the whole circle of the horizon was empty but for ourselves, and as there was absolutely nothing to be done (for it would have been madness to hoist a scrap of sail, and as for trying to make a jury-rudder, we simply could not have done it whilst we were pitching and tossing so violently) we four sat comfortably on the poop, dried ourselves, and watched the Arabs squatting close to the foot of the mast. They had asked Jaffa's permission to search for food, and had found some dried dates. They seemed to enjoy them, and the sight of food of any sort made us remember that we had not had any that day, and that we were as hungry as hunters.

Jaffa found a large store of these dates under the poop, and, though they looked unappetizing to a degree, we enjoyed them hugely, washing them down with another drink out of that kerosene tin.

I was so hungry that I could have eaten a cat.

The sun was now blazing down on us. Unfortunately we had not brought our helmets or topees,
having left the *Bunder Abbas* at daybreak. Our
caps were little, if any, protection from it, in spite
of our constantly dipping them into the sea, and my
head was burning and throbbing. Salt water got
into that wound, and I did not dare to take off the
handkerchief for fear of it bleeding again. Wiggins
complained a good deal of his ribs.

The nakhoda, too, recovered consciousness, and
begged for water, sitting up and moaning when he
saw all the wreckage round him. He had such a
cruel, cunning face that I could not trust him for'ard
with the crew, but kept him aft with us. He looked
as if it would have given him a great deal of joy to
cut our throats, and no doubt it would.

Every half-hour or so Dobson or I would go
for'ard to see that the hawser to the sea-anchor was
not chafing in the "fairway," taking stock of the
weather at the same time. Every time I said: "I
think it's easing off," Dobson would shake his head;
"'E ain't finished with 'is tantrums yet, sir."

However, at last I felt sure that the gale was
moderating. There were not such high waves, they
did not boil down on us so furiously, they were longer
too, not so steep, and we were certainly riding more
easily. Dobson at last agreed: "'E's in a good
'umour, I do believe."

The nakhoda's wicked old face was a good enough
barometer. As the wind and the sea fell, so did his
face look more glum, until at last, when there was no
manner of doubt that the gale was fast dying down,

C 697

THE FOUR OF US TRIED TO HAUL THE YARD AND SAIL ON
BOARD, HAULING FOR ALL WE WERE WORTH

he scowled angrily. What idea he had in his cunning old head, I did not know.

"We'll be able to start rigging a jury-rudder soon," I told Dobson, "hoist a bit of sail, and bear away towards Jask."

I had given up any possibility of beating up to the *Bunder Abbas*. If I could get into Jask the political agent would soon charter me a dhow to go back and look for her.

Well, we made that jury-rudder. It took us two hard-working hours, and without the help of the Arab crew we could not have made it. A clumsy thing it was; a triangle made of balks of timber, with one long projecting plank at each corner for the steering ropes. We also managed to secure the lower after end of what remained of the sail, binding a rope round it to act, later on, as a sheet.

There were still six able-bodied Arabs, not counting the nakhoda. The wounded man (the one who could not walk) had been washed overboard by the first big sea which struck us. The wounds of the others were not worth troubling about. As far as I remember, Dobson's fists had made them; certainly they had not been struck with bullets, because Jaffa was the only one on board who had shown himself able to hit a haystack at ten yards.

Having completed the jury-rudder we rested until the falling wind and sea allowed us to use it. We took it "turn and turn about" to keep watch, Jaffa and I, Dobson and Wiggins—nothing to do and two to do it. The only thing we had to do was to keep an eye on the treacherous old nakhoda.

The afternoon slipped by; the sun began to set in all its grandeur, and only a few gloriously-tinted clouds, scudding across the sky, were left to remind us that nature had been in such an angry mood. The wind and the sea seemed to sink to rest with the sun; only an occasional sobbing gust moaned through the rigging, and, rising from the sea, a huge full moon, like a burnished silver plate, set deep in a dark indigo sky, flooded us with light.

It was now possible to try to bring the dhow under control; so, first of all, overboard went the jury-rudder, with two hawsers lashed to those projecting planks, and led to either side of the poop. Then we hoisted a little of our tattered sail, cut away the grass hawser to the sea-anchor, and, the breeze—it was only a breeze now—blowing steadily and softly from the north-west, filling the sail gently, we squared the yard and let her " rip ".

But the jury-rudder would not act as a rudder. It was too clumsy, and the ropes attached to it too heavy. Twenty men on each would have been scarcely sufficient to work it. However, it kept our stern to the wind—acting as a drag on the dhow—and we scudded merrily away to the south-east at about three knots. I imagined that we were about eighty miles to the south-west of Jask, and hoped that as the breeze backed, as it generally did for some time after a shamel, we should be presently blown away to the east.

Up to now the Arab crew had been helping quite willingly: but whilst they were working aft with the jury-rudder I noticed that the sly old nakhoda took every opportunity of speaking to them, and that afterwards, though they still worked, they worked sullenly and unwillingly.

I had thought of allowing him to go for'ard with them, but after this, and after Jaffa had warned me not to do so ("He only make a mischief," he said), I kept him aft where he was, much as I disliked his company.

I rather fancy that that knock on the head had made me sleepy. I could hardly keep my eyes open during my first turn of watch-keeping. It was beautifully cool, the "shamel" was now nothing more than a respectable breeze, and the long subsiding swell made a most heavenly sight in the moonlight. Jaffa and I talked—it was the only way we could keep awake—he telling me more about the peculiarities of the winds which blew in this region. Then he went on to tell me some of the experiences he had had during the nine years he had served in the British service as an interpreter. Though they were very interesting I was more interested in him and in his quiet aristocratic method of telling them. After the wonderfully cool way he had handled his Mauser pistol that morning he was not to me the same Jaffa who had boarded the dhow with us.

Dobson and Wiggins relieved us presently. "The jury-rudder is keeping our stern into the wind well enough," I told Dobson; "the sea is nearly smooth, the wind mostly gone, and the Arabs are all sound asleep—the nakhoda under the poop, the rest for'ard."

Then I slept like a log until Dobson called me for another spell of watch, and Jaffa and I were again on duty.

It was as wonderful, enchanting a sight as I have ever seen. Above us the great, dazzling, silent moon; around us the sea, a rippling surface of silvery white, stretching away to the circle of the horizon. The little dhow, with her white deck and black shadows, was the centre of it, her sail a great patch of white, casting its clear-cut shadow to starboard over the bows and over the water under them, as sharply cut where it fell on the water as across the deck.

In the bows, beyond the foot of the sail, the sleeping Arabs lay in its dark shadow; in the stern, in the shadow of the poop, Dobson and Wiggins were soon fast asleep—the nakhoda had crawled under the poop and slept there.

It was all so silent and so beautiful—the embodiment of all that is lovely and peaceful and good in nature—that the perils and tragedies of the day before seemed almost unreal, and it seemed impossible to realize that, unless we kept wideawake and alert for the first suspicious movement, we might have our throats cut at any moment.

What we could realize—only too painfully—was that we were very hungry.

Probably that helped to keep us awake more than anything else.

At any rate we did keep awake until I thought that two hours had gone by, when I woke Dobson, coiled down on deck again, and was asleep in a second.

Something touched me. I woke up. Dobson was bending over me. "There's summat going on for'ard, sir. I don't like the sound of it. I've been for'ard under the foot of that 'ere sail twice in the past 'arf-'our, and those noises leave off. I find them Arabs a-lying there as quiet as mice in a nest, and I don't understand it."

I rubbed my eyes, sat up, and rose to my feet—very stiff I was.

The sea was absolutely calm now; the moonlight flooded our decks. Every seam and knot in the planks was distinct; every stitch and ragged tear showed out clearly in the drooping sail, whose shadow swallowed up the whole of the bows.

"Listen, sir!" Dobson whispered, pointing for'ard.

I heard a soft rasping sound, as if pieces of rough wood were being drawn across each another. I crept for'ard close to the gunwale, and had not taken two paces before the noise ceased.

Dobson joined me. "It always leaves off directly I start to go for'ard, sir."

"Come along," I said, and we both walked along the deck, and, lifting the foot of the sail, peered underneath. When our eyes were accustomed to the darkness we could see the figures of Arabs huddled up close together on top of the fore hatch. We waited for several minutes, but no one stirred.

We crept back again.

"Where's Wiggins?" I asked, and Dobson pointed under the poop. "He felt so bad with his ribs, sir, that I told him to go and lie down."

"See if the nakhoda is under there," I told him, and he crept in.

He came back again, white in the face. "'E's not there, sir."

I crawled under myself, crawled all over the beastly place.   He certainly was not there.

"I never saw 'im go, sir!" Dobson whispered apologetically.

However, he was gone; there could be no doubt about that.   He was certain to have crept for'ard among his men, and it was as certain that mischief would be brewing.

"We'll turn 'em out and see what it is," I said, pulling my revolver from its holster and opening the breech to see that it was loaded.

We went for'ard again, and as we bent down under the sail, our revolvers in our hands, there was a rush of bare feet and the whole crowd of them leapt at us. Three or four were clinging to me, throttling me round the neck, clutching my arms to my sides, and pulling my legs from under me.   In spite of all my struggles I was thrown to the deck on my face; someone bent back my wrist to wrench the revolver away, but before it was dragged out of my hand I managed to get my finger on the trigger and pulled it.   As my head whirled with the choking of those iron fingers round my throat I did not know whether I had actually fired it or not.   I was banged on the deck, twisted round and round under a heap of grunting Arabs; something was forced into my mouth; I nearly lost consciousness, but when the grasp on my throat was relaxed I managed to draw a breath of air and found myself next to Dobson, both of us lashed up like mummies, lying on our backs on some coils of rope.

We were both gagged, unable to speak, much less

able to shout and wake Jaffa and Wiggins—lying perfectly helpless.

Two Arabs were squatting on their haunches on either side of us. Like a fool I tried to struggle, and the one near me bent down and drew something across my forehead—a knife; I felt its edge jag along the bone and the blood running down the side of my temples and matting on my eyebrows.

I lay still, terrified lest the next time I moved that knife would be across my throat. I really was horror-struck.

I saw the remainder of those brutes stealing aft noiselessly, under the sail into the moonlight, and had an awful fear that in our struggles we had made so little noise that Wiggins and Jaffa would not have waked, and that they, too, would be caught unawares. I did not know whether my revolver had fired or not. I tried to imagine that it had, but everything was too horribly blurred for me to be sure.

Then my heart gave a great bound of relief, for, as the last of those Arabs had stooped down and shown himself in the moonlight, I saw a flash and heard Jaffa's Mauser pistol—and a louder one, Wiggins firing too. Shots banged out close to us, from the foot of the sail. An Arab gave a yell of pain, and the others came stampeding into the shadow again.

Thank Heaven! They had not caught them asleep.

Two of the Arabs—two with revolvers, mine and Dobson's I imagined—knelt down by us and hunted for more ammunition, pressing the muzzles against our foreheads to keep us quiet. The muzzle slipped into that gash; how it did pain! I had no more cartridges—none, thank God! Dobson had an un-opened packet of twelve rounds, and we saw them carefully dividing these between each other. A cartridge dropped between us, and they hunted for it among the coils of rope, pulling us away roughly. An Arab pounced on it with a hiss of delight. I saw the Arab with a revolver take it and place it in his chamber, so I knew that they only had twelve rounds between them. Then these two armed men crept along, one on each side, to the edge of the shadow of the sail, stooping down to see under it, whilst the others, with knives in their hands, lay flat down on the deck between them.

I was half-dazed and mad with mortification and rage. I would have given my life to have known what Jaffa and Wiggins were doing at the other end of the dhow. There was a dark shadow under the poop platform, I knew, and trusted with all my heart that they had retreated there. But not a sound came from aft; they might both have been hit for all I knew. And not a sound did the Arabs make either. The only noise was the creaking of the yard against the mast and its huge sleeve of rope. The sail drooped down absolutely motionless, blotting out the moon.

How long this silence lasted I have not the least idea. It seemed ages.

"They have only twelve cartridges," was the only thing I could think of, and waited to count the shots, holding my breath for fear the thudding of my heart would prevent my hearing them.

The dark figures of those Arabs suddenly seemed

to stiffen, and then, from either gunwale, where the shadows were darkest, the revolvers flashed and banged, twice on my right, three times on my left.

"Seven cartridges now, only seven," I thought joyfully, and each flash had been answered by more flashes from aft, and bullets ripped along the deck close to where Dobson and I lay.

An Arab gave a low sob, and I heard a revolver clatter to the deck on my left. A dark arm stretched out to pick it up, where it lay in the moonlight, and as the dark hand seized it and hurriedly drew back into the shadow a bullet splintered the deck where it had been.

A long period of silence followed. Except for an occasional groan from one of the Arabs, and the creaking of the yard above us, no sound came to relieve the extreme tension of my ears.

Seven more they had. How many had Jaffa and Wiggins? That was all I could think about. Wiggins would probably have very few, but Jaffa—I knew nothing about him. My ears were throbbing with the strain of listening to count pistol shots which never came. Then they crept aft again. I thought they were going to kill us. They dragged us aft until we lay among them, just in the edge of the shadow of the sail, and one of them began calling out. Though there was no reply from aft, I knew well enough that they were telling Jaffa that he would probably hit us if he fired any more.

So long as these Arabs did not recapture the dhow, I did not care in the least whether I was hit or not.

The answer came with a single pistol shot from

aft. As it flashed, both the Arab revolvers went off. Probably they were waiting for this, and fired at the flash. I was too dazed to count the number of shots. Was it two or three? Had they five or four cartridges still? My brain was whirling and numb. I could not be sure.

They were probably as bad shots as ourselves, and appeared to be getting nervous.

There was a hurried consultation among them; they drew back farther into the shadow, and all of a sudden began stripping off their loose cloaks, five of them, two with revolvers, the others with knives, and I could make out the figure and beard of the nakhoda as he gesticulated and encouraged them.

I knew that they were standing by to make a rush aft, when suddenly they gave a hoarse cry and stiffened where they stood, pointing over the sea. They stood like dark statues for a moment, and then the whole darkness disappeared. They stood out in the glare of a searchlight, naked to the waist, their eyes glittering, their lips drawn back in fear, showing their white teeth, and their shadows thrown against the now lighted sail.

In another moment the searchlight—for it was a searchlight — had passed and it was dark again. Jaffa and Wiggins fired half a dozen rounds very rapidly; the bullets did not come for'ard, so probably they were firing in the air; they yelled, too, and back the searchlight swept and remained, whilst a small shell, bursting with a roar close to the bows, threw up a column of fire and water. In a second those Arabs had dropped on their knees, crouching below the gunwales and hiding from the glare of the light—all except the nakhoda, who, yelling something like "Allah", rushed at me with a long knife.

He would have stuck it into me had not the others thrown themselves on him and pulled him to the deck.

As they did so Jaffa and Wiggins, shouting and cursing, rushed forward.

In a minute I was free, Dobson was free. Wiggins had cut the ropes, whilst Jaffa stood guard over the Arabs, and as I staggered to the deck, bleeding like a pig again, a boat rasped alongside, and Popple Opstein's great red face appeared as he climbed over the gunwale, followed by half a dozen men.

"Four more! They've got four more — or is it three?" was all I could think of to say as he came for'ard. I had to sit down to prevent my legs giving way.

"Thank God you came along in time!" I said, as he shook some sense into me and gave me something to drink.

I was all right again in a few minutes, and whilst the Arabs were being securely tied up, to prevent any unpleasant mistakes, I was able to tell him what had happened.

"What about your edge of civilization, Martin, old chap?" he laughed. "You nearly toppled over the edge of it that time, eh? We spotted you in the moonlight, and saw the revolver flashes, so knew something was wrong. We never thought it was you."

"Man, she's full of rifles. I'm dead certain she is,"

I burst out, "and I haven't been out here ten days! Isn't it splendid?"

"You don't look very splendid," my chum smiled grimly. "The sooner you get on board to our doctor the better."

I really felt almost intoxicated. I could not stop talking. "Look at that one-eyed interpreter of mine," I babbled, turning to Jaffa, who was leaning up against the gunwale cleaning his Mauser pistol. "Look at him! He saved the whole show. He's simply grand with that pistol of his. Aren't you, Jaffa?"

He smiled his inscrutable, dignified smile.

"You saved all our lives. We should not have pulled through without you," I went on, and for the life of me I do not know whether he looked pleased or not.

The *Intrepid's* men were going round collecting the knives which the Arabs had dropped on deck. Dobson and I found our revolvers.

For the life of me I could not keep silent.

"How many cartridges are there in yours?" I asked him, opening my breech. "There are only two in mine."

"Not a blessed one, sir!" he grinned; so, after all, I had miscounted.

"How many have you?" I asked Wiggins.

"Not a blessed one either, sir! I did have two, but fired 'em when we sighted the *Intrepid*—that 'ere Pershun told me to!"

Commander Duckworth of the *Intrepid* now came on board the dhow, and I had to tell him the yarn all over again. In spite of feeling absolutely "played out", I talked as if I should never stop, telling him detail after detail, imploring him to go right away and hunt for the *Bunder Abbas*. I rather fancy I suggested that he should leave us in the dhow to sail into Jask.

However, I found myself, Dobson, Wiggins, and Jaffa climbing down into his boat and being pulled across to the *Intrepid*. I know that I talked to them all the time, and to Nicholson, the staff surgeon of the *Intrepid*, whilst he was probing and stitching those wounds of mine. When he had finished these he stuck the needle of a syringe into my arm. "That'll send you to sleep all right," he said, looking at me curiously.

When I went aft he was commencing work on three wounded Arabs who had been brought over. The rest of them were in the battery surrounded by inquisitive bluejackets. The old nakhoda squatted on deck by himself, covered up in his burnous, with only his eyes showing. He did not even deign to look at me.

The *Intrepid* was already steaming ahead, her boats hoisted, and the dhow ("My dhow, old chap," I said, slapping old Popple Opstein on the back) was safely towing astern; I could see her mast.

"Rifles, my dear chap! She's simply chock-full of them!" I laughed.

I was famished—starvingly hungry—and they got food for me down in the ward-room, although Nicholson tried to make me lie down. The ward-room chaps, in their pyjamas, sat round me as I talked to them. I could not leave off talking, and I found that I didn't like anything they had on the table, so could not eat.

Nicholson took hold of my wrist and shoved another beastly syringe needle into my arm. He made the fellows go away too, although I had not told them nearly all that had happened, and in a little while I did let Nicholson take me to a cabin—just to humour him. That is the last I remember—I certainly don't remember undressing—but I woke in broad daylight to find myself in pyjamas belonging to somebody else, feeling rather shaky, my head covered in bandages, and Nicholson standing over me with a satisfied smile on his fat face.

My aunt! how hungry I was!

"Food, Nicholson, that's what I want," I said. "I haven't had anything worth speaking about for twenty-four hours."

He felt my pulse, smiled, and went away. I called him back. "How about the *Bunder Abbas*? Have you found her yet?"

"She's been alongside us for the last forty hours or more," he said. "We are anchored off Sheikh Hill. She's all right."

I looked puzzled. I had not noticed that the engines were not working.

"My dear chap, you've slept solidly for nearly three days. I've seen to that."

Popple Opstein came in, looking anxious, until Nicholson told him that I was as "right as rain".

"Man, you are lucky!" he cried, his face growing violet with excitement; "she had nearly four hundred rifles on board. Look! I've brought you one," and he held up a brand-new Mauser rifle.

I handled it lovingly—my first capture. "You

won't 'pot' at any poor wretched sentry on the Indian frontier, my beauty," I thought.

"How did you find the *B. A.*?" I asked; and my chum explained that the *Intrepid* had taken my dhow in tow, steaming to the north'ard; that at daybreak the launch had been sighted, and though she had raised steam again she could not use her engines as something had fouled her propeller, below the water-line of course, where Mr. Scarlett could not get at it.

"The result was," old Popple Opstein went on to tell me, "that we had to tow her as well, and when we anchored here sent our divers down to clear it."

Later on Nicholson allowed me to dress, Percy smiling out of his great eyes when he brought me some clean clothes. Afterwards I went aboard the *Bunder Abbas* to hear Mr. Scarlett's account of what had happened and to see what repairs were still necessary. I found people from the *Intrepid* busily straightening the bent stanchions and fitting a new after-awning cut from an old awning belonging to the cruiser.

"She'll look all right in a couple of days," Mr. Scarlett said, as he and I watched the last few boxes of ammunition being hoisted up through the dhow's hatches and transferred to the *Intrepid's* battery deck.

It was a most comforting sight.

"Thought I'd seen the last of you, sir, when that big squall struck the dhow, and thought you'd seen the last of the *Bunder Abbas* when she half-filled herself with water, her fires had been put out, and that hawser coiled itself round the screw.

"My, sir, but I was being sick every few minutes with pure fright—I was that frightened that
I wanted to jump overboard and get the drowning
over quietly, without a lot of lascars howling and
clawing round me—as I was waiting for 'em to do
when she did sink. We made some kind of a sea-
anchor with what was left of that awning and some
spars, got her head to the wind, and baled her out
with buckets—with buckets, sir! Three mortal hours
that took, and another six to raise steam again, the
lascars all preferring to drown up on deck, so not
a blessed one would go below.

"We never noticed that hawser round her screw
till we let the steam in her engines, wound a few
more turns round her screw, and brought them up
all standing. Thank God! we hadn't cast off our
sea-anchor, or we'd have had all the making of
another over again—and dead tired, tired as dogs,
we all were."

There was this to say for Mr. Scarlett—I never
doubted him. Whenever he told me of anything,
I felt perfectly sure that he had told me all. However, I was inquisitive to know how he himself had
actually behaved, so could not help asking Corporal
Webster later on what kind of a time they had had,
hoping that he might have something to say about
him.

"Awful weren't the word for it, sir; the worst time
I've ever had in my life. We none of us thought
she'd float, and she wouldn't have but for the gunner
—sick one moment, working like half a dozen men
the next. Why, sir, when we steadied her into the

wind, an' baled her out, he laid the fires in the boilers himself, no one else knowing how to do it, them lascar chaps funking going below, and we chipping up a mess table (the only dry bit of wood on board) and passing the bits down to him."

I learnt still more of that extraordinary man by watching Percy, the Tamil boy. His eyes showed the most unbounded admiration for the gunner. He simply slaved for him all day long, and seemed to be perfectly happy so long as he was doing something for him: pipeclaying his helmet, or washing out his vests—anything, in fact.

I don't pretend to be a judge of character—luckily —and he certainly puzzled me. That gale had told me more about Mr. Scarlett, Dobson, and Jaffa than I should have learnt in six months of ordinary cruising.

CHAPTER VI

The Edge of Civilization

FOR two more days the *Intrepid* remained at anchor, three miles off Sheikh Hill, within sight of the open shallow creek running up to Bungi village and of those cliffs from which the Afghan, a week before, had wasted ammunition on the *Bunder Abbas*. The launch remained alongside of her and the dhow astern. Why we were thus delayed I am not certain, but from the many curious and inquisitive questions Nicholson continually asked me, and from the many times I caught him watching me, I imagine that it was principally on my account, and that Commander Duckworth would not send me away cruising by myself until Nicholson had reported favourably.

At the end of this time both the *Bunder Abbas* and I were in first-class condition: the bandage which covered my wounds had been replaced by what Nicholson called a collodion dressing, and the *Bunder Abbas* showed no signs whatever of her recent hard usage. I was ordered to tow my empty dhow out to sea, set her on fire, and sink her. This I did with very great regret, for, although she was old and rotten, she was my first capture, and I wanted her to be con- demned and sold properly by a prize court. However, it was not to be; so she was burnt to the water's edge, and her stone ballast quickly sank her.

We all knew that her cargo of arms and ammunition represented not a tenth of the great number reported to have been brought down to Jeb for shipment to the Makran coast, and everybody felt certain that sooner or later—probably sooner—more dhows would endeavour to run across.

We were therefore very grateful when we did at last receive orders for patrolling between the two inlets.

Two cutters belonging to the *Intrepid*, with a Maxim gun in the bows of each, had to patrol the creeks, keeping out of rifle shot from shore during the day and running close in at night. My chum, Baron Popple Opstein, commanded No. 1; and Evans, a little rat of a lieutenant, full of "go", but all nerves, No. 2.

I was ordered to patrol from one to the other, backwards and forwards, on a line about six miles from the shore, during the daytime, and to close to within a mile of the shore at sunset. I was also ordered to communicate with both cutters each morning, as soon after daylight as possible, to receive reports of any happenings during the preceding night. Still farther out to sea the *Intrepid* herself would patrol a line twenty miles long, also closing at dusk to within sighting distance of a Very's light, should we want to communicate with her by firing one.

All being ready, Evans, Popple Opstein, and I went aboard the cruiser, fully expecting that Commander Duckworth would give us a great deal of unnecessary advice, as though we were a lot of babies, not to be trusted a hundred yards from him; instead of which he simply asked us if we understood his written orders, and when we answered that we did, merely said: "Right you are! You can get away as soon as you like. Good night!"

"He's a splendid chap to serve under," Evans said in his nervous, hurried way of talking. "He's always just like that."

It was grand to be sent away entirely on one's own, without being tied down this way and that before ever the conditions which might conceivably happen had happened.

"Imagine anything like this in the good old Home Fleet!" my chum said as we parted. "We should be fathered and mothered day and night."

So, an hour before the sun set, I took the two cutters in tow, dropped *Intrepid* No. 1 close under Sheikh Hill, and steamed down to Kuh-i-Mubarak with No. 2, leaving her there in the mouth of the deep creek running up to Sudab, the village where I had seen the camels.

"Good night and good luck!" I shouted, as I steamed off to sea to commence my own job.

No one expected a dhow to slip across during those first days, because there were so few hours of darkness; but the moon, of course, was rising later each night, and every twenty-four hours increased our chances.

However, nothing came in sight, and on the seventh day—a Thursday it was—according to my orders, I fetched *Intrepid* No. 2 back to the anchorage off Sheikh Hill, and found the *Intrepid* herself anchored there, with my chum's boat already alongside.

I made fast to her, and immediately began the job of filling up with coal, water, and provisions; whilst the crews of the two cutters went inboard in order to get a good meal and a comfortable sleep whilst their boats were being revictualled. Sleep in a cutter crammed with gear is not a success. It does not matter how comfortable you try to make yourself, there is always something sticking into your back; and a chum's foot in your face, though quite an unimportant detail, does not induce slumber, especially if the owner happens to be restless.

I went aboard to have my wounds dressed. Nicholson took out the stitches, and said that both gashes were healing well. I wanted him to let me take Wiggins back again. I had had to leave him behind with his broken ribs (very much against his wish), but he was not yet well enough to rejoin.

Then my chum came aboard the *Bunder Abbas* and smoked his dirty old pipe with me on the little platform deck outside my cabin. We sat in those two easy canvas chairs under the awning and had a good time.

"Enjoyed the week?" I asked.

"Splendid," he said, beaming and showing his white teeth. "Splendid."

"Did that Afghan chap have a shot at you?"

"Once or twice," he nodded. "He's a rattling poor shot."

"Shoot back?"

"Once or twice; never hit him."

He was on board for three hours, and I don't believe he said another word (as a matter of fact he slept most of the time); but as he was going away he wanted to know whether I had seen Mr. Scarlett's snake again.

I had not. He kept a bandage round it now. If he did uncover it, he did so at night.

Popple Opstein was evidently still very interested in it.

"I wish he'd let me try that dodge of a pair of pincers and a bit of tin slipped under it, or wiring its head or something," he said.

I shook my head, and told him that it was useless to suggest that again.

Just before sunset I towed both cutters back to their positions, leaving them there.

Nothing happened during that week, although the darkness was very favourable for any dhow to try to creep in. At sunrise every morning I waited inshore to see that the two cutters were safe and had nothing to report, then pushed farther out to sea to steam slowly up and down, whilst the men not on duty scrubbed decks, cleaned guns, or washed and mended their clothes.

It was fearfully hot all this time, and I learnt that Moore was right after all, and that one could hardly keep awake in the afternoon. From noon until four o'clock the heat, even under the awnings, was at times almost unbearable. I could not keep awake myself, so had to let the men sleep too, and Moore did not hide his satisfaction at my first defeat. The crew was so small, and, what with men on watch and those wanting extra sleep after a night's watch, there were seldom more than three or four "hands" to employ at odd jobs, so precious little cleaning was done either, and I even began to wonder whether it would not be wiser to paint the water jackets of the Maxims, and even the six-pounder, as they were so difficult to keep bright.

"There is either too much wind or not enough" is a sailor's saying about the Persian Gulf; and although we were actually outside the Gulf itself, yet the saying held true enough here. Hardly a puff of wind ruffled the glassy, glaring surface of the sea for those first fourteen or fifteen days: the sun blazed at us all day from an absolutely silent, monotonous, burnished sky. I began to curse it when it rose, and when it did set, and give me a chance to cool down, to dread its reappearance and the heat of the next day.

Mr. Scarlett told me that I should soon become accustomed to it. He himself simply revelled in it. He advised me to drink as little fluid as possible, if I did not want to be covered with prickly heat, and I did my best to follow his advice, although the desire for liquid was sometimes almost unbearable.

Another Thursday we spent alongside the *Intrepid*, my chum coming aboard me to sleep and smoke, and occasionally make some contented remark. Then back we went to our stations for another week of patient watching.

On Sunday morning I edged in as usual, to see whether the Baron had anything to report.

It was about half-past four, still dark, but the darkness rapidly disappearing, when he flashed a signal lantern, and I answered him.

In ten minutes he was alongside. He had a sick man whom he wanted me to take on board, so we hoisted him in and put him down below.

"It's only a touch of the sun," the Baron said; "but we can't make him comfortable here. You can give him back to-morrow."

This occupied perhaps ten minutes. It had become appreciably lighter, and I could see the sheikh's house or fort looming above our heads as I started off to go along to Evans.

We had not steamed a mile before we heard a Maxim firing very rapidly. Looking inshore I could see the cutter pulling in under those cliffs from which that Afghan had fired at us.

"Put your helm over and wake up the engine-room people," I ordered, and round we swung. The cutter had now disappeared round the base of the cliffs, but as we hurried after her we could still hear the Maxim firing.

We all were grandly excited—all except Mr. Scarlett. As he went down to see that our guns were ready I saw that his face was a muddy, grey colour. He would not look me in the face, and his hand was shaking as he steadied himself by the rail. My former feeling of contempt for his cowardice came back.

Percy came up with two cups of cocoa and some biscuits, grinning delightfully; but his face fell when Mr. Scarlett refused any—he thought that he had not made it properly.

It was quite light now, and I steered wide of the

cliffs, in order to be able to look up the creek more quickly and to be able sooner to help the Baron if he was "busy".

Then, as the mouth of the creek opened out, there was a shout from for'ard of "Look, sir; look there!" and I was astonished to see a large dhow—a very large dhow—lying half in, half out of the water on the beach, two thousand yards away. A red flag was trailing down from her ensign staff, and her bows were surrounded by a great crowd of camels and natives. The cutter was about nine hundred yards away—between us and the dhow; pulling like mad her men were, and tut-tut-tut-tut went the Maxim in her bows. I could see the line of bullet splashes, first in the water, then in the sand among the camels, then in the water again. They were making bad shooting —a Maxim is always a troublesome weapon in a moving boat.

"Give them a shell!" I yelled down to Mr. Scarlett. The little six-pounder barked, and its first shell burst in the water, but the second sent up a cloud of smoke and sand right among a tangled mass of camels and men. We saw some camels struggling on the ground, and broke into cheers as the rest of them were driven frantically up the beach and the sand-hills, to disappear behind them.

A few chaps, their loose cloaks flapping about, scampered after the others, until not a single living thing was left in sight.

"She's a fine dhow that," Mr. Scarlett said, coming up the ladder to me, his voice very shaky. "We shall have to be very careful, sir."

"Careful!" I shouted. "Why, man alive, they've run away! There's not a soul to stop us. Look at the cutter, man; they're almost up to her."

Mr. Scarlett looked and shivered.

I saw that the cutter had taken the ground. Her bluejackets, with their rifles in their hands, were jumping into the water and wading ashore, racing ashore, my chum struggling to get ahead of them.

"Go it, Popple Opstein!" I yelled, unable to control myself, and wished that the old "*B. A.*" would go faster, so that I could be alongside him.

My aunt! What luck! Two dhows in less than a fortnight!

"We shall be millionaires in no time," I said, turning to Mr. Scarlett, to cheer him up; but he had gone down on deck again.

Then I had to stop my engines. I dared not go in any closer; there was not a foot of water under my keel.

I shouted for the dinghy to be lowered.

The Baron and his men—eight of them—were on the firm sand now, running along towards the dhow, cheering and whooping, when suddenly I heard rifle-firing—rifles from behind the tops of those sand-dunes, rifles from the tops of those beastly cliffs, and saw the sand spurting up all round them as they ran. Through my glasses I could see heads peering over the sand-dunes and rifles firing over them. I yelled to the men to leave the dinghy and open fire again with the six-pounder.

Then two of those running figures fell; one rose and went on, the other lay where he fell.

"Lie down and shoot back, or you'll all be killed,"

I shouted, like a fool, as if they could hear me eight hundred yards away.

Then I realized that if they could reach the dhow they would obtain some shelter from the fire.

I saw my chum fall, sprawling, and get up again, stoop to pick up his revolver—he never would put the lanyard round his neck—and go on again, slowly, limping. Two men stopped to help him, but I saw him waving them to leave him, and they dashed to the side of the dhow, flung themselves flat down, half in, half out of the water, and commenced shooting. My Maxims were busy now, and keeping down the fire a little; but for a couple of seconds poor old Popple Opstein was alone on the beach, with bullet-spirts jumping up all round him. Those two seconds seemed like ages, till, with a gasp of relief, I saw him gain the shelter of the dhow and throw himself down among the others.

Thank goodness! he could not be very badly wounded.

But the dhow only gave shelter from the men behind the sand-hills; my chum and his people were still entirely exposed to a dropping, long-range fire from the tops of those cliffs, and bullets still splashed and spurted all round the dhow.

The six-pounder shells were bursting well along the tops of the sand-hills, and three men, left behind in the stranded cutter, were also peppering them with their Maxim. These two guns kept the people on the beach fairly quiet, so I cocked up my two Maxims and opened fire on the cliff, the people up there immediately paying attention to us. A bullet splintered the deck close to where I was standing, several whistled through the awnings, others flattened themselves against the funnel. Griffiths and I were standing there by the wheel and compass absolutely exposed. I do not know how I looked, but I do know that I was chiefly frightened lest I should look as frightened as I felt. I wondered what Mr. Scarlett was doing. He was under the awning, so I could not see him. A bullet smashed Percy's coffee-cup and broke it to atoms—bullets were flying all round us. There was nothing for me to do; that was the worst of it. To relieve the strain of being idle, I sent Griffiths to bring up a rifle and some ammunition, and took the wheel myself.

Before he came back I saw the figures close to the dhow rise up and dash into the water, wade round her stern, and disappear from view. Seven figures I counted; that little white heap halfway along the sand only made eight; so another must have been badly hit. But now they were safe for a time, entirely sheltered by the dhow.

The natives, Afghans, Baluchis, whatever they were, thereupon turned more rifles on to us and that stranded cutter—both from the sand-hills and from the cliffs. The range from the sand-hills was well over twelve hundred yards, and most of the firing was very wild; but one of our chaps, Jones, a marine, working one of the Maxims, was shot through the arm about this time. However, our high gunwales kept off most of the bullets.

It was very different with that stranded cutter. She was not more than six hundred yards away from the sand-hills, closer still to the foot of the cliffs, and almost immediately one of the three men still working her Maxim fell and was pushed aside or crawled away—I couldn't see which.

Griffiths came up with his rifle. "Go on, fire yourself!" I shouted, and he lay down and began potting at the people on the cliff, over our heads. The shooting now slackened from there, and I quickly understood why, for I saw fifty or sixty natives scampering down a cliff path and wading through the shallow mouth of the creek. By the time I had ordered a Maxim to swing round on them most of these had joined the others behind the sand-hills. We bagged two or three, however.

I knew that we were in a horrid mess, and didn't want Mr. Scarlett to come up to me—absolutely yellow in the face—and tell me so. Just as he was blurting and stuttering out something about a falling tide and getting that cutter afloat, people down below began shouting: "Look! Look!"

Griffiths, peering over his shoulder with frightened eyes, pointed, and I saw a regular horde of Afghans pouring over the tops of those sand-hills and racing down the beach, straight for the stranded cutter. I looked at her. Only one man was now working that Maxim, or trying to do so, and making a bad job of it. Something had gone wrong with the belt. He tried desperately to jerk it clear, failed, then gave it up, caught sight of the yelling Afghans charging down on him, and hid under the gunwale.

The six-pounder fired as rapidly as it could, and must have killed many, but one of our Maxims had

jammed and the other would not bear. Mr. Scarlett's
piercing voice was shrieking for me to turn the *Bunder
Abbas* round so that he could use the second Maxim.
I gave the wheel a turn and rang down to the engine-
room. Before I was able to turn her side farther
towards the beach that fierce rush had reached the
water's edge. Scores of wild Afghans were splashing
through the sea. We could hear them yelling as they
waded knee-deep—waist-deep—towards the cutter.
Then we saw the two men still alive in her peer over
the gunwale, and one seized a rifle and began firing,
but the other crawled across the thwarts, let himself
down over the stern, and commenced to swim towards
the *Bunder Abbas*.

A six-pounder will not stop a rush: its shells are
not deadly enough. I thought the Maxim would never
fire. Looking at the dhow to see whether our people
were safe, I saw rifles sticking out from under her
poop railings, so knew that Popple Opstein and his
men had climbed on board. They, too, were firing
on the Afghans charging through the water. On
these came; they were not thirty yards from the cutter;
the man inside it had his face turned appealingly to
us.

Then Mr. Scarlett started the Maxim. He found
the range in a twinkling—he only had to follow the
splash of the bullets till they fell amongst the natives,
and then wobble the gun—and it was impossible to
miss. Their shouts of triumph changed to wild
shrieks of terror. It was just as if a scythe had swept
over them. They subsided under the water—they
disappeared—only a few, crouching till their heads

hardly showed above the surface, regained the beach and the protection of the sand-hills.

There was no time for thinking of this sickening slaughter; my chum and his men had to be brought off, his cutter had to be refloated, and that dhow had still to be destroyed.

"Land and help him!" The thought did come into my head for a second, but it would have been idiotic. We should only be putting our heads into the same trap that he was in.

The Afghans had had such a terrible lesson that for a short time only a few ventured to the edge of the sand-hills to fire on us. The fire from the cliffs, whilst our Maxims were no longer keeping it down, became somewhat more vigorous, and I knew that now was my chum's chance to rush back along that beach and regain the cutter.

I shouted to the signal-man to semaphore across to him, but he must have also realized that this was his opportunity, for almost immediately we saw the blue-jackets sliding down the dhow's side—two had to be helped down—and then they all—seven of them— came back along the water's edge. Very slowly they came, for one man was being carried and my pal was limping badly, though managing without assistance. Only a few Afghans were firing at them, and these we stopped by mowing the edges of the sand-hills with Maxim bullets wherever a head showed.

They seemed to be taking hours. I found myself yelling to them to try to go faster. They kept on stopping to fire at the sand-hills. Then, at last, they began wading out, and we cheered as we saw them climb aboard the boat without further loss, get out their oars, and try to push off. Our joy died down when we saw that they could not move her. The tide had fallen, and the cutter was on top of a sand-bank with not a foot of water covering it. They jumped out again into the shallows and strained and heaved, but not an inch could they shift her.

All this time the Afghans on the cliff were firing at them. They clambered back into the boat and replied to this fire with rifles: something had evidently gone wrong with their Maxim. Afghans now appeared over the sand-hills immediately behind the cutter, where we dare not fire for fear of hitting my chum's people. These, too, opened fire on the cutter, and the water all round it was alive with bullet splashes. Another man fell down in the boat and his rifle overboard.

Unless something was done very quickly they would all be killed. I yelled for volunteers to pull the dinghy across and take them a rope. Dobson, the leading seaman, and Webster, the corporal of marines, jumped into her first. "Take the wheel and don't go farther inshore," I called to Griffiths, and rushed down on deck to supervise the rope being passed into the dinghy and coiled down in her stern-sheets. On my way I saw Jaffa, standing at the foot of the ladder, aiming at the top of the cliffs with a rifle. He was as calm as ever.

The dinghy was on our shore side, away from the cliffs and sheltered from fire. We coiled all the ropes we had into her stern, bending one to the end of the next. I rushed back to the wheel and moved the *Bunder Abbas* in towards the cutter until my bows touched the sand. Then I gave the word to Dobson and Webster and they shot ahead of the bows, the rope uncoiling and paying out as they pulled.

Directly they had cleared our bows the whole of the rifle fire was turned on them, and they had not taken fifty strokes before Dobson was hit. He dropped his oar, but grabbed it again, pulling with one hand. A moment later he was struck a second time and fell forward.

Webster seized his oar and went on, but I shouted to him to come back, and with a brilliant thought he made fast the rope and we hauled him back. As the dinghy came near I saw that Dobson was dead. We lifted him out and Mr. Scarlett jumped in.

"I'm going, sir," he said, and I was so astonished that I could say nothing.

We laid Dobson on deck and jumped back to work our guns, whilst Mr. Scarlett and Webster pulled madly towards the cutter, paying out the rope and steering wildly. We yelled with delight when they reached the cutter and passed the rope inboard.

In a moment the cutter's crew had clambered into the water again to lighten the boat. They held up their hands to signal my rope made fast.

I gave the "*B. A.*" a touch astern and stopped her engines; the rope tautened, the cutter's crew shoved and pushed and yelled that she was moving. In half a minute we had her afloat, her men scrambling in as she slid into deep water; in ten minutes we were out of range, and in half an hour she and the dinghy were both alongside, and I had dropped anchor two miles from the cliffs and out of sight of the dhow. The cutter was peppered with bullet holes, her gunwales, sides, and oars splintered and grooved in a hundred places. She leaked like a sieve, and water filled her to her thwarts.

She had one dead man on board—one of those left as boat-keepers—the one I had seen shot when working the Maxim; one man shot through the chest and leg; four others wounded (one with three bullet wounds through soft parts), besides Popple Opstein.

"It went clean through my calf muscles," he told me. "It's nothing."

Not until then did anyone remember the man who had started to swim back towards the *Bunder Abbas* when those Afghans charged down. He had not been seen since, and must have been drowned, or perhaps killed by a bullet in the head. Two of the cutter's crew had been left on shore dead, so these made the cutter's total casualties three killed, one missing, and five wounded. Only four had escaped untouched.

The dead man and the wounded were all brought aboard the *Bunder Abbas*: the dead who might only have been wounded, the wounded who so easily might have been dead. A turn of the head, and a bullet which would have only grazed your ear blows out your brains; you drop a cartridge, stoop to pick it up, and a bullet which would have gone through your heart wings on its way without your knowing that it had ever come and gone.

Whenever one sees dead and wounded brought back by the untouched men who have been fighting alongside them, one cannot help thinking queer

thoughts, and casting enquiring glances at the sur-
vivors to see what qualities they have which spared
them. I must admit that I have never yet noticed
anything particularly noble about those who have
escaped. Since those gun-running days I have seen
much fighting and many killed and wounded, and
the untouched have generally been cursing something
or somebody, giving relief to the strain on their
nerves by cursing hard. Thoughts take longer to
write than to think, so they don't, in actual practice,
waste much time.

We were obliged to take every heavy weight out of
the cutter to prevent her sinking, and then tried to
stop the bullet holes below the water line.

Webster, the corporal of marines, was as handy
with the medicine chest and its bandages as he was
with anything else I ever saw him try his hands on.
In half an hour he had made the wounded chaps as
comfortable as it was possible for them to be. Percy,
too, was in his element bringing them water, tinned
milk, and coffee. He was like a dog in his admiration for white men. If he had had a tail he would
have wagged it off that morning.

Until that cutter was safe I did not care how many
rifles the Afghans took out of the dhow in our absence;
but directly she was fairly watertight I left her at anchor
with the dinghy, Moore, the timid Goanese carpenter,
and a couple of hands, to carry on repairs, and steamed
inshore again.

I kept wide of the cliffs (from which a terrific fire
burst out) until the beach and the dhow herself came
in full view.

The shore was again alive with Afghans and their camels. Through my glasses I could see sacks of rifles being thrown from the dhow on to the sand, snatched up by eager men, and rapidly packed on the camels' backs. A long string of heavily-laden camels was already disappearing behind the sand-hills.

But I was not going to worry about them or Afghans. I was going to set that dhow on fire with my shells.

At twelve hundred yards I opened fire.

"At the dhow!" I shouted to Mr. Scarlett. "Don't worry about people."

Her woodwork began flying, and I knew that the shells were bursting inside her. It was only a question of time—the people aboard and close to her had vanished at the first shell—and presently smoke began to pour from her hatches. We cheered at this—those of us on deck working the gun, Griffiths at the wheel, and poor old Popple Opstein supporting himself against the deck rails. The rest I had sent down below under cover.

We kept on firing at her, and soon there was a rush of black smoke, small explosions took place aboard her, her stern blew out, her masts came tumbling down, and she took fire fore and aft. Every other minute some ammunition must have exploded, scattering fragments of wood and broken rifles round her on the sand. It was courting death to go near her; but, even so, some Afghans now and then rushed towards her, seized a rifle, and rushed back again. What plucky fellows they were!

By half-past ten o'clock there was no doubt that not

a round of ammunition remained in her, nor a rifle that was not entirely useless; so, with a parting shot dropped behind the sand-hills, I went back to the cutter and dinghy, running the gauntlet of the cliffs without receiving any damage.

Hoisting in the dinghy, and taking the empty, waterlogged cutter in tow, I steamed very slowly seawards to find the *Intrepid* and Nicholson.

Four men killed, one missing, and five wounded among the cutter's crew, one man killed and one wounded aboard the *Bunder Abbas*, was the price of that Sunday morning's work.

As we left Sheikh Hill behind us reaction set in, and we were very depressed.

The edge of civilization! I could not help thinking of that. At home people were just getting out of bed, wondering what Sunday clothes they should wear. I wished that some of them could have seen how we had spent that morning. If only I could have got hold of the people, English, French, or Germans— I didn't know and I didn't care—who had manufactured those rifles or sent them out there, I should have enjoyed torturing them.

Poor old Popple Opstein sat moodily outside my cabin under the awning, with his elbows on the table and his face buried in his hands. If I had been in his place I know that I should have done exactly as he had done; but, poor old chap, he knew as well as I did that he had bungled the whole affair, that we might have destroyed the dhow and the rifles without landing or losing a single man. He was suffering the tortures of the damned.

I put my hand on his shoulder and squeezed it. Nothing I could say would do him any good, and nothing did either of us say.

I dared not ask him if he was certain that those two men who had been left on the beach were actually killed; the thought of them having fallen alive into the hands of the Afghans was too horrible. Instead, I asked one of his men, and, thank God! he was certain that they were both dead. The one who had dropped halfway along the beach had been shot through the head, and the other, the one shot whilst lying half in the water under the dhow's stern, had been lying next to him, and his head was under the water all the time they were there.

The only touch of humour about the whole tragic business came from Percy. Dressed in his best, and looking very important, he had come up to me as we were in the middle of destroying that dhow and asked, pointing to my chum: "Master have guest to breakfast?" I had laughed like a fool, till I hurt myself.

As we were eating the food he had prepared for us —on the way back to the *Intrepid* that was—I turned to the gunner. "Mr. Scarlett," I said, "if you are a coward you are the bravest coward I have ever heard of."

"I do things like that just to try and beat it down, sir," he mumbled; "but it's just as bad when the next show comes along. I can't help it, sir; I really can't. I know I look frightened; but I don't look half as frightened as I really am."

Percy looked upon him as a demigod—that was very evident.

CHAPTER VII

The Battle of the Paraffin Can

WE were only able to tow that waterlogged cutter very slowly, so we did not sight the *Intrepid* until three o'clock that afternoon. Half an hour later we crawled alongside, and my chum and I went on board to report. He looked as if he was going to his execution, and though I did my best to make him " buck up ", and tried to hammer it into his head that we had done our best, and could do no more, he seemed more "down in the mouth" than ever.

Commander Duckworth made us tell him all that had happened, and I thought afterwards that if only people at home — just coming out of church they should have been at that hour—could have peered down into that luxuriously-furnished cabin of the *Intrepid* in the middle of the Straits of Ormuz, could have heard the story which my chum told, and seen the agony in his face as he told it, how it would have impressed them!

Cool, grey-green silk curtains kept out the glare from the port-holes and skylight; green-silk lamp-shades on the tables fluttered in the grateful breeze from the electric fans; pictures of English scenery, old naval prints, photographs of beautiful women in evening and Court dress, and photograph groups of

polo teams and their ponies covered the white bulk-
heads. From photographs in silver frames, standing
on the tables between silver cups and trinkets, more
delicate women looked out with smiling sympathetic
eyes, whilst backwards and forwards past them paced
the commander in his spotless white uniform. The
Baron and I were sitting on a dainty, silk-covered
sofa, digging our bare feet and toes into a soft Persian
rug. We had no clothes on except dirty, open cotton
shirts (the sleeves rolled up), and a pair of dirty duck
"shorts" halfway up our thighs. Our bare legs and
knees, our sunburnt chests and arms, looked very
much out of place among the luxurious surroundings.
Tied below his left knee Popple Opstein had a blood-
stained handkerchief, and on my head and forehead
was the dressing which Nicholson had put there three
days ago.

My chum still wore his revolver belt and holster,
and, for once, the dirty lanyard was round his neck.

"I made a fool of myself, sir," he blurted out; "I'd
never had a chance before, and I went straight for
her." His face was drawn with pain and shame at
his want of discretion.

"You both want a brandy-and-soda," was all Commander Duckworth said when he had heard our tale.

He made us drink one—it was iced, and it was
grand—and said not a word of reproof for our fool-
hardiness. If he had stormed and cursed us, I do not
know what we should have done.

I dreaded terribly that my chum would not be
allowed to take his cutter away again on account of
his wound—if for no other reason—but I think that

the commander realized his distressed state of mind, and I breathed freely when he quietly told us to repair all damages, that fresh men would be sent to replace casualties (my chum winced), and that we were to report as soon as we were ready to return to our stations.

I saw Popple Opstein's face flush with gratitude. He said, tremblingly: "Thank you, sir!" and limped out.

Commander Duckworth stopped me. "I don't know whether I am doing wisely or not in allowing him to go away again. Just have a look at him every daybreak, and, if that wound goes wrong, bring him back. Tell Nicholson to report to me what he thinks of it before he does go, and—and—just let him know how things stand."

"Very good, sir. Thank you, sir, very much! He's rather a strange old chap, fearfully sensitive, and he'd break his heart if you stopped him going."

The cutter was hoisted to the davits, and, whilst all the carpenters and ship-wrights in the ship were re-pairing her, the *Intrepid* slowly steamed inshore, towing my launch astern. Nicholson found time to look at the wounds in my scalp and forehead. He told me that they had healed splendidly; but when I saw them in a looking-glass—a great red line across my forehead and another on the side of my head across a patch of half-grown hair—I could not help making a grimace.

"It won't show in a month's time," he said, laughing. "Don't you worry about your beauty being spoilt; the girls will like you all the better for it."

Strangely enough, I did happen to be thinking

that perhaps if that little, yellow-haired lady saw me now, her mocking grey eyes might look a little serious—for once. At any rate she could not possibly treat me as an infant. I grew quite red—though that I should have done so was perfectly absurd, because I scarcely knew her, had only spoken to her once or twice, and then she had treated me as if I were a midshipman or a mere child.

Nicholson read my thoughts—or thought he did—and chaffed me till I grew more red than ever, and wanted to kick him.

Five miles off Sheikh Hill the *Intrepid* lowered the repaired cutter, the *Bunder Abbas* came alongside for me and to take in more ammunition, my chum and an entirely fresh crew manned his boat, and I towed him back to his old billet. He looked so sad and "rigid" as the cliffs opened out and he saw the blackened mass of woodwork, all that remained of the dhow which had caused that tragedy of the morning, that I felt very nervous to leave him alone for the night.

It was quite dark when I yelled "good night" to him and steamed away down the coast to Ruh-i-Mubarak, to try to find Evans.

We found him surely enough—or rather he found us. He mistook the "*B. A.*" in the darkness for a dhow, and fired twenty or thirty rounds from his Maxim before he saw my flashing lamp.

He was awfully apologetic; though, as no damage had been done, it did not matter. He had not seen a suspicion of a dhow, nor had he heard the noise of our firing, so went nearly "off his head" with excitement when I told him what had happened.

Having found that he was safe and sound, I went back to my patrolling line.

For several weeks everything went on extremely quietly. Every morning I would hail old Popple Opstein, and find how things were going with him; sometimes, when there was no hurry, he even came aboard for a cup of coffee. Every morning I visited Evans, and these two events were about the only excitement we had; except, of course, the weekly Thursday afternoon alongside the *Intrepid*.

The weather was monotonously fine, and it really was monotonous work. Neither was Mr. Scarlett exactly the type of man I should have chosen to live with. We agreed very well, indeed, but he was of a morbid disposition, never laughed except cynically, and seldom talked much unless something or other stimulated his rather brooding, sluggish mind. Then, as you already know, it was difficult to make him stop.

I liked talking at meals—he didn't; and, as a matter of actual fact, I, being a cheerful kind of chap, found him rather a "damper".

Wiggins had returned to the *Bunder Abbas*, and a leading seaman named Ellis, a sturdy, hard-working, little man, rather opinionated and fond of "gassing", had taken Dobson's place. He and Moore, the petty officer, did not "get on" at all well together. Moore was jealous of him, and was for ever coming to me complaining that "that 'ere Ellis took too much on 'isself."

Several times Moore brought him up to my platform deck (which we used as a quarter-deck) and reported him for disrespect. Precious little sympathy did he get from me, however. Still, in such a tiny little ship it was unpleasant to know that they were not on friendly terms. The jealousy first started, I fancy, when we had a "sing-song" one night. Both of them had sung songs, and Ellis had been more often "encored" than Moore. The reason seems perfectly inane, but full-grown men, under conditions such as these were, often behave in the most childish way possible.

During these first weeks Mr. Scarlett and Jaffa, between them, put me up to all the tricks of the gun-running business. What one didn't know of the Arabs' dodges for concealing rifles the other did; so I became quite an expert, theoretically.

One evening when it was fairly cool—after a regular furnace of a day—Mr. Scarlett became communica-tive. We had been speaking of boarding suspected dhows.

"Now take the case, sir, of a dhow flying the Turkish flag. You steam up to her; down goes her sail; over you bob to her in the dinghy with Jaffa, and tell the nakhoda to show his papers. You dare not board until you have seen them. He hands them down to you. You look through them—written in Turkish, English, and Hindustani; all three prob-ably—and so long as they are in order, whether you know for certain that she's brim-full of rifles or whether you only suspect that she is, you dare not board and search her.

"I remember," he said, "running up against a fine dhow one morning—I was away in the old *Pigeon's* cutter then—a long time since. We ran her down, headed her off till she couldn't get away, felt sure that she was going to be a fair prize, and yelled "Hallib! Hallib!" until she lowered her sails. And that reminds me, sir; never go alongside any dhow until she's lowered her sail. They Arabs have a nasty trick of waiting for you to come alongside, and then lowering the sail so that it and its big yard drops into the boat and smothers it. I've known 'em carry away a cutter's mast that way. Whilst you are helpless under the sail they pot at you, hoist it up again, and sail away. I've been 'had' like that myself once.

"Just you see that sail properly lowered and then make them hold up the halyards to show you that they are 'unbent', because they are as nippy as sharks a-hoisting it again.

"Well, as I was saying, we were as keen as mosquitoes over that 'ere dhow, but, as we caught hold of her with our boat-hooks, she hoisted Turkish colours and we dared not board her. The nakhoda, grinning at us, leant over her side and handed down his papers. These were in perfect order, so we no more dared board her than we dared stop the mail-steamer. What riled us chiefly was the brazen-faced way they did things. The cargo was put down as one hundred cases of champagne, consigned to a dirty little Persian village of about twenty miserable fishing-huts. We knew it well, we did, before—and after. We felt jolly well 'had'. We were as certain as 'eggs is eggs' that she was chock-full of rifles and ammunition, but they were as safe where they were as if they'd been on top of the Eiffel Tower.

"The lieutenant in charge of us cursed the Arab nakhoda, and called his ancestors dogs and sons of dogs, hoping he knew enough Hindustani to understand. Then off we had to shove.

"Our only chance was to catch those rifles on their way to the beach whilst the dhow was unloading, or when they once got there. All we could do was to pull off again and follow her, and it was about all we could do to keep up with her until she reached her blessed village just before dark.

"We'd been there a week before—for water—so we knew what it was like. If there had been thirty half-starved fishermen then I'd be overshooting the mark; now the beach was crowded with rascally Afghans and their camels, and no sooner did the dhow drop her anchor, close in to the beach, than those cases of champagne—about five feet long they were, each holding a dozen fat rifles we felt sure—were bundled into boats.

"We had a Gardner machine-gun in our bows, and opened fire with that and our old Martin Henrys; but there must have been a couple of hundred Afghans letting rip at us, so we had to pull out of range and watch those cases of champagne being lashed on the camels' backs until it was too dark to see anything more. At any rate, all those rifles got ashore, and you can guess what they were used for later on—for potting at British Tommies trying to keep order on the Indian frontier.

"Don't you go away with the idea that we English don't have a hand in the game," Mr. Scarlett continued gloomily. "Why, sir, many's the time I've seen captured rifles with the old 'Tower' mark on them, showing that they'd been made in England— old-fashioned Army rifles some of them, others not. And the tricks they're up to! My word, they are as artful as a bagful of monkeys! I've helped search a couple of hundred dhows or more in my time, and that's taught me a thing or two."

"The first dodge as I remember bowling out—and the simplest of 'em," Mr. Scarlett told me another evening, as he sipped his tot of rum—for it was not until Percy had brought along his rum and he had taken several "sips", when the crew had "piped down" and everything was quiet, that he generally started his "talking machine"—"they built double bottoms in their dhows, made 'em so cleverly that we used to think they were the real inner skin. But we happened to have emptied one of her cargo, and walking about inside her she sounded hollow under our feet, so we ripped up a board and found a snug little collection of rifles lying there. Of course the nakhoda swore he knew nothing about them; he and his crew called upon Allah and most of the minor prophets to testify to that, but it didn't prevent them doing their five months 'chokey' or losing their dhow. A nice little haul that was, and the word was passed along to 'sound' the bottoms of all the dhows we overhauled. We used to bang 'em with the butts of our rifles. They gave up that dodge after a while and invented something 'cuter' still. They'd fasten ten or twelve long ropes to the keel, outside her, bringing them over the side on deck, and they'd lash the free ends to sacks of rifles. If they sighted a

gunboat or a launch, or any of our people, and there
was a risk of being caught and searched, they'd
simply drop them overboard and let them hang down
in the water suspended from the keel.   Along we
would come, and find nothing wrong;   search her
high and low, and let her go, with our blessing or
the other thing.   Then one of our launches happened
to come upon a dhow unexpectedly, and caught them
doing it, heaving the sacks of rifles overboard—took
her by surprise—and that game was 'up'.   Never you
leave a dhow, sir, till you've 'underrun' her.[1]   You'd
be surprised how many rifles we picked up that way.

"Then there's another dodge they have round
about these coasts.   All along the Arabian side there
are plenty of mangrove trees, and a great trade in
firewood is carried on with the Persian coast.   So
what was easier for a dhow than to stow a dozen or
more rifles at the bottom of the hold and fill up with
firewood on the top of them?   They'd chance us
getting tired of unloading them;   a cutter cruising
by herself couldn't do it, because you daren't throw
any of the stuff overboard, and there wasn't room
on the dhow's deck for all the wood stowed below.
Why, sir, I've seen the whole of the *Pigeon's* upper
deck on both sides full up to the level of the 'nettings'
with chunks of firewood.   Just imagine the amount
of work that meant—five or six hours in the horrid
heat—every chap feeling as limp as putty with the
climate and the monotony.   A cutter cruising by herself either had to let her go or stand by the dhow,

---

[1] Underrun = drop a bight or loop of rope over the bows and haul it along
under her keel.

wasting perhaps three or four days, till her gunboat came along to victual her.

"However, we did search them, and we did find rifles, which meant 'Good-bye' for that dhow and 'chokey' for her crew. They found that trick not worth the risk, these people being generally law-abiding people (more or less), simply tempted every now and then to make a larger profit by carrying a few rifles. They weren't what you might call reg'lar hands at the business.

"And there's another thing they do, sir; on top of the firewood they often load a small cargo of their dried fish, thinking the British sailor won't stomach the smell of it. Ugh! the stink from some of those dhows! Why, we sometimes never got rid of the smell of it for weeks.

"You never heard about the mail-steamers—the Royal British Mail—carrying rifles themselves, I suppose, sir?" he asked, a little less gloomily as the incongruity of it appealed to him. "Why, sir, for one whole six months the mail-steamer brought up regular consignments of sugar from Karachi to Bushire and landed them there for a respectable firm of merchants. One fine day a careless chap at a winch, who was lowering a cask of sugar into a lighter, let it drop. The cask was stove in, and instead of sugar they found half a dozen rifles stowed in pieces, packed in saw-dust. That was an eye-opener, I can tell you. The mail-steamers don't carry so many casks of sugar now as they did then," Mr. Scarlett finished, smiling sardonically.

Another night he became talkative and began:

"You remember that chap who fired at us—the first time we shoved our nose under the cliffs at Sheikh Hill? I told you for certain he was an Afghan and couldn't possibly help firing his rifle at a white man. Well, sir, they often send one or two of these fellows across to the Arabian coast in the empty dhows, just to see that the rifles are brought to the proper place. You can always tell if there's one of these chaps aboard a dhow when you come along to search her, because he'll fire at you for a dead 'cert'. What we did was to make the crew line the side nearest us, after they'd lowered the sail and unbent the halyards. Our sportsman, the Afghan (or Afghans) dar'n't fire then for fear of hitting his friends, or had to climb up where we could see him, which didn't give him much of a chance, we being standing by waiting for him. Still, he didn't mind being riddled with bullets so long as he got in a shot at us English, more especially if he'd hit any of us.

"The only thing in this world he does fear and does mind is the sea. If there's a bit of a lop running you may bet your life that Mr. Afghan is as sea-sick as a dog, and you'll find him coiled up like a cat somewhere under the poop, without a kick left in him. He'd give anyone, white man or no white man, all he possessed, if he'd only kill him right out—that's when he's sea-sick.

"He's a terrible bad sailor, is the Afghan!" Mr. Scarlett said reflectively; "that's the only good point about him except being such a born fighter."

Mr. Scarlett, as you know, would talk about gun-running occasionally, but never once in those weeks did he mention that bracelet snake of his. It was covered with a bandage which he used to replace very carefully every morning; sometimes I happened to catch him doing this and saw it, but as he never referred to it neither did I.

Percy, I am sure, was very inquisitive to know what was the matter with his arm, because, as I said before, everything about Mr. Scarlett was of absorbing interest to him; though, after he had been kicked out of the cabin once or twice when Mr. Scarlett was dressing, he never ventured near it again until he was called.

Things went on like this for three weeks—three weeks of calm, intensely hot weather. Popple Opstein's wound had healed without anything going wrong with it; my scars were becoming less marked. Jones, the private of marines, was well—as were all the other wounded. Popple Opstein was quite himself again, and in fact everything was going on very comfortably if monotonously. It certainly was monotonous, because during all that time we never sighted one single dhow, and although the *Intrepid* had stopped and searched a few farther out at sea she had not found a single rifle over and above the proper number a dhow is allowed to carry for her own protection.

Then, to vary the tedium, it began to blow. A shamel got up very quickly, and blew steadily for eight or nine days. It was not so bad that the *Bunder Abbas* couldn't keep the sea and do her patrolling, but the two cutters had to hug tight at anchor in their two little creeks.'

However, Evans grew restless after the third day, and put to sea one morning, leaving the shelter of Kuh-i-Mubarak and beating into the shamel long after he ought to have run back again. A squall carried away his foremast when he was already to leeward of it, and he rapidly began to drift farther to the south. Fortunately I happened to sight him, went down to help him, and took him in tow. Towing him back into shelter against a heavy head sea strained some of the planks in the bows, below the water-lines, and the boat began leaking badly. We had only left the *Intrepid* four days previously, so that she would not be coming inshore to revictual us for another three; and, as it would have been foolish to attempt to tow the cutter right out to sea to find her and repair damages, we decided to beach her, do a little amateur caulking, and try to repair the foremast if that was possible.

There was a jolly little sandy beach about half a mile up the creek, so we beached her there after Evans had transferred his Maxim, ammunition, and stores to the *Bunder Abbas*. I anchored close by, in case he was attacked. There was little chance of that, however, because the village of Sudab lay more than three miles away behind the sand-hills, not a single living soul was in sight, and none could approach without being seen for at least a mile.

His men were soon busy working and skylarking, stretching their legs on the strip of sand, and thoroughly enjoying themselves. Not a sign of an Arab or an Afghan, not even of a miserable Baluchi, did we see all that day. In fact, things seemed so safe and pleasant that I landed most of my fellows too, and we got up a cricket match, with an empty paraffin tin for a wicket, a ball made of "spun yarn", and a bat made out of a broken oar. ‚ We equalized numbers with my lascars, and had a most exciting game, the *Bunder Abbas* winning the championship of Kuh-i-Mubarak just before the "spun-yarn" ball was worn out completely.

The work on the boat had been finished, the seams recaulked, and the mast repaired; but Evans decided, as it was going to be a perfect moonlight night, to stay there until next morning, in order that his men might have a change from the cramped cutter and get a good night's sleep.

At sunset I took all my people back to the *Bunder Abbas*, leaving the cutter's crew playing football with that paraffin tin, with their bare feet, until they grew tired of that, and kicked it into the edge of the sea. They then made themselves snug for the night, lying down on the crest of the beach with their rifles by their sides, in case they were attacked, and with one man doing "sentry go", to give warning if necessary.

When the moon rose I could see them all lying comfortably there, one sleepy-looking figure sitting up among them, and some way along the sand the cutter, with the sea—it was just about high water—lapping against her stern-post. Having seen my own "look-out" man "standing by" with a loaded belt in the Maxim, in case he was needed, I lay down on the deck, outside my cabin, and slept gloriously.

I was awakened by a rifle shot, and jumped up. More rifle shots spluttered out. I looked ashore and saw the cutter's crew lying flat on their chests firing along the strip of beach—showing up in the moonlight as clearly as if it was daytime—and heard Evans shouting out excited orders by the dozen. (I told you what a "nervy" chap he was.) One of his men came crawling down towards us, yelling to us to open fire. It did not want his shouts to alarm us; my fellows were already on deck, looking wildly up and down the creek to see who was attacking. Not a sign of an enemy could I see, and it was light enough to see half a mile; but the hummocks of sand stretching inland and along the beach cast such very dark shadows that whoever was attacking could lie there absolutely hidden.

To judge by the amount of ammunition the cutter's crew were expending, Evans was evidently certain of his enemy. Spurts of sand were flying up just in front of his men, although I could not see any flashes coming from out of those dark shadows. I admit that I felt considerably flustered; Mr. Scarlett's face looked ghastly in the moonlight, and I wished with all my heart that I had not allowed Evans to sleep ashore. I could not help thinking of how Popple Opstein had been caught, and was very fearful that something of the same kind was going to happen again.

If we could only have seen something to fire at it would have been less frightening, but there was nothing.

Then Evans himself came rushing down to where the cutter lay, and yelled to me to open fire whilst his men shoved her off.

I thought he could not possibly have made a mistake, so banged away with a Maxim at those shadows.

"There, sir, there! Look there, sir!" Moore suddenly rushed at me, pointing excitedly to a dark object apparently crawling along just by the water's edge not a hundred yards away.

The cutter's crew had seen it too, their bullets were spurting close to it, but Evans shrieked for them to come down and shove off the cutter, so I started the Maxim. We saw our bullets splashing all round, ceased fire, and waited for anything else to appear. Whatever that was, it never moved again.

By this time Evans had got the cutter afloat, and had come alongside the *Bunder Abbas*.

"Arabs crawling along the beach!" he shouted. "The sentry saw them first, fired at them—we've all fired at them—we've not seen any more since."

"Were they firing at you?" I called down, when he left off shouting at me.

He didn't know—he was not certain of anything except that his fellows had managed to kill at least one man.

At any rate, whatever had happened, no one was attacking us now. I stopped the Maxim, and together we waited on the qui vive all night, in case we were attacked again.

When the moon sank, an hour and a half before the sun was due to take her place, it became extremely dark, which made it most trying and nervous work waiting for daylight. Instead of the good night's sleep we had all promised ourselves, not a soul among us so much as closed his eyes after the alarm.

At daybreak not a sign of any living thing could be seen on those desolate sand-hills or on the beach, so we ventured ashore to pick up the cutter's masts and sails, which had been left behind in the panic.

I went too, to have a look at the chap we had shot, and guess what we found — fifty yards along the beach—that paraffin tin! just where we had thought we had seen the enemy crawling along to attack us— simply riddled with bullets. It was like a nutmeg grater, and the sand all round it was scored and tossed about by hundreds more.

I simply sat down and laughed and laughed till I thought something would crack. The whole thing was so obvious. It was high water when the men went to sleep; as the tide fell it left that tin high and dry: the sentry, suddenly catching sight of it and its shadow, lost his head, thought it was someone crawl-ing along the beach, let off his rifle at it, woke the others, and in their excitement they fired at every shadow they saw.

"You killed him, sure enough," I roared, holding up the perforated tin; "the attack was repulsed with great slaughter."

It was not until we had walked behind the sand-hills, and found not a single trace of footsteps, that Evans would allow that the whole thing had been a false alarm.

"Your Maxim fired at it too," he said angrily. "You've made a fool of yourself as well."

Evans never heard the last of his paraffin tin, nor did his boat's crew; and, later on, when the yarn (with additions) spread aboard the *Intrepid*, we all came in for a great deal of chaff. For months afterwards, a messmate hankering after a black eye had only to ask a man belonging to that cutter's crew, or to the *Bunder Abbas*, what kind of an Afghan a paraffin tin was most like, and he got one.

However, we had made the cutter watertight and mended the foremast (after a fashion), though it was not strong enough to "look at" the shamel still blowing; so, leaving Evans to wait until it had blown itself out, I struggled up to wind'ard to have a look at Popple Opstein and find out how he had fared.

I found him snugly anchored under the lee of Sheikh Hill. He was so close inshore that when I poked in to have a yarn, the "*B. A.*" could not get within half a mile of his cutter.

I pulled across in the dinghy.

"Has no one fired at you?" I asked him, seeing that he was within easy range of the shore and even of those high cliffs.

"Not a soul," he told me. "I've not seen a man, woman, or child these five days. Just look at those palm trees!" pointing in the direction where Bungi village lay. "They seem to have changed colour: they're browner than they were; and we cannot see anyone moving about among the sand-hills, not even from the top of the mast. I can't make it out."

I had to tell him the yarn of last night's brilliant little battle with the paraffin tin, and left him and his crew intensely amused.

When I went back to the *Bunder Abbas* I climbed her mast (much higher it was than the cutter's masts), and through my glasses very carefully searched the flats behind those sand-hills. Not a single living, moving thing did I see, although I watched for quite a quarter of an hour.

I sent Jaffa up to the masthead, and he came down puzzled, wanting me to land him so that he could find out what had happened.

He smiled when I suggested danger. "You wait, sir," he said, and disappeared down below.

My chum began making a signal to me, asking if I could spare any matches, so I forgot about Jaffa until, going back to the cabin, I came across him rigged out as a coast Persian or Baluchi—I didn't know anything of the different tribes, and I don't now—a regular low-caste, unkempt, miserable creature, dirtier than the dirtiest. The only thing remaining of the immaculate Jaffa was his dignified smile.

"You send me shore, sir, when dark comes. I go Bungi; find out things; come back to-morrow night —same time."

Mr. Scarlett told me that no self-respecting Afghan would waste a cartridge or blunt a knife on him in that rig, and that he would run very little risk; so, after sunset, and before the moon rose, I took him ashore myself in the dinghy, feeling rather ashamed to let him disappear behind the sand-hills alone, and promising to be there for him the next night.

At sunrise next morning, just as we were preparing to go to sea for the day, he was seen strolling calmly over the sand-hills, not even deigning to wave his arms to attract attention. One thing was certain: he could not be in any danger.

I stopped heaving in the cable, lowered the dinghy,

and pulled ashore myself, jolly glad to get some exercise.

"What's the news?" I called out, as the dinghy took the ground.

"Bungi all gone—houses burnt—men and old women lying all round—killed—no one else there—no young women—no children—only dogs and some goats—no Baluchis—no camels—no Afghans—all nothing."

"What's the meaning of that?" I asked in horror and astonishment.

He shrugged his shoulders.

"Afghan take revenge—lose many fighting men—cannot have rifles so take young women and children—take them to mountains—come and see."

I was only too keen to go, and followed him over those same sand-hills from behind which the Afghans had fired at Popple Opstein that horrid Sunday morning. We walked nearly a mile across the sandy wastes—very hot they were to my bare feet—and as we neared the clumps of palm trees which showed where Bungi had stood I saw why they had changed their colour—nearly all had been scorched by the heat from the burning thatched roofs. Their big leaves, red and yellow and black, hung low, mournfully.

The whole village was destroyed and the scene was too horrible to describe, but I saw enough to know that Jaffa was right.

Some half-jackal half-wolf dogs went yelping away when we disturbed them; nothing else lived.

The cruel Afghans had not even been satisfied with this. It was plain that they had driven their herd of camels up and down the patches of cultivated ground until not a trace of them existed. Jaffa explained this, and pointed out the innumerable hoof-marks.

The one well was heaped with dead bodies.

He said, in his quaint way, that that was a proof that "the Afghans had been very angry"!

Then he took me out of the village and showed me the broad track of camel marks leading across the ford towards the mountains.

The sooner the captain of the *Intrepid* knew of this the better; so back to the dinghy and the *Bunder Abbas* we went. I signalled across to tell Popple Opstein (we now knew why he had not been fired at) and went to sea, steaming down to Kuh-i-Mubarak. The shamel was still blowing strongly, so Evans was taking shelter in the creek close to the site of the "battle of the paraffin can". As we passed him I shouted out to tell him the news, and that I was going to find out whether Sudab had met the same fate.

I steamed up until the lagoon opened out and the water became too shallow to go farther. Then, landing with Jaffa, Webster, the corporal of marines, and two privates, all armed, we advanced very cautiously inland towards those palm trees under which I had seen the camels many weeks ago. Long before we reached them we knew by the burnt leaves and the sickening smell which pervaded everything that Sudab had met the same fate as Bungi. Even the fishing-boats had been smashed or burnt. We were very glad to get away from it, tramping back through the hot sand, and meeting Evans on his way to explore on his own account. I tried to dissuade him from going, but he was too excited to listen.

"I'm going along to find the *Intrepid*," I shouted after him.

"I'll come along too, directly the shamel has finished," he called back.

In an hour the little "*B. A.*" was plunging and burying herself into a head sea, making two knots, over the land. We went at it all the rest of that day and all that night, sighting the *Intrepid* next morning.

I signalled across my news, and was immediately ordered to close. It was too rough to go alongside. I was ordered to steam to Jask with telegrams for the Admiral and to find out if the telegraph people had any news.

Of course, it was evident to everyone that the Afghans had given up any idea of landing more rifles at either of these two places, so the sooner the Admiral knew of this and the sooner we found out what fresh schemes were under way, the better.

But I was short of coal, and it took nearly two hours to fill up from the *Intrepid*, making fast with a hawser to her stern, and passing small bags from her poop to our bows along a running whip—no light job with such a nasty sea running. Then I was off again for Jask.

I looked at myself in the cracked glass inside our cabin. That scar across my forehead still showed very plainly, and for the life of me I could not help wondering what that little yellow-haired lady would say when she saw it.

CHAPTER VIII

Ugly Rumours

AT daybreak next morning we were off Jask Point,
with its square white telegraph buildings and its low
sand-hills jutting out into the sea. As the shamel was
still blowing hard from the north-west I anchored to
the east'ard of the point, close to some rocks, and
among a number of dhows sheltering there.

Percy pipeclayed my shoes and helmet, laid out my
last clean white suit of uniform, and, having made
myself look as smart as I could, I landed close to the
old ruined fort (or sheikh's house) and walked up
towards the telegraph buildings, meeting the political
agent, in pyjamas, smoking a cigar and looking criti-
cally at the earth breastwork and the line of wire
entanglements.

"Hallo!" he called out cheerily; "they told me
you were coming in. You people have made it
hot for everybody along the coast, and no mistake!"

He did not want me to give him any news. He
had already heard of the capture of one dhow and the
destruction of the other, of the terrible losses of the
Afghans, of our men being killed, and that Bungi
and Sudab had been destroyed. The Afghans had

got the idea into their heads that the poor, wretched Persian villagers had given the "show" away, so had taken this ghastly revenge.

"You can't keep anything secret in this country," he said; "the way news travels is simply marvellous. I even heard that an officer had been wounded.

"Was that you?" he asked, looking at my forehead. "I heard that one of you had been seen to fall whilst running along the beach."

I shook my head. "I did not land. It was my chum. Shot through the calf he was. He's all right now."

"Those Afghans came along this way before they went home," he continued; "camped round the new fort, halfway to old Jask; hanged a couple of Persian customs people who lived in it; hanged them from the top of the wall to show their contempt for the Persian Governor; looted it and went away next morning with their camels and the women and children captured in those villages. They had a great number of wounded, those you had wounded—poor wretches!—and threatened to come along and cut our throats later on. A few of them did actually ride up here and fire their rifles—but that was nothing. They put down their losses—they had more than sixty killed —and their ill luck with the gun-running business to the telegraph cable—about right they are too—and would do anything to destroy it and us. Before they went away they cut the land line running along the coast to Karachi, just to give us the trouble of repairing it."

"Aren't you rather nervous?" I asked him.

He shrugged his shoulders.

"We have twenty fellows here who can handle rifles—Eurasians and people like that—besides Borsen and myself. The governor of Jask, too, has fifty or sixty border police, Bedouins, whom the Afghans hate more than they hate us, so we could rely upon them at a pinch!"

"I suppose they will not attempt to run more rifles into Bungi or Sudab?" I said enquiringly.

"No, no! they've had enough of those two places. They'll get news across to the Arabian coast and lie quiet for some months. Come along and have 'chota-hazri'," he said, changing the subject. "You needn't say anything about those Afghans or about them coming along here. My wife knows nothing about it, nor does Miss Borsen; I don't want them to know."

He took me up to his house and sent off the telegrams for the Admiral. The old head boy brought us tea, bread and butter, and fruit, and I quite enjoyed myself, except that the old gentleman was wearing a yellow-silk turban, and every time he came out on the veranda it caught my eye, and I thought he was Miss Borsen.

However, I might have spared myself the trouble of constantly turning my head and expecting to see her, because she was not even living in that house, but with her brother.

Afterwards, on my way down to the beach, I saw her there, a slim little figure on the shore, dressed all in white, with a big white helmet almost covering her yellow hair, looking strangely out of place among a motley crowd of Arabs, Persians, and Zanzibaris, loading and unloading the dhows.

" Her brother ought not to let her come down alone," I thought angrily.

She had a camera with her, and was taking pictures of the natives and their camels. She smiled when she saw me, and every mortal thing I had in my head seemed to go out of it. I couldn't think of any blessed thing to say except that it was a fine morning.

Then she laughed until I grew red and uncomfortable. It was a relief to shout across to the " B. A." for the dinghy, but whilst it was coming she made me pose for my photograph.

" I have a snapshot of your little steamboat (boat!— mind you); I must have one of its captain too," she said, as if it was a great compliment to be photographed by her.

If there is one thing I hate more than another it is having my photograph taken. Especially did I hate this, because she arranged me and rearranged me, with Griffiths in the dinghy for a background, and all the time he was grinning at me till I felt the idiot I looked. She never mentioned the scar on my forehead, so I took my helmet off so that she must see it, and then all she said was: " Do put your hat on again, and turn side face; that nasty scratch quite spoils the picture."

Hat! Nasty scratch! Spoils her picture! My word, what irritating things girls are! I'd gone ashore wanting her to see the wound, perhaps to say something nice about it, and hoping that she would treat me, for once, as though I were a man; and she'd made me cover it up in order not to spoil her picture, and made me stand there, like a baby, whilst she took the snapshot.

I felt very irritated, and when she said: "Let me come aboard and photograph that dear Mr. Scarlett," I felt more annoyed than ever. At that time of the morning the *Bunder Abbas* wasn't clean and tidy, so I answered rather cuttingly that I'd send the gunner ashore to be photographed, and suggested that perhaps she'd better wait until her brother or the political agent's wife could bring her on board some other time.

She smiled again her mocking smile, and, curtsying derisively, watched me clambering clumsily into the dinghy, trying not to wet my feet. With her eyes on me I felt like an elephant trying to get into a canoe, and one of my feet slipped and went into the water. That buckskin shoe was pretty well spoiled.

When Griffiths shoved off—still grinning the brute was—I looked back to salute; but she was already walking away from the beach and did not turn her head.

"She's offended now," I thought. "Serve her jolly well right! Fancy asking herself aboard like that; no English girl would have dreamt of doing such a thing!"

However, I was not really in the least pleased, and Mr. Scarlett soon found out that I was in a pretty bad temper.

Commander Duckworth had ordered me to lie at Jask until replies to his telegrams had been received from the Admiral, so there I had to stay—possibly for days.

The morning went by very slowly. I was in a

thoroughly bad temper, and didn't care a "buttered biscuit" whether the six-pounder's recoil springs wanted adjusting or not; and when the lascar first-driver reported that the packing in the high-pressure piston-rod gland was not as tight as it should be, dragging me down below to see it, I cursed him till he salaamed a hundred times a minute to appease me. Moore, too, reported Ellis again for giving him "lip", and went away "with a flea in his ear".

I could not get the idea out of my head that those Afghans would come back and attack the place. Those wire entanglements and earthworks looked such puny things to keep back those fierce chaps who had faced our Maxims and six-pounder near Bungi, that if they really meant business, fifty rifles would not keep them out.

It was such hard luck on those two women. The political agent and Borsen did not count. They'd gone into the job with their eyes open, but the women —well, that was different. They should never have been allowed to come to this desolate, exposed, out-of-the-way spot, on the very edge of civilization.

Those mountains, too, were only twenty miles away; the Afghans could swoop down from them in a night, appear as unexpectedly as a vulture, get between the telegraph station and old Jask, with its fifty Bedouin border police, and cut it off entirely.

I sent for Jaffa and asked him what kind of fellows these border police were. He shrugged his shoulders, as much as to say that they were useless, and volunteered to go to Jask and find out, in the bazaars, what news there was. I let him go, and he borrowed a

camel from a friend on the beach and rode away
inland, his black lambskin fez disappearing among
the palms surrounding the ruined sheikh's house.

That afternoon Mr. Scarlett and I enjoyed the luxury
of a thoroughly good sleep, lying back in our canvas
chairs under the awning outside our cabin until Percy
woke us for afternoon tea—tinned milk, bread (stale)
buttered with liquid tinned butter, rancid at that.

There was a little sandy cove among the rocks
close alongside, so I sent the whole crew ashore there,
natives and all. They were soon enjoying themselves
to their hearts' content, bathing and skylarking, scrubbing their clothes, drying them on the hot sand, and
having a thoroughly good time.

"I'm hanged if I'm going to land at Jask again,"
I said to myself; but I did go, bawling ashore for someone to bring off the dinghy, and wearing my one
respectable flannel suit of "plain clothes"—the very
first time I had worn "plain clothes" since joining
the *Bunder Abbas*.

I left Mr. Scarlett in charge; he never wanted to
go ashore. He said, quite openly, that he was afraid
of meeting Jassim, and felt sure that he would do so
sooner or later. He was not a man one could argue
with. Once he had made up his mind that something
gloomy was going to happen he'd stick to it, and
when it didn't happen he would be more certain that
something worse still would take its place. This silly
business about Jassim and the bracelet was, of course,
at the bottom of it all. It seemed so absolutely
childish for him to imagine that he would meet the
man, or that anyone would remember the beastly

thing, after all these years, to say nothing of the fact that whatever poison was left in the fangs after they had bitten those two could not possibly have retained its powers, that I lost patience with him.

I landed, but never intended going near the telegraph station, not by a long chalk. I did not want to be treated like a child by Miss Borsen—you bet I did not—so I wandered off to explore the ruins of that sheikh's house or fort among the palm trees.

It was a great square building with a tower at one corner, built up of red sandy bricks, all rounded by age, and the mortar, or whatever it was which bound them together, so friable and crumbling that I could loosen a brick with the end of a stick in no time. An entrance under the tower (from which the door had long since disappeared) led into a courtyard covered with rubbish, and all round it were the remains of dwelling-rooms, storehouses, and stables. Some still had roofs to them. A great high wall with crumbling battlements and platforms seemed to shut out every trace of breeze and shut in every ray of heat. The place was like an enormous oven. I climbed up some rough brick steps leading towards the battlements and base of the tower and had a good view over the surrounding country.

Beyond a few miserable palm trees was the open narrow piece of flat ground forming the neck of the peninsula. It gradually rose towards the telegraph buildings, and about halfway between—something like three hundred yards from where I stood—were the line of wire entanglements and the earth breastwork, stretching right across from the rocks under which the *Bunder Abbas* was anchored to the shore on the other side, where the shamel was still driving white breakers up the beach with a continuous roar.

Still higher was that strong, loopholed wall surrounding the buildings themselves.

Away to the east'ard ran the telegraph line on its bare steel poles: the line which ran along the coast to Karachi, and which the Afghans had cut only a few days ago. I could follow the line of telegraph posts till they dwindled into "nothing", and felt very thankful that it was not my job to go along that appallingly lonely coast to repair damages.

I suppose I was seen from the telegraph station, for a servant came running down the peninsula, came into the middle of the courtyard, and I'm hanged if I didn't get an invitation to tea with the political agent's wife.

I climbed down and followed him, pretending that I was unwilling to go, and grumbling to myself that if I did meet Miss Borsen we should probably have a row. In half an hour I found myself playing tennis with a borrowed racket and borrowed shoes, which flopped about like canoes on my feet, with Miss Borsen playing opposite me, and beating me time after time with her low drives along the side lines. She seemed to take a positive joy in seeing me falling over my own feet in my attempts to return balls much too good for me. I hate being beaten at any game, especially by a woman, so that did not improve my temper.

"What about your gunner?" the political agent said, when at last I was allowed to "cool off" out of range of that little torturer's eyes. "Doesn't he ever come ashore?"

This made me think of Jassim, the bracelet, and of snake poisons.

"Do you know anything about poisons?" I asked. "How long do you suppose a cobra's poison would remain deadly?"

"In a dead cobra, do you mean? I don't know; but I should not care to keep a dried one without having his poison gland removed."

"No," I said. "If you extracted the poison and kept it in a—a bottle, for instance."

"Not for long, I should imagine," he answered; and then I was fairly startled, for he began to tell me the story of the very cobra bracelet on Mr. Scarlett's arm. I did my best to appear as if this was all quite unknown to me, for fear he should guess that I knew something about it, and drag more information from me than Mr. Scarlett would care I should tell.

"I've never seen it," he went on, quite unsuspiciously; "but an old friend of mine, skipper of a tramp steamer doing a queer business in the Gulf many years ago, saw it once, and told me that he'd never seen such a beautiful piece of workmanship. It will turn up some day at Christie's or at some other curio dealer's in London, I expect, and I'm rather sorry for whoever buys it. If he is known to possess it the news will come along out here, and I don't mind saying that it will disappear again within six months. The present Khan of Khamia, the real owner, is not the wealthy chap some of the former khans were, but he offers a reward every three months in the bazaars of every town on both sides of the Gulf —a reward of thirty thousand rupees—to whoever brings back the 'twin death', as it is called. That's two thousand pounds, and there's not an Arab born yet who wouldn't give his body to earn that, to say nothing about his being certain of Paradise if he helped· to restore it to its rightful owners."

I mopped my perspiring face often enough to prevent him noticing how his confirmation of Mr. Scarlett's yarn had stirred me, and was quite glad to be called away to play tennis.

I played worse than ever, and Miss Borsen grew more provokingly successful.

After all my determination never to go near her again, I found myself weakly consenting to stay to dinner. The political agent rigged me out in clothes of his own, and the meal was a most delightful change after "pigging it" on board the "*B. A.*" for six weeks on tinned grub, with only the gunner's black-bearded, morose face in front of me. After such fare as we had had this dinner was luxury, but still more of a luxury than the food was the daintily decorated table with its soft candlelight.

It would have been absolutely enjoyable if Miss Borsen had not been there too. She had a most irritating effect on me. Whether she intended it or not she always seemed to be "pulling my leg", and I instinctively "bristled up" and wanted to get the upper hand, and put her in her proper place as a very dainty little lady who should listen, very respectfully, whilst I talked.

I tried to tell them about being carried away to sea

in that dhow; but when I came to the part where I climbed along the struggling yard, instead of looking impressed, she merely giggled: "I wish I'd been there; you must have looked like a frog." This put me "off" telling any more yarns, and made me so annoyed with her that I disagreed with everything she said.

Every time I did so she came off best in the argument, in spite of not speaking English very fluently.

By the end of that dinner I felt that I wanted to pick her up—I could have done so with one hand—and give her a thoroughly good shaking, just to make her realize how strong I was, and that though she could defeat me with her clever little tongue, she was, at any rate, helpless physically.

It was a most gloriously cool night, with millions of stars shining, and they all walked down to the beach to see me go aboard. We came to a dark patch close to the beach, where the tide sometimes washed across, and when the political agent called out: "Be careful of your feet; it's swampy," the temptation was too great. I whisked little Miss Borsen off her feet, and, before she had time to make more than an angry protest, had carried her twenty paces across it and set her down on the dry sand.

She never spoke a single word after that, and I chuckled to think that, at last, I had stopped her tormenting little tongue. I would try that dodge again if necessary.

I hailed the "*B. A.*"; the dinghy came ashore for me, and off to my launch I went, shouting good-night to them all. My little tormentor's voice was not among the chorus of "good-nights" shouted back. She still had her tongue tied.

Mr. Scarlett was waiting up for me, looking more saturnine than ever. His dark eyes gleamed maliciously when I came into the light of the lamp, because a little blue-velvet bow had caught in a button of my coat. It was one she had worn, and I got red, looked an ass, and untwisted it. I kept it, too, as a trophy of the first victory I had won.

"Brute force is better than brains—sometimes," I chuckled to myself.

"Jaffa come back?" I asked.

Mr. Scarlett shook his head, and I felt rather nervous about him, although that was quite unnecessary, because he arrived next morning, safe and sound, but with very little definite information. The townspeople in Old Jask were in a state of alarm at the threats of the hill tribes, and the Khan or Mir had called in the border police from outlying villages. He had actually served out ammunition to them—a thing he did not often do for fear that they themselves would plunder Jask. I went up to see the political agent to tell him of this. He knew it already, but it was a good enough excuse to go, for I wanted to know if I had offended Miss Borsen and apologize if I had done so.

However, I did not see her; and although the replies to those telegrams did not come from the Admiral for another four days, and I went there every day, I never did see her. There was always some excuse: that she had a headache, or was resting; but it was plain enough that I had mortally offended her, and my victory seemed much more like a defeat.

So it was quite a relief when the cipher telegrams did arrive, and when the "*B. A.*" steamed away north-west again, to look for the *Intrepid*.

These telegrams ordered Commander Duckworth to proceed immediately to Muscat. He wasted no time in picking up the two cutters and departing, leaving me to cruise up and down that same strip of coast for another fortnight, without seeing a sail—until, in fact, I had to run across to Muscat myself, for coal and water.

I found the *Intrepid* there anchored under the black cliffs and the old fort, and hoped to get ashore, but was ordered to fill up as quickly as possible and to cruise off a place called Jeb, about forty miles to the north'ard, where those rifles were originally reported to have been stowed. A miserable native chap, with a grudge to repay, had come along from there to say that a dhow was filling up with rifles for the Makran coast. So off I had to go.

This coast was entirely different from the one I had just left. Stupendous barren mountains towered up to the sky; their ridges and shoulders, sweeping down to the sea, ended abruptly in stupendous cliffs whose feet were eaten away by the continual beating of the south-west monsoon waves, until they looked as if they must soon topple over. Forbidding-looking inlets here and there made very comfortable shelter to lie in for a few hours, though I could not stay in them for long without being "sniped". My orders were not to go within five hundred yards of any inhabited place, because the people along the coast were so well armed, and even in these desolate inlets they would discover me, after a very short time, and compel me to go out into the heavy seas again.

Thank goodness, they were execrable shots!

Luck was not in our way, for when we returned to Muscat we found that the *Intrepid* herself had captured that dhow, and all we had to do was to tow it out and burn it—not a very heroic task.

The next fortnight was spent still farther to the north'ard. Sixty miles of coast we had to examine, and we started from the farthest point, gradually working along towards Muscat. Wherever there was a gap in the cliffs, or a valley running down to the sea, in we would go and be sure to find a village, perhaps a dozen huts, perhaps fifty, nestling under a few date-palm trees or along the banks of a stream. The natives (fishermen, for the most part, owning perhaps a few sheep or goats, which they guarded day and night from wolves and jackals) were an inoffensive, absolutely ignorant lot of people. Even Jaffa could make very little out of them except that they lived in perpetual fear of Bedouins or other raiding Arab tribes and of wild animals. They did not want money—they did not seem to know the use of it—and for a few dates and a few pounds of rice—especially rice—we could get enough fish for the whole crew.

I had to search all these villages for concealed arms. It was supposed that the Arabs—Bedouins or whoever they were—knowing that it was useless to try to send any more rifles away from Jeb, would take them farther up the coast in caravans, distributing them in small numbers among these villages and compelling the natives to store them in their huts, until dhows should come along and take them away.

However, we found nothing whatever except a few old muzzle-loaders, dating from the year "one".

There was such an entire absence of danger that whilst a couple of bluejackets or marines, under Moore, Ellis, or Webster, went from hut to hut, searching, I would take the head man of the village away up the slopes of the mountains and try to get a shot at a wild goat. I managed to bag one or two, and when, one day, at some wretched place which I don't believe possessed a name, I shot a leopard (I had only a shotgun with me), breaking its hindlegs so that it could not get away and the natives could surround it and beat it to death, I was looked upon as the saviour of the village. They filled the dinghy with fish, and actually brought along a sheep. Jaffa and Mr. Scarlett said it was a sheep; I thought it was a goat; and I'm hanged if it was possible to tell, by eating it, which it was.

The news of my shooting the leopard spread along the coast, and whereas, previously, the villagers had been half-frightened out of their lives when the "*B. A.*" appeared, flying hurriedly with their women and children, goats and sheep, to the mountains, now, when we anchored off a village, the beach would often be lined with people to welcome us and implore me to go and shoot leopards or jackals.

On the last day of this cruise, the last morning before we had to return to Muscat for more coal and food, I took the *Bunder Abbas* into a most marvellous gorge in the cliffs. Just imagine enormous, perpendicular, sea-worn cliffs, eight hundred feet high, with the south-west monsoon swell roaring at their feet, and a cleft, not fifty yards across, cut straight down through them, as by some enormous knife.

Into this the "*B. A.*" shoved her nose, twisted and turned, with those huge walls on either side, until long after the sea had disappeared and the booming of the breaking swell had ceased. Gradually the walls trended downwards, until a last turn disclosed an inland basin, quite a mile long and nearly as broad. Mangrove trees came down all round it nearly to the water's edge; what looked like rich grass-land ran up the slopes of the mountains until it faded among the gaunt bare rock; and at one place, where a little stream opened, there was quite a large cluster of huts, with many fishing-boats drawn up on the beach in front of them. I anchored in front of this village—marked on the chart as Kalat al Abeid—lowered the dinghy, and pulled ashore, with Jaffa to interpret, and the three marines (armed with rifles) to do the usual searching.

I took my shot-gun, but the head-man—a tall, wizened, old chap with a scarlet sash round his waist and a scarlet turban on his head—as soon as he saw it, shook his head, patted one of the marine's rifles, and jabbered away excitely to Jaffa, pointing up to the mountains.

Jaffa interpreted: "He say plenty leopard in mountain—come down every night—kill sheep and goats —two nights ago killed a woman. Want you get rifle from ship—go shoot them—want all men go— kill many leopard—he show you where they sleep in daytime."

"Right oh, old cock!" I said, sent the dinghy back for another rifle, and hurried away the marines and Jaffa to get their searching done.

The villagers were so eager for us to go shooting that they had actually stripped their huts of everything movable, bringing the things outside, so that all we had to do was to stoop down through the low doorway, see that the floor was bare and had not been disturbed lately (no rifles buried there), then back out again and search the next.

It was the quaintest sight in the world to see the excited children—little brown naked urchins—staggering out with big clay cooking utensils and brass cooking pots as big as themselves, as happy as the day was long at this new kind of game.

One or two huts were so dark inside that we could not see; but the natives tore away some of the palm-leaf roof to let in light, in order that nothing should delay us.

Griffiths came back with the dinghy and my rifle, bringing a spare one on the chance that I would let him have a day's sport too. I let him come, and away inland we started, the head-man, Jaffa (with my shot-gun), and myself leading, followed by Webster, his two marines, and Griffiths, surrounded by a dirty, happy mob of natives, armed with short, clumsy hunting spears, some only with boat's paddles. Innumerable children followed, shrieking with delight, and a dozen or more women, hooded so that we could only see their eyes, bearing vessels of water—big earthenware chatties—on their heads, brought up the rear of the expedition.

If I had had any idea whatever of treachery the
fact of the women coming along would have dispelled
that.   We were just as safe as if we had been going
shooting among a lot of country people in England.

Directly we had reached the limits of cultivation the
children were sent back very quickly.   No leopard
could have slept comfortably within a mile of the
noise they made.   Then we commenced to wind up
a track towards the mountains themselves, and the
nearer we came to them the more rugged and barren
they looked.   Very nearly black they were in places;
great rents split whole shoulders from the main ridge;
huge masses of rock were poised on each other like
vast columns, looking as though a bird perching on
them would upset them.   Indeed the slope we were
ascending was so strewn with gigantic blocks of black
rock that one knew that they, at one time, must have
fallen from just such columns.

The head-man began talking volubly to Jaffa, and
he, turning to me, said: "Leopards there—come down
at night—go back sleep close by."

I told Jaffa that whatever happened I must be back
by sunset.

The old man understood and nodded—so we pushed
on.   It was very hot work scrambling up that vast,
debris-strewn slope, over smooth rocks which gave
scarcely any foothold, twisting round great boulders
or half-wading through loose sand, worn from the
face of some steep, precipitous part by countless years
of exposure—everything too hot to put one's hands
on comfortably, and the sun always scorching on
one's back.   I called a halt long before the old

head-man had begun to show the slightest sign of fatigue.

I looked back. My three marines and Griffiths were some way below us, among the admiring villagers, wiping their perspiring faces. Lower down was the little group of women crouching together, with their water chatties in front of them; a thousand feet below, beyond the dark, green fringe of mangrove trees, the *Bunder Abbas* lay in that inland basin, and, winding out like a dark snake, the channel wriggled through the cliffs to the sea. The blazing sun poured down relentlessly from a cloudless sky.

Jaffa touched my arm, pointing out to sea and to a faintly-showing trail of smoke. Unslinging my glasses, I followed the line of smoke till I saw a steamer. It was the *Intrepid*, evidently making for this same harbour.

"Why the dickens is she coming here?" I thought, and would have stayed; but the head-man was impatient, so we shoved on again, though I kept turning back to watch her until she disappeared under the shore-line. In half an hour Jaffa, whose one eye seemed better than my two, swung me round to see her emerge from the channel into the basin itself.

Well, the old "*B. A.*" was safe enough now. It did not matter how late we got back; when he heard about the leopards Commander Duckworth would be too good a sportsman to be annoyed that I was not there. I felt quite at ease.

So on we scrambled, in Indian file, higher and higher, until a turn of the track round a shoulder of the rocks shut out the sight of the sea, and also, thank goodness, gave us shelter from the sun. It was like going from brilliant sunlight into a darkened room.

We now found ourselves in an extraordinary hollow, more like being at the bottom of a huge well or cup— a coffee-cup with a crack in it, the crack the ravine through which we had just entered—its bottom strewn with a jumble of rocks which had fallen in the course of ages from the precipitous walls which shut out the sky. It was very gloomy and silent but delight- fully cool.

Craning our necks backwards we looked up through the rim of our coffee-cup to the burning sky overhead. That rim must have been a thousand or twelve hun- dred feet above our heads if it was an inch, and at one point, immediately opposite us, there was an extra- ordinary gap in it. Just as the cleft in the cliffs through which the *Bunder Abbas* had steamed three hours before looked as though some giant had chipped it out with an enormous axe, so this gap looked as though the same giant, on his way to the sea, had pinched a piece out of the edge as he swung himself across it.

Strangely enough, Jaffa discovered afterwards that there was a local tradition something to that effect.

The villagers began to crowd round us, jabbering excitedly. The old head-man drove them away, whacking them with his long stick. Then he began talking to Jaffa.

"Villagers stay here," Jaffa explained. "Head- man take you and us up to gap—leopards lie among rocks all about here—when we climb up to top villagers make noise—leopards try escape through gap —you shoot."

What a grand idea! I would have gone anywhere with the sporting old chap, although I had not the faintest idea how we were to get up there without wings.

"Right oh! Lead on!" I cried, and the old fellow began leading us farther into the gloomy bottom of the "cup", clambering round the boulders, Jaffa, myself, the three marines, and Griffiths following him. Then he began to ascend the precipitous wall itself by a path—if you could call it a path—so steep and so narrow in places that it was as much as I could do to keep my feet or climb up it. It zigzagged up that wall in twenty or more zigzags; looking down from the upper ones we could see those below; looking upwards we could see no trace of any foothold, nothing whatever but rocks rising sheer above us. At one or two of the worst places the edge of the track actually overhung, and small stones dislodged by my feet fell plumb down until I dare not watch them far for fear of feeling dizzy.

Presently we had scaled the rocks sufficiently high to come to the edge of the shadow cast by the eastern rim of the "cup". Here I called a halt, perhaps three hundred feet below the gap, and we leant back against the rocks and rested. I felt like a fly on a wall, and only wished that I had suckers on my hands and feet, or were a goat.

"This isn't a proper track, is it?" I asked Jaffa.

He smiled, and at the time I didn't believe him

when he said: "The only way out of the valley—only way inland from the village—for men or camels!"

"Camels! What nonsense!" I thought.

The old head-man was much too energetic for me. Off he went again, and led us into the full blaze of the sun.

Great snakes! In a minute or two I was dripping with perspiration, and when we did at last reach that gap, and I threw myself down on some rocks there, I don't think that I had ever felt so hot in my life.

However, a grand current of air whistled through the gap, as though this, too, was the only way the sea-breezes could pour inland. I soon cooled down.

"What a climb!" I said to Webster, as we looked down at the extraordinary chasm beneath our feet—the "coffee-cup", as I have called it—and tried to trace the zigzag path up which we had climbed. It must have taken us an hour at least to ascend, and I confess that, as I looked down, I did not in the least relish the idea of having to crawl down again.

At the bottom it was dark and gloomy and silent; not a trace of villagers could we see among the rocks there, nor could we get a view of the *Intrepid* or the sea beyond, because the crack in the "coffee-cup" was shut in by another shoulder of the mountains.

The gap was about five yards wide, its sides about twenty feet high, and I took twelve paces before I looked down into the valleys on the far side. Deep and misty they were, and beyond them stupendous ranges of barren, naked mountains lost themselves in the distance.

The old man made us take up positions on the

crest on either side of the gap, myself, himself, Jaffa, and Griffiths on one side, the three marines on the other; and was just going to give the signal to the men below to commence their drive—a leopard drive, mind you; think of it, and think how happy and excited we were—when, turning to look down the far side, his face became a muddy-yellow colour—just as Mr. Scarlett's often did. All the life seemed to die out of it, and he gasped out: "Bedouin!"

We all turned, and through my glasses I saw what at first looked like some huge snake winding up the valley towards us. Then I saw that it was an apparently endless caravan of heavily-laden camels, wearily trailing one after the other. Among them were many horsemen—a hundred or more, although it was impossible to count them.

Then I knew why the *Intrepid* had turned up so unexpectedly. These were the very fellows we had been hunting for, bringing their rifles from Jeb to hide them in the village at our feet, until dhows could be sent to take them away. And they must pass through this gap, on either side of which we were lying, in order to get there. Some wretched brute must have taken the news to Muscat, and given away the scheme (there were always plenty of these fellows mean enough to sell their own fathers for a few rupees).

The old head-man, half-paralysed with fear, was worming himself down into the gap. I clutched him.

"Ask him how long before they reach here!" I told Jaffa.

The old chap could hardly speak, he was so frightened.

" In two hours!" Jaffa told me.

My brain was hot with the fluster of wondering what I ought to do.

Webster, the corporal of marines, came scrambling down across the gap and up to me, his eyes gleaming. He was bursting to suggest something.

" Out with it!" I said.

" Beg pardon, sir, but the five of us could hold this here gap against a whole regiment, and we'd drive these chaps off like winking.   They can't outflank us, they must come along in single file.   It would be grand if we could stop 'em."

I could see that for myself; but at the first shot back would go the whole caravan, and if those camels were laden with rifles and ammunition not one should we capture.   A better plan rushed through my head —to let them get through and then prevent them getting back!

I would send the head-man to tell Commander Duckworth.   He would come along with every man he could land, and do the whole business whilst we stopped their retreat.   It would be the grandest haul that had ever been made.   Instead of the villagers driving leopards up to us, the *Intrepid* should drive these Bedouins and their camels; instead of getting a few mangled leopard skins, we would bag the whole caravan and its rifles.

I told Webster.   He grinned with delight.

"How many rounds of ammunition have we?" I asked.

We had nearly six hundred between us; that was enough.

Hurriedly I explained to Jaffa what we intended doing. I tore a leaf from his note-book, and with his pencil wrote a message to Commander Duckworth.

"Give it to the old man! Tell him to take it to the *Intrepid* as quickly as he can; tell him to take his villagers and the women back with him."

Jaffa's eyes sparkled as he passed the orders to the trembling head-man and gave him the note.

I let go of his cloak, and he slid down the rocks like an eel, and was off down the dizzy zigzag path, like a goat, to where his people lay hid.

Then Webster, with a grin on his face, went back to his side of the gap with orders to conceal himself and his two men farther along the edge, not to expose themselves on the sky-line for a single moment, and on no account to fire until I fired.

I knew that I could trust Webster.

Jaffa drew out his beloved Mauser pistol to see that it was loaded, and we had nothing to do but wait whilst those weary camels and their escort wound their way up towards the gap.

CHAPTER IX

Trapping a Caravan

FROM where I lay, sprawling on my stomach, on the very edge of that vast ridge, like a fly clinging to the rim of a cup—my "coffee-cup"—I could look down on both sides. Inland, the sides of the ridge fell away steeply but not precipitously; the track from the gap did not zigzag down, as it did on my other side, but wound and sloped at an easy angle until I could trace it no farther. The leading horseman of the caravan was, possibly, two miles away, and perhaps a thousand or fifteen hundred feet below me—one could not judge heights or distances with any accuracy—the middle portion of the winding caravan was hidden by a swelling of the mountain slope, and the tail end, indistinct, lost itself in the stifling haze which filled the valleys below. I watched those first few mounted men. They kept on halting and waiting, going on again and stopping, as though the camels could not keep pace with them.

I turned my head the other way, and looked down the precipitous curtain of rocks which fell almost sheer into the extraordinary hollow below me. The red turban and flowing white cloak of the old villager showed up—a bright spot against the dark rocks—as he scrambled hastily to join his people, tiny little dots moving about between the boulders which strewed the bottom of the "coffee-cup". I could not see the crack through which we had entered the hollow, because the huge walls surrounding it overlapped there, but I marvelled how we had managed to climb the path without slipping and being dashed to pieces below. I really did not believe it possible for a camel to negotiate it in safety.

"Surely a camel cannot go there?" I asked Jaffa.

"Yes, camel go down, safe; horse cannot; Bedouin leave horses behind them."

"Will they bring them up to the gap?"

Jaffa did not think they would, and I devoutly hoped that they would not.

I thought how old Popple Opstein's face would have beamed, and his yellow hair stood up, if only he had been here with me on that edge of rocks. Yes, here I was literally on the edge of civilization, where all my life I had longed to be. How my chum would have chaffed me about that if he saw me now! Perhaps in a few hours, if he had the luck to be landed, he would see me.

And, thinking of yellow hair, perhaps little Miss Borsen, if she too could see me and could realize what might soon happen, would treat me as a man. More likely than not she would only have smiled in her tantalizing, irritating way, and told me how uncomfortable I looked.

Jaffa touched me. "Bedouin see very far; very good sight; see us soon."

What an ass I was! I had ordered Webster and

his fellows to conceal themselves below the crest, and here I was still sprawling on the sky-line myself.

I crawled lower down; so did Jaffa and Griffiths.

Until I had left the ridge it never occurred to me that probably the advance party of Bedouins would scale the sides of the gap and scatter along the edge. If they did that they would certainly see us; so it was necessary to hide much farther away from it and take no such risk.

I whistled softly to Webster, and he came crawling across to me, keeping well below the sky-line.

"Take your men a hundred yards along the ridge," I told him; "hide among those rocks there, below the edge, and for Heaven's sake don't show yourselves, not until the last Arab and the last camel have gone halfway down the zigzag, and not until you see me move."

"I understand, sir," he answered grimly, and presently I saw him and his two men scramble to a cluster of detached rocks much farther along.

When they were safely hidden, Jaffa, Griffiths, and myself crawled in the opposite direction, away from the gap, behind some more boulders. We shifted about among them until we found a position from which we could see that gap, and also look down the zigzag path. We were about one hundred and fifty yards from the gap, and practically on a level with it. Of course we could see nothing of the approaching horses and camels, but I trusted to my ears to hear them.

Lying there under these conditions was an extraordinary trial to my nerves, and I thanked my stars that Webster had come ashore with me that morning and not Moore. Moore would have made a hopeless muddle of his job, and could not have controlled his own nerves, let alone those of his men. As it was, I presently found the strain of waiting and listening so great that I had to hang on to those rocks, like a maniac, to prevent my legs making me crawl up to the sky-line, twenty feet above us, to have one more look at the caravan.

I do not believe that if I lived a thousand years I could be more excited or "jumpy".

I breathed more freely when I saw the head-man reach the bottom of the "coffee-cup", gather his villagers together, and disappear with them, like a lot of white ants, out of sight round that projecting corner of rock which marked the huge crack or rent giving exit to the path. I relied upon the old sportsman hurrying down to the village as quickly as he could, and hoped that in another hour Commander Duckworth would receive my note. In another forty or fifty minutes afterwards he might be able to land his men, and in another hour and a half they might reach the entrance to the "coffee-cup".

Then the fun would begin.

My wrist watch was, of course, still smashed—there had been no chance of having it repaired—so I could only judge by the height of the sun that the time was about eleven o'clock. At the earliest the *Intrepids* could not reach the bottom of the zigzag path for another three hours; and, if the head-man had been accurate, the head of the caravan would be at the gap an hour and a half before they arrived.

The only thing that troubled me then was whether the leading Arabs would have descended it, turned the corner, and sighted the *Intrepid*, and perhaps the advancing bluejackets, before the rear of the caravan had passed through the gap and had begun the perilous descent.

Once the rear-guard was below us I felt that we could prevent them climbing back; but if it should happen that the *Intrepids* were sighted and the alarm given when only a part of the caravan had passed us, then our position would be perilous.

If they searched the ridge before even commencing to send their camels down I knew that we should be discovered, and in that case there would be nothing for it except to sell our lives as dearly as possible. But I did not think they would take the trouble to do this, nor did Jaffa, and the chief danger lay in the alarm being given before all the camels and Arabs had passed through the gap.

If this happened, I made up my mind to shoot as many camels as possible, to prevent the Arabs getting away with all their rifles; and I told Jaffa that if anything went wrong, I relied upon him and his Mauser pistol to prevent either Griffiths or myself falling alive into their hands.

Somehow or other I could rely upon Jaffa, and it was a comfort. Webster would have to look after himself and his two men; I knew that he would not fail.

Writing this now, the fact that I really thought this ending possible, or prepared for it, seems almost unreal. Time has quickly blurred the remembrance of the extraordinary peril of our position at that time, and only left vivid recollections of the wonderful feeling of exhilaration which took hold of us as we lay there feeling almost like wild beasts waiting for our prey, and listening for the first sound of their approaching feet.

A large bird appeared above us, circling with motionless wings. Suddenly he came gliding downwards, disappearing behind the crest. Looking up again into the burning sky I saw more specks coming from all directions. Soon there were ten or twelve of the ugly brutes circling round. So close to us did they come that I could see their heads and their naked necks stretched towards the ground. They were vultures, and one by one they slid downwards in huge spirals and disappeared.

Jaffa whispered: "A camel or a horse has dropped; they must be driving them hard."

He told me that the speed of a camel caravan was about two and a half miles an hour. As the crow flies, Jeb was probably thirty miles away from the spot where we lay. It was inside the mark to add another fifteen for the turns and twists of the track through the mountains and valleys; this would bring the probable march to forty-five miles, and if the camels had been pressed forward day and night, as Jaffa imagined likely, the poor beasts must be very weary.

Jaffa had noticed when he first looked through my glasses at them that their necks were very straight. He now explained to me that the halter of one camel is secured to the one next in front, and that, as the leading camels of a gang were always the best, when the others tire they tend to be dragged along, and the ropes stretch their necks until they are almost straight and not curved.

"They were very straight," he said.

This waiting was a tremendous strain. To know that the caravan was approaching on the other side of that ridge, behind and above us, made the longing to climb up and look over simply maddening.

To pass the time we made little loopholes between the rocks, through which we could fire towards the gap and down the zigzag path without being seen ourselves. Griffiths asked me, under his breath, if he could smoke his pipe. He asked simply to hear himself speak. He knew that I would refuse, but it was a comfort for him to whisper and a comfort for me to whisper back that the blue smoke might show —a fact he knew well enough.

Then a horrid thought struck me. When we had first reached the gap I had lighted a cigarette, and the burnt match and the end of the cigarette must be lying somewhere there still. If either of them were seen the alarm would be given at once. My whole mind became tortured with picturing them lying there on the bare stones, and I would have given anything in the world to be able to crawl across and try to find them. I did not fear that our tracks would be found: the rocks were quite bare; what loose stones there were between them would not leave a foot-mark; but even now, as the scene comes back to me, I remember that the fear of the burnt match and cigarette end being discovered was horrible at the time.

Just as the strain became almost unbearable, and the impulse to crawl to the gap almost more than I could resist—I had actually risen to my hands and knees—Jaffa gave a low sound, and pressed me down.

Looking through my loophole I saw a tall, fine-looking Arab standing erect at our side of the gap, with a rifle in his hand, turning his head from side to side and then peering below into the chasm beneath.

I felt certain that the white cigarette end must be lying there at his feet, and that in another second he must see it. My heart seemed to stop beating and my ears buzzed. He turned and looked intently at the very heap of boulders behind which we lay. I could have sworn that our eyes met. I had to put my hand to my mouth to prevent me giving way to the frantic desire to yell. Then he disappeared back into the gap, and I breathed more freely.

"He tell others—all safe—see nothing—camels come presently," Jaffa whispered.

In two or three minutes more Arabs—ten, then twenty—crowded through the gap, their rifles held ready and their fierce eyes scanning every rock.

Thank goodness! The towering sides of the "coffee-cup" hid the *Intrepid* from view.

They moved stiffly, as though tired, talking quietly and squatting on the rocks for a few minutes, until they suddenly stood up, looked back through the gap, slung their rifles over their shoulders, and commenced to scramble down the zigzag path.

They had hardly left the gap when, with a light scraping noise, the ugly head and neck of a camel appeared. He hesitated as he saw the steepness of the path below him, but the camel leader beat him about his head and lips until he condescended to move out of the gap, and with hesitating paces, putting down his huge feet with very great care, started the descent. As his body came into view we saw long sacks or bundles of matting—containing rifles, we felt sure—strapped one on either side of him.

From his quarters stretched taut the halter of the camel "next astern", and another supercilious, scornful, ugly head appeared. Camel after camel (all with their bundles), Arab after Arab (some armed, others simply leading camels) squeezed after each other through the gap in the crest and started down the zigzag path.

I was thankful to notice that the advance-guard seemed in no hurry to reach the bottom, but would go on for a hundred yards, wait for the leading camel to overtake them, and go on again. The longer the time which elapsed before they sighted the *Intrepid*, the more chance would there be that the end of the caravan had already passed through the gap before the alarm was given.

Fifty camels I counted; sixty; sixty-two—three; but as the sixty-fourth head emerged into sight it sank down to the rocks. The wretched brute had fallen on his knees, his neck stretched quite straight as his halter to the camel ahead took the strain. He was dragged bodily forward for a few inches on the smooth rock, then the halter "parted", and his neck curved again.

C 697

LOOKING THROUGH MY LOOPHOLE I SAW A TALL, FINE-LOOKING
ARAB PEERING INTO THE CHASM BENEATH

Another ugly camel's head appeared over his back, but there was no room to pass—the gap was too narrow—and he stopped, swaying his head angrily from side to side.

The Arabs called shrilly one to another — half-dazed they seemed to be, probably from fatigue—and a dozen of them, surrounding the kneeling camel, tried to make him rise to his feet. They prodded him with their rifles and spears, howling execrations, hauled on the broken halter, and beat him on the nose and face. They actually fired rifles close to his face; but he took not the slightest notice. He never even moved his head, holding it up quite motionless, with that extraordinary sarcastic, supercilious look which camels always have, and appeared to be quite unaware of the cruel treatment.

"Camel—finish—much tired—never get up—stay to die," Jaffa whispered.

Two vultures—appearing from nowhere—perched silently on the rocks behind which lay Webster and his two men, saw them, and flapped across to another rock. The Arabs were too busy to notice this or they might have been suspicious.

Then a fine-looking, very richly dressed Arab, with a flowing red[1] patriarchal beard and a green turban pushed past the camel and began to give orders. The ropes securing the bundles were unlashed, the bundles were dragged aside and propped up against the projecting rocks, and then, hauling on those ropes (they passed under the camel's belly), shouting and yelling

[1] The sheikh must have visited Mecca three times, as only after three such pilgrimages are beards dyed red.

as though hell had broken loose, the Arabs tried to hoist him to his feet.

The sheikh, or whoever he was, climbed to the top of the gap, the better to superintend operations. A grand-looking chap he was, with a fine "fighting" face, beetling eyebrows, and a great hooked nose.

For a moment I thought again of that cigarette end, and grew sick with fear lest it was there and he should see it. But he was too much interested in the camel to see anything else. Although his men heaved with all their might they only raised the poor beast a few inches, and down it would sink again.

Then the sheikh gave more orders. Men began calling down to those on the paths of the zigzag, immediately underneath the helpless camel, and I saw these hurriedly making large gaps in the line of camels. Two men took hold of the poor brute's halter and hauled the head round until it was touching the hind quarters; the others, gathering at the side of the camel farther from the precipice below, using their rifles as levers and also pressing against his lean flanks, shoved "all together"; the men on the head-rope tugged the head still farther round, and the helpless brute toppled over the edge. Rolling and falling, sliding through the gaps in the lines beneath, bounding from boulder to boulder, he at last "fetched up", two hundred feet below, against a rock, and lay there a shapeless mass of broken back and neck and legs.

The two vultures hopped about excitedly and flapped a little farther down, eyeing the remains with twisted heads.

At another order from the sheikh those bundles were torn open, and I simply "thrilled" to see at least two dozen rifles—brand-new rifles—hauled out. Each man, taking one or two of them as he passed, started off again along the zigzag path after the rest of the camels. The sheikh, clambering down to the path, followed them slowly, and that procession of camels commenced afresh through the gap, camel after camel, until I had counted eighty-three. After the eighty-third came many more, pace by pace, with weary feet, but these were loaded with boxes of ammunition. No attempts had been made to conceal that fact; the boxes were just as they had left the manufacturers, slung in great nets across the camels' backs.

One hundred and thirty-four passed through, counting both those with rifles and those with ammunition; and, last of all, led by two men, a magnificent camel, splendidly caparisoned, with a scarlet, silver-embroidered cloth and with silver-mounted harness, stalked angrily through, followed by two smaller ones with unwieldy burdens. These three were doubtless the sheikh's own camels, his riding camel and the two which carried his tent and the cooking gear and food which he might want on the march.

No more camels came.

I could hardly believe our good fortune. Everything had turned out as we had planned. Looking down into the "coffee-cup" I could see the zigzag of painfully-descending camels; and still farther below them the white figures of the advance-guard, not yet near the bottom or that corner beyond which they would be able to see the *Intrepid*. Not one of those

Bedouin Arabs suspected that we six were lying there above them, or that the *Intrepids* were—possibly— hurrying up to drive them back to us. I would have given much to know what was happening beyond the mountain screen, whether the *Intrepids* had actually landed, and, if they had landed, how near they were. I reckoned that, by now, if all had happened as I hoped, they would be about halfway up from the village, and in another quarter of an hour, or less, the first of those Arabs would have scrambled out of the bottom of the "coffee-cup" and should see them.

What the time was, or how long it had taken those one hundred and thirty-seven camels to pass through the gap, I had no idea; but the sun was already slant- ing downwards in the west and was no longer light- ing the rocks at the bottom of the "coffee-cup". In fact they had disappeared for some time in the shadow cast by the ridge on which we were hidden, and as the sun gradually sank, so did the sharply-outlined shadow of the ridge and the gap, rising upwards along the opposite face of the chasm, gradually shade the zigzag path higher and higher.

We were fearfully thirsty, but we still dared not shift our cramped positions to get at our water-bottles and make ourselves more comfortable. We simply lay where we were, peering through our loopholes between the rocks at the caravan crawling down the path. Vultures, perched on the rocks around us, craned their bare necks downwards and watched too. It looked like some huge centipede or caterpillar, as each camel carefully felt for his next foothold and swung his long ungainly legs stiffly and cautiously forward. I caught sight of one, the third in a gang or string of five, evidently making very "heavy weather" of it. Whenever the path was sufficiently broad I noticed that an Arab would take hold of his halter to steady him. I pointed out this camel to Jaffa, and scarcely had he whispered: "He fall—soon," when the poor brute stumbled, tried to recover his feet, and fell on one knee, the other leg sprawling over the edge, violently pawing space. The Arab guiding him sprang away, clinging to the rocks, and in a moment the camel had toppled over. I heard wild cries of alarm; the camel leaders on the zigzag below tried desperately to make a gap in their line as they saw what was happening over their heads; but too late. The camel fell; the two camels behind were dragged after him, and the three slid like an avalanche down the rocks, sweeping more camels and one or two Arabs from the narrow zigzags below, bursting their bundles and scattering rifles until they disappeared in the gloom beneath.

It was a horrid sight, and for two or three minutes there was the utmost confusion. The frightened drivers pulled the camels' heads this way and that, and how the poor stupid creatures could keep their foothold at all was marvellous, especially as in many places the path was so narrow that, even from where I was, I could see the "inner" bundles of rifles scraping against the rocks.

We were so intent on watching this that we never turned our heads; but when I did again look across the gap to see whether Webster and his men were still hidden, I had a terrible fright.

Squatting right in the mouth of the gap, and on both edges of it, were a score or more of Arabs, their rifles slung over their shoulders.   Jaffa saw them; Griffiths saw them.   If they were as frightened as I was they did not show it.

We hardly dared to breathe.   There they were, the nearest of them not fifty yards away.   They evidently meant to stay, for they had brought firewood, and some of them were trying to set light to it, whilst others were pouring water from a skin into a brass cooking pot.

That anything such as this should happen had never entered my head.   I never thought that they would have taken the precaution of leaving a rearguard to protect their line of retreat, and to have done so entirely altered the whole situation and upset all my calculations.

If they took to wandering along that ridge we should be discovered, and if they simply remained where they were we could not fire on the caravan without exposing ourselves to this new force.   At the very first shot they would take cover, find out where we lay, and then crawl to the rocks overhead and shoot down.   In those first few moments my whole idea was to kill as many as possible before being killed myself.

We watched them with straining eyes.   If they had scattered and come near us I should have opened fire. My fingers clutched my rifle to draw it to me, and then loosened again, because they all collected round that cooking pot; the blue smoke came curling up among them, and they evidently had no other thought than to rest and make coffee. They never even troubled to look down to see whether their comrades and the camels were recovering from their disorder, but huddled close together, sheltering their heads from the sun with their dirty cloaks.

There was no immediate danger, so I turned to watch the caravan. Down at the gloomy bottom of the "coffee-cup" I could just distinguish little white figures moving among the boulders — the advance party had at last reached the gorge which led them out into the open. Three or four disappeared round the shoulder of the rocks which shut out my view of the gorge, and I knew that in a moment or two they would sight the *Intrepid* lying at anchor—and perhaps her advancing men.

I was right. Hardly had they disappeared before back they came into view, very hurriedly, and in a marvellously short space of time the whole of that "coffee-cup" rang with strange cries and shouts as they passed the word up and up its precipitous sides. Along the zigzag path — from one zigzag shouted to the next above—we could hear the news being passed. The camel leaders seized the heads of their camels and stopped them; the Arabs crouching round the gap sprang to their feet as the shouting disturbed them, unslung their rifles, and began talking excitedly.

Down below I saw the green turban of the sheikh as he worked his way along the lowest zigzag, until he too reached the bottom and also disappeared from view.

I would have given all I possessed to know what he could see.

Whatever he had seen I quickly knew that he had seen something which convinced him that the caravan could not hope to escape downwards, because more orders—flurried and high-pitched—were shouted upwards along the zigzag until the deep ravine re-echoed from side to side with them. The camel leaders began unfastening the long halters from the camels, and, very nervously, began to try to turn the tired animals round to face upwards again. Some had room enough and managed to do so; others were in places so narrow, with steep rocks so close to the path, that it was a pure impossibility for a camel to turn. Many camels absolutely refused to try, sinking to their knees; two or three tried, toppled over their clumsy feet, and fell, increasing the horrible confusion as they crashed below.

I realized now that the caravan could neither move upwards nor downwards. If only Commander Duckworth and his people could come quickly the whole of these rifles and ammunition would be theirs. In the joy of knowing this I cared not a jot what happened to us.

The shouting and confusion below us grew greater; every armed Arab was trying frantically to reach the bottom of the path, squeezing past the standing or crawling over the kneeling camels. Directly they reached the bottom they hurried away round the shoulder out of sight.

Some unarmed camel men began shouting to the men round the gap, and ten or twelve of these left the group round that cooking bowl and began the perilous descent. They had not gone more than a hundred yards along the first arm of the zigzag before more shouts came from below; they turned and called back to the others, and the remainder of the rear-guard rose and followed them.

In five minutes we six were alone on that ridge, with the blue curling smoke of that Arab fire between our two little parties.

I had to hold my breath to prevent myself shouting with joy; Jaffa's face was beaming; I heard Griffiths chuckling with delight.

The relief from the awful strain of having that rear-guard so close to us was too much for Webster or one of his men, because for a moment I saw the barrel of a rifle appear behind their rocks and almost expected to hear a cheer. The rifle disappeared as if someone had pulled it down violently.

By this time the caravan was in a state of the most hopeless confusion, totally unable to move either upwards or downwards; many camels had fallen, others were kneeling and refused to move; some were facing one way, some the other. The frightened camel leaders had given up any attempt to restore order and were gradually moving up the path as if to escape themselves, even if they could not bring their camels with them.

Only the upper few zigzags were now in sunlight; the gloom down at the bottom was increasing very rapidly, and unless the Arabs there had worn fairly white clothes we should not have been able to see them as they scrambled among the boulders, to disappear out of sight round that corner.

I realized now that when the sun sank still lower,

and the gloom increased still more, we should be able to see nothing whatever to fire at down below. And, too, I had never thought that if they tried to defend the approach to the gorge they might take up a position round that corner where our fire could not reach them. They were evidently doing this, and it upset my scheme still more.

I knew enough of soldiering to know that a small force, well posted behind rocks, could hold the mouth of that ravine (the crack in the "coffee-cup") for an almost indefinite time against a very much superior force. If the *Intrepids* were actually advancing, and had not brought Maxims or field-guns, these Arabs, with their "backs to the wall", could keep them at bay for the three and a half or four remaining hours of daylight. If so, they might be able during the night to withdraw a remnant of the caravan, and in the dark our five rifles and six hundred cartridges would not stop them.

There was only one thing to do. It sounds heroic, but there was no thought of heroism. Those men still scrambling to the bottom and the men of the rear-guard must be stopped. We five must open fire on them and compel them to remount the zigzag to attack us, and therefore prevent them joining those who had already issued from the "coffee-cup" to defend it against the *Intrepid's* people.

If I could only have been certain of what was actually happening down there, outside our line of vision, we might have waited; but I did not know, and it was absolutely necessary to do something, and to do that something quickly.

We had to take the risk that perhaps after all the *Intrepids* had not landed, and that directly we opened fire the whole force of Arabs would turn back and overwhelm us.

I told Jaffa and Griffiths that we must open fire. Griffiths nodded. "Just as you like sir; I'm ready."

Webster must be told, and Jaffa was the man to tell him, because, if he was seen, his clothes at a distance might be mistaken for those of an Arab.

I told him to make his way to the top of the ridge, find out what was happening down in the valley, how far away the horses were, and how many men had been left with them. Then he had to work his way along beneath the sky-line to Webster, and tell him to separate his men, station them on the top of the ridge so that they could not be seen, but, if possible, be able to fire down both ways, and, when I opened fire, to do so himself at every armed Arab in sight.

Jaffa understood, took my field-glasses, and wriggled away up to the ridge, whilst Griffiths and I listened to the noise of grating stones. Then there was silence and what seemed a very long period of waiting whilst we anxiously watched that rear-guard descending. If we did not open fire soon it would be too late.

At last I could stand the strain no longer. Jaffa must have had time to reach Webster, although we had not seen him crawling over the ridge.

Already the leading men of the rear-guard were indistinct in the gloom of the lower zigzags.

"We must chance it," I whispered to Griffiths. "You scramble up till you get a comfortable place where you can see both ways. I'll go halfway to-

wards the gap. When I open fire you commence;
aim awfully carefully. Now go!"

We both rose stiffly to our hands and knees, dodged
round the rocks, and separated. Some cartridges fell
out of my bandolier. I stopped to pick them up: one
cartridge might make all the difference. I crawled to
the top of the ridge.

I gave one hurried look into the valley, but not a
sign of horses or Arabs could I see. I threw myself
down and crawled to the edge of a rock from where
I could point my rifle into the darkening "coffee-
cup". As I did so I saw Webster and his two
marines leave their shelter and clamber up the crest
on their side of the gap.

There was no time to wait; the excitement was too
great to think what would be the result of this new
move, too great to realize anything. Not twenty
armed Arabs were in sight down in that vast hollow
beneath us, little, dirty, whitish, moving figures
threading their way past the motionless camels.

I took a very careful aim at the nearest and fired.

CHAPTER X

The Fight in the "Coffee-cup"

As I fired so did Griffiths; our two rifles went off almost together. We fired again. Three shots also came from Webster's side of the gap.

The effect was immediate.

Those camel-drivers who were abandoning their camels and creeping up to what they thought was safety, stopped; those still squatting among the camels scrambled to their feet; the little string of moving figures, the last of the rear-guard (it was at them we had fired) turned, looked up, and tried to find cover. Unfortunately for them there was no cover where they were, and they showed up against the rocks sufficiently well to make fair targets. We kept on firing at them, firing almost vertically downwards, and presently saw one stumble and fall off the path among the boulders strewn at the bottom. The rest managed to crawl safely down the last "leg" of that zigzag and scattered among those same boulders, hiding one by one.

I had no fear that they would "spot" us yet, because the Lee Metfords made scarcely a streak of smoke. For the same reason they would not be able to know how few we were.

Jaffa, having given my message to Webster, returned and crawled to my side, and told me the comforting news that he had seen the horses, quite two
miles away down the valley, with very few men left
to guard them.

As I peered below I could see the camel-drivers
seeking cover all along the line, squeezing themselves
behind rocks or underneath the motionless camels
themselves. We made many of them hurry still
more by firing at them, until in less than a minute
after we had opened fire there was absolutely nothing
to be seen on the wall of precipitous rocks except the
zigzag line of camels—some standing, others kneeling,
some facing upwards, others downwards.

Jaffa cried for me to look.

At the bottom, hastening back round that projecting
corner of rock which hid the outlet from the "coffee-
cup", many little moving dots appeared. I seized
the glasses, and believed I could see the green turban
of the sheikh. Dropping them I called to Griffiths
to fire, and emptied my magazine into the middle of
the group.

It was grand, it was just what I had wanted. The
more men we forced to come back within sight the
fewer would remain to defend the ravine out of sight,
where we could not get at them.

Now if only the *Intrepids* would hurry up!

I pricked up my ears. One solitary report of a
rifle came up from below, dull and muffled. More
followed rapidly, and I fully expected to hear bullets
coming our way, thinking that the sheikh's party had
commenced firing in our direction. However, none

came, nor could I see any spurts of flame from among those boulders, although it was so gloomy there that I certainly should have seen them had those fellows been firing at us. The only explanation could be that the firing was outside the ravine, and must be *at* the *Intrepid's* people—or perhaps *from* them. My ears tingled as I tried to decide which.

The volume of fire increased so rapidly that soon I could not distinguish individual shots; there was one continuous grumbling rumble, and suddenly whatever doubt I had was swept away, for I heard the tut-tut-tut-tut of a Maxim—faint but unmistakable.

That settled the question. Griffiths shouted: "They've come, sir; that's their Maxim," and a moment later, to make still more certain, a sudden flash of flame burst out among those boulders at the bottom of the "coffee-cup" and the noise of a bursting shell came bellowing up to us.

I found myself waving my arms and cheering; the others were doing the same. Some vultures which had remained indifferent to the noise of rifle firing flapped heavily up from below. The camel-leaders were peeping down to see what was happening; the camels themselves showed no signs of alarm.

Several more shells bursting there in quick succession so filled the hollow beneath us with smoke that we could see nothing until, very leisurely, the white cloud began drifting upwards, clinging to projecting rocks in little eddies, just like the morning mist in some deep valley before the sun has quite driven it away. Eventually we could actually smell that powder smoke as it escaped over the "rim" of the "coffee-cup", and it was the most beautiful scent we could wish for.

Good little nine-pounder! I'd often seen it on the *Intrepid's* poop.

The noise of the firing continued without cessation, rising and falling in fierceness, and although we could still hear shells bursting we could not see them. Probably those first few had been fired before the *Intrepids* knew where the Arabs lay concealed.

Occasionally a different sound came up to us—the puff of a bursting shrapnel—and as I pictured the little balls flinging themselves down among the rocks, and finding out the defending Arabs, I wondered how long they would stand such a trial.

The worst of it was that we could take no part.

Those Arabs who had come back with their sheikh— and the rear-guard, too—had probably wormed their way out of the hollow and were taking part in the defence. There was no one for us to fire at. A few of the camel-leaders were in view, though, as they were unarmed, we did not waste ammunition on them.

All five of us had ceased fire and were listening to the noise of fighting. We tried to distinguish some difference between the Arab firing and the shots from our own people, but that screen of rocks seemed to muffle them and make this impossible. We could not even tell whether the rattle of the Maxim was getting nearer to us; nor could we distinguish the firing of the nine-pounder at all.

Whether hours seemed minutes or minutes hours I could not tell. All I did know was that we were not helping, and that it might be impossible for the

Intrepid's people to dislodge the Arabs. What could we do to compel some of them to come back? I racked my brains but could think of nothing.

Then Jaffa suggested shooting the camels. "You shoot camels—they fall down—break rifles—Bedouin lose camels and rifles as well—must come back to save them!"

I did not know; but we might try, however cruel and inhuman it was.

I sent him across to tell Webster to single out the nearest standing camel and fire at it until it fell. I called to Griffiths to fire at the second standing camel, and chose the third myself. It was that magnificently-caparisoned one belonging to the sheikh, standing perhaps four hundred feet below me, entirely unconcerned, and unmistakable in its gorgeous crimson cloth.

I fired very carefully at him. At my second shot he swung his head round as if a fly had bitten him; at my third he lurched forward, fell over the edge, and plunged down. Almost immediately one of those smaller animals toppled over, and both, crashing across zigzag after zigzag, swept more camels in front of them. The bottom was so filled with powder smoke that we could scarcely follow the confused mass of bodies as they hurtled downwards.

The utmost terror broke out among the unarmed Arabs. We could see them leaving their camels and taking shelter under any projecting rock they could reach. I fired at another wretched brute, standing with his bundle of rifles so closely pressed against the side of the precipice that I knew that the path must

be very narrow there.   Immediately below him, on the
next zigzag, was a confused group of animals clustered
on a broader path.

At my second shot he staggered, fell right among
them, swept three or four off their feet, and another
avalanche swept down.

I felt almost sick at what I had done and stopped
firing to see what would happen.   The others ceased
firing too.

Jaffa came back and lay down near me.   His one
eye was better than my two, so I gave him the
glasses.

Then—all at once—bullets came whizzing our way,
striking rocks below, above, at each side of us, and
screaming away out of the "coffee-cup".   The noise
of this rifle fire was very different—each shot was a
roar, magnified a hundred times, and multiplied
a hundred times as it re-echoed from the walls of
the chasm.

Thank goodness!   At last we had compelled the
sheikh to weaken his defence by trying to save his
caravan from destruction.

Griffiths and I began firing at more camels;
Webster and his men followed suit; more went
hurtling down.

We had to do this, however cruel and beastly it
was.   Unless we kept those fellows away from the
mouth of the ravine, the *Intrepids* might never force
their way in.

I could now see the flashes of many rifles—it was
a beautiful sight.

Jaffa, excited for the first time, told me that twenty

or thirty armed Arabs were climbing up the zigzag. I wished that fifty or a hundred were coming—the more the better. They could not possibly see to aim at us, nor could they know how few we were, and as they emerged from the gloom we could pick them off like starlings on a fence.

Several more camels were hit and fell. Absolute panic had broken out among the unarmed men; many of those on the upper zigzags began creeping and crawling downwards, and I knew that when they met the Arabs coming up to attack us, the confusion on that awful path, and in that awful obscurity below, would be appalling.

After this events began to follow each other very rapidly.

The number of bullets whizzing round us was great, and proved that very many men must have been withdrawn already, back into the hollow; I felt certain that the noise of the Maxim gun seemed louder. If this meant anything it meant that the Arabs were gradually being forced back and that the line of bluejackets was advancing.

Very shortly afterwards the character of the noise of rifle firing altered entirely. There was very little of that muffled rumbling which we had heard before; the noise was sharper and very much louder, and amongst it, quite distinct, I could hear the most distant sound of our own rifles, much like tin tacks being driven into wood with single blows of a big hammer. The bottom of the ravine, too, was lighted up with hundreds and hundreds of rifle flashes, and shells began bursting there again. This made it certain that the Arabs had actually fallen back into the bottom of the "coffee-cup", and I knew that they must be so bunched up together that the shrapnel bullets would soon compel them to scatter up the lower legs of that zigzag.   Once there it would be difficult to reach them, but I did not bother about that.   They would have to come up and attack us if they wanted to save a single camel.

Jaffa quietly told me that they were already beginning to do this, and then, almost before he had spoken, I heard the faint sound of cheering, and knew that the *Intrepids* were rushing the mouth of the ravine.

Oh, what a grand, comforting sound that was!

The nine-pounder had stopped firing; so had the Maxim.   Probably the guns' crews could not keep pace with the last rush of our fellows, or could not fire without hitting them.

Then I saw spurts of rifle flame spitting out into the gorge, in the very opposite direction from which they had been spluttering before, and knew that they came from our own people.

It was grand!   It meant absolute victory and the capture of the entire caravan.   I turned and grinned at Jaffa and Griffiths.

"Bedouin come up very fast—plenty come," Jaffa said.

"Well, let them come; so much the better," I thought; but then it struck me that in my excitement I had not noticed how rapidly the sun was setting. The shadow of the ridge above us had long since swallowed up the whole of the opposite face of the walls of the "coffee-cup". What with the powder smoke and the shadow I could not see farther down than about the third zigzag. In the morning it had taken us a full hour to scale the path when it was clear; now these people had to do the same thing when it was blocked with camels. They could not possibly do this in less than two hours, and by then I knew that the sun would have set and that it would be completely dark before one of them could put foot in the gap.

This difficulty now faced us, and I had not foreseen it.

If those Arabs intended to abandon their camels, scale the path, and endeavour to escape back to their horses in the valley, what should we do, or, rather, what would become of us?

So long as they only thought of escape, all would be well. They were probably well beaten now, but directly it became impossible for our people to keep them "on the move" with rifle fire—owing to the lack of light to aim at them—they would begin to recover from their panic. Once they came up to where we were we dare not fire on them, because the flashes of our rifles would have told them immediately that there were only five of us.

If we did not fire they would imagine that we had evacuated the ridge, and the obvious thing for them to do was to occupy it themselves, and wait until morning. If they did that, I realized very well that we could not escape, and, more important still, I knew that it would be impossible for Commander Duckworth to remove a single camel from the path under the fire of their rifles, and that all the nine-pounders and Maxims in the Navy could not dislodge them.

Already rifle fire was dying down at the bottom. It was too dark to aim there, and it would soon be too dark for us to aim either. No bullets had come our way for some time, so I had not them to disturb me as I tried to think what to do.

At first I thought that we all should gather in the gap itself and defend ourselves there, but I gave up that idea because I felt sure they would scale the ridge above it on either side, shoot down, and make an end of us pretty soon.

I did not know what to do.

All I could see now, except for the very occasional flash of a rifle, was a frightened group of camel-drivers huddled together on the third zigzag, apparently waiting for the armed men to join them before they plucked up sufficient courage to start the ascent. It was too dark farther down to see a single camel.

Then Jaffa turned to me and said simply: "I go down path—speak to camel men—tell them you no want kill Bedouin—Bedouin throw rifle away—you won't shoot—if they no throw rifle away you kill them all."

My aunt! What a chap! What a scheme! If it would only work, and if only the camel men could get the Arabs to listen!

"I tell them you have a hundred men on top—they no know—very frightened—very much frightened."

"But they might kill you," I said.

He shook his head, and drew his beloved Mauser pistol. "I go and speak to them."

"All right! Good for you! Go along!"

He did not stand up and scramble down to the path; he wriggled himself below the farther side of the crest, and presently appeared through the gap, walking coolly along the path, his white suit making him very conspicuous.

I crawled over the crest myself, and made my way to the gap. So did Griffiths.

We saw Jaffa holding up his hands to show that he came in peace, and heard him calling loudly. Then some heads appeared much nearer than I imagined any Arabs to have reached, and gazed at him. He stopped and harangued them, pointing along the crest where we had been lying, sweeping his hands from side to side as if there was a bluejacket behind each rock.

The Arabs were answering him, and he was arguing with them like a father. Then, as the last rays of the sun streamed through the gap, he came sauntering back to us. Webster and his marines had joined me. "They believe me," Jaffa said. "All very frightened—will tell Bedouin—Bedouin throw away rifles."

"You are a splendid chap!" was all I could say.

I told Webster what Jaffa proposed to do, and at his suggestion we all began to show ourselves at different points along the crest—one here, two there, all of us at another place—dodging backwards and forwards, dividing into parties, and going to opposite sides of the gap. I felt as though we were a lot of "supers" in a pantomime, trying to "make believe" that we were an army.

Breathless, we all collected again at the gap.

It was not quite dark yet—not behind us—where the twilight lingered a little, and we could see perhaps fifty yards along the path into the "coffee-cup".

Presently Webster proposed that he and I should take station at either side of the mouth of the gap, and that the two marines should do the same at the other end of it. He suggested this because if we all stayed where we were there would be no room for the Arabs to pass. Griffiths I sent up to the ridge above it, with orders to fire only when told to do so. He did not like leaving us, because it was so dark. In fact we could hardly see each other, and, looking down into the hollow, the darkness seemed like black velvet.

Up from that blackness came sounds of men calling to each other; once or twice there were yells of pain or fright, and we strained our ears to hear whether anyone had fallen down. The noises were still far below, but gradually approaching.

We waited, and, with nothing else to do, began to grow fearfully nervous. When one is frightened one gives an enemy credit for all the virtues and valour and skill imaginable, and thinks that he must be cool and collected. At that time I could not conceive how we could escape being killed, and was only certain of one thing—that I'd account for as many Arabs as possible before that happened.

I wondered what our fellows were doing at the bottom, and whether old Popple Opstein was there. I knew that they dared not attempt to climb the path at night.

Jaffa began to coach us as to what we should say

when the Arabs came. He made us repeat after him: "Khalli bunduk 'ak", meaning "Throw down your rifle"; "Ist agel", meaning "Hurry up"; and "Ma kattle kum", meaning "Won't shoot you".

We repeated these after him till we knew them. Shall I ever forget them!

Then he said it was time for him to go, and asked me for a box of matches. Luckily I had one—nearly full it was. Why he wanted matches I did not know.

We heard the stones rattling under his feet as he slipped away down the path.

"Can you see me?" he called out.

I shouted back: "Yes."

He went farther down the path, asking at every two or three paces whether we could see him. When our eyes had become accustomed to following his white clothes we could distinguish them at quite a distance.

At last he had gone too far.

"We can't see you!" I called.

He retraced his footsteps until he was again visible. Then he seemed to rise in the air.

"I stand on rock by side of path!" he shouted; "path is under my feet—to my right—very narrow—Bedouin must pass one by one—I speak to them—make them throw away rifles—if no give up rifle I strike match—you see match—fire below match—kill Bedouin."

"Come back!" I yelled. "It's too dangerous!"

"No! I stay!" and nothing would induce him to give up his plucky scheme.

Plucky! Why, it was the bravest job any man could have taken on himself.

Quite close beneath us men began shouting. I hoped these were the camel men warning the armed Arabs to throw away their rifles if they wanted to save their lives. I knew that in a few minutes the first of them would reach Jaffa, and that then the crisis would come. Webster was fidgeting with the bolt of his breech-block and breathing hard.

Already Jaffa was beginning to call out: "Khalli bunduk 'ak! Khalli bunduk 'ak! Ma kattle kum! Ist agel! ist agel!"

Our nerves were very much on edge.

Then footsteps began to approach, softly, cautiously. Jaffa altered his tone of voice. One could almost imagine that he was imploring someone, for his own safety, to throw away his rifle, just as a father might have done. We heard the noise of a rifle falling on to the rocks, then another and another, and, before Webster and I realized it, dim, cloaked figures came up to the gap and stopped there, as if frightened and uncertain what to do.

My heart was in my mouth then, and I said as firmly as I could: "Ma kattle kum! Ist agel!" Webster chipping in with a quaver in his voice, and the two marines and Griffiths bellowing these words behind and above us.

For a moment the Arabs still hesitated, but then they commenced to pass through the gap between Webster and myself.

One, two, half a dozen, a dozen panting figures glided through, and more came—twenty or thirty more—and all the time Jaffa's voice sounded—as calmly as if he were aboard the "*B. A.*"—"Khalli bunduk 'ak! khalli bunduk 'ak! Ma kattle kum! ma kattle kum!"

Then I heard Griffiths moving among the rocks overhead, probably shifting himself into a more comfortable position, and the fool must have had his finger on his trigger, because his rifle went off, right in our faces, almost blinding us.

Of course the approaching Arabs thought that we were firing at those who had passed through the gap, and believed that they were going to be murdered.

I cursed Griffiths, and shouted: "Ma kattle kum! ma kattle kum!"

Jaffa yelled to us not to shoot—but no more Arabs came.

Out of the darkness Jaffa's voice sounded, higher pitched now: "Khalli bunduk 'ak," and voices at his feet answered him, angry voices, despairing voices; a crowd of Arabs seemed to be collecting all along the path, and people were calling up from below. I realized that they were refusing to part with their rifles, preferring to have a chance for their lives, or to die, if they had to, with them in their hands.

We were all shouting: "Ma kattle kum! Ist agel!" The two marines, knowing that something was wrong, ran to us.

"Stand by to fire! Be very careful; fire below, and to right of the match, if Jaffa strikes one."

There was a very ominous murmur now. Jaffa was haranguing, expostulating; then he stopped.

"Stand by!" I shouted, bringing my rifle to my shoulder.

A tiny light showed. Jaffa had struck a match.

"Fire!" I yelled, and our four rifles went off together.

We heard groans, a yell of pain, and a body falling.
Some of our bullets had gone home.

Jaffa's pistol flashed once; we fired again; it flashed
a second time, and then, with a glare and a startling
roar, a shell burst not fifty yards below us, and for a
second or two lighted up the whole scene—Jaffa on
the rock, and those Arabs, a whole line of them, surging up to him.   Wild screams came up from a lower
path, and told us that men there had been wounded;
and Jaffa began in his old voice of calm assurance,
"Ma kattle kum!   Khalli bunduk 'ak"—he never
once stopped talking.

"No shoot," he called to us; "they throw away
rifles—they come:" and with the most intense relief
from the strain of those few awful seconds I heard the
welcome clatter of rifles on the rocks, and that weird
procession began again to pass between us.

In their hurry to escape this new terror of the bursting shells the Arabs actually swept the two marines
back to the farther end of the gap.

Another shell burst, some way from us, but near
enough for all to hear the fragments smashing against
the rocks, and enough to break the nerves of any who
had already suffered as those poor wretches had done.

I realized now that they were absolutely panic-
stricken; they were throwing away their rifles long
before they reached Jaffa.   They came in one continuous line through the gap, struggling with each
other to escape those shells, and to escape from that
awful inferno below them.

They were mere terror-stricken fugitives, with no more fight left in them, and Webster and I had to step aside, out of the mouth of the gap, to prevent them carrying us along with them in their flight. We were shouting: "Ist agel! Ma kattle kum!" more to let them know the way to the gap than anything else, for the glare of those shells (which burst dangerously close to us every four or five minutes) blinded everyone, and they could not see the way. In fact, we four standing there, and Jaffa on his rock, were now doing nothing more dangerous than a policeman does in calling out to a crowd to pass along. The marines at the farther end of the gap had forgotten their Arabic words, and forgotten their fright—if they had been frightened—and were shouting: "'Urry up there! keep a-moving! 'Ere, you won't get no front seat if you don't 'urry. Pass along, please! First turn to the right takes you to the 'orses. 'Urry up! 'urry up! The show's about to begin."

Griffiths, on the rocks above, had altered "Ma kattle kum," into "Call the cattle home," and was droning this out under the impression that he was talking the proper "lingo".

As one shell burst I had seen a group of men on one of the paths apparently bearing a comrade. In time they came up to Jaffa, and I heard the sound of voices entreating something. Jaffa called to me that it was the sheikh's son, badly wounded and asking for water.

With shuffling footsteps they bore him up to the gap, and laid him on a rock.

I could well imagine the awful experience he must

have had whilst being carried up there amongst his terrified followers, and the tremendous pluck of those who had stuck to him.

They now began crying "Pani! ma!" and Jaffa called out that the sheikh's son wanted water. He, poor chap, did not deign to ask; but for a half-suppressed groan, when they laid him on the rocks, he was absolutely silent.

We had no water (our water-bottles had been emptied long ago), but I remembered that brass cooking bowl in which the rear-guard had started to cook coffee.

It had been placed between some rocks, so had not been upset, and I groped round and found it. There was still some liquid "of sorts" in it. I gave the bowl to the men, and they scooped up a little fluid with their hands and poured it into his mouth. They finished the remainder themselves. Then they picked him up and bore him through the gap as he muttered something, apparently to me—though whether a blessing or a curse I did not know.

The two marines hurried them on with cruel jests, and, before they had passed through, the blaze of another shell lighted up the mournful little band and the red-stained beard of the sheikh. I looked for the green turban, but that was gone.

During the next few minutes perhaps twenty limping, hard-breathing men passed us. After that, though we waited and watched the zigzag path whenever a shell burst, not a single man could be seen.

It was time to stop those shells. They were meant well, but they had done their work and had scared the Arabs; now we should be very relieved if no more came, because many were unpleasantly close.

I ordered the two marines, Webster and Griffiths, to fire three volleys into the air, giving them the word of command, and firing myself. Whether the *Intrepids* saw these volleys or not, or whether they understood that we were "all correct" or not, I did not know, but they ceased firing.

Then, at last, we knew that we had won, that the morning would show us our prize—the caravan of living camels strung along the zigzag path and the dead ones below. But we were too worn out with the strain of that day's work, and that last hour or more in the gap, to feel any exultation. All we wanted to do was to lie down and sleep, and all we wanted to see was the rising of the blessed sun. We had cursed it a good many times during the last three months; now, how we did long to see it again!

Jaffa came back to us, and we made much of him, praised him, and told him that it was he who had saved us and captured the caravan, that all the credit was due to him.

He simply lay down and slept. Praise from us seemed to mean nothing to him. I let every one of them sleep. I only had to say the word, and they simply subsided where they stood, and straightway fell asleep.

Backwards and forwards by myself I paced from one end to the other of that gap, my rifle in my hand, looking down into the black obscurity as I came to the opening on each side.

Away down in the valley which had swallowed up

those panic-stricken Arabs I sometimes heard voices, gradually growing fainter and fainter in the distance. Below, in the "coffee-cup", occasionally weird noises came up, perhaps from those poor wretched camels still huddled on that awful path, with their unwieldy burden of rifles flattened against the rocks. Once or twice a momentary twinkle of light flickered far below; probably the bluejackets were striking matches to light their pipes. It was a comfort to think that some-one down there still kept watch.

Presently a land-breeze began gently sweeping through the gap, on its way to the sea; so warm and heavy was it that it made the desire to sleep an agony. How I could have remained awake without my pipe, I do not know; that, and perhaps my hunger, kept me going.

Hyenas, jackals, or wolves began howling in the valley; others, along the walls of the "coffee-cup", answered them. They must have scented blood, and appeared to be gathering all along the ridge, but did not venture down, staying there howling and whining in piercing cadences. I set their hateful music to a tune of "Keep awake! keep awake! one turn more! twelve paces! one turn more!"

There was no means of judging the time, but per-haps it was an hour after I had been left to myself when two wretched Arabs came stumbling up, or hopping up, dragging broken legs after them, and supporting each other. Poor, wretched, miserable creatures! the agony they must have suffered would have made me feel pity for them had not my brain been absolutely numbed with the craving for sleep, and unable to think of anything except the necessity for fighting it.

At last, when I thought that I must have done more than my share of "sentry-go", I simply collapsed on top of Webster. I remember him scrambling to his feet, but I am certain that I was sound asleep before I lay flat on the ground. It was no use being ashamed of myself; I was not. It was physically impossible for me to keep awake any longer, and, as it turned out, it was physically impossible for any of us to keep awake.

When I did awake it was broad daylight; the sun was just appearing over the opposite rim of the "coffee-cup", and dear old Popple Opstein was bending over me, shaking me. The gap was full of the *Intrepid's* bluejackets, and they were trying to shake life into the others. Jaffa was leaning against a rock.

"Water! water!" was the first thing I said, and Popple Opstein, with his face that strange violet colour, his eyes ablaze with excitement, gave me his water-bottle.

"We couldn't climb the path in the dark, Martin, old chap," he burst out. "We tried, but we couldn't do it. Two of our chaps fell over and broke legs or arms, so the commander brought us back."

"Thank goodness that he did call you back!" I said. "You would have all been killed. It's bad enough in daylight, with nothing blocking it."

"It took us three hours to get up," he said. "We counted more than a hundred camels on the path, and you knocked over any number. They are lying in heaps at the bottom!"

He gave me a ship's biscuit. Nothing I have ever tasted tasted so appetizing as that did, and he spared me another mouthful of water to wash the last crumbs down my throat.

Then I lighted a cigarette, and together we walked through the gap to see if there were any traces of the disarmed Arabs. The valley was empty and silent, shrouded in shadow. Not a single living thing could we see except a few vultures.

We walked back again and looked into the "coffee-cup". The zigzag path was now swarming with villagers and bluejackets trying to restore order among the camels. Close to the rock where Jaffa had stood, rifles lay scattered everywhere.

"We must have captured a couple of thousand rifles and thirty or forty thousand rounds of ammunition," my chum said exultingly. "It's the finest haul, they tell me, that's been made for years."

I don't mind saying that if he had told me that there was a steaming hot dish of bacon and eggs and a potful of coffee waiting for me round the corner I should have been much more excited—just at this time.

CHAPTER XI

The Cobra Bracelet Again

TAKE the whole world over, and you would not have found a more happy group than we made that morning, sitting in the gap, yarning whenever our jaws were not busy crunching the ship's biscuits the *Intrepids* had brought us; Webster, Griffiths, Jaffa, and the two marines surrounded by a crowd of blue-jackets eager to learn every detail of the adventure, and the Baron and myself squatting on a rock, he beaming at me like an old mother hen who had just found her long-lost chick, and watching me munch his biscuit as if it was the most pleasant sight in the world.

"When darkness came on," he was saying, "We gave you up for 'finish'. We thought they'd rush you; we thought you'd have not the slightest chance of escape. You remember firing rifles—at the beginning—when it first got dark? We were waiting for them. We tried to help you with those shells of ours—it was the only thing we could do—but we made so certain that it was the beginning of the end for you that, when no more rifle flashes showed up, we thought you all were killed. We felt sick that we couldn't climb up and kill a few Arabs to revenge you, so we kept plug-

ging away with the nine-pounder in sheer desperate
anger. Man! we never guessed for a moment what
was really happening.   Look down there at that litter
of rifles; the path and the rocks for a hundred yards
are simply smothered with them.   It's splendid!
splendid, old chap!"

In his excitement my chum leant forward and
gripped my shoulder till I winced.

" If you'd seen Jaffa standing there on his rock, and
heard him calling out: ' Khalli bunduk 'ak. Ma kattle
kum! Ist agel!' you'd have thought him splendid.
He's the hero of the affair," I said, pointing to Jaffa,
who was extricating himself from the crowd of his
admirers and stalking solemnly away to perch himself
on a rock, where no one could come and worry him
with questions. "We shall never forget those words;
we shouted them till we were hoarse. Didn't we,
Webster?"

Webster smiled.   " Pretty ticklish work—part of
the time, sir!"

"Those shells of yours just did the trick," I went
on, telling him how Griffiths's rifle going off acci-
dentally had nearly brought about a catastrophe.
"They were simply hideous in the darkness; the
chasm looked a perfect hell, and the half-crazed
wretches fled through the gap from them like a flock
of sheep. How the dickens did you manage to train
the gun and aim it? That's what beat me."

He explained that before it was too dark to see the
gap from the bottom of the "coffee-cup" they had
found a rock which gave, more or less, the proper
elevation when the muzzle of the gun rested on it,

and when the trail of the carriage was pushed up against another, the gun pointed somewhere in the right direction. After every shot they had had to drag it back, feel about for the rocks, and trust to luck. That was why the shells were so erratic and the firing so slow.

"We were very nearly as frightened of them as the Arabs were," I laughed, "and were mighty glad when you stopped your fireworks and bits of iron-mongery flying round us."

Recollecting those volleys we had fired when all was over, I asked my chum whether they had seen them, and how they knew what we meant.

The Baron shook his head. "Too much smoke down there; we saw nothing. We only stopped firing for the simple reason that we'd fired every blessed shell we had. Why, my dear old chap, we thought you'd been 'deaders' long before. Even this morning we thought we should have to fight our way here; it was a kind of a forlorn hope; the commander didn't want me to come, and it was not until we were halfway up without being fired on that we had a glimmer of an idea that the Arabs had 'hoofed' it during the night. And you and your fellows were so fast asleep you never heard us cheering as we scrambled up the last fifty yards.

"When we saw you six huddled here we thought it was a burial party wanted—nothing else. Why, dear old ass, I was just turning you over to see where you'd been killed, when you began muttering some outlandish gibberish."

"Ma kattle kum!" I suggested, smiling.

"Something like that," he grinned. "Ugh! it was a bit of a shock," and his cheeks flushed that curious violet colour.

"What was a shock?" I asked. "Finding me alive?"

"No, you fool! Thinking we'd have to bury the lot of you, and not an inch of ground where we could stick a pickaxe, let alone a spade, for miles."

The Baron lifted his helmet and wiped his forehead.

The sight of his yellow hair reminded me of Miss Borsen, and I told him how I had managed to silence her tormenting little tongue. "Just picked her up like a feather, carried her twenty yards before she could say 'knife', and never a word more did she say. I thought I'd got the best of her for once, but she only thought me a horrid cad, and wouldn't even let me apologize, wouldn't even let me see her again. So she came off best after all."

"Women always do," the Baron grinned. "Irritating things, women."

We were both agreed on that point.

Then he told me his part of the yarn. It was just as I had thought. Some skunk of an Arab with a grievance had come along to Muscat and sneaked, given the whole show away, and the plan of taking all the rifles and ammunition still remaining at Jeb to Kalat al Abeid (the little village whose head-man had brought me up here to shoot leopards). That was why the *Intrepid* had hurried round. Even before Commander Duckworth had heard from Mr. Scarlett that I was up in the mountains he was preparing to land his men, and when he received my scribbled note it had been a case of hurrying ashore in double-quick time, to try to take possession of the mouth of the ravine leading to the "coffee-cup" before the Arabs reached it.

As you know, they did not, in spite of the villagers clapping on to the nine-pounder and Maxim and dragging them up those baking slopes. They had been met with a very fierce fire, and it was not till the resistance began to weaken (when many Arabs had been withdrawn to defend the camels from us) that the *Intrepids* could make any impression. But once an Arab leaves his first position for one farther in the rear, his chief anxiety is to keep his eye on a still safer place behind him; so, once they had begun to retire, the job was comparatively easy.

Before they gained the mouth of the ravine the *Intrepids* had lost two men killed and five wounded. My chum told me that Nicholson, the staff surgeon, did not expect one of those to pull through safely.

"It's jolly hard luck on them," the Baron said, his face falling.

We sat silent for some time, looking into the "coffee-cup" and watching the very tedious and dangerous work of getting the remaining camels safely down to the bottom.

Then a message was semaphored that the commander wanted to see me and my party; so I gathered them together and left the Baron and his men to keep watch at the gap in case the Arabs recovered from their fright and came back. There was precious little chance of this.

The zigzag path was the most extraordinary sight, littered with rifles, bandoliers, water-bags, turbans, and cloaks, showing how hurriedly the poor wretches had tried to escape. It was dangerous work there, and worse still when we reached the camels. Each poor brute thought we were bringing him food, and was furious when he saw we were not, swaying his neck and making an angry rumbling noise somewhere from halfway down his neck, scraping his bundle of rifles or ammunition-boxes against the rock. We had to squeeze past each one very carefully indeed, with an eye on his head and neck and a hand gripping at his bundle. Lower down we came to the villagers trying their best to shift the camels, make them get on their feet if they were kneeling, or turn them round if they were facing upwards. Poor devils, they were only fishermen, and were evidently making a poor job of this. Among them was my old friend the head-man, shouting orders by the dozen. He smiled affably, and gabbled a lot of weird words as I squeezed past him. Jaffa explained that he was comparing me "to the sun for strength and the jackal for cunning". I smiled back, and as Jaffa followed he commenced another long rigmarole, which I did not stay to listen to, but which Jaffa afterwards told me was to the effect that the Bedouin would be very angry, and would come back presently, when the *Bunder Abbas* and *Intrepid* had gone away, and kill them all.

That was the worst of it. I knew enough about the temper of those gun-running fellows—hadn't I seen what had happened at Bungi and Sudab?—and the Arabs are no whit less ferocious and revengeful than the Afghans. It seemed such hard luck to get those villagers to help us and then leave them to certain vengeance. These especial people were so simple, and had been so useful, that it would be a shame to leave them unprotected. But what could we do? Neither the *Bunder Abbas* nor the *Intrepid* could stay there for ever.

Lower down still, quite close to the bottom of the zigzag, I met the commander, very pleased with himself and with me too.

"You should get promotion out of this," he said, as I saluted; "it's the finest haul that's been made for years—three thousand rifles at least, and more ammunition than we've destroyed in the last twelve months."

He made me tell him the whole yarn over again, and then ordered me to take my men back to the *Bunder Abbas*. I did not want to go, but had to.

At the bottom of the "coffee-cup" I saw the mangled remains of many of the camels which had fallen down the precipice. Rifles from their burst bundles were scattered round them, and some of the *Intrepids* were still moving about among the boulders, searching for dead or wounded Arabs. Then at the very entrance to the gorge, round the corner where the Arabs had taken up their first position, I found Nicholson busy with the wounded, and showing some natives how to make litters.

The man who had been so desperately wounded was dead. "Nothing could have saved him," Nicholson told me, as though I might think he had not done enough for him. He brightened when he saw how little the scar on my forehead showed.

"A good bit of work—that," he said, quite pleased, and wanted me to take the other four wounded back to the village.

So off we started with them. Two could walk, and we took it in turns to carry the others, for the villagers were much too excited and impatient to realize the necessity for gentleness. They wanted to run along with them as if they had been sacks of potatoes.

Fifty or sixty of the camels were already slowly tramping down the rocky slope ahead of us, and when we reached the village we found them kneeling under the shade of some trees, looking quite contented—that is, if a camel can look contented. The youngsters who had brought them down, and all the women and children in the village, were gathered round in a state of wonderment. The women covered their faces when they saw us; but the children came crowding round us, clapping their little brown hands, and followed us down to the beach, dancing and jumping with glee.

I took the wounded men on board the *Intrepid*, and then went aboard the *Bunder Abbas*, where I had a great reception. Even the dismal cook and his still more dismal "mate" showed symptoms of pleasure, and Mr. Scarlett's face — for once — was beaming. His claw-like hand shot out and gripped mine like a vice. "I've had a terrible bad time of it for the last twenty-four hours, sir. Never thought to see any of you alive again. We all wanted to come along and lend a hand, but you

know that we dursn't leave the "*B. A.*", sir, don't
you?"

He was terrified lest I should think he had failed
me. Of course he hadn't.

I sent him, and as many men as could be spared,
up to Commander Duckworth, in case they should
be needed.   They went ashore like a lot of boys,
Mr. Scarlett one of the youngest, but had had enough
of the sun and hot rocks before they eventually returned. By dark every camel had, somehow or other,
been brought down to the village, and by midnight all
the rifles and ammunition were aboard the *Intrepid*.

As I looked shorewards to the grim dark mass
of mountains towering into the starlit sky, I was
most thankful that I had not to spend another night
on top of them. We all had had enough excitement
to last a long time.

I went across to the *Intrepid* to gloat over the rifles
piled in her battery, and had supper with the Baron.
A most joyous and hilarious meal it was. Afterwards
Commander Duckworth sent for me to give me orders
to proceed to Muscat next morning.

This gave me the chance of putting in a good word
for the villagers.

"It does seem precious hard," he said, shrugging
his shoulders. "These hundred and thirty or more
camels are not the slightest use to them; they dare
not take them inland to sell, and those Arab chaps
are certain to wipe out every man of them. But what
can I do? I can't stay here for ever."

I suggested that he should let them have some of
the captured rifles.

"They won't know how to use them," he said·
"they'll only shoot each other."

However, he changed his mind next morning, for
as I weighed anchor he signalled across: "Am sending fifty rifles and two thousand rounds of ammunition to the village".

If the inoffensive, childlike villagers would only
learn to use them properly, and would guard that
gap night and day, they would be safe; but—I knew
they would not. They were simply fishermen; they
could not spare men from the boats; and after the
first few days had passed without anything happening
they would imagine themselves safe, or, still more
likely, never take any precautions whatsoever, considering it wrong to interfere with "fate".

Just as the *Bunder Abbas* was shoving off, a native
boat came paddling furiously from shore. I stopped
my engines, and it came alongside with a couple of
sheep — a parting present from my old head-man.
Sending back a message of thanks, and dragging
them aboard, I went ahead again, wound my way
through that extraordinary channel in the cliffs to
the open sea, and by sunset found myself once more
anchored in Muscat harbour.

It was too late to report myself to the political
agent that night, so I went next morning. He heard
my news with great satisfaction, said very nice things
about my part of the "show", and expressed the
opinion that the loss of the valuable caravan would be
such a blow to the inland tribes that the gun-running
trade would be dead on that part of the coast for many
months. He agreed with me that something ought

to be done for the villagers, but shook his head when I suggested that the "*B. A.*" might be spared to protect them for a few weeks.

"Can't anything be done for them?" I asked anxiously.

"The most I can do," he said, "is to let the local Arab camel dealers know that they have all those camels to sell—almost for the asking. Once they have got rid of them there won't be so much temptation for the Bedouins to attack them."

He did this, and during the afternoon six or seven large trading buggalows glided out of harbour. I hoped that they were off to my village, and, one passing close to the "*B. A.*", Mr. Scarlett hailed her to know where she was going.

"Yes," he nodded, after much shouting backward and forward; "they are all on their way there as quickly as they can. They aren't going to let the chance slip; they don't expect those Bedouins will leave the camels there many days."

Poor devils! Precious little profit would they make out of their assistance to us, and precious little would those traders give them.

We "coaled" and "watered" that day, having a good deal of trouble with the natives in the lighters. There was such a swell running into the harbour that we were banging against those lighters rather heavily, and the natives were often frightened to carry the coal on board. Jaffa was ashore, so Mr. Scarlett had to do all the persuading. He was in his element at "persuading". I don't believe he had any more feeling for those chaps than if they'd been dogs.

"There now, that comes of knowing the 'lingo'!" he said cheerfully, when at last the eighteen tons of coal had been stowed below, and he came up on deck to have a drink. "I told them a few things about their grandfathers and fathers, grandmothers and mothers, which fairly got them on the raw."

He was a very strange chap. He would be cheerful and talkative one moment, morbid and taciturn the next—one never knew. I often tried to chaff him out of these fits of depression, told him they were worse at full moon, and joked him about being in love. The moon may have had nothing to do with them; but I often noticed that he grew silent and morose towards sunset, and have often seen him go and hide himself in the cabin or turn his back to it.

Once I asked him why.

"I can't help it, sir; every time I see the sun setting I remember those shadows racing down from the mountains that time Jassim's wife was killed with this," and he tapped his left arm where the bracelet was.

He happened to be quite cheerful that evening, after his successful day's work with the lightermen, so when it was cool I simply forced him to come ashore.

"Come and have a walk; it will do you good," I said, and took him with me in the dinghy. Directly we landed, between the Custom House and the Sultan's palace, he started off along the shore at a great pace, pushing in and out of the Arabs busy loading and unloading dhows as if he never even saw them. As I caught up with him I saw that he was in one of his morbid fits again.

"What's wrong now?" I asked.

"This is the very spot where I stood eighteen years ago and saw the cursed snake for the second time. The Khan of Khamia came down here, and his wives were carried along that passageway—the arm with this bracelet on it showed up just there—there!" and he gripped my arm and pointed, his eyes glittering as if he could really see it again.

"Come along, man; don't be a fool!" I cried angrily; "people will think you mad," and dragged him reluctantly away through narrow, tortuous passages, jostling natives of every black or brown nationality under the sun, and pressing back occasionally against the walls of the miserable houses to let laden donkeys pass. The Eastern smell pervading everything delighted me; it was splendid; but I do not suppose he noticed it. At last we came to the main gate of the town, with its armed guard of ruffianly Arabs, and turned to the right along an open space where many horses were tethered, until we found ourselves close to a wretched mosque and a crowd of idlers lazily listening whilst a decrepit-looking old chap, standing on the steps, read from a paper he was holding. As we pressed through the people I caught the words "Khamia", when Mr. Scarlett stopped suddenly, gripped my arm fiercely, and literally pulled me away. He was shaking all over, and that muddy, frightened expression had come back.

"What the dickens is the matter now?" I asked, very irritated.

"Come back; get back to the '_B. A._', sir; I can't breathe here."

He let go of my arm and simply ploughed his way through the crowd, and when clear of it actually began running.

I caught him up and stopped him. I was furious.

"Didn't you hear what he was reading?" he said, trembling. "It was the proclamation offering a reward for the 'Twin Death'?"

"That's nothing, man; you know they read it out every few weeks."

"I can't help it, sir; don't leave me, sir! For God's sake get me back to the '*B. A.*'! That's not all. I've seen something else."

He would not tell me what, but walked as fast as he could, looking back every other second, with wild eyes, as if he was afraid of being followed. He walked so fast that I could barely keep up with him, and in one street or alleyway, which was fairly empty, he broke into a run again.

He was in a pitiable state of terror, and I was mighty glad when we did at last reach the beach, jump into a shore boat, and get aboard the *Bunder Abbas*.

It was not until he had had a glass of brandy that he began to calm down, and presently he apologized most abjectly for spoiling my walk.

I knew that I should never take him ashore again; I was very irritated. The whole business was so childish. He might take the bracelet off—I would guarantee to have it off in ten minutes—without the least risk.

I tried to argue with him; but it was not of the least use; he only became more agitated. He shut himself in our cabin, and I left him there till Percy announced dinner, with a grin of importance at having provided a special feast for us from one of the sheep those poor devils of villagers had given us.

"Kid-ney on to-ast," he said, his eyes and mouth wide open with delight.

"Come along, Mr. Scarlett!" I shouted, and tried to make him come out.

"I durs'n't yet, sir; I'll wait till it's dark."

"What on earth are you frightened of—now?"

"Of being seen, sir; I durs'n't show myself. Look at those boats there, sir," he said, pointing through the cabin door at some native boats which were passing—such boats were passing at all hours of the day. "He might be there."

"Who? Not that decrepit old chap we saw this afternoon?"

"No," he said, clutching the side of his bunk and looking half-mad; "Jassim! Jassim himself!"

"Jassim? You haven't seen him, have you?" I asked, startled.

"Yes," he groaned; "and he saw me! We came face to face in that crowd outside the mosque. I knew him directly, and he knew me—I'll swear it."

"You're mistaken, man; it couldn't have been he."

Mr. Scarlett shook his head. "No, no! I recollect his face as though it was yesterday—he has a scar on his upper lip, too. No, no! I couldn't make a mistake! He shot out an arm, felt above my elbow, then turned away without a word."

"Touched the bracelet; made sure it was still there, did he?"

Phew! I whistled, and shivered in spite of the terrible heat inside the cabin, for there was something so uncanny about the whole business. If Jassim had recognized him there might be danger—might be very great danger, unless Mr. Scarlett would let me or someone take the cursed thing off his arm. We could not hope that we had escaped by hurrying away. Two Englishmen couldn't walk through the town of Muscat without everyone knowing from where they came. There was not a mail steamer in the harbour, and even if there had been, and we might have been taken for passengers, the native boatmen who had brought us off from shore would give us away. It was very awkward.

"Kid-ney get cold, master," Percy pleaded, with a disappointed look in his face; so I went and tried to eat, sending Mr. Scarlett's share into the cabin.

I ate but little; he ate less. His nervousness and fright were infectious. I began to feel as nervous as a cat. Fearing lest Jassim—if indeed it was Jassim—should try to force his way on board, I gave very stringent orders that no native boat should be allowed to come alongside and no one allowed on board without my permission. I also stopped the leave of the native crew, lest they should be tampered with.

Webster, Moore, and Ellis, who acted as quartermasters, were provided with revolvers, and ordered to use them if anyone did attempt to come aboard during the night. I don't know what they thought had suddenly made this precaution necessary. Certainly the whole crew knew that something had happened, and every one of us was in a horrid state of nerves.

When the sun had set, Mr. Scarlett ventured out for a breath of the hot air. I had a terrible night with him. I had never seen anyone so unmanned as he was. Eventually he did go to sleep, but woke screaming in a hideous nightmare, and there was no more sleep after that—for either of us.

Next morning he would not be content until he had rigged a screen round the little upper deck where the cabin was, and there he stayed, hour after hour, peering through a slit in the canvas, with a pair of field-glasses at his side to scrutinize any approaching boat. This made me more "jumpy" than ever. But a screen would not keep Jassim away, nor did it, and during the forenoon a native boat came pulling towards us with a single Arab in the stern-sheets. Mr. Scarlett called out for me, and I found him yellow with fear, peeping through his screen.

"That's him, sir. He's coming."

"He can't do anything; I won't let him aboard!" I said. "For goodness' sake don't be such a confounded coward."

"But I am a coward! I told you I was a coward. I am, sir; I can't help it;" and he slunk into his cabin and fastened the door.

"No one allowed to come aboard," I reminded Ellis, who happened to be the quartermaster at the time. He waved off the boat, but the Arab forced the boatman to bring it closer, and as I saw him more clearly I gasped with amazement, for I had seen him before; he was the sheikh who had commanded the caravan we had captured—the red-bearded man to whose wounded son I had given water. There could be no possible mistake. His beard was not dyed now, but once having seen this man Jassim—if it was Jassim —there was no forgetting him.

To meet him under these conditions was startling, to say the least of it, and I was quite thrown off my balance. To gain time I told Jaffa to ask him what he wanted.

A long conversation followed, and then Jaffa said: "Say he want very great talk—must have very great talk."

In my own opinion it would have been better to let him come aboard, have the matter out once and for all, and hear what he proposed doing; but the door of the cabin overhead slid back and Mr. Scarlett whispered through the screen: "For God's sake, sir, send him away; don't let him come near me."

So, as my head really was rather dizzy with my discovery, I sent him away, and back he went, never moving a muscle of his face to show that he was disappointed.

I certainly was disappointed; one doesn't meet such people every day, and I should have liked to find out whether his son was alive. One thing, only, I determined on—not to let Mr. Scarlett know that it was his caravan of rifles we had captured, because I knew this would only add to his fright and his fear of impending calamity.

That afternoon a letter was brought off addressed in sprawling letters to the "Officer with black beard, His Britannic Majesty's ship, *Bunder Abbas*."

The quartermaster brought it to me and I took it up to Mr. Scarlett, who seized it with trembling fingers and tore it open. Presently he called me to come to him.

"I've translated it, sir. He wants the snake; he offers me five thousand rupees if only I will let him take it off my arm. He says he does not want to do me any harm, but that he is desperately hard up and must and will have it. It's really a threat, sir," he said, his hands trembling violently.

I guessed why he was so desperately "hard up", though I did not tell Mr. Scarlett, but spent the whole day trying to argue with the poor chap, going over the same old arguments which Baron Popple Opstein and I had used so often—with the added inducement of his now being able to make money by getting rid of the snake.

Every now and again he would almost yield. Then he would remember seeing Jassim's wife dying and that bluejacket clawing his way down to the sea, and he would rock himself from side to side, like a woman in despair, shouting at me that he would sooner be killed than die such a death.

I really thought that he was going mad—as his predecessor had done.

So when Jassim came next morning I sent him away again. Not a flicker of disappointment crossed his face, but as I watched the retreating boat and his motionless back I could not help feeling that we had done a very foolish thing indeed, and that trouble would certainly follow.

Not a soul stirred out of the *Bunder Abbas* all day; there was a strange sensation of impending trouble, and as darkness fell and the lights of the gloomy, unruly town twinkled out, I felt an unpleasant, gruesome feeling that we had let him go, had lost touch with him, and should not now know when danger threatened or from where. Whether my mind had gradually been influenced by association with Mr. Scarlett or not, yet although I did my utmost to induce myself to believe that there was no danger, the effort was extremely unsuccessful. Jassim now had good reasons for revenge on both of us, and he badly needed money. If he had turned out to be an insignificant nonentity or a mere cadging loafer whose only trace of his former power and dignities remained in his remembrance of them I should not have feared him; but this Jassim was evidently a man of great influence still (you must remember that gun-running or slave-running were then the only aristocratic occupations the sheikhs of the various tribes indulged in), and must even now have powerful friends scattered everywhere who would be only too glad to assist him.

I do not mind saying that it caused me most unpleasant thought, and I was more than ever sorry that we had rebuffed him twice already.

Luckily the *Intrepid* came in next morning, and I was extremely pleased to receive orders to return to Kalat al Abeid for a fortnight.

Whilst our lascars were raising steam I saw the commander going ashore to call on the political agent, and on his way back he came aboard the *Bunder Abbas*.

"The political agent's delighted with our haul," he said, as I saluted him. "He's mentioning your name in his dispatches to the Indian Government. You ought to get something out of it. You got my orders. Well, you can go there for a fortnight; you can't be spared for longer. Don't get into trouble. You can finish off those leopards. I killed a couple; there are plenty more."

I thanked him very warmly, and as he was shoving off he called out: "They're getting nervous at Jask again. Some brigands of 'sorts' from the hills have been cutting the telegraph line and threatening to burn the telegraph station."

"Is nothing going to be done?" I asked.

"No," he called back. "We've advised them to send away those two ladies—two are there, I hear—but nothing else. They're always crying 'wolf', and we can't keep a ship tied to the telegraph-posts all the time."

I had intended telling him that Jassim was in Muscat, but this news made me forget him and spoilt my pleasure at getting away from Muscat and being able to help my friends the villagers. It made me very uncomfortable to think of those two fragile ladies exposed to such dangers in those sunbaked telegraph buildings on the little promontory of Jask.

We were not ready for sea until next morning, and that night I dreamt that I had to rescue those two ladies, or, rather, choose which I should rescue, and I picked up the little yellow-haired lady with the grey eyes and tried to carry her down to the *Bunder Abbas*; but my foot wouldn't move properly, and an Arab with a flaming-red beard and a knife in his hand would have caught me had I not woke up.

However, if one always worried about dangers

which might happen at some uncertain future one's time would be pretty well occupied. When once we were out at sea, and the little "*B. A.*" was tumbling about with the tail end of the south-west monsoon swell sliding under her, our cares and troubles seemed quickly blown away. The whole crew had caught some of yesterday's gloom, and they too were now as cheery as schoolboys. Even Moore and Ellis—still enemies—exchanged a few friendly remarks, and the dismal cook and his "mate" chattered to each other as they carried on their everlasting scouring of pots and pans. Mr. Scarlett was a different being altogether. He was his natural colour again, and I could have sworn that he was fatter than the day before. As for Percy, his glistening brown cheeks were split with a smile which extended from ear to ear. He knew that there had been something wrong, that his hero had been in some danger, and his two solemn great eyes followed Mr. Scarlett wherever he moved. To him the gunner was the most wonderful thing his little world held, and if you had seen him squatting in a shady corner outside our cabin, whitening Mr. Scarlett's shoes or helmet, daubing here and there, then waiting for the damp places to dry in the sun, holding them up to see the effect and trying to make them look whiter than any shoes or helmet had been before, you would have felt a great liking for the little chap in his queer surroundings so far from his home and people.

All that day we steamed along that tremendous coast line of cliffs, and whenever some particularly barren rock stuck out into the sea I could not help,

for the life of me, picturing the white telegraph buildings at Jask, and remembering the fluttering of a
white handkerchief I had once seen waving "good-
bye" from the corner near the flagstaff.

"No other tune you know?" Mr. Scarlett asked me
cynically, whilst we were thoroughly enjoying the
lunch Percy had furnished. "You've been whistling
and humming the same old tune for the last three
hours."

I'm hanged if I'd known it at the time, but it was
"Two Eyes of Grey". Well, to know that those
treacherous Afghans were threatening that isolated
telegraph station was enough to make anyone think
of the little grey-eyed lady imprisoned there.

In the afternoon we passed quite close to one of
those buggalows which had gone to Kalat al Abeid
to purchase the camels, and her deck was crowded
with them. We met another as we threaded our
way through the channel cut in the cliffs, also laden
with camels. She was drifting out with the tide, and
we had some difficulty in passing her.

When we anchored off the village itself, three more
were half in, half out of the water, and we could see
our friends the villagers trying to persuade more
stubborn brutes to climb aboard along sloping gang-
ways.

The head-man was along in a jiffy, bringing another
sheep with him. I hardly recognized him for a moment in a green turban and a scarlet burnous with a
flaming scarlet belt, into which he had stuck silver-
mounted daggers (the green turban I found out afterwards was the one Jassim had lost that awful night,

and I remembered that he was not wearing it when he followed his wounded son through the gap). Across his knees he had one of the rifles we had given him—each man in the boat had one—and he was treating it as if it was a baby or something alive. When he stepped on board, all smiles and friendliness, he brought it with him, and kept on patting it affectionately, shaking a bag slung from his shoulder by a piece of coarse string, and smiling like a big baby when the cartridges inside it rattled.

He was vastly amusing in his new finery. He told Jaffa, for my edification, that "men of Kalat al Abeid no fish—so much good things no work any more—Arab trader from Muscat bring so much food—dates, rice, cloth, beads, bracelets for women—brass cooking-pots; never want nothing no more. No fear Bedouins —taffenk—fishenk[1]—kill them all."

Jaffa soon found out that, as I thought, he never bothered to keep even a few men posted in the gap in the mountains. "It was absurd to keep them there in the daytime: surely they could see the Bedouins coming down from the ravine and shoot them; and as for at night, why, everyone knew that devils and horned dragons breathing flame came and went through that gap during the dark hours."

If he had spent the night with us up there, whilst the *Intrepid's* shells were bursting, he might have had some foundation for his yarn.

At any rate, not a man of the village dared stay there after dark, and it was useless work trying to chaff the old chap out of his superstitions. He cer-

[1] Rifles, cartridges.

tainly had not seen any devils or horned dragons breathing flame—no one alive had; but their fathers had told them about them, and that was good enough for him.

"Sometimes hear big noise of wind rushing through the gap," Jaffa interpreted, as the old man evidently tried to back his superstition with some tangible facts.

"Well, ask him about the leopards. Tell him I want to go there and shoot some," I told Jaffa.

He was quite willing to talk about them, but did not want to give me the trouble of climbing all that way. He patted his rifle, pointed to those of his men, and Jaffa explained, without a smile on his face: "The white sea-lord shall recline in the shade of my hut whilst I and my men go and shoot leopard— bring back plenty skins, and plenty claws to make necklace for white sea-lord."

"But the white sea-lord jolly well wants to do the shooting himself," I laughed, "and to-morrow too."

When this was interpreted to the old man—I must call him sheikh, now that he was so important—he smiled, as though he thought me rather a mad ass.

"Well, tell him I'll come ashore to-morrow an hour before sunrise, and we'll have a great day together."

That was arranged satisfactorily, so I gave him a packet of cigarettes, and he went ashore, still patting and fondling his rifle, to hurry up the embarkment of the remaining camels.

CHAPTER XII

Mr. Scarlett Bares his Arm

MR. SCARLETT was in such high spirits at getting safely away from Muscat that he declared his intention of coming shooting with me, and he did. I left Webster, the corporal of marines, in charge of the "*B. A.*", and took Moore, the petty officer, Hartley, the lazy signal-man (who was so fat I knew he'd sweat his soul out climbing up the mountains), and the two marines, Jones and Gamble. Of course Jaffa came with us; we could do nothing without our aristocratic Persian interpreter.

Early as it was, we found the shore swarming with the villagers, helping the crews of those dhows to embark the last of the captured camels, and making enough noise to prevent any respectable devil or horned dragon venturing within a hundred miles of them.

When they saw us they hastily rushed back to their huts, and by the time we had landed and found the sheikh waiting for us near his white-domed well, they came running back—the whole crowd of them— every man with a rifle and a bag of cartridges. At a word from the beaming sheikh they began firing their rifles to welcome us. How it was that no one was hit was a marvel, for they knew less about hand-ling them than I do of a sewing-machine.

You may bet your last dollar that I was not going shooting with that little lot, and it took Jaffa at least a quarter of an hour of talking before they stole away to their huts, and came sorrowfully back without their rifles, but with much more useful spears and sticks.

I asked Jaffa how he had managed this.

"Tell them in England country sheikh ask great man shoot—insult if villagers shoot too."

I could not help laughing at the idea of a day's "shoot" at home when all the beaters from the countryside carried rifles. It would make some "shoots" a good deal more exciting than they often are.

The sheikh himself would have sent his rifle away as well, though I saw that it would almost break his heart to do so. However, I explained by gestures that I wanted him to shoot with me, and his pride and joy were comical to see.

Eventually we shoved off for the ravine, followed by hooded women bearing huge chatties of water, and every "toddler" in the village carrying a bigger or smaller bundle of dry date-palm leaves. It was as quaint a shooting party as ever I had seen.

As we traversed the rocky slopes across which the *Intrepids* had advanced to the attack of the mouth of the ravine, the natives spread out to pick up battered bullets and empty cartridge cases. They were lying there in hundreds, and every big stone had one or two white marks where bullets had struck it. At the mouth of the ravine, at the spot where the

Arabs had first taken up a position, the stones and rocks were white with splashes and fragments of nine-pounder shells, and fuses and shrapnel bullets lay among them. Close by were three cairns with wooden crosses. These were the graves of the three who had been killed, and the sheikh explained that he and his people had piled up those big stones so that the wolves and jackals should not disturb them.

Passing through the ravine we once more entered that vast hollow, left the sunshine behind us, and craned our necks upwards to see the gap. Six days ago, when I was there, it and the path had been full of living creatures and ringing with shouts from one zigzag to another, as the bluejackets and villagers tried to bring down the camels. Now the gloom was haunted with silence and loneliness. Except for two or three bloated vultures, which flew heavily upwards and disappeared over the rim, not a thing moved. The not-yet-whitened skeletons of several camels showed what a feast they and the jackals had made.

As we did on that first memorable day, so we did on this. The villagers were ordered to remain at the bottom whilst the sheikh, Mr. Scarlett, myself, and the rest of the men climbed up the zigzag. We left Hartley below; he solemnly shook his head when he saw what kind of a path it was, and, as he was already pretty well "done up", I let him stay. He promptly went to sleep.

When we did reach the top, walked through the gap, and looked down into the valleys beyond, I almost expected to see the huge snake of a caravan wriggling up to us again. I showed Mr. Scarlett where we had first seen it, and pointed out the rocks behind which we had crouched nearly all that day; also the rock on which Jaffa had stood calling out in the dark: "Khalli bunduk 'ak! Ma kattle kum! Ist agel!"

He was very interested, but the sheikh was still more impatient, so we spread out along the crest just as we had done before, and then he gave the signal for the villagers to beat up towards us.

I don't know what I imagined they would do. They were not flies, or even goats, so I could hardly expect them to climb up the precipice; but what actually occurred was that, after spreading over the whole of the bottom of the "coffee-cup", yelling and throwing stones into any places likely to conceal a leopard, they all made for the zigzag path and came up it very swiftly, one behind the other, yelling like fury, beating the rocks with their spears as they passed them, the ones in rear beating the rocks which had already been struck a hundred times already, just as vigorously as the first. Occasionally they threw blazing bundles of date-palm leaves into crevices and caves; but, except for this and the noise they made, their ideas of what was wanted were very laughable.

The sheikh had lain down close to me. Presently he gave an exclamation and pointed. I saw a leopard slinking round a rock just ahead of some shouting villagers; he was at least four hundred yards away, and before I could stop the old man he had fired his rifle, regardless of the fact that if his aim was anywhere in that direction he was far more likely to hit one of his own people than the leopard. I need not have worried myself. The bullet struck a rock close below us and shrieked away into the sky, whilst the recoiling butt struck his cheek. First of all he looked to see whether the leopard was dead, and as it had disappeared behind a rock he was as pleased as "Punch"; then he felt his cheek and patted his rifle reprovingly as if it were a naughty boy. But he smacked it a moment after, when the leopard appeared again, bounding up the rocks.

I roared with laughter, which of course upset him. Holding the rifle more gingerly than ever, and keeping his face well out of the danger line (he could not possibly have looked along his sights) he fired again, and of course "thump" went the butt against his shoulder. At that he laid the rifle down, sat up, and gazed scornfully at it, jabbering something to me which I, of course, did not understand.

The leopard was now standing on a rock, entirely unaware that he had been fired at, watching the advancing beaters, twitching his tail, and uncertain what to do.

I nodded to the sheikh to watch how it should be done, took a steady aim, and fired.

The animal was two hundred yards away, if an inch, and I did not expect to hit him, but luck was with me. He sprang up, pawing the air, gave two or three huge bounds from rock to rock, then just missed the edge of a boulder, clawed frantically for a moment, and fell on the zigzag path dead.

The wonder and amazement showing in the old man's eyes were the greatest compliment I had ever had paid to my skill. He handed me his rifle and

wanted to try mine, taking it with an awed expression
as if it were a live thing.   Then he noticed the difference in the breech (mine was a Lee-Metford, his a
Mauser), and a cunning smile flickered across his face,
as if that was the reason why mine had behaved so
much better.   His eyes simply danced from rock to
rock, watching for something to appear, so that he
could show me that with the same rifle he was just as
good a shot as myself.   Presently a wolf or jackal
trotted along a narrow ledge of rock below us.   He
threw up my rifle, pressing the trigger at the same
moment, and, as he never even held it tightly, and
was sitting up on his haunches, was nearly knocked
over by the recoil.

Where the bullet went goodness knows, but his
look of abject disappointment when he recovered himself and saw the beast still running along was too
comical for words.   He gave the rifle back to me,
waved his hands as if to say that he would have
nothing more to do with such works of Satan, folded
his cloak round him, and sat sulkily indifferent.   His
green turban and crimson cloak made him a quaint
figure in the glaring sunlight.

The others fired a few shots (though at what I could
not see) and I only hoped that they would not shoot
the villagers.   Nothing more appeared for us to shoot
at, till presently a vulture, coming from nowhere,
perched heavily on a rock not fifty yards away—a
splendid target for a rifle.   He was quite indifferent
to our presence.

I made the sheikh lie down—he was as excited as
a child again—showed him how to hold the rifle,

press it into his shoulder, and look along the sights; the bird watching us all the time, looking like a ragged tramp sitting for his photograph.

When he at last fired, the bullet hit a rock at least ten yards below the bird; but the report frightened it and it flew away.

The old man evidently thought he had wounded it, for he recovered his affability and patted the rifle approvingly, smiling at me.

Whether or no there were as many leopards as we had believed, at any rate we saw no more there, and presently they brought my dead one up to the gap and commenced skinning him. Whilst they were doing this the sheikh led us down to some craggy rocks on the other slope, and a leopard was frightened out of them but broke back through the frightened villagers, and only gave me a long and hopeless shot whilst he was travelling very fast. I am sure the old gentleman was rather pleased that he wasn't the only one who missed.

This was a disappointing day's shooting, but the exercise did us all the good in the world, and we went back to the village quite content. As we drew near, the villagers rushed ahead to exchange their spears and sticks for their beloved rifles, came back to meet us, and fired another *feu de joie*.

At a word from Mr. Scarlett the sheikh, seizing a stick, rushed in among them and whacked left and right till they stopped. If he realized the danger it was a very plucky thing to do, because bullets were whizzing all round us.

It was very evident that if the villagers went on

expending their precious cartridges as they had this day, they would soon have none left to keep the Bedouins away. This waste of good ammunition so outraged Mr. Scarlett's professional feelings that he actually spent the greater part of the next week teaching them the elements of rifle shooting. I had never seen him so happy for so many days together.

Under the shade of some "nabac" trees close to the well he rigged a tripod and a sand-bag for a rifle to rest on, painted some black bull's-eyes on the side of one of the huts, and every evening showed the villagers how to look along their sights and get them in a line with the bull's-eye.

At the end of the week he rigged a target some way along the beach and invited me to see the results of his training. I do not suppose that there was a single man, woman, or child but had come down to join in the excitement. They were all gathered round the firing point, some eighty or one hundred yards from the target, jabbering noisily—the children not being more childish than the "grown-ups".

Then in absolute silence—even the children held their breath—the first man lay down and aimed very carefully. He fired, and every single soul scampered pell-mell along the beach to the target to see where it had been hit.

In spite of actually seeing most of the bullets striking the sand, they had the most implicit confidence in each other's marksmanship; and I nearly burst myself with laughing, when, after a little while, they began to tire of running to and fro after every shot, and actually gathered round the target itself with their heads as close to the black bull's-eye as they could get them, waiting for the next shot.

Mr. Scarlett managed with difficulty to bring them back, but at this rate the millennium would have arrived by the time each man had fired the three rounds he allowed them. As a matter of fact this exhibition of the result of his training did take three evenings, and I do not remember that any man hit any part of the canvas more than twice. Most of them never hit it at all. However, they were not in the least disappointed; they were all too ignorant and stupid to mind what became of the bullet so long as the noise and recoil were big enough. Not even when Mr. Scarlett put the target four hundred yards or so farther along the beach, and he and I fired a dozen rounds and hit the bull's-eye seven times between us, did they show much appreciation. Every one of them—even the children—put their fingers in the holes and shouted with glee; but they evidently considered the whole performance due to magic—not our magic, but the rifles' magic.

The sheikh refused to fire, evidently not wanting to disgrace himself before the tribe, although his explanation, given to Jaffa, was that it was quite unnecessary—"that if he could hit a vulture at twenty paces, of course he could hit a huge piece of canvas."

Well, even Mr. Scarlett could not be expected to train those poor ignorant fishermen in three or four days. I do believe that they imagined that all that was necessary was to put a cartridge in the rifle, show it the object, and pull the trigger. Allah would look after the bullet. If he did not mean it to hit—

well it wouldn't, that was all—and Mr. Scarlett and Jaffa had not sufficient command of their language to make them believe otherwise.

Even after this fatuous display the sheikh confidently told Jaffa that he pitied any poor Bedouins who tried to attack his town—town! mind you; not collection of hovels, as it actually was. His own house and the dome-shaped well were the only two structures you could lean against without risk of falling through the sides. He and his silly simpletons of villagers really believed that they were now a formidable tribe—with their rifles, their new finery, their sacks of dates, and the flocks of sheep the Arab traders had given them in exchange for the camels. They suffered badly from "swollen heads", were too proud to fish, and loafed about the village with their rifles and silver-mounted daggers—doing nothing. The women were just as foolish over the stores of food and the unaccustomed finery they now had, and all had lost any fear of the Bedouins swooping down through the gap to take revenge.

Every camel except one had been taken away, and that one the sheikh kept for his own use, fitting it out with the gorgeous trappings belonging to Jassim's own riding camel—the one I had killed on the zigzag path. When he was perched, insecurely and uncomfortably, on top of all this splendour, he thought himself the finest fellow in the world, in spite of the fact that the brute could only be induced to move, and that only at a snail's pace, by being pulled along by his halter.

He used to mount it and come along with me when

I went shooting along the mountain slopes; but he could never keep up with me, however much the attendant villagers hauled on the head-rope.

One evening, as our fortnight's stay was drawing to a close, we saw from the *Bunder Abbas* two little dots moving rapidly down from the mouth of the ravine. As they drew nearer we saw that they were two camels, and that a man was riding the first and leading the other. Darkness swallowed them up; but next morning there were three camels kneeling under the shade of the dark-green "nabac" trees alongside the well—the sheikh's and the two strange ones. And whilst we were wondering who the man could have been, a boat paddled off with a letter for Mr. Scarlett. As he caught sight of the hand-writing he actually seemed to shrivel; the lines in his face became drawn and haggard, his eyes positively sank into their sockets, and that horrid, frightened, muddy colour spread over his face and down his neck. I knew then who had written the letter —Jassim.

Mr. Scarlett staggered into the cabin and slid the door across. It seemed hours before he opened it —just a crack—and beckoned to me.

"Same thing, sir, only more threatening. Says he will take it off without hurting. That he must have it, and he'll give me still more money."

I had not the patience to try to persuade him to run the slight risk and get rid of the beastly bracelet once and for all, so said nothing. It was he who at last, trembling and sweating with fright, suggested that Jassim should be allowed to come on board and talk things over—" if—if you'll stand by with a revolver, sir, and kill him if he tries to seize it."

It was the only sensible course to take; and, later on, Jassim did come aboard.

What a grand-looking fellow he was in spite of his age, and how he must have hated me and the *Bunder Abbas* for the part we had played in capturing his caravan! If he did, he showed no sign, salaaming to me as to an equal. I took him up to our little deck, to Mr. Scarlett, and the two began yarning very earnestly, whilst I stood by to see fair play. Jassim was evidently explaining how he proposed to take off the bracelet, and produced two pairs of thin pincers—the same idea that my chum and I had suggested a hundred times.

Some extraordinary excess of courage seemed to come to Mr. Scarlett, and he actually bared his arm, uncovered the bandage, and showed the snake. As it glittered in the sunlight I saw Jassim's eyes flash with something which was not all greed. He slid on his knees, bent down till his lips touched it, holding out his hands and muttering something. Then he rose to his feet, his chest muscles working under his muslin shirt, walked to the rails, and stood for a few moments looking towards the mountains. Mr. Scarlett's arm was stretched across the table, the muscles clenched so hard that they stood out in lumps. He looked at me appealingly, said something to Jassim, who came back to the table, lay half across it to steady himself, and took up those two pincers. Very, very gently he began to insert the jaws of one under a coil of the bracelet, whilst with the other he held fast the head of the snake. I noticed Mr. Scarlett shudder as the pincers touched his skin, and great drops of sweat gathered on his forehead. Then Jassim gently pulled at the coil until it began to come away from the skin. I was looking on, fascinated, my eyes riveted on the head, which, although it was gripped by the other pair of pincers, seemed to be fighting to twist itself backwards and wriggle itself free. At an unlucky moment those pincers slipped off the head, and as the iron dug into Mr. Scarlett's arm and the head flattened itself against the skin, Mr. Scarlett's self-control gave way.

Clenching his free hand over the snake, and seizing the pincers which held the coil, he tore them out of Jassim's hand and jumped away. His chair and the pincers fell with a clatter on the deck, and he stumbled blindly into the cabin, crying to me to send Jassim away, and closing the door behind him.

I turned towards the Arab. He too seemed to have grown older. His face was not pleasant to look at. I managed somehow or other to get rid of him, but there was no peace for me. Mr. Scarlett would not let me leave him all that day nor all through the night. I think he must have been mad. He sat crouched in one corner of the cabin, clutching the snake with his right hand, and moaning for me not to leave him if ever I stirred.

I did everything I could to rouse him—taunted him with cowardice, told him that he was not fit to be called an Englishman, let alone an officer; but he only whimpered like a child, and moaned that it was the Arab blood in him, rocking himself backwards and forwards, cursing himself for ever having allowed Jassim to see the snake.

When day broke after that horrid night those two camels had disappeared from under the nabac trees. Seizing my telescope and looking towards the mountains I could see them entering the gloomy mouth of the ravine. Mr. Scarlett was just in time to see them too, and some of the terror in his face faded away as they were lost to view. All day he followed me, cringing and apologizing in the most abject manner. Twice he came to me, with his face set and determined, to ask me to take off the snake; but at the sight of it round his bare arm he would alter his mind and say: "Not now, sir; let's wait till Jassim shows his hand again; let's wait till we go back to Muscat!" I lost patience with him completely, and would not speak to him.

The whole crew were, of course, aware that something mysterious had occurred, and Percy guessed that danger threatened his hero. It was quite pathetic to watch him following Mr. Scarlett with his big brown eyes, and looking wistfully sad at not being able to help him.

This affair of Jassim completely upset me, and made me wish that the *Bunder Abbas* should be sent patrolling again. However monotonous that might be, there would not be the dread of such a scene and such a horrid night as I had just spent with the gunner. Our fortnight at Kalat-al-Abeid had now come to a close, so I went ashore to wish my old friend the sheikh good-bye and to give him a few parting words of advice—through Jaffa. I pointed out to him that if a man and two camels could come riding down from the gap without anyone seeing them, five hundred could do so just as easily and just as unexpectedly. However, he only smiled a superior smile and patted his rifle, so I left him complacently oblivious to his danger, and took the *Bunder Abbas* through the channel in the cliffs out into the open sea once more. Once out there Mr. Scarlett quickly recovered his composure, but I very much dreaded what would happen should we be detained at Muscat for any length of time.

However, we were in luck. When I went aboard the *Intrepid* to report myself, and told Commander Duckworth that, so far, the Bedouins had made no attempt to attack the village, and amused him by describing the results of their rifle practice and the grand appearance of the old sheikh on his walking camel, he said: "Well, Martin, you've had a fortnight's rest, and now I have rather an amusing job for you. There's a place called Sur on the chart; it's thirty miles to the south'ard, a deep backwater with two towns—Heija, on the north-east side, belonging to the Beni-Bu-Ali tribe; and, on the west, Shateif-al-Kabira, inhabited by the Beni Janaba. They hate each other like poison, and are always having rows. There is only one decent well for both towns—half-way between them—and the old Sultan has a fort and keeps a garrison there to protect it and keep order. A few months ago he sent a son of his there to command, and the harum-scarum young ass got himself into a mess, enraged both tribes so much that they've joined forces—for the first time on record—and surrounded his precious fort. As a personal favour the Sultan has asked the political agent if he will get him out of this trouble; so there's your job, and off you go as soon as you're ready. The Sultan is sending off a few thousand rupees, and if you find these won't do the trick, and the tribes are bent on getting the young scamp's blood, just bring him back with you. The *Bunder Abbas* can get quite close in to the fort, and you ought to have no trouble. At any rate, fix things up as best you can."

"Thank you very much, sir!" I said, and asked him if there was any more news from Jask.

He shook his head. "The political agent is always hearing rumours of trouble—nothing more. They haven't sent those ladies away. I wish they would."

So did I.

I stayed on board to lunch with Popple Opstein. He was beginning to find lying off Muscat rather dull work after the exciting times we had had, and almost wished we had not captured all those arms. "The gun-running business has been knocked on the head for the next few months or so," he told me, "and things are as dull as ditch-water."

The *Bunder Abbas* had taken nearly all her coal, water, and provisions on board by the time I went back to her, and I found Mr. Scarlett in another of his nervous saturnine fits. Moore told me he had shut himself in his cabin ever since the coal lighter had come alongside. When he came out to speak to me he was so nervous and shaky that I was more than ever anxious about him.

To come back from the noisy, cheery mess aboard the *Intrepid* to be cooped up alone with him again made me feel extremely miserable. I was beginning to dread Percy announcing a meal. The food, generally speaking, was horrid—horrid to look at and horrid to eat. The gunner would sit on one side of the table, I on the other, and we often never spoke a single word all through a single meal except to curse Percy or the cook or the flies or the sun blazing through the awning. At least once every day the wretched cook would be sent for by the gunner and slanged in Hindustani or Urdu or some such queer dialect or other until he slunk down the ladder trembling with fear. Often to avoid a row with the gunner I would go away and leave him to finish his meal by himself. Latterly, when I saw Percy laying the cloth for " food ", I would find myself a job of work to do, hoping that Mr. Scarlett would finish before I came. But that was no good; he would always wait for me.

I was, in fact, heartily sick of him. I don't mean to say that I actually disliked him, but we had nothing whatever in common once we had told each other all the yarns we knew and when the subject of gun-running was worn threadbare.

It suddenly occurred to me to ask old Popple Opstein to get leave and come along with me for this trip to Sur, so I signalled across, and presently back came a semaphore: " Right oh! leave granted. What time do you sail?"

I was not going until the morning; it was no good spending a night at sea along that coast. So I signalled: " Daybreak—delighted."

He made me dine with him; we had a great sing-song on the poop, with the ship's company chipping in, and after it he came back with me, bringing his bedding and other gear.

The night was as hot as Hades, without a breath of air, but the old "*B. A.*" standing out in the moonlight was a different ship with Popple Opstein climbing up her side and with him to yarn to before we lay down on the little deck outside the cabin (inside which Mr. Scarlett had again shut himself) and tried to sleep.

Not much sleep did we get, so much had we to talk about, and so pleasant it was for me to have someone to talk to.

CHAPTER XIII

Rounding up a Prodigal

AT daybreak next morning our little steam-winch ran the anchor out of the water merrily, and off we went for Sur, its two towns of irrepressible Arabs, and the young scamp of a Sultan's son who had caused all this bobbery. Old Popple Opstein, in his pyjamas, lay back in my easy chair, smoking his noisy pipe— the deck all round him soon strewn with half-burnt matches—and looking happy and contented to sit there and watch me take the *Bunder Abbas* out of harbour. Mr. Scarlett, his old self once more, was in the bows under the awning, securing the anchor, and I'm almost certain he was whistling a cheerful tune; the crew, both black and white, were skylarking and singing snatches of song whilst they scrubbed and holystoned the decks; Percy's big, shy eyes were dancing with fun as he brought three cups of tea up the ladder to our little deck; and even the despondent cook seemed to have made a better brew than usual that morning.

"Here's luck to the '*B.A.*'!" Popple Opstein cried, as he drank his, and the *Bunder Abbas*, not intending to be left out of the lightheartedness and gaiety he had brought with him, dipped her bows into the swell and gambolled and sported like a porpoise.

It was a very joyous morning, and though the monsoon was in a rather too playful mood we made five knots against it as we steamed along that grand coast line. By noon Jebel-al-Khamis, towering into the burning vault of blue sky, showed that we were abreast the opening in the cliffs which led to Sur, so over went the helm and inshore we steamed, with the swell catching us up, sliding under us, and hastening ahead to crash itself to a foaming dazzling death. A cairn perched on the top of the naked cliff, and a vast jumble of rocks, piled on each other like a heap of enormous broken bricks, at its foot, marked the entrance to the actual channel. In half an hour we were inside just such another ravine as the one leading to Kalat-al-Abeid, only the walls were not so high nor so bold. The roar of the breaking swell outside died away: we twisted this way and that, and saw by the chart that in a few minutes we should turn another corner, enter the open backwater, and see right ahead of us the fort which guarded the well, and the two towns whose people were trying to "do for" the Sultan's son, or the "Prodigal Son" as my chum called him.

By this time we were both in uniform—if one could call it uniform: white topee helmets, white cotton shirts with the sleeves rolled up, white cotton "shorts", bare legs, and canvas shoes. We only had to put our neck through our revolver lanyards and buckle our revolver belts round our waists to be ready to land and demand the Prodigal Son; quite ready even though ten thousand Arabs wanted to keep him. The chart showed three fathoms of water quite close to the fort which he was so gallantly, or otherwise, holding out against such odds; the little "*B. A.*" only drew eight feet at the stern, so we could run up almost alongside, and the one thousand or ten thousand Arabs would, we feared, soon alter their minds when they heard the chink of those dollars. Both of us sincerely hoped that they would not and would give the six-pounder and the Maxims a chance of arguing it out with them. We were doing this for the Sultan as a personal favour, so knew he wouldn't mind how many of his faithful (?) subjects went to Paradise during the argument. We certainly did not.

"My dear old chap," Popple Opstein said, smacking me on the back as this thought struck him, "there'll be no red-tape business about this little job; none of your beastly waiting for them to fire at you first, no worry about 'papers' and nationality or rot like that. Just go straight in, see how things are; if he's in a tight place, and they won't take the old man Sultan's bag of dollars, pull the Prodigal Son out by the scruff of his neck—and there we are. We ought to have fine sport."

Presently we ran clear of the channel into a big backwater or "khor", not so big as that at Kalat-al-Abeid but longer and more narrow, its shores thick with scraggy, dried-up-looking mangrove trees, with here and there a clump of darker almond trees, the everlasting bare hills rising behind everything.

"There's the fort," we both cried, pointing to the top end, where we could see a big, square, battlemented building about two miles away, standing alone on a waste of sand in which even the mangrove trees apparently could not exist, for they stopped short perhaps five hundred yards from either side of the fort. Almost at the same moment we spotted the two rebellious towns—one on each shore—nestling under the trees. Through my telescope I saw that the red flag of Muscat drooped down from the flagstaff over the fort, so we had not arrived too late! Not another sign of life appeared, no figures were moving about behind the parapet of the fort, and not a single soul showed on the open sandy space. As we drew nearer, a dark patch close to the edge of the sea turned out to be a couple of trees half-concealing a dome-shaped well—the well for the guarding of which the fort had been built.

It all seemed so peaceable that we were rather disappointed, until suddenly that open space round the fort simply swarmed with crawling figures, hundreds of little white "puff-balls" of smoke seemed to grow out of the sand, and great spurts of white smoke leapt out from the battlemented parapet of the fort itself. The dull booms coming across the water told us that the Prodigal Son must be firing his old muzzle-loading cannon. To judge by the amount of firing, he was having a very bad time of it indeed.

"Just in time, Martin, old chap," Popple Opstein chuckled, his face becoming violet in his excitement. "Shove the '*B. A.*' ahead and we'll chip in."

Mr. Scarlett, sucking in his breath and looking unhappy, wondered why they were fighting in the heat of midday.

"They never do so," he said. "It must be a very fierce attack."

But I was not going to shove on any faster. To begin with, I had to go carefully, because there were many shoal patches marked on the chart; and, to end with, I couldn't go faster, because the packing in the high-pressure piston-rod gland had opened out on the way down. The lascar engine-drivers were already terrified at the escape of noisy steam, and if we shoved her on faster the packing might blow out altogether. So I just sent along two or three six-pounder shells— or, to be accurate, four—two among the people on one side, two among the people on the other.

"The white sea-lord metes out even justice," old Popple Opstein chuckled (of course I had told him the yarn about the "white sea-lord jolly well wanting to shoot his own leopards").

The little shells burst beautifully, and their result was magical. The dark crawling figures making "puff-balls" tore back to the cover of some huts at the edge of the mangroves, whilst the defenders of the fort gave it them hot with the little cannon.

As we anchored within fifty yards of the shore—just abreast the big fort with its red flag, and the white-domed well close to it—the big door at one corner was flung open, and out streamed a crowd of men laden with water-skins and chatties—any mortal thing which would hold water—hurrying to the well. They began working like the very dickens to fill them, and staggered back again into the fort with anxious glances to right and left, to see whether the tribesmen were going to attack again.

"We were just in time, old sonny," my chum grinned; "they were short of water."

"That's why they were fighting at noonday," Mr. Scarlett explained. "It must have been a very close thing."

I prepared to land. Where I went my chum went too. We both buckled on our revolver belts, and I saw to it that he put his lanyard round his neck this time. Jaffa, clean as a new pin, standing at the side waiting for Griffiths to bring the dinghy alongside, was making certain that the magazine of his Mauser pistol was full. Mr. Scarlett remained in charge; Moore had to "stand by" with the six-pounder, and Webster and his marines manned one Maxim, Ellis and his bluejackets the other. With the knowledge that they would shoot straight and quickly there was no danger in landing, and I knew that no Arab would play the fool with us.

It was my chum who suggested that we should lay out a kedge-anchor astern, in order to bring the "*B.A.*"'s broadside to bear. This delayed us for a quarter of an hour, but at last we were ready, and with a white ensign flying in the stern of the dinghy—almost as big as herself—we landed on the beach: Popple Opstein, Jaffa, and myself. My aunt, but it was hot! The sand seemed to burn through our rope-soled shoes as we tramped up towards the well and its two weeping "nabac" trees. Footmarks in thousands were all round it; one deep trail leading to the door of the fort, two more leading away along the sand to the towns on either side.

As we left the shade of the trees the door at the angle of the fort opened, and out came four Arabs, armed to the teeth with rifles, belts of cartridges,

swords, and huge curved daggers. They advanced to
meet us, salaaming a hundred times. The leader
fixed his dark eyes on me whilst he jabbered away to
Jaffa.

Jaffa translated, to the effect—more or less—that,
thanks to the all-seeing benevolent kindness of the
Prophet, whose name be praised, who always shielded
the true believer and scattered his enemies just as they
were cock-sure of having won in an innings with runs
to spare—or words to that effect—we, rulers of the sea
and sons of the Great White Queen, had unexpectedly
turned up and scored the winning goal just as time
was called. He implored us to demean our noble
selves sufficiently to take some abominable refresh-
ment (he was pretty well right in that) under the
wretched roof of his cowardly and entirely despicable
master, the mighty fighter, the heaven-born leader of
men, born with a double-edged sword in his hand,
and destined to bring joy to the heart of his noble
father, the Sultan of Muscat, "to whom all we pigs
and nobodies own eternal allegiance—Mohammed be
praised!" There was another long rigmarole to explain why the Prodigal Son could not come to receive
us, but I gathered that he had been wounded in this
recent attack, and was having his wounds dressed
even now.

"Right oh! We'll go along with them," I told
Jaffa, cutting him short. "Tell him that we didn't
come here by chance, but at the request of the Sultan."

The sheikh, or whoever he was, received this news
with astonishment.

"He say they all lay down lives for Sultan—love

Sultan very much," Jaffa interpreted to me with impassive face.

Off we went, and, my word, it was a most unpleasant place! The foot of the walls of the fort was piled with all kinds of rubbish—cast-off blood-stained clothes, bones, skeletons of dogs and camels, all the filth one could imagine — and the stench was horrid.

Popple Opstein pointed out any number of bullet marks in the crumbling bricks of the forts, and we made grimaces as we realized what a very tough defence they must have been making, and how excessively uncomfortable they must be.

Two solemn, weary-looking Arabs—one bandaged about the head—opened a little door in the big one, which had been closed again, and we passed into a large passage, which opened out into the court-yard in the centre of the fort. Stone benches on either side of this passage-way were thronged with more tired-looking soldiers, most of them asleep, and very many of them evidently wounded. In the court-yard itself the heat and the smell were awful. Thirty or forty lean horses were tethered in the open, a dozen camels knelt stolidly in the shade which a mat-screen gave them, whilst hundreds of goats and sheep wandered about feeding on whatever garbage lay about. As we passed across, and tried to avoid falling over sheep, being kicked by a horse, or bitten by a camel, a score or more battle-stained Arabs raised themselves wearily from the ground and leant on their rifles.

"A beastly place to be cooped up in," Popple Opstein whispered, as we followed our guides through

an archway into a delightfully-cool chamber or hall,
and up some winding stone steps to the upper story.
This was evidently where the officials and officers
lived—much more handsomely decorated it was, with
carvings, and lattice-work of stone, wood, and iron,
elegant pillars and arches forming a delightfully-
cool, creeper-covered balcony above the four sides of
the crowded court-yard, from which, however, the
smell and the noise of all the animals below were still
too unpleasantly evident.   Fifty or more soldiers were
lying on this balcony in every attitude of weary sleep,
and as we hurried along it after our silent guides we
could catch a glimpse of the battlements on the flat
roof above our heads, and a motionless sentry standing out vividly against the sky, watching to give the
alarm did the tribesmen make another attack.

We passed several elegant door-ways screened with
matting, and then, at last, a richly-embroidered curtain was drawn aside and we were ushered into a long,
darkened room, the wooden floors carpeted with splendid rugs, on which six or seven magnificently-dressed
Arabs were seated.   They welcomed us gravely.   Most
of them appeared to have been wounded: one had his
arm in a sling, another had his leg swathed in white
cotton and tried to repress a groan when he moved.
We, in our very rudimentary costume, must have made
a comical appearance in the midst of all this magnificence; but we didn't care "tuppence" about that.
On a raised, rug-carpeted platform a very handsome
Arab stood erect, his left arm bound closely to his
chest under his white linen shirt, his right hand
grasping the hilt of a gold-mounted dagger stuck in

his belt.   Salaaming gravely, he stepped down to meet us with outstretched hand, drew us to the platform, and made us sit beside him.

We almost fell over ourselves when he burst out with: "It's awfully good of you fellows to come along —awfully lucky, too; just when things were queer. Another hour of it and my chaps would have burst out to get water or die—you saw them scurrying out. I can never be too grateful.   You are on your way to Muscat, I suppose; if you can see my father, the Sultan, or get hold of the Chief Wazir, tell him you have saved his son's honour.   He will do anything for you, I know."

"Oh no!" I said, when I'd recovered from my astonishment at hearing him speak such English. "We've come straight from Muscat, at the Sultan's special request, to get news of you."

I did not like telling him that we'd come to rescue him.

"Really!" he said, his eyes glowing.   "We are all the more in your debt.   But when you return, do not say anything about this," he touched his left arm; "it's nothing.   A bullet splintered the bone.   It will do quite well.   My father will only worry if he knows of it.   Have some coffee and cigarettes," he continued, as a Zanzibar slave brought round a tray.   "Now you've given me the chance of stocking my fort with water we can hold out until these tribes leave us alone to fight each other.   They're certain to do that soon. I need hardly tell you that we are all very grateful indeed."

He turned and spoke to the others, who answered

with a murmur of respectful and dignified acqui-
escence.

Coffee was brought in tiny little enamelled metal
cups, more cigarettes were handed round, and the
Prodigal Son kept us busy answering questions about
the latest news from Muscat; and, when he discovered
that we were practically ignorant of anything that was
happening there, asked questions about European
politics, of which neither Popple Opstein nor I knew
much more.   It seemed really most extraordinary that
though he was wounded and surrounded by the tribesmen from those two towns, thirsting to eat up him and
his handful of soldiers, he should interest himself in
events so far away.   To show him that I was not
altogether ignorant of Court "goings on", I told him
of the two sums of money which the Sultan had
already tried to send him overland.

"The Sultan is a good father; he deserves a better
son," he said with such engaging frankness that he
raised himself tremendously in our estimation.   To cap
all, I told him that he had sent five thousand rupees
with us, not daring to trust them by land again, and
that if he thought they would be of any use in pacify-
ing the two tribes, I would send them ashore directly
we returned to the *Bunder Abbas*.

"If not," I added with a great show of importance,
"I have orders to take you back to Muscat."

He smiled, such a jovial frank smile that I could not
wonder why he was such a favourite with his father.

"What would you do in my place?" he asked.
"Here I'm given a fairly important job, to protect
this well and keep peace between the two towns.   I've

C 697

BOWING IN THE MOST DIGNIFIED MANNER TO THE PRODIGAL SON
AND OURSELVES, THEY SQUATTED IN A CIRCLE ROUND US

Page 266

done it so successfully that they are as thick as thieves, and are so hot-headed with the imagined strength of their combined forces that they dare to revolt. Would you give up the job until you were compelled, now that it has turned out a failure? A few more weeks, perhaps months, a little money paid out here and there—now that you have brought me some—and I shall be able to report that all is peace again, and commence to levy taxes, of which (he shrugged his shoulders) I have not sent to Muscat enough to buy a skinful of wine—not for the last five months."

There was no necessity for us to tell him what we should do if we were in his place—he knew; but the interview was becoming rather prolonged, so I hinted to him that unless we showed ourselves outside the fort fairly soon that six-pounder on board the *Bunder Abbas* might " go off".

He smiled delightfully, apologized, and immediately led us out, down the stone staircase, across the court-yard, through the passage-way with its sleeping soldiers, and out into the glare of the open waste land. I could have sworn that I heard some women's voices singing to the twang of musical instruments, and women's merry laughter coming from an upper, lattice-hid window. What a place for women, and how brave they must be to be merry under these conditions! I could not help thinking of Jask and those two ladies there, and wondered whether they kept up their spirits as well as these did.

At last we were again in full view of the *Bunder Abbas*, and I guessed that the sight of us must have been a great relief to Mr. Scarlett.

A brilliant idea struck the Prodigal Son.

"How much money did you say you brought? Five thousand? It's not much, is it? but we'll see if the Khans of the two towns are open to a little bribing. They often are, in spite of them being such important people," he laughed.

"I'll send messengers to them at once," he said. "Come down to the well. We always discuss things there."

He gave some orders, and before we had reached the grateful shade of those two nabac trees, two mounted Arabs, bearing white flags fastened to spears, came out from the fort, separated, and galloped away along the sands.

We sat down, thoroughly enjoying our amusing experience, and whilst we were waiting I sent Griffiths in the dinghy to bring back the money bags. Before he returned with them, nine or ten splendidly-mounted Arabs had galloped up from the two towns and dismounted. Bowing in the most dignified manner to the Prodigal Son and ourselves, they squatted in a circle round us, keeping their eyes fixed on my chum's yellow hair and blue eyes—in evident admiration. More coffee was brought from the fort and more cigarettes were rolled, and a discussion—a very heated discussion—took place, of which we, of course, could not understand a word.

However, the Prodigal Son seemed to soothe them, and when Griffiths came up the beach with four fat bags of rupees—making two trips with them—and dumped them down at my feet, they became very affable indeed. To watch those dignified Arabs—half of them wounded and all of them scarred—try to pretend not to be interested in the four bags, when all the time their eyes kept turning towards them, evidently calculating how much was inside, was as good as a play.

Eventually, after innumerable cups of coffee, everything seemed to have been arranged peacefully. They rose to their feet, bowed to us, to the Prodigal Son, to each other, mounted their horses, and rode back to the two towns, leaving us alone.

"Well, I cannot thank you enough," he began, his face twitching as he pressed one hand against his broken arm, as though the pain was very great. "With your help, and with the money my father sent me, I have patched up the quarrel, and I trust it will be lasting."

"The quarrel or the patching up?" Popple Opstein interrupted admiringly. "I do really believe you'd prefer the first."

I'm certain that he was right too.

We induced him to come aboard the "*B.A.*", which he did in the uncomfortable little dinghy, first having sent the bags of silver into the fort, and he made himself so agreeable to Mr. Scarlett that the gunner's dark eyes glowed with pleasure.

"Will you do me one more favour?" he asked before he went ashore. "The Sultan will be anxious to hear how things are—you have seen for yourself. He is an old man, and he worries. Both of us will be the more grateful if you let him know as soon as you can."

We were so carried away by his delightful personality that within an hour the "*B.A.*" was steaming back to Muscat, going so fast—to save daylight—through that tricky channel that the lascar drivers were scared to death by the noise of steam escaping through the piston-rod gland. We saved daylight right enough, and were soon tumbling about in the swell outside; but the gland gave so much trouble that we could only manage to go dead slow, with barely enough way to prevent the *Bunder Abbas* being driven on the rocks, where the roar of the breaking swell boomed in our ears all night. We had a most horrid time of it—old Popple Opstein and I—not knowing from one minute to another when the engines would stop entirely. It was not the slightest use to try to reach Muscat, and I only waited for the first streak of daylight to crawl back through the channel into safety.

My lascar first-driver said he could repair the gland in two days at anchor, and I intended anchoring close to the fort again; but before we were clear of the channel the packing blew out altogether, the engine-room was filled with steam—the whole launch seemed to be in a cloud of it—and the engines stopped entirely; so there was nothing to do but anchor where we were. It was a beastly nuisance, because I was so anxious to take the news to Muscat as quickly as possible; otherwise I did not care a rap.

Popple Opstein suggested that we should sail the dinghy up to the fort and spend the day with the Prodigal Son. No sooner said than done. Out went the dinghy; Griffiths stepped the mast and put up the sail; my chum and I jumped in with a loaf of bread, a tin of tongue, and some sardines, and off we went, only to pull back again for water and for Jaffa—we had forgotten both, and both were 'necessities. We drifted and sailed, pulled round corners, and sailed again until we came out into the open "khor", met a fairly-steady breeze—a soldier's breeze—which filled our little sail, and made us bubble through the water.

In a couple of hours from leaving the "*B.A.*" we were hauling the dinghy on to the sand, close by the well, and were tramping up to the fort as happy as schoolboys, leaving Jaffa to guard the boat from a crowd of loafing Arabs who surrounded it. We noticed one thing immediately—the horses, camels, sheep, and goats were now outside the fort, so we knew at once that all was peace.

However, the Prodigal Son was not at home—we imagined that he had perhaps gone to distribute the money; so, as the silly soldiers at the big door would not let us inside, we amused ourselves by examining the outer walls, walking all round them and looking up at the battlements and the muzzles of the silly little cannon sticking out from the towers at the corners. The walls were pitted everywhere with bullet marks, especially round the loopholes, and we felt that we had underrated the Arab marksman-ship. The heat thrown back from those lofty bare red-brick walls was so great that soon we were only too glad to go back to the shade of the nabac trees near the well, until the attentions of the crowd gathered there became rather irritating and the beastly flies almost insupportable. So off we went for a short walk to have a look at Heija.

Whilst we were wandering round it, feeling like a couple of trippers, we turned round a corner, and, clatter, clatter, with a smother of dust, a dozen or more Arab horsemen dashed madly past us. Behind them, at a more dignified pace, cantered others, and among these we at once recognized the Prodigal Son, who, catching sight of us, drew his horse back almost on his haunches to speak to us. On his right wrist was a hooded falcon, and he was holding the reins with his left hand—holding in a troublesome, fiery horse with the arm we had seen bandaged to his side the day before, the one he had said was broken. Athough we recognized several of the cavalcade, not one now had a bandage or a sign of a wound; even the man whose leg had been swathed in cotton was joyously curveting and pirouetting on a splendid horse.

For a minute neither of us quite realized the real truth. Then, when we looked enquiringly at his left arm, the Prodigal Son burst out laughing, and even the older, more dignified among them smiled grimly.

They lent us a couple of horses to ride back with them, and old Popple Opstein disgraced himself by falling off, but afterwards managed to stick on until we reached the fort. There we were taken up to that same audience-hall and had more cigarettes and coffee. The Prodigal Son never gave us a chance of asking for an explanation of the marvellous recoveries, and presently we found ourselves sailing merrily back to the "*B. A.*", so delighted with his amusing, frank manner that it was not until we were halfway there that we even began to wonder what was the meaning of it.

Jaffa's dignified face had been gradually relaxing, as if he was bursting to tell us something amusing.

"Out with it, Jaffa," I called. "What is it?"

"Very much laughter—in Heija—in Shateif also—make much fool of Sultan—poor people very angry—sheikhs and soldiers much joy. Plenty men from Heija and Shateif come to well—tell me. All pretence—the fighting—surround fort—much powder play—news goes Muscat—Sultan's son in much danger—want money—buy peace—money comes—son rob caravan—Sultan think wild Bedouin rob caravan—send more—son rob that—writes letter that he in much danger—Sultan thinks money never come to him—so send more money in *Bunder Abbas*."

"But we saw them fighting like 'billy loo', going it 'hammer and tongs' yesterday. You mustn't believe everything you hear," I said, incredulous still.

Jaffa shook his head. "All game—make pretence to fight—all men know *Bunder Abbas* bringing more money—runner come from Muscat in early morning—when they see her come, begin pretend fight—fort fires powder from cannon—men fire rifles—take no aim—only make noise. Then hurry, pretend have many wounds when masters land—take money—send masters away with good tale for Sultan."

"Nonsense!" Popple Opstein blurted out; "the walls are peppered with bullet holes. We've seen them ourselves."

Jaffa smiled again. "Make them—themselves—when merry—fire at loophole for target—all play."

My chum was the first to believe the yarn. He roared with laughter. "It all fits in like a puzzle.

The Prodigal Son! What a name for the chap! That's why they all looked like cripples yesterday, and left off their bandages to-day. My holy Moses! the whole thing was a 'plant', simply to delude us. What a chap! Didn't you hear those girls singing and laughing? They wouldn't have been there if there had been real fighting—or they wouldn't have been so cheery. D'you remember the rush for water? My sacred aunt!"

He kept on roaring with laughter every few minutes.

As he had said, the whole thing fitted in like a puzzle. It amused him, but it did not amuse me to be made a fool of. I was very angry, though with my chum in the boat it was impossible to remain angry for long, and soon I, too, saw the funny side of the expedition, and was laughing as much as he was.

And the Prodigal Son had been so anxious for us to hurry back to Muscat, and so anxious for us not to mention his poor wounded arm to his father! Of course not! It was all as plain as a pikestaff now. If the Sultan heard of it, back to Muscat he would order him, and evidently the fatted calf there was not half so much to his liking as the spree he was having in that fort.

On our return to the *Bunder Abbas* we told Jaffa not to breathe a word of this to anyone.

By next night the steam gland had been repacked, so, threading our way out again to the sea, we steamed back to Muscat.

I went across to the *Intrepid* and told Commander Duckworth everything. He, too, roared with laughter, but quickly checked himself.

"That's all right. It doesn't matter one way or the other. You saw the battle; you got there just in time to stop it; the money was just in time to make peace; and you saw the Prodigal Son, as you call him, out hawking. That is all the Sultan wants to know, and he'll be just as grateful to us as though you had actually rescued him."

And he was, too, and sent me a Mauser pistol, just like Jaffa's, as a present.

CHAPTER XIV

We Deal with Jassim

THE packing in the high-pressure piston-rod gland blew out again as we anchored at Muscat. As a matter of fact, the whole of our engines required a thorough overhaul after practically four months of almost continuous steaming; and though the lascar engine-drivers had done their best—a very poor best—it was now entirely beyond their capabilities to put things to "rights", and make all the necessary readjustments and the *Bunder Abbas* again fit for sea.

In these circumstances, and as neither the political agent nor Commander Duckworth had anything very pressing for us to do, artificers were sent across from the *Intrepid* to carry out the necessary repairs. Whilst they were opening out the engines, working and sweating down below, there was, of course, but little to do on deck, and I had at first a very pleasant, lazy time indeed—pleasant, at any rate, after five o'clock in the evening. Before five o'clock the heat was much too great except to pant and perspire under the awnings; after that hour one's muscles began to call out for exercise. Then, with Popple Opstein and the rest of the *Intrepid's* officers, we would often pull across to a sandy beach—where no sharks ventured — about a mile from the rock on which the southern of those two old Portuguese forts stood, and have grand bathing picnics—in and out of the water for a couple of hours at a time. Occasionally fifty or sixty of the men would come with us and drag the seine-net, for the sea was simply alive with fish. If we did not do this, we would go up to the political agent's house and play tennis in the compound there —on a concrete court—in the most terrible glare; or perhaps we would wander out through the main gates of the town and scramble about the ravines and defiles leading inland.

I have never in my life been in such a hot place as this was. The little white town of Muscat is surrounded by bare, razor-backed, volcanic, rocky ridges; the harbour itself is enclosed by more black, naked cliffs, and these seem to collect the violent heat of the sun all day to give it out all night. The temperature in the shade on board seldom fell below a hundred degrees during the day, and seldom dropped more than four or five degrees at night. Sleep under these conditions was very difficult, very unrefreshing, and often I have tumbled and sweated on my grass mat till daybreak, kept awake by the oppressive heat and the weird chants of the watchmen calling across the harbour from the towers of the two great forts.

Several of my men went sick. Little wounds (a scratched mosquito bite, for instance) simply would not heal; and Wiggins, the broken-rib man, had to be sent down to Karachi suffering from fever. He was very loath to go, poor chap.

For the first two or three days Mr. Scarlett was

quite happy. I let him take some men ashore to paint the name of the launch on the rocky face of one of the sides of the harbour. He painted it in white letters, four feet long—"BUNDER ABBAS"— among the names of a hundred other ships which had done the same during the last twenty years, and this kept his mind occupied; but after he had finished, he shrank into his usual saturnine self, his dark eyes seemed to sink farther back than ever beneath his shaggy eyebrows, and he spent his whole time watching lest Jassim should come again. For fear of seeing him, and for fear of any violence, he never ventured on the mainland.

Jassim had sent him another letter, increasing his offer to fifteen thousand rupees if only Mr. Scarlett would let him have the bracelet. My chum happened to be on board when the letter arrived, and we both went over the same old arguments as before, doing our utmost to persuade him to take the risk, and holding out before him all he could do with the money—a thousand pounds would be a fortune to him—and how with that and his pension he could retire and live comfortably ever after. If he had been an ordinary warrant-officer we might have argued with him successfully. But he was not; he was more than half-Arab, by nature and upbringing if not by birth; and if our arguments were met at first by a half-shrinking consent, the possibility of a fatal result would so terrify him immediately afterwards that he always ended with a flat, sullen refusal.

"Kismet," he would groan, and once he had used that word we knew it was impossible to move him.

If he did agree to accept the increased offer we were to hoist a red flag; and the mere knowledge that evening that Jassim's gloomy eyes were watching us from shore, awaiting his signal, made even my chum and myself feel nervous. It drove Mr. Scarlett into the locked cabin, where he stewed all night.

As you can imagine, this state of things was bad for his health, and when one day he ran a rusty nail into the palm of his left hand the wound festered, and the hand and the whole of his arm swelled tremendously.

He was so ill that Nicholson, the staff surgeon of the *Intrepid*, determined to give him chloroform, and make deep cuts into both hand and arm. The snake, of course, would have to be exposed during the operation, and Mr. Scarlett was so desperately anxious that no one else should know anything about it that he only consented when Nicholson promised (I had told him about it) to come across to the *Bunder Abbas*, and, if Popple Opstein and I would stand by and give him a hand, do it there. He came that very evening, when the great heat of the day was over, and we (with Percy terrified and sad) cleared a space on the little upper deck, just outside the cabin, for the operation. Having kicked Percy down the steps and screened the deck from observation, Nicholson began.

It is not necessary to go into all the details, but when Mr. Scarlett, lying on the deck, was thoroughly insensible, we unwound the bandage and found the beastly snake almost sunk in a deep groove of the mottled, swollen skin, clinging ever so tightly. I noticed Nicholson run his finger along it until he

came to the head, when he tried to pass one finger
under the jaw, but my nerves were very much on
the stretch. I saw him pick up a knife, and, not
being used to such things, turned away my head.
It was not till Mr. Scarlett had given one or two
sudden, half-conscious moans that I turned round
again. There were the deep cuts in the arm and
hand, but—I almost started out of my skin—the
snake had disappeared, and only the deep groove
round the arm remained, the scale marks showing
how tightly the snake must have buried itself.

Nicholson quietly pointed to a corner of the deck
close to the funnel, and there, sparkling in a patch
of sunlight coming under the edge of the awning,
was the bracelet—writhing, coiling, and uncoiling,
drawing back, and striking with its head.

Popple Opstein's face was blue, his mouth wide
open, his eyes staring at it, his great red hands
shaking violently.

Nicholson went on with his work.

"Good God!" I at last managed to gasp. "Did
it bite him or you?"

Nicholson did not answer. Mr. Scarlett was recovering consciousness now, and he was working
very rapidly. Popple Opstein and I had to fly
round and do this and that as he bade us. There
was no time to ask questions or answer them.

At last Nicholson, starting to bandage the arm,
asked for a piece of rope—a couple of feet of signal
halyard.

"Now a needle and thread," he called, and, when
I fetched them, sewed the bandage very securely.

Not till then had I time to look at the snake again.

It was now lying perfectly still, coiled closely like a watch-spring, the flat head pressed over the coils and the light flickering in its green opal eyes and playing on the enamelled scales.

Nicholson, busy holding Mr. Scarlett's head, jerked out: "Hide it!

"Pick it up," he said irritably, as my chum hesitated to touch it; "the confounded thing won't hurt you."

Popple Opstein stooped and took hold of it very gingerly. As it did not move he held it in the palm of his hand, and we were both examining its marvellous beauty when Nicholson again jerked out: "Hide it somewhere—lock it up—Mr. Scarlett's coming round—he mustn't see it."

I took it very nervously from Popple Opstein, and in the excited state of my nerves, its scales seemed to press themselves into my hand and wriggle. I could only just prevent myself dropping it, and darted into the cabin and locked it in my one drawer.

"Now, help me to lift him," Nicholson called out, and in a couple of minutes Mr. Scarlett lay moaning in his bunk, with the bad arm swathed in cotton-wool and bandages.

"He'll do all right now. Give me a drink, and have this mess cleared up," Nicholson said gruffly.

"How did you do it?" I asked him.

"Feel that," he answered, and with a blood-stained finger and thumb pinched the end of one of my fingers.

I winced—he might have had hold of me with pincers.

I shouted for Percy, and sang out for Moore to send up a couple of hands, and whilst Nicholson kept an eye on his patient my chum told me what had happened.

"He took up his knife. I set my teeth; but just as I thought he was going to use it he dropped it, and before I could wink an eyelash he'd nipped the jaws of the snake—just as he nipped your finger—bent four inches of its neck right away from the arm, and, with the fingers of the other hand, swept round under the coils and unwound it. For a moment or two he held it in the air, the jaws in between his finger and thumb, the body coiling and twisting—I could hardly breathe—then he threw it away where you saw it, and it lashed about like a live thing. It's done now; what danger there was is over. Won't he be thankful?"

"We'll tell him directly he's round," I said. "My country, won't he be pleased! He'll be a new man."

Nicholson, coming out of the cabin, sang out: "No, you won't, unless you want to kill him. He's bad enough now, and he'll fancy the swelling is due to poison, whatever we tell him. He must not know until he's well again. As many people die of sheer fright, after being bitten, as from the poison itself."

"Is that why you coiled the signal halyard round the groove?" we both asked excitedly.

"Of course it was. He'll feel it under the bandage, and think the snake's still there. I sewed the bandage so that he couldn't take it off to make certain. Don't you tell him till I give the word."

A very anxious week followed, for Mr. Scarlett was

so ill that he had to go aboard the *Intrepid*. Whilst he was away, several more letters came from Jassim, and at last Jassim himself came aboard.

On the chance of his coming I had given very strict orders that no one should say where Mr. Scarlett had gone, and when I took him all round the *Bunder Abbas* his face fell as he realized that he was not on board. Not a word would he say about the snake, never so much as a hint to Jaffa; but as he left the ship he spoke to him, looking at me, and Jaffa repeated: "Twenty thousand rupees". I could not resist asking him, through Jaffa (who, if he had a shrewd suspicion that he was the red-bearded leader of the caravan, never mentioned it), how his son was —the wounded man who had been carried through the gap.

At the question Jassim gave me a glance of such terrible hatred that I knew at once that the poor chap was dead, and that he blamed me for it.

This could not help but worry me, and another worry came along about this time: there was disquieting news from Jask. Mr. Fisher, the acting political agent, had telegraphed across that the Baluchis were causing trouble and constantly threatening to come down from the hills and attack the place. The land wire had been cut in several places, and a party of native employees had been beaten and robbed about twenty-five miles to the eastward. He had borrowed a few of the border police from the Mir of Old Jask, but they were such brigands and so much of a nuisance that he had sent them back again.

It really made me angry to think of keeping Miss

Borsen and Mrs. Fisher there. I actually asked if the "B. A." could not go as soon as ever her repairs had been effected, but Commander Duckworth shook his head.

"It's just as it always is at this time of year," he said. "Those tribesmen keep on threatening, hoping to get 'backsheesh'. They do it every year; but nothing will come of it. They won't risk their skins."

However, this did not relieve my anxiety. I seemed to have a personal interest in little Miss Borsen, because, I suppose, she had come out from England with me, and possibly because we had quarrelled.

One day Nicholson signalled across that he and Popple Opstein were bringing Mr. Scarlett across that evening. They came, he looking desperately ill, although his arm was practically well. When we four were alone he pulled out another letter—Jassim had evidently soon found where he had gone.

"He offers me twenty thousand rupees," he said wearily. "It's a lot of money."

He thought that we should commence the same old arguments again, but, Nicholson winking at me, I went into the cabin, unlocked my drawer, and brought out the bracelet. I handed it to Nicholson, for it was "up" to him to tell the good news. He simply laid it on Mr. Scarlett's thin knees and said quietly: "It's been off your arm for ten days. I took it off when you had the operation."

Mr. Scarlett shrank from it and clutched his arm. "But it's there—I can feel it—I've felt it a hundred times in these last days."

Nicholson smiled, pulled up his sleeve, cut through the bandage, and showed him the signal halyard.

Mr. Scarlett gave a wild look at each of us, dropped the snake on the deck, bolted into the cabin, and we heard him sobbing like a child.

Nicholson yelled for Percy. "Brandy and soda for Mr. Scarlett."

"For all of us," I said, because we needed it.

Eventually Mr. Scarlett came back and asked to see the bracelet, handling it tenderly. He was much too disturbed to talk coherently, or to thank Nicholson or either of us. It was pitiful to watch him. He had not found his "bearings"; did not realize all that it meant to him, and kept on rolling up his sleeve to look at his bare arm as if he did not believe his own eyes.

He gave way again, buried his face in his lean hands, lying half over the table, which shook with his sobs. It was very distressing to watch.

"Can't we hoist that red flag, sir?" he asked presently, lifting a haggard face.

I nodded.

He jumped to our signal locker, picked out a red-and-white flag, tore off the white part like a maniac, bent it to the halyard, and hoisted it to our little yard-arm, where it drooped in the heated air. Seizing a pair of glasses he watched the shore as though he expected Jassim to come paddling out. But Jassim did not come, and in his nervous condition Mr. Scarlett worked himself into a terrible state of agitation lest he had disappeared, and was, even now, preparing violent measures to regain the bracelet.

I think that before Nicholson went away he had

taken the precaution of giving him a very strong sleeping-draught, because he eventually became calmer and went to sleep.

When he was asleep I took the bracelet away from him and locked it in my drawer, hoping most devoutly that Jassim would soon come and claim it; and next morning, without saying anything to him, I took the precaution of sending the bracelet across to the *Intrepid*, so that the sight of it should not upset him, and that Jassim, if he came, should not be able to terrorize him into giving it away before the money was produced.

Jassim did come that day, and his manner was mysterious and threatening; nor did I like the look in his eyes when Mr. Scarlett bared his arm and he realized that the bracelet had disappeared and that the gunner had not now the fear of taking it off.

Jassim evidently wanted to get rid of me; but I would not go.

"When he puts down his twenty thousand rupees he shall have it, not before," I told Mr. Scarlett. "The bracelet is not on board, and I shall not tell you where it is. Never you mind where it is." I stopped him enquiring. "You tell him to bring his money and he shall have it."

As I imagined, Jassim could not produce the money, nor do I think that he ever intended doing so, hoping all along so to work on the gunner's fears that he could get it for nothing. The two of them began talking very excitedly, waving their arms and thumping the little table. From the fierce looks which Jassim occasionally turned on me I was evidently being talked about, and was not very popular in that quarter.

I saw that hateful muddy colour spread over Mr. Scarlett's face and his eyes narrow with fear. He turned to me, hardly able to speak.

"For God's sake, sir, give up the wretched thing," he stuttered. "Tell me where it is and I will give it him. I don't want any of his money; all I want is to be quit of it."

"When you've got your money, not before," I said.

"But, sir, remember we are not in England. He swears he'll kill you; that if you land he will kill you; if you don't he'll find other ways of killing you. He won't touch me, because I gave his wife that drink of water. But, sir, it's different with you."

"I gave his son water a month ago," I said, with a sudden inspiration.

Mr. Scarlett was too much agitated to enquire when or where. He turned to Jassim and asked him something. Jassim replied bitterly.

"He says you shot him, and he died; the drink of water made no difference. You don't know these people out here," he implored. "Don't run any risk. I don't want the money, indeed I don't."

Jassim had risen to his feet and stood not three feet from me, glaring at me as if he would willingly kill me then and there. I saw in his eyes that what Mr. Scarlett had said was true. I don't know what made me do it—I certainly never thought, and regretted it immediately afterwards—but I suddenly locked my arms round him, and before he could make a move

I had tripped him over the railings and dropped him overboard.

The boat which had brought him off was close there, and he scrambled on board like a drowned rat, sat down in the stern-sheets, folded his clinging wet burnous round him, and, without deigning to turn his head in our direction, was paddled ashore.

"You've done it now, sir," Mr. Scarlett moaned, burying his face in his hands and sprawling across the table. "For God's sake let's get away from Muscat."

I tried to pacify him by pointing out that if Jassim killed me he would lose all chance of finding the snake. "He won't be such a fool as that," I said.

"He'll want revenge—revenge more than the snake —now, sir," Mr. Scarlett groaned.

There are times in plenty in most men's lives when, either through anger or stubbornness, danger does not influence them. This was a case in point. I had suffered so much from Jassim and his wretched snake that his threats simply stiffened my back to such an extent that I much preferred to be killed than give in. The mail steamer was leaving next day, so, to make certain that Jassim should not get it, I went aboard the *Intrepid*, told Popple Opstein what had happened, and after one last look at the bracelet we packed it up and sent it home to my bankers in London. At any rate, whatever happened to me (and I did not really believe that anything would happen) Jassim should never have it, and later on we might be able to negotiate for the reward of thirty thousand rupees with the rightful owner, the Khan of Khamia himself.

I breathed more freely when the mail steamer left the harbour, and not until it had gone did I tell Mr. Scarlett what I had done.

He and I stood watching till she disappeared behind the rocks at the entrance, and, drawing a deep breath of relief, he said:

"It seems wonderful, sir; don't it, sir? Here for thirteen years it's been part and parcel of me, and now I'm finished with it. I never want to set eyes on the beastly thing again."

From that moment Mr. Scarlett began very rapidly to mend. He grew stouter, his eyes lost their hunted look, and though he worried much about the risks I was running, still it is a different thing to worry about other people's risks from worrying about one's own, and he rapidly recovered his spirits.

I made light of any danger and took no precaution whatever, until one night, shortly afterwards, I was awakened by the noise of a scuffle and a splash in the water alongside.

"What's that?" I sang out, springing up.

Webster answered out of the darkness: "It's all right, sir. It's that Arab chap you hove overboard the other day. He was trying to creep on board over the stern. I spotted him, sir, and popped him back into the 'ditch'."

Another day I was bathing with the *Intrepids*, and we were skylarking afterwards on the beach, when a bullet hit the sand close to me and we heard the report of a revolver. Spotting someone moving behind a rock we all darted in that direction, but when we reached it saw no one.

I don't mind saying that those two things happening made me extremely nervous, and made me stick pretty close to the "*B. A.*".

I could now realize what mental agony Mr. Scarlett had suffered, and though perhaps I did not show it as much I felt it most acutely. The boot was on the other foot now with a vengeance, and it was I who, when it grew dark, looked longingly at the little hot oven of a cabin and felt a great temptation to lock myself in until daylight.

A few days after the revolver-shot incident Mr. Scarlett astonished me by asking leave to go ashore for a walk in Muscat itself. Remember that he had not dared to land since he and I had had that first walk there and had run across Jassim. Away he went, taking Jaffa and Webster with him, and they did not return on board until long after I had finished dinner.

Mr. Scarlett was chuckling—I had never seen him so pleased with himself—Jaffa had a contented smile on his face, and Webster so far forgot himself as to wink at me.

"Hallo, what have you been doing?" I asked.

"He's all right, sir," the gunner said, rubbing his hands. "Mr. Jassim won't be worrying you again for some time."

"What has happened?" I asked eagerly. "Have you killed him?"

"Well, sir, not exactly, but we just happened to meet him—after we'd been hunting round for him all the afternoon—and we just happened to have a bit of a row, and there just happened to be a couple of the Sultan's soldiers handy. I made a bobbery, Jaffa and I calling out that he had stolen money from us, and off they took him up there," and Mr. Scarlett jerked his thumb towards the big fort on the right, whose towers and battlemented walls showed out in the moonlight over our heads. "There he'll stay, sir, as long as we like to pay for his keep. It cost us five chips to the soldiers and another twenty to the sheikh in charge of the fort. It was well worth it. Don't you think so, sir? So long as we pay the governor of that fort or jail, call it what you like, five rupees a day he'll keep him there and feed him," Mr. Scarlett said, emphasizing the "feed him" as if that made his action quite meritorious.

Well, it was a very "low-down" game to play, and if I had known they were going to play it I should have put a "stopper" on it; but now the man was under lock and key it was so much a relief that I had not the honest courage to blame the gunner or take steps to have Jassim set free.

After that Mr. Scarlett visited the jail nearly every day, to assure himself that Jassim was still there; nor was he content until he had peered through a grating overlooking the court-yard in which untried prisoners were kept, and seen him. He seemed to take a fiendish delight in those visits, and I must say that I fully shared his satisfaction, for, to me, the resulting comfort and relief from anxiety was cheap at the price—only five rupees a day. It may have been a cowardly, despicable thing to do, but I don't believe that any.

one placed in the same circumstances would have done otherwise.

We had now been very nearly a month at Muscat, and the artificers from the *Intrepid* had not quite finished my engine-room defects, when one morning, four or five days after Jassim had been secured, an urgent signal came from Commander Duckworth that he wanted to see me at once. I had a presentiment that something had gone wrong at Jask.

I was right. As I went into his cabin the Commander sang out: "You'll have to go across to Jask after all, and as soon as ever you are ready. There's more trouble there. One of the European telegraph people has been killed somewhere along the coast by a marauding lot of brigands who have cut the wire again. Fisher dare not send his people to repair it without an escort, so you had better go across and see what you can do. When can you start?"

"By midnight, sir," I told him, having taken the precaution of finding out before I left the "*B. A.*".

"Right you are! Off you go! I don't fancy that there is anything serious. If there is you can telegraph for me and I will bring the *Intrepid* along. Good-bye! Good luck!"

What a grand chap he was! I left his cabin feeling that he had not hampered me with any restrictions whatsoever, and had placed entire confidence in my judgment. If only senior officers would always treat their juniors in that way they would not so often have to grumble at the way they are served—and, what is more important still—they would make more efficient officers of them.

I met Popple Opstein outside. For once he had shipped a long face.

"Did the skipper tell you who has been killed?" he asked. "I'm afraid it's our poor little friend's brother. What rotten hard luck on her if it's true!"

In my excitement at getting this job I had never thought. Of course it must be Borsen; he was the only other European there. Poor fellow! Poor little sad-eyed slip of a girl, she would be weeping her heart out.

I had a burning feeling inside me, and I wished that I could have started off then and there to blow a dozen or more of those cowardly treacherous Baluchis to atoms.

"I wish I could come along with you," my chum said wistfully. "I'd love to have a 'go' at them!"

He tried to get leave, but without success, so back I went to the "*B. A.*", angry, and impatient to get away.

"Good-bye, old chap! Tell her how very sorry I am," he called after me.

"Right you are!" I shouted back, but had an uneasy thought that perhaps she was still too angry to allow me to speak to her.

I told Mr. Scarlett the news, rather expecting him to show the old half-frightened expression, and was quite taken aback when he smiled and said: "A chance of our seeing a bit more scrapping—eh, sir?" He said it as if he, too, rather looked forward to such a thing happening, and I had to look again at his face to make sure. Well, his disposition seemed to be changing, and as there was nothing else to account for the change except the parting with the snake I put it down to that.

It was splendid the way those artificers and lascars worked to finish their job. They knew why they had to hurry, and they toiled and sweated in the heat of the engine-room like demons.

By half-past ten that night we were ready. I sent the *Intrepid's* artificers back to their ship with something inside them to warm their stomachs, flashed across the "Permission to part company", and steamed out of the harbour.

"He won't be there very long now," Mr. Scarlett grunted, jerking his thumb towards the fort, whose towers and walls showed up above us in the moonlight.

I really had forgotten Jassim, and did not care how soon he bribed the jailers and got free. I despised myself for having allowed him to be kept there.

Off we went to Jask—easily at first, to give the engines a chance of settling down; later on as fast as they would whizz round.

We were all so impatient to get there that however fast they went the "*B. A.*" seemed to crawl along.

At ten o'clock next morning we met the fortnightly mail-steamer coming from Jask, on her way to Muscat, and Hartley semaphored across to ask if all was well there.

Someone on board took in the signal and answered "Yes," to our great relief, and then I asked if the two ladies from Jask were on board.

"No," was semaphored back, and I was half-glad and half-sorry—glad to know that I should see them, sorry that another fortnight must elapse before another steamer would give them a chance of escaping.

By noon the little white telegraph buildings showed up over the horizon, and two hours later I steamed close in under the rocks on which they stood, and anchored. No white handkerchief fluttered from the signal-mast. Poor little lady, if it was her brother who had been killed she must be somewhere inside those white walls in a terrible state of grief.

I landed immediately.

CHAPTER XV

A Tragedy of the Telegraph

As the keel of the dinghy grated on the sand, and I scrambled ashore, Mr. Fisher, the acting political agent, came down the path to meet me, looking so thin and haggard I scarcely recognized him.

In answer to my eager questions he told me that he feared Borsen had been killed, but was not yet certain.

"Five days ago the poor chap went down the coast on his usual monthly duty of paying the local people at the different relay stations along the telegraph-line. He took with him a Goanese telegraphist and half a dozen native employees. The party rode away on their camels, and the next I heard of them—two days later—was a telephone message that they had seen some wandering parties of Baluchis or Afghans and had been warned, by a friendly village where they had halted, that they might be attacked and robbed. He intended to send the pay-chest, that night, secretly, to the next village and to push on after it next morning.

"A message came from him to his sister, next morning, saying that he was thoroughly enjoying himself and wished she was with him—that was to allay her anxiety. Within an hour the Goanese telephoned in that he had been killed, but the message was then interrupted, the wire was cut, and we have heard nothing since. Quite probably this man was killed as well.

"All we know is that the wire was broken somewhere about twenty-eight miles away, and that when I took a large party out to try to reach the spot, we found the coast swarming with brigands and were glad enough to get back safely. We only returned a few hours ago, and now I want you to take us down there as quickly as you can. It is our only chance of finding any of the party alive—and a very poor chance, I'm afraid."

Of course I was ready to go anywhere or do anything. He and his party were "standing by" to embark, and some ten or twelve natives were already coming down from the telegraph-station with folding-ladders, a portable telephone apparatus, coils of telegraph-wire, and repairing tools. They also brought with them a roughly-made coffin, and, as fast as they arrived, I sent them aboard the *Bunder Abbas*. Whilst Griffiths was pulling the dinghy backwards and forwards I asked Mr. Fisher how his wife and Miss Borsen were bearing up.

"Wonderfully well," he said, his face twitching. "Women sometimes make us men almost ashamed of ourselves—they are so patient and brave."

The dinghy had returned for us, and just as we were stepping in we heard a girl's voice calling, and saw poor little Miss Borsen standing behind us, looking the picture of misery and distress, so sad and so pale

under her big, white topee that I felt horribly sorry for
her. I saluted and tried to show my sympathy. As
I did so she flushed scarlet, and as quickly every trace
of colour left her face; she seemed to freeze, and only
bowed in the most distant manner. I knew that she
meant this as a direct "cut", to remind me that she
had not yet forgiven me for carrying her over the
swamp that night.

Speaking to Mr. Fisher, and ignoring me, she
implored him to take her.

He tried his best to dissuade her, but she insisted
on coming.

"Do you mind if she comes?" he asked, turning to
me.

"Not at all," I answered coldly, as if she were a
complete stranger. "Anybody you care to bring may
come."

I looked to see if that hurt her, but she gave no
sign whatever that she had heard. I felt angry to be
so snubbed, and a brute to feel so enraged with her
just when she was so miserable; but I could not help
it.

So they both came aboard with me, and an extremely
uncomfortable trip it was—squeezed up together in the
little dinghy as we were, with Miss Borsen ignoring
me completely.

However, I was sitting where I could see her pro-
file, and she looked so utterly woebegone and lonely
that my anger died away, until we got alongside, when
she smiled so sweetly on Mr. Scarlett, as he helped
her out of the boat, that I was furious again. I beat
the feeling down, and, as she evidently loathed the

sight of me, kept away, giving her and Mr. Fisher the use of the cabin and the little deck aft of it, and rigging up a screen for'ard of it, so that she need not see me whilst I took the "*B. A.*" out of harbour. Percy fetched my pipe and tobacco, and I smoked furiously and fumed inwardly all the way down the coast, unable to avoid hearing Mr. Scarlett, on the other side of the screen, spinning one of his most exciting yarns and trying to take her thoughts away.

However, he soon found that was no use, and came for'ard to me shaking his head. " Poor little lady! Poor little soul!"

Percy was a fickle youth. Whilst Popple Opstein had been aboard, on that amusing " Prodigal Son " adventure, he had transferred his worship from Mr. Scarlett to him. Now he transferred it again to Miss Borsen, and waited on her hand and foot, standing by with his big eyes fixed on her as if she was some beautiful angel come straight down from heaven into this little world of his. He was such a nuisance that Mr. Scarlett had to drag him out and drop him down the ladder on to the fo'c'sle.

Mr. Fisher joined us presently, and we three, through our glasses, examined the shore and desert plains running inland behind the line of telegraph-posts. Before we had steamed ten miles we saw numerous bands of mounted men moving about the dreary wastes, and Mr. Fisher was on thorns to get back as quickly as possible to the telegraph-station (which was now without a white man), and kept on saying: " I must send my wife and Miss Borsen away by the very next steamer. I don't like the look of things at all." He also told me that he had tried to make them go by yesterday's mail-steamer—the one we had "spoken"—but that Miss Borsen would not go until she had definite news of her brother's fate, and his wife would not leave her at Jask alone. "They'll have to stay there for another fortnight now," he said, shrugging his shoulders.

"She doesn't seem very pleased to see me," I said bitterly.

"I'm afraid you rather annoyed her the last time you were here."

"How? Carrying her over that swampy place?"

"Yes," he nodded; "she thought it an insult."

"If she never gets a bigger insult than that she won't do badly," I answered angrily. "However, I'm sorry; but she won't let me tell her so."

At last, about half-past four, Mr. Fisher thought we were abreast the place where the last telephone message had come from—the five hundred and twentieth telegraph-post I think he said it was—so I turned the "*B. A.*"'s bows inshore, with Ellis heaving the lead every few seconds, to warn us of shoaling water.

It was a shallow, sandy bay with nothing to be seen on the desolate shore except the endless line of telegraph-posts. I anchored three hundred yards off and took ashore Mr. Fisher, a native telegraphist, and the portable telephone apparatus.

They connected this to the telegraph-wire and tried to call up Jask. If Jask answered, we were on the near side of the cut wire; and, as Jask did answer, it showed that the spot where the tragedy had taken place must be still farther away.

So back to the "*B. A.*" we went, and I heard Miss Borsen asking Mr. Fisher, with a half-sob, whether he had found anything.

We weighed anchor and felt our way, carefully, still farther along to the east'ard.

Presently the signal-man shouted to me that he saw someone on the beach, and, looking through my telescope, I made out a man hopping down towards the water's edge on one leg and waving his arms to attract attention.

I called out to Mr. Fisher that we had found the place, pushed the "*B. A.*" in as far as I dared, anchored, and he and the man with the telephone-box came ashore with me.

"The wire's cut about two hundred yards on the left," Mr. Scarlett shouted after us. "I can see it trailing on the ground."

Griffiths pulled us in to the spot where the man—a Goanese he was—was waiting for us, squatting down close to the sea. As I jumped ashore I realized why he had been hopping—his left foot had been roughly hacked off above the ankle. He was gesticulating and sobbing, jerking his head backwards and forwards. Raving mad I thought him; certainly he was half-delirious, and as he held out both his arms towards us I shuddered, for he had no right hand, only a stump of a forearm.

"Right hand, left foot—a common custom," Mr. Fisher said, quite calmly, as he let him sip from his water-bottle and tried to calm him.

Presently he was helped upright, and went hopping through the sand to the top of the beach, where he clung to a telegraph-pole, close to the foot of which were the remains of a wood fire and what I took to be charred sticks.

He began speaking very rapidly.

He stopped, and Mr. Fisher led me away just as the repair party landed about two hundred yards farther along the beach.

"Would you mind going and giving them a hand? They will work better if you do. I must stay here."

I thought his request strange. His manner was very strange: his eyes were burning with fear and disgust.

I did as he asked me and walked along to where the telegraph-wire lay on the sand, coiled in spirals like a snake. The repairing people were very smart at their job, fixed a rope and tackle from one cut end to the other, and then hauled taut the great length of wire between the two nearest telegraph-posts, mounting their portable ladders and fixing things in a most seamanlike way, until they had the wire as taut as they could haul it, with six or seven feet of rope tackle bridging the gap and the two cut ends of the wire hanging down. Then they commenced to put in a splice, and worked so cleverly and systematically that I was quite interested.

The sun was getting close to the horizon by the time the wire was properly joined together and their work finished. Mr. Fisher came to see the job, and the telephone-box was brought along and messages sent into Jask and to the nearest relay station on the other side.

" Well, that is done," he said, with a sigh of relief, "until they cut it again."

The repairing people took their gear back to the " B. A." and we were left alone. He took me to where we had landed, and I saw the mutilated Goanese sitting close to the coffin, which I had not noticed being brought ashore.

" Did you find Borsen's body?" I asked.

He nodded very sadly. " Yes; all that was left of it—a few charred bones. They had cut him in pieces and burnt them."

I shuddered, and knew that what I had mistaken for charred sticks had been bones. That was why he had sent me away.

There was nothing more to say, and we stood looking out over the sea, with rage burning within us, at the thought of the hideous, useless tragedy which had taken place at this spot only two days ago.

The glorious sunset was bathing everything—the sea, my little launch, the shore—in a flood of molten gold, shading to the tenderest pinks as it reached the barren mountains standing up so clear and sharp against the silvery, green sky behind them. The radiant glow threw our shadows and the shadows of those gaunt telegraph-poles slanting across the sands, far across the trackless desert towards the feet of the mountains. If we moved our bodies, our shadows swept in huge arcs across the infinite silence, and, as we moved our arms, shot out huge, ghastly tentacles horrid to see. The setting sun seemed to mock us in its beauty, to laugh and say: " See, I rejoice in the wild wastes of eternal sands. I wash their edges with my golden sea. I paint them with my wondrous tints, and your ghostly shadows, and the shadows of the telegraph-posts you have dared to place there, are the only blots on my fair handiwork."

A beautiful sunset generally gives me a feeling of hope and of trust in a glorious future. That evening I felt myself trembling with an ill-defined fear of impending danger, and as though we and that lonely telegraph-line had trespassed, had forced ourselves and our civilization upon a land where nature, primitive and unchanged, held her sway, and that we too should have to pay the penalty of our vandalism, even as poor Borsen had already paid for his.

The dinghy was coming ashore, her sides glowing with light, the blades of her oars dropping showers of golden spray as Griffiths lifted them from the surface of the sea.

I stirred myself as the bows rasped on the beach, and helped to carry the coffin into the boat, not daring to look behind me. It was very heavy, and I looked enquiringly at Mr. Fisher.

"Sand," he said, and I understood.

The poor Goanese had crawled a little distance away, and was digging at the sand with one hand. We found that he had buried his telephone-box— the one by which he had sent that interrupted message into Jask, and we quickly brought it to light. I knew what the look of satisfaction in his eyes meant—he had saved it from falling into the hands of the brigands, and had been faithful to his trust. The fellow deserved a V.C., but seemed perfectly contented when Mr. Fisher spoke a few words of praise to him.

We pulled away from the appalling loneliness of the telegraph-wire and gaunt poles, and as we came alongside, the sun slid down below the horizon, and Hartley, the signal-man, struck our little ensign.

What Mr. Fisher told Miss Borsen I do not know. I heard him take her into the little cabin, slide the door across, and leave her there. The port-holes were close to me as I stood by the compass giving orders to the helmsman, and her broken-hearted sobs seemed to tear their way right through me. Poor little fragile, lonely thing, and I had been so fiercely angry at her scorn of me! I would have given the whole world for her to forgive me and to be able to comfort her.

Presently her sobs ceased; possibly she slept. I dared not look through the port-holes to see, and gave my orders in a whisper lest they should disturb her. You could not hear a sound aboard the *Bunder Abbas* except the noise of the engines and the occasional tinkle of cooking-pots as the dismal cook went on with his everlasting washing of them.

On the way back to Jask Mr. Fisher told me all that he had been able to learn from the Goanese. The morning after Borsen had sent off the pay-chest all his native employees deserted, so he and the Goanese had to continue their inspection alone. They thought that the brigands would not molest them; but when these cruel brutes galloped up and found the money-chest gone, they were so enraged that they had killed Borsen, mutilated the Goanese (as you know), and galloped away again. They probably thought that the wretched telegraphist would die of sun and thirst, and so he would had he not bravely crawled to the wire, dragging the telephone-box after him, and with consummate pluck, considering the horrible agony he must have been in, had thrown up the connecting wire till its hook caught the telegraph-wire overhead, and enabled him to send the message into Jask. This was the message which had been telegraphed to Jask, from there to Muscat, and had brought us a hundred and twenty miles across the sea to save his life. He had not been able to complete it, because the Baluchis—some of them—had ridden back and cut the wire between him and the telegraph-station. There he had been for more than forty-eight hours without one drop of water. It was indeed marvellous how he had survived.

On the way back, Percy and the dismal cook prepared as lavish a meal as our little meat-safe and a small store of tinned food (kept for special occasions) could provide, but I was in no fit mood to eat, and stayed alone at the wheel. I steered to the south'ard, to get well away from the land before laying off my course to Jask, picked up the light shown from the telegraph-station some time before midnight, and anchored close in under the rocks.

I believe that Miss Borsen slept all the way back. Poor little lady, the strain of the last two days must have been awful, and she must have been dead tired. I thought that the sight of me would increase her misery, so I did not go down on deck when Mr. Fisher took her ashore.

Leaving Mr. Scarlett to see that everything was fixed up for the night, I turned in, weary in mind and body, and dreamt once more that I was carrying Miss Borsen down the path from the telegraph-station, pursued by a score of mounted Baluchis, and that Griffiths was trying to bring the dinghy ashore, but had lost one oar and was turning circles. I was yelling for him to come my way, when Jassim suddenly appeared between me and the sea.

I jumped up in a perspiration, and found Mr. Scarlett bending over me.

"What's the matter, sir? You're making a terrible noise. I had to give you a shake."

I murmured some apology, and he left me to sleep again.

Mr. Fisher had asked me to go up to the telegraph-station early next morning, and so I did, landing in time to have some "chota-hazri" with him in the veranda. The old head-boy, wearing his best yellow turban, came forward for my helmet, and smiled a greeting.

"Have some coffee; there are some bananas too —yesterday's steamer brought them," Mr. Fisher said.

I asked him how Miss Borsen was, but he did not know. His wife had been with her all night, and he had not seen her.

He tried to talk of many things, but with manifest effort. At last he blurted out: "The truth is, affairs are in a very unpleasant position. It's impossible to disguise the fact any longer. Our coolies, and even some of the house boys, are leaving us. They all say the same thing: don't want to go, but they have wives and children, and they don't want to be killed. They are going to their village, and presently, they say, they will come back. 'Presently' means," he said bitterly, "if the tribesmen don't kill us all. There is no doubt in my mind that they intend to attack this place. Almost daily I get warnings from the Mir of Old Jask, who's a feeble, well-meaning old chap, with all he can do to look after his own town, and quite unable to spare us any of his soldiers. Not that they would be of any help. I've tried them, so know.

"You see," he continued, "I have no absolute proof of any rising more formidable than what has just occurred. No one knows what is going on behind those beastly mountains. I've sent plenty of warnings both to Karachi and to Muscat (I knew that), even to Teheran; but the answer is always the same: Sit tight, and if anything definite happens, let us know.

"Well, you are here, that's something; and I don't mind telling you that the presence of your little launch makes all the difference in the world. Up there, right away beyond those hateful hills (he had risen and was pointing away towards the gaunt Baluchistan ranges), in every village for a hundred miles or more, it is known you are anchored here; and the head-men at this very moment probably are deliberating whether they had better not keep quiet till you steam away."

"I'm hanged if I'm going!" I said, rising too. "If I'm ordered away I'll break down my engine and take a month to repair it."

He smiled. "I want you to come round our little defences with me and make suggestions. We have nineteen Eurasians here who can be trusted with rifles. If the worst came to the worst we might hold out for a week until help came; but I wish with all my heart that those two women were not here. It's getting on my nerves. I find myself peering through the big telescope up there hour after hour, searching the desert. I can't tear myself away from it, and at night I can't sleep. This place at the best of times is one of the worst holes in the world, and after being stuck here for two solid years my mind is so enfeebled that it is almost impossible to concentrate my thoughts.

"Oh, I forgot to tell you!" he continued; "I sent a telegram to Duckworth last night informing him of yesterday's proceedings."

I had forgotten all about doing this, so, before any reply could be received, I wired again that I considered it advisable to remain at Jask on account of the disturbed condition of the surrounding district. Commander Duckworth might laugh at my self-assurance for imagining that the little "*B. A.*" could be of much use, but I did not think that he would—nor did I care, so long as he did not order me away. My whole aim in life now seemed centred round the forlorn little lady with the sad grey eyes; and even if she would not make friends with me again, I hoped to be able to protect her. I knew perfectly well that this was the impelling force which decided me to remain there.

The telegram having been sent, Mr. Fisher took me round the whole position.

As you know, the telegraph buildings were built on the rocky end of the peninsula and surrounded by a strong, loopholed wall. He explained to me that there was no probability of an attack either from the sides or from the end, because the Baluchis and Afghans hated the sea, and nothing would induce them to get into a boat.

If they came, they must attack along the neck of the peninsula, and up the open, sloping space below the wall. Across this, as you already know, there was a small breastwork of earth, with a still smaller trench behind it, looking much more like an elongated vegetable-marrow bed than a defence work, and, fifty yards lower down, two rows of barbed-wire railings stretching across from sea to sea.

Five hundred yards away, on the narrowest portion of the peninsula, and commanding the landing place to the east—on our right as we looked inland—was the ruined sheikh's fort, or Old Fort, which I had explored on my first visit. It was half-hidden in a fold of the ground and by some date-palm trees. A thousand yards away on the western side—our left-hand side—commanding the beach and landing place there, was the new sheikh's fort, or New Fort, where the custom-house officers had been hanged by the Baluchis on their way back from destroying Bungi and Sudab. Between these were perhaps a score of native "matting" huts. The whole of the sloping neck of the peninsula afforded no cover whatever; but on the right side of the slope, just between the line of barbed-wire and the baby entrenchment, was a line of more substantial huts belonging to the coolies and other servants of the telegraph staff.

I don't pretend to be a soldier; but it struck me immediately that this line of huts must be destroyed. It interfered with the fire space from the loopholed wall. Also I told Mr. Fisher that the half-ruined sheikh's house — the Old Fort — must be pulled down, as it would give grand cover for an attacking force.

He shook his head. "I daren't do that; it belongs to the Mir of Jask."

"If you don't pull it down, blow it up," I said, smiling. "You can tell him it was an accident."

All sorts of plans ran through my head. I suggested this and that—twenty different schemes—and rather swept Mr. Fisher off his feet with suggestions.

"The first thing to do?" he asked, passing his hand nervously across his forehead, as if he only wanted to be told one thing at a time.

"Blow up the Old Fort!" I told him, and he promised to start right away, as soon as he could get hold of his people. He took me up on the roof of the signal station, where the big telescope stood on its tripod, and I had a grand view of the surroundings of Old Jask, eight miles away, and the wriggling track which led to it round swampy inlets of the sea; of the dreary wastes of sand stretching east and west as far as the eye could see till they lost themselves in the mountains; of the interminable telegraph-poles dwindling away in the distance along the shore line to the east'ard and to the west'ard (to our left as we looked down), of the little *Bunder Abbas* under her now trim awnings, and of a cluster of dhows moored close to the new sheikh's fort and the village of New Jask.

From force of habit Mr. Fisher slued round the telescope and diligently searched the plains at the foot of the mountains, in whose ravines and valleys the wild tribesmen were concealed.

"Can't see a single band of them this morning," he said with much relief. "The *Bunder Abbas* is the cause of that."

Afterwards I returned aboard her and sent Hartley, the signal-man, to the telegraph-station, so that I could communicate with Mr. Fisher and he with me at any time. I also sent Jaffa to Old Jask to try to obtain news in the bazaar there.

That done, I had a yarn with Mr. Scarlett. A great change had come over him since he had got rid of his snake bracelet. I am sure he was fatter; the lines in his face were certainly not so deep, nor his eyes so sunken. He had lost that furtive look in them and that vulture appearance. He received the news that I was going to stay here, and that there would probably be some fighting, with positive pleasure.

"Anything we can do to help the poor little lass, sir! Now, a Maxim, that's what's wanted up there (pointing to a prominent corner on the flat roof of the main building); from there it could sweep the whole approach. We might lend 'em one of ours if it came to the pinch. Eh, sir?"

"Right oh!" I told him. "Directly we get permission to stay, you can mount one there."

Permission did come, Hartley semaphoring the

telegram that very afternoon, and Mr. Scarlett waking me to give the good news. I could swear that he was as pleased as I was.

For the next few days I spent most of my time on shore, landing at sunrise and supervising, in a sort of way, the destruction of the ruined sheikh's house, and the strengthening of the breastwork and the wire entanglements. I say "in a sort of way", because neither Mr. Fisher nor I knew which of us should take entire charge of the defence preparations, with the result that there was a lot of unnecessary work done and some muddling. At any rate the one or two charges exploded in the walls of the Old Fort did not do much damage, and I did not care to interfere.

Meanwhile Mr. Scarlett busied himself preparing the corner of the roof of the telegraph buildings and placing big balks of timber behind the parapet to receive the mounting of a Maxim, if the occasion arose. In spite of the desertion of most of the servants, labour was plentiful, natives of all nationalities and shades of colour clamouring for a job. Many of them were Afghans and Baluchis, and probably were spies; but the only information they could give was that we were expecting an attack and preparing for it, which it was good for them to know. We set these people to work strengthening the barbed-wire fence and the "vegetable-marrow" trench.

At first I had most of my meals with Mr. Fisher and his wife—Miss Borsen never joined us. In fact, I never saw more of her than a flick of a skirt as she fled round a corner one day when I had appeared unexpectedly. She was so obviously avoiding me that it became most unpleasant, and later on I never went to the house unless I was obliged to do so.

This worried me a good deal—the fact of her refusing to forgive me, I mean—and took away a great deal of my enjoyment.

In spite of this the days went past very quickly. Hartley occasionally saw bands of mounted people wandering about the plains and the coast, but the telegraph-wire was untouched. Jaffa could report nothing more definite than a general feeling of uneasiness; trading dhows came and went, and, day after day, trains of camels and donkeys shuffled backwards and forwards through the eight miles of sand to Old Jask, loading or unloading them.

Indeed, the only exciting incident was the sudden bursting of a strong "shamel", which scattered the dhows and compelled me to raise steam and take shelter from it round the other side of the peninsula.

A fortnight passed, and the mail-steamer had called and left again without either of the two ladies. This time it was Mrs. Fisher who would not leave her husband, and Miss Borsen who would not leave Mrs. Fisher; so they both stayed—out of a mistaken and foolish sense of duty—much to Mr. Fisher's secret grief.

Then the blow fell, the morning after the steamer sailed.

Of course I always slept on board, and just as daylight was dawning I was awakened by hearing a tremendous fusillade. Mr. Scarlett and I jumped up, peering ashore in the direction from which the noise came, and saw a great number (a multitude they looked in the indistinct light) of people on camels streaming right along the peninsula, firing rifles as they rode, whilst a furious burst of firing farther away, in the direction of the new village and the New Fort, told us that another band must be attacking that.

The crew of the *Bunder Abbas* were tumbling to their guns, and Mr. Scarlett jumped down on deck to see that everything was ready.

Fascinated, I watched that mad rush of shrieking, firing natives. Leaping off their camels, two or three hundred of them began advancing up the slope towards the telegraph building, stopping to fire, moving on, and stopping again.

"For God's sake get those guns going!" I yelled down.

"In a minute, sir, in a minute!" Mr. Scarlett's voice, calm and collected, came back.

I clutched the railings and gasped as I thought of those two women up there and wondered whether the door through the loopholed wall was closed or not—it was not light enough for me to see. If it was open— God help them!

By this time the leading Baluchis—or whatever they were—were almost up to the line of the barbed-wire; but then I was intensely relieved to hear a few shots popping off from the telegraph buildings, so knew that some of the people had had time to seize their rifles.

"What the devil has gone wrong? Why don't you open fire?" I bawled, as the first of the attacking party reached the barbed-wire. It stopped them for a moment, but then they began throwing their loose cloaks across it and scrambling over.

Now was our chance, and, mad with fury, I dashed down below, yelling to the six-pounder and Maxims' crews to open fire. Mr. Scarlett was not there, nor Moore. Someone told me they were below, aft, and I heard a smashing of woodwork, jumped down, and found them smashing open the door of the magazine. I seized a box of Maxim cartridge-belts and simply heaved it up through the hatchway. In a mad rush of Mr. Scarlett, myself, Moore, and two or three others we were on deck again with a box of six-pounder ammunition between us. As we dragged it forward the marines and Ellis, with his seamen, were pulling the Maxim belts through the breech-blocks; and as we wrenched off the cover of the six-pounder cartridge-box I saw that the crowd of Baluchis were already swarming over the line of breastworks. The long cartridge was thrown into the empty breech of the six-pounder, and as I darted up the ladder to the upper deck it fired. A moment later both Maxims opened too.

CHAPTER XVI

The Siege of Jask

FORTUNATELY the *Bunder Abbas* was lying broadside on to the shore, so that all three of her guns were able to bear on the ground leading up to the telegraph-station — about fourteen hundred yards away. I reached the upper deck and looked ashore just in time to see the first six-pounder shell bursting on the open slope, close to a group of fifty or sixty of the enemy, who had already reached the breastwork. Some had jumped down into the little trench, others were still clambering over the earthwork. Most of them were firing their rifles, though (as far as I could see through my glasses) without taking the trouble to aim—in fact they were practically firing in the air. As the shell burst among them they swerved aside, just as minnows do when you drop a stone among them, but still went on. Another shell made them swerve again and scatter a little more widely, but did not stop them. A Maxim was wanted—not shells.

Although both Maxims were firing very rapidly, Ellis and Webster did not seem able to find the range. This may have been due to excitement or the uncertain light. At any rate, from where I was I could see, quite plainly, the bullets tearing up the ground near the end of the barbed-wire fence, some two hundred yards this side of where the Baluchis were crossing it.

I yelled down that they were going short, and actually watched the furrows advancing until in another moment those streams of bullets had reached the poor wretches and simply ploughed lanes through them. These people made such a fine target that Ellis and Webster instinctively kept firing at them, and more time was lost before I could make one of them slue his gun round to support Moore's shells. When he did so, the rushing, yelling crowd, who were scrambling across and beyond the trench, seemed to melt away, and only a few were left alive—some to fall back into the trench, where they lay comparatively safely, and others to take refuge among the mat shed huts belonging to the telegraph employees—the huts I had so often implored Mr. Fisher to burn. Ellis—I think it was Ellis—was still "playing" the Maxim on the barbed fence, and was not able to see, or too excited to realize, that he was only firing on dead men lying heaped in masses, or sprawling singly over the fence. I shouted down to tell him not to waste more ammunition.

At this time there were not more than perhaps twenty of the enemy to be seen, and these were doing their best to escape, crawling and creeping, dodging towards those confounded huts.

I stopped the Maxims and ordered Moore to fire a few shells among the huts, hoping to set fire to them, or at any rate turn out the Baluchis taking shelter there. Before he could do this my fellows began shouting: "More are coming, sir; look, sir!" and I saw another horde of chaps dash out from the Old Fort and the dip in the ground round it, rushing up the slope as the others had done, but keeping away to their left, to avoid the mangled heaps of their tribesmen huddled near the barbed-wire fence.

They were already within fifty yards of the huts before we could swing our guns round, only to discover that whilst they kept on the far side of the slope the curvature of the ground protected them to a certain extent, and we could not reach them easily. Only their heads could we see, their heads and their arms brandishing rifles.

We let rip at them without doing much damage, if any, for I never saw the rush waver. But then they came to the barbed fence, and climbing over it they made a better target. They must have suffered horribly, but at least a hundred passed it and disappeared among those huts to join the remnant of the first rush.

I guessed what would happen. Directly they had regained breath the whole crowd would dash for the loopholed wall.

I yelled for everybody to "stand by" and train their guns on the upper slope.

"They'll be in the open in a minute!" I shouted, and glued my glasses to my eyes. It was quite light now. Turning for a moment to the telegraph-station, I saw Hartley trying to semaphore something from the top corner. Rifles were poking out through the loopholes, and, thank goodness, that door in the wall was shut.

Shooting was still going on everywhere—one could not distinguish exactly from where.

"Drop a shell among the huts and turn 'em out," I called down. "Stand by with the Maxims to follow them when they break cover."

Moore fired twice. Then, as I expected, a regular horde of Baluchis rushed out from among the huts, yelling and firing their rifles, making a most appalling din as they swarmed up the slope.

But they were in full view and entirely exposed. The Maxims swept through them; the six-pounder scattered bits of iron and stones amongst them and tumbled many over like rabbits. But we could not stop them all, and before I realized it the wave of men —thinned, it is true, but still numerous—had swept to the foot of the white, loopholed wall itself. The desperate savages were leaping up to grab the top, climbing on each other's backs, poking their rifles through the loopholes, and hammering at the door with their rifle butts. And at this very time the Maxims stopped firing; so did the six-pounder.

I dashed below.

"Go on!" I shouted. "Go on! Why the devil ain't you firing?"

"We'll hit the telegraph people, sir!" they called.

"Don't worry about them—fire—fire—carry on the Maxims," I yelled, "or they'll be inside in a moment."

I cared not a rap whether we killed all the telegraph people, so long as we kept the Baluchis outside. Miss Borsen wouldn't be anywhere near the wall, so we should not hurt her.

The Maxims began pumping out more lead—by good fortune they worked splendidly, the belts jerking through like lightning—and in less time than it has taken me to write this the Baluchis had begun to fall back. Once they were clear of the wall Moore opened on them with shell, and though these shells do very little damage in the open they kept them on the run whilst more Maxim belts were being slipped in.

They fled back to the huts almost too quickly for the guns to follow them. From the rear of the huts they burst forth, trying to keep out of sight; but as they came to the wire-fence they had to climb over it, and one of the Maxims was waiting for them and played terrible havoc. The remnant simply flew down—their heads showing beyond the contour of the slope—till they disappeared among the date-palm trees round the Old Fort.

My fellows began to cheer—they had been too busy before — and the lascars and all the other natives danced about and cheered too—Percy wildly excited; all except of course the cook and his mate, who were busy preparing the men's cocoa, and were apparently still contemplating their usual early suicide directly the saucepans had been cleaned again.

Jaffa, left to himself, had been firing a rifle. He looked pleased and happy. As for Mr. Scarlett, he was beaming.

"Drove 'em 'Balooks' back all right, sir!" he said, rubbing his hands. "They've learnt a lesson or two, those poor wretched devils," and he jerked his thumb towards the open sloping ground, which now looked as if a fierce gust had blown the washing out of a laundry and distributed it unevenly over the ground.

I asked him what had been the matter at first, and why he had broken down the doors of the magazine. He told me that as Moore had run aft with the key he had dropped it overboard in his excitement. This was Moore all over. Just like the idiot he was!

We now had time to look towards the village and the New Fort.

Only a very occasional shot came from that direction, and through our glasses we saw that the parapets and battlements were black with figures, so knew that the Baluchis had captured it. The trading dhows were being hauled off-shore and were putting to sea, their crews working desperately to save them from falling into the hands of the Baluchis; the bay was full of their frightened cries as they hoisted their clumsy sails and tried to gain safety.

Just then bullets began to fall round us, and soon we were under a brisk, long-range fire—apparently from the fugitives round the Old Fort. It was so badly aimed that it was hardly enough to disturb us, but a badly-aimed bullet is just as dangerous as a well-aimed one—if it happens to find a billet. So, whilst the Maxim crews were getting up more ammunition and reloading belts, I made Moore throw a few shells close to the Old Fort. The first few they stood, but at the seventh we had the gratification of seeing them bolt back into a fold of the ground close to the landing-place on the other side of the peninsula. They drove their frightened camels into this shelter, and were safe from any tokens of "esteem" we could send them.

Just then someone called my attention to the telegraph buildings. I looked and saw the door in the loopholed wall thrown open, and men began filing out and racing down the slope—a man in pyjamas leading them. It was Mr. Fisher. Why they were coming out goodness only knows; but down they ran, apparently with the idea of manning the trench and breastwork. They had almost reached it before I remembered that some of the enemy might possibly be there still; and, sure enough, as the leading ones leapt into the trench on one side, I saw thirty or forty Baluchis, who had been hidden from us on the other side, spring up, fire point-blank, and leap over, dropping their rifles and slashing with swords as they jumped down among them. We could not possibly give assistance; we could not fire into the mêlée, and stood stock-still, holding our breath, watching the hand-to-hand struggle. It probably did not last fifty seconds, though it seemed more like fifty minutes, and at last the telegraph staff began to retreat uphill. Luckily very few—not half a dozen—followed them; the rest contenting themselves with lying down and firing.

Mr. Scarlett, without orders, took the risk and fired a shell among this lot, and made them scramble over the breastwork again out of sight. The others stopped as well and came back.

Mr. Fisher, in his pyjamas, tried to lead his people to charge down once more; but they would not follow him. Instead, they fell back inside the loopholed wall—the white figure being the last to enter—and I breathed again when the door was once more closed.

We now had all we could do to prevent the *Bunder Abbas* being damaged by the fleeing dhows. Their crews had quite lost their heads. One fouled us amidships and tore a stanchion out before she drifted clear; another, having cut her "grass" hawser cable, drifted helplessly right across our bows, with our little cable tautening under her bottom. Every single soul of us was trying to shove her free, and I had to veer cable before she eventually scraped past, hanging up for a moment as her projecting stern caught in the stem-post and carried away another stanchion, which let the whole fore part of the awning fall over the six-pounder gun—and over us too. If only the Baluchis had taken advantage of this moment we could have done nothing. Luckily the poor wretches were disheartened, or perhaps they never even saw their chance.

Away inshore, by the New Fort, there was much yelling and screaming. The whole village was humming like a hive of bees disturbed—the inhabitants fleeing along the beach and staggering under their valuables, until some shots, apparently from the New Fort, fell among them, when they dropped their burdens and fled all the faster. The enemy in that fort commanded the track to Old Jask, and these poor wretches had to make a great circuit before they could hope to reach safety.

Honestly, I had not imagined that an attack would have been delivered with so little warning. As Mr. Scarlett said: "It was not at all like their usual way of doing things." They ought to have come along in the daylight, settled themselves across the base of the peninsula, and then sent in a messenger to ask for a ransom, failing which they would storm the place. That had always been the custom in this part of the world, so both Jaffa and Mr. Scarlett assured me.

It was not very flattering to our own military instincts and preparation for defence to realize that if they had not begun firing their rifles almost before they had reached the neck of the peninsula, and long before they ever commenced to dismount from their camels to charge up the slope, they must have taken the telegraph-station by surprise. We should have heard or seen nothing until too late; and I really went cold "all over", to think what would have happened inside those walls with the *Bunder Abbas* absolutely powerless to interfere. I knew now, though I did not know it before, that none of these people can control themselves; they must let off their rifles to work up their courage to the charging-point, and must continue wasting ammunition to keep it there.

The extraordinary thing was that Jaffa had ridden nearly twenty miles inland only yesterday, and had actually visited several villages at the foot of the mountains, without obtaining any warning whatever.

Hartley began signalling again from the top of the roof.

"Two men killed and two missing," I read. "Mr. Fisher wishes to know if you can clear the trench. There are fifty or sixty of the enemy still there?"

I'd forgotten them.

I called out to Mr. Scarlett and asked him whether

he thought we could turn them out with shell and Maxims. We both agreed that we could not do so without expending more ammunition than we could afford.

"Right oh! We shall have to land and drive 'em out!" I said.

He was very anxious to come with me.

"Don't leave me this time, sir," he pleaded, and I could not help but wonder at the change which had come over him.

He saw my look of surprise and burst out with: "I am a different man now, sir; I feel a different being altogether since I got rid of that," and he touched his left arm. I shook my head and told him that he would have all he could do to keep the main body back if they had the heart to come along again.

I semaphored to Hartley to tell Mr. Fisher to keep up a fire on the trench, so as to occupy the minds of those chaps still there, and in half an hour landed in the dinghy, just below some rocks at the end of the barbed-wire fences, with Webster, Jones, and Gamble. Sending the dinghy back for Ellis, Andrews, and Griffiths, we dashed to the top of the beach and lay down between the end of the fence and the breast-work. Until they came it was a very ticklish position to be in; for if those fifty or so "Balooks" had spotted us, and had the "heart of a worm", they might have "done for" all three of us.

We lay there absolutely motionless, glued to the ground, whilst the noise of casual firing from above told us that the telegraph people were doing what I'd asked them—firing at the trench farther along.

Not a hundred yards from us rifles began answering them. It was a great relief when the dinghy came back and Ellis, Griffiths, and Andrews joined us.

Then we rose, fixing bayonets and rushing up and across the open to the wretched breastwork, much too excited to worry about how many chaps we should find there. I knew that the trench had no traverses— we had never thought them necessary; so once we scrambled over and into it we should be able to sweep the whole length of it with our rifles.

We just caught sight of the ghastly heaps of dead lying at the foot of the fence a little farther along, some actually leaning over as if they were alive. Then we saw some live Baluchis lying down on our side of the breastwork, too busily engaged plugging at the loopholed wall to think of danger behind them.

Directly we saw them we yelled—we could not restrain ourselves any longer—and as we rushed for them they saw our bayonets, squealed with fright, and leapt across the breastwork into the trench. We were after them in a moment, each racing to be first, jumping the breastwork with a bound, and seeing them flying helter-skelter to the far end. I jumped clean on a wounded man, who wriggled up and tried to slash at me with a sword; but I was away before the blow touched me. We simply emptied our magazines into these chaps and they never gave us a chance to close. A few fell, but our aim was too wild to account for many, and most of them scrambled out, over, and down towards the barbed-wire, like a lot of rabbits making for their "bury". We knocked over one or two as they flung themselves over the wires, and the rest simply dashed down the slope to join the main body hidden in the hollow.

A faint cheer came from the loopholed wall, and I heard a cry of disgust from my own men. Looking back I saw them bending over the corpse of what had been one of the Eurasian telegraph people. It was horribly mutilated.

A little farther on another lay dead, mutilated in the same hideous manner. It made me sick to look at them.

In fact the whole place was a shambles. There must have been nearly a hundred—perhaps more—bodies dotted about in little white heaps near the fence and the breastwork, the heaps being more scattered between the breastwork and the wall where the Maxim had caught them in their final rush. Along the foot of the wall corpses lay singly. What grand-looking men they were, too, with fierce high-bred faces. It was a horrid business.

The edge of civilization! Yes! I was there again, and the only satisfaction this slaughter gave was the knowledge of what the fate of those two poor frightened women would have been had the attack succeeded.

I don't want, in this yarn, to worry anyone with the thoughts which flashed through my head on this or that occasion, but I should like to write just this, and have done with it. To stand quietly, as I was doing then, on that slope where not many minutes previously four or five hundred raging men in the prime of life had rushed up with the one idea in their souls to "kill or die", "kill or die", and to see now the huddled, white-cloaked figures lying all round, so calm and still and dignified by death, made me feel wearily sad.

It was my duty to kill them—I was sent there, on the edge of civilization, to do so—and it had fallen to my lot to do it. "Kismet!"

It was only one more wave of fanatical, unthinking, misdirected barbarism broken again as it tried to wash back the advance of civilization, and civilization cannot and must not cease to roll back such waves, in the eternal progress of the world. I remembered the day I had walked so jauntily out of the Admiralty with every contempt for the roar and bustle of traffic and trade, and every nerve tingling with delight at soon leaving it for the edge of civilization; and now that I was there, and had done a man's work with the tools and engines of war which civilization had put in my hand, I was neither pleased nor proud.

It was all too cruel, too brutal, all so meaningless and useless a waste of life. These men had died because we prevented them, by every means in our power, from obtaining more rifles. They only wanted them to carry on their family and tribal blood feuds, to raid other tribes, and to shoot our own soldiers across the Indian frontier. But to these poor wretches this was their whole duty in life, and they knew that the telegraph-cable was one of their chief enemies—it could give warning of attempts to land arms; it could summon ships from below the horizon to prevent them being landed: so they had laid down their lives in the endeavour to destroy it, and had left their waiting wives to teach their fatherless children black

hatred of the white man, and to bring them up with
the one idea, later on, when they were big enough
to hold a rifle, of trying to revenge their fathers' deaths
and beat back—in their turn—advancing civilization.

Standing among all these heaped-up corpses I
could not help thinking what a wailing there would
be when these grand men did not return to their
village fastnesses in those grim mountains standing
up like a huge wall against the horizon.

A rifle suddenly went off close to me. Turning, I
saw Webster open his breech and jerk out a cartridge.

"A wounded chap tried to stab me, sir," he said in
explanation.

That was the worst part of it. The wounded never
expected anything but death, and wanted revenge
before they died. It was not the slightest use trying
to attend to their wounds, in fact it was dangerous to
go anywhere near a man, even though he looked as
dead as a stone—he might only be pretending to be
dead and waiting his opportunity for you to get close.
I ought to have given orders for my men to go round
and shoot every one with any sign of life in him, but
this I absolutely refused to do. The poor, ignorant
wretches should have the chance of crawling down
among their own people—if they could.

I called my men away, and, carefully avoiding
every patch of tumbled, distorted bodies, went up to
speak to Mr. Fisher, whom I saw coming towards
me—still in his pyjamas—a revolver in his hand.

He was quite cool. "Thank you very much!" he
said simply.

"How is Miss Borsen," I asked eagerly, "and

your wife?" but he did not know. He had not seen them since the first alarm.

"What will these Baluchi chaps do now?" I asked.

"Baluchis!" he said. "Most of them are Afghans, the real fighting Afghan; there are only a sprinkling of Baluchis. I don't know what they will do, but they've had such a lesson that they'll probably be off again to the hills to-night. I've sent off a wire to Duckworth to tell him that we've been attacked and that you beat them off by fire from your launch."

He seemed undecided what to do. He still hesitated about burning those confounded huts which had already caused so much trouble. He did not want to irritate the employees who lived there, and kept on saying: "We'll wait till the morning; there probably won't be a sign of them then."

But he gladly accepted my offer to mount one of my Maxims on top of the station, and I went back to the *Bunder Abbas* with my people to send it ashore as quickly as possible.

Already some at least of the Afghans were recovering their fright, for as we marched down to the beach we came in for a sharp "sniping", and Jones the marine was shot through the arm. He dropped his rifle and swore at Gamble, thinking he had struck him; then he looked at the place, shook his fist towards the Old Fort, picked up his rifle with the other hand, and came on.

It was the same arm which had been hit during the engagement with the Afghans at Bungi whilst we were trying to get old Popple Opstein out of his trap.

Once aboard the *Bunder Abbas* I took charge and sent Mr. Scarlett ashore with the Maxim.

He was delighted to go, unshipped it and lowered it, with two thousand rounds of ammunition, into the dinghy, and set off ashore with Jackson and Ellis to help him.

Some of the telegraph coolies were waiting to carry it up the slope, and as I ate some breakfast which Percy had ready for me, and afterwards smoked my pipe, I watched the three of them busy mounting it at the corner of the parapet.

Before leaving the *Bunder Abbas* I had ordered steam to be raised, and directly the lascar first-driver reported the engines ready I signalled to Mr. Fisher that I intended to steam round to the other side of the peninsula and try to teach the enemy another lesson.

This I did, and, as I expected, found them totally unprepared for my approach. They must have seen the *Bunder Abbas* getting under way and steaming out, but possibly imagined that she was going to sea. At any rate, as I suddenly appeared round the head of the peninsula and the rocks there, I found them crowded together, almost on the shore, among their camels.

They appeared to be asleep, but woke with a fright when Moore let rip a shell among them.

As they rose to their feet I turned the *Bunder Abbas* round and gave them a taste of the Maxim as well.

They had had one lesson at daybreak; they now, at midday, had a still harder one. It was pure, undiluted slaughter; but, though sickening, was absolutely necessary. They fled helter-skelter inland, leaving their camels to fend for themselves, rushing behind the ruins of the Old Fort, and, when a couple of shells drove them out of that, flying panic-stricken in a long straggling line—the devil take the hindmost—through the sand-dunes towards the mainland, many of them making a long detour in the direction of the New Fort. What I did hate to see was the poor, wretched, wounded camels hobbling about, falling down, and struggling to their feet again.

Having cleared this side of the peninsula I went back and anchored at my old billet. From there I could see the remnant of the enemy huddled round the walls of the New Fort. I might have stirred them with a few more shells, but did not. Mr. Scarlett signalled presently that the Maxim was mounted and ready, so I ordered him to bring Jackson back to the ship; Ellis and Hartley between them would be able to work it, and I was too short-handed already to spare anyone else. Mr. Scarlett was very pleased with himself and with the splendid fire zone which the Maxim he had just mounted could sweep. He had seen the ladies, and said that though they were very white they seemed fairly cheerful.

I asked if they'd sent any message to me.

"Mrs. Fisher did, sir, but I'm hanged if I remember what it was exactly."

"Did Miss Borsen?" I asked, trying to hide my nervous anxiety to know whether perhaps what had occurred might have made her show signs of forgiving me.

I felt miserable when he shook his head. "Not as I remember, sir."

There were two things that troubled him: those confounded huts, which rather interfered with his beloved Maxim, and that breastwork. He pointed out that there were not nearly enough men to defend the breastwork, and that it formed admirable cover for an attacking force.

"We ought to level it in, that we ought," he said, shaking his head.

Of course he was right. Hadn't we seen what had happened that very morning?

"Mr. Fisher expects them to clear away back to the hills to-night," I told him. "What do you think?"

He shook his head again. "They don't seem to be carrying out their usual routine; not a bit of it. They ought to retire—that is, if experience is anything to go by. I don't like the look of them occupying the fort; it looks as if they meant to stay."

When I asked him whether he thought the Mir of Old Jask would attack them, and endeavour to recapture his fort, he only made a grimace.

All that afternoon there was absolute quiet except for an occasional shot from the New Fort and also a few shots fired on the slope itself, where the telegraph coolies were busy dragging the dead into heaps and burning them. These last shots told me that some of the wounded Afghans had had to be dispatched.

Mr. Scarlett was so anxious for me to try to get

a "move on" Mr. Fisher about burning the huts and levelling the breastworks that I went ashore later in the day and again urged him to do this.

Nothing I could say could make him realize the necessity. "I am certain they'll all have cleared away home by to-morrow morning. We'll wait till then. Besides, I dare not overwork the coolies. If I do they will desert," was all I could get out of him.

I suggested that it might be advisable to send Mrs. Fisher and Miss Borsen on board the *Bunder Abbas* for the night; but he declined for the same reason as he declined everything else—that he expected the Afghans to disappear before morning.

"Do you know that you are responsible for much of this?" he said, as he walked backwards and forwards with me outside the loopholed wall.

"Responsible! What do you mean?"

"Why," he said, "they all know of the loss of that huge caravan over on the Muscat coast—the one you and the *Intrepid* captured between you. If they had got those rifles and all that ammunition through to the Indian frontier there would have been another 'rising' there. They were only waiting for them before giving the signal to the tribes along a hundred miles of the frontier to pour down through the passes and lay waste the valleys and murder the tribes living there under British protection. They all know this, and to-day they have been trying to revenge themselves for their lost opportunity. I've seen among the killed several men I know: powerful sheikhs, Arabs from the other coast, leading men from Afghan villages. It is a bigger business than I thought at first.

"However, they will probably be gone by the morning, and you may pride yourself that but for your capturing that big caravan the other day, the Indian Government would have had another little war on its hands.

"Oh," he added, "I'd almost forgotten! I had a wire from Muscat. The *Intrepid* has gone off up the coast after some more arms."

I went back to the *Bunder Abbas* rather elated at the idea that I had helped to stop a little war, and remembered what Commander Duckworth had said: "They ought to do something for you." It was rather early to expect promotion, but it would be grand if it came.

"Can't budge him," I told Mr. Scarlett. "He still thinks they'll have gone back home by the morning. The *Intrepid* has gone after some more arms, so we shan't be disturbed till she gets back. That's one good bit of news."

Just before sunset a small dhow came drifting slowly into the bay. She was flying the Muscat red flag and did not seem to notice anything unusual, or that the anchorage was deserted of shipping, so I sent Jaffa across to warn her nakhoda of what was happening. Jaffa came back to say that he was very grateful and would put to sea again, but had several passengers for Old Jask who preferred to land and would take shelter at the telegraph-station until things were quiet. I saw them later on—three cloaked figures—land on the beach and make their way up towards the loopholed wall.

We also saw numerous little spirals of blue smoke rising into the air round the walls of the New Fort, so knew that the tribesmen were preparing food; and Hartley, just about this time, signalled that he could see a large mass of mounted people moving across the plains in our direction. This did not worry us. We, Mr. Scarlett and I, were quite happy. From what he told me it was out of the question that, even though they did not retreat that night, they would attempt an attack. Their ideas of war and sieges were to attack at dawn; it was a tradition to attack at dawn, and seldom had they been known to attack at any other time.

The sun was setting now in its usual magnificence; everything—the rocks, the telegraph - station over them, the sandy shores, the walls of the New Fort, were flooded with delicate rose tints. The mountains behind and the few wisps of clouds overhanging them were suffused with the same delicate colours, and out from behind them rose the moon—nearly full—and we knew that directly the sun's light vanished her light would take its place and enable us to defeat any attack (almost inconceivable) that the Afghans might attempt.

We only had to keep vigilant watch, and if they tried to rush the slope again we should see the white-cloaked figures as plainly as in daytime.

I kept the first watch that night, Griffiths with me. At about ten o'clock flames burst out ashore, in the direction of the New Fort, and soon it was evident that the whole of the village was on fire. It was a grand spectacle as the flames spread from hut to hut, leaping high in the air, lighting up the walls of the fort, even the white walls of the telegraph buildings, and making the water of the bay and the brasswork of the *Bunder Abbas* glow red.

The flames and crackling were still fierce when Mr. Scarlett relieved me at midnight.   In his opinion the Afghans had set the huts on fire purposely, and were probably retreating inland under cover of the heavy cloud of smoke which lay above them.

I had four hours in which to sleep, so, stretching myself on my bed, I lay down on that little upper deck outside our cabin, leaving him and Gamble to keep the "middle" watch.

CHAPTER XVII

Jassim Takes his Revenge

AT four o'clock in the morning Mr. Scarlett shook me and reported all quiet and the fire on shore dying down. I scrambled to my feet to take over the "morning" watch, feeling as fresh and wakeful as though I had not been to sleep for a fortnight!

The moonlight was very brilliant, so brilliant, indeed, that the telegraph buildings on the dark rocks and the New Fort on the white sand stood out quite as boldly as in the daytime; and all that could be seen of the remains of the fire was a glowing line of red-hot ashes extending along the beach, where the village had been.

The slope leading up to the loopholed wall was so flooded with light that I could distinguish even the barbed-wire fence and the shadows of the wires and uprights.

Of the Afghans themselves nothing whatever could be made out; but this did not imply that they had gone away, because most of them might be sleeping inside the fort and the others behind it, and at the base of the peninsula the fringe of date-palms threw such extremely dark, puzzling shadows that the camels might have been concealed among these, or even been driven farther along behind the sand-hills without our having noticed any movement.

At any rate, whatever had or had not happened, I was not going to leave anything to chance, or take any risks: so the rest of the hands were called and stood to their guns; cocoa was served out; and to make sure that Ellis and Hartley were on the alert I made a flashing signal to them. As it was answered I knew that they, too, were "standing by" their Maxim.

After this there was nothing to do but strain our eyes shorewards and wait for daylight. In the half-hour when the increasing light of dawn is absorbing the light of the moon and rendering the outlines of objects uncertain and ill defined, this waiting for an attack is always most scaring. It makes no difference how often one experiences this feeling of acute tension, it always seems to occupy one so completely that not a soul moves or speaks; even breathing is a difficult matter, and breaths come in deep jerks, only when they can be held no longer.

But if the strain is great when the moon is there to help, it is ten times as great when there is no moon and the first glimmer of daylight distorts everything so strangely and forms such strange weird shapes.

How grateful we were to the moon that morning!

Daylight did come at last. The fading shadows under the fringe of date-palm trees showed us hundreds of motionless lumps which gradually outlined themselves into camels; figures began moving about among them, and out from the door of the fort streamed many more to kneel on the sand, facing the glory of the rising sun, throw their arms above their heads, and bend at their devotions.

This might only be the preliminary to an attack; so still we remained at our guns, until the sight of many little spirals of blue smoke rising in the calm morning air, and the little groups of men seated round them—evidently cooking—made it absolutely certain that they did not intend any such thing— not that morning.

"That finishes the business," Mr. Scarlett said, drawing a deep breath, and letting it out again with a jerk.

We had been so certain—Mr. Scarlett and I—that they would have done the one thing or the other, and now they had done neither; they had simply stayed where they were, in complete possession of the base of the peninsula, and entirely cutting it off from any assistance from Old Jask.

Mr. Scarlett shook his head and shrugged his shoulders. He could not understand these tactics.

"It ain't like 'em, sir; it ain't like anything I've seen or heard of before, and I don't care about it," he said, as I dismissed the men from the guns to get their breakfasts and scrub decks.

Whilst they were doing this we were startled suddenly by the sound of rifle firing, a long way off, in the direction of Old Jask, and drawing rapidly nearer. Without waiting for the order, the crew tumbled up from below to their guns, but no one could see anything happening. At first we made sure that another band of Afghans were attacking

the old town; but this could not be so, because the
people round the New Fort seemed even more startled
than we had been.   They sprang to their feet, seized
their rifles, and whilst some began to "round up"
the camels, driving them close to the wall, others
poured into the fort itself.

Whilst we were wondering what all this meant,
the battlements of the fort became alive with dark
turbans; puffs of smoke darted out from them, and
the reports of their rifles came across to us.   At what
they were firing we could neither see nor guess.

At last, after firing had been going on continuously
for four or five minutes, Mr. Scarlett saw a cloud of
dust, and, looking in the direction of his finger, I
made out a number of mounted men—some on horses,
others on camels—advancing over the plain from Old
Jask.   Spurts of light, showing in the cloud of sand
dust over their heads, told us that it was from them
we had heard the first firing.

"It's the old Mir's border police coming to recapture the fort," Mr. Scarlett sang out.   "Now
you'll see some pretty fighting.   Just remember, sir,
that they are mostly Bedouins from the other coast,
and they and the Afghans hate each other like poison.
Now watch what's going to happen."

I did; we all did.

The line of men came charging up to the base
of the peninsula, sweeping away to the right and
wheeling round the bend of the swamp lying there,
until they were not more than two thousand yards
from the fort.   Firing from both parties was continuous.   Then for a moment I lost sight of them

behind some sand-hills, and expected, when next they appeared, to find that they had dismounted, left their horses and camels in rear of those sand-hills, and were attacking properly—with short rushes or something of that sort—although I was puzzled to think what they could effect against the thick walls of the fort.

Instead of this they reappeared in sight—in somewhat looser formation certainly, but still mounted—and galloped madly along the intervening sand, firing rapidly, whilst the fusillade from the parapet and towers of the fort swelled furiously, and the people who had driven the camels under cover of the walls lay down to fire as well.

The attacking party came to five hundred yards—to three hundred; none of them seemed to have been hit. Still they galloped, the men on camels bringing up the rear left far behind. Then the horsemen suddenly divided into two parties, and, yelling and firing their rifles, they circled completely round the fort, enveloping it, meeting in the rear of it, and dashing round again. A continuous splutter of musketry burst out from the walls above their heads, without, as far as we could see, doing the faintest damage. In fact, the firing was so wild that a good many bullets began falling round us, and one banged against the funnel close to where I was standing.

The circling rings of horsemen grew larger as they curveted and pranced in the clouds of dust kicked up by their own horses' hoofs, until they all swooped off like a flock of birds and gathered in a knot about half a mile from the fort; whereupon the firing died down almost completely. Every now and then a horseman darted out from among them, dashed towards the fort, gave a display of horsemanship, fired his rifle, performed some circus tricks, and then dashed back again.

I was so interested and amused that I forgot that the fort was well within range of our six-pounder.

"Let's help them," I shouted, ordering Moore to "plug" a shell at the fort.

Mr. Scarlett only laughed. "You'll see what happens."

Our first shell burst short, burying itself in the sand; the second blew a hole in the soft bricks of the fort; and before we could fire a third the whole covey of those border police had whirled round and galloped rapidly away, quickly disappearing in another cloud of dust on their way back to Old Jask, still firing their rifles furiously.

I don't believe that a single man of them had been hit.

"Shall we cease fire, sir?" Mr. Scarlett asked. "We haven't enough ammunition to waste any more on the fort."

"Right oh!" I nodded.

The horsemen of the party had galloped off, but the few men on camels who had been left in the rear had evidently "rounded up" some of the Afghans' camels, for they now reappeared beyond the sand-hills trying to drive a dozen—perhaps more—in front of them.

Immediately there was a stir among the Afghans outside the wall; more poured out through the door of the fort, and in a twinkling they were after them on foot, wading across the swamp so as to head off the party with the camels. Firing burst out more furiously than ever, and it was not many seconds before the captured camels were abandoned and the other fellows followed the horsemen.

"Well, sir, that little 'show' was what they call a battle—a regular 'pitched' battle," Mr. Scarlett said. "How they decide who's won beats me. It's an accident if anyone gets killed or even wounded, but those Bedouins will go back and pour out a long yarn to the old Mir; every one of them will have to give an account of the fierceness of the fight, and probably they'll all desert during the day and go looting on their own account—looting peaceful villages, which is much more in their line. We may as well let our chaps, and the Afghans too, go on with their breakfasts."

In ten minutes the whole of the tribesmen were squatting round their fires again as though nothing had happened.

Now that we knew they had not retired—had no intention of doing so—Mr. Scarlett was as anxious as I was that those huts should be burnt, the breastwork levelled, and the trench filled in; so I went ashore to try to persuade Mr. Fisher to make a start on these jobs.

I found him much more surprised at the non-retirement of the Afghans than we had been, and very much more disappointed. In fact, he looked about as worried as any man could look. He took me up to the house so that I could personally assure his wife that the *Bunder Abbas* would not leave them.

She was in a terrible state of alarm, almost beside herself; her eyes were terrified, and she clutched my arm so tightly whilst she was imploring me to stay that her finger nails left deep marks.

"Why don't you send for the *Intrepid*? We shall all be killed," she said in the most agitated manner; and it was quite useless to tell her that the *Intrepid* had gone up the coast and that we could not communicate with her. When she did let go of my arm her hands worked convulsively at her sides, and I no longer wondered why her husband looked so worn.

Miss Borsen was not there, of course, and I had not the courage to ask after her. In fact, I was very glad to tear myself away and go up to the Maxim on the roof, to see for myself whether it could sweep the whole slope.

Mr. Scarlett had told me correctly. The Maxim had a grand position, and no one could approach without coming under its fire except towards the right, where it was possible to creep up unseen behind those huts.

Ellis and Hartley had filled old flour-sacks with sand and placed them along the parapet, on each side of the gun. They were busy bringing up more, and were quite happy. "If only those huts were out of the way, sir, nothing could get near us," Ellis said; and though I again implored Mr. Fisher to burn them he still refused. He took me to see the two wounded Eurasians—one shot through the arm and the other badly slashed about the head. They were bandaged in very "shipshape" fashion, and looked comfortable enough.

"Who did that?" I asked, pointing to their dressings; and when he told me that Miss Borsen had looked after them, as she knew something of "first aid", I envied them for a moment.

He had now only fifteen of the telegraph staff remaining, and, as he said, none of them knew anything about fighting. He was doubtful about trusting rifles to the servants and telegraph employees, because these were of all nationalities—Zanzibaris, Baluchis, Tamils, and various half-castes; but he had collected the rifles strewn over the slope yesterday when those fellows had been shot down—nearly a hundred of them there were, of all patterns. Very little ammunition had been found on the dead bodies, and that, too, was all mixed up—Mauser, Mannlicher, Le Bras, Lee-Metford, Martini—all in a hopeless jumble. He promised to have them sorted.

Then I was taken all round the outside of the loopholed wall, and discovered—what I had not thought of before—that it was possible for an enemy to crawl along the rocks on the eastern side—the right side looking inland—without being seen, to clamber up them, and attack that flanking wall without exposing themselves. However, the man who designed the wall must have realized this and had built it nearly fifteen feet high, so that unless they brought ladders with them it would be difficult to scale. The cable-house—a little square building into which the cable from Muscat wriggled out of the sea—stood isolated on the rocks, and could be attacked at night with impunity.

Walking round the rear wall I satisfied myself that

no attack could be made from that quarter, because
the rocks at the end of the peninsula could only be
reached in boats, and as the sea was always rough
there at this time of year a landing was out of the
question.   The western side—the one looking over
the bay where the *Bunder Abbas* was anchored—was
fairly safe, though here again a daring enemy might
creep round by the beach (where I had just landed)
and attack from short range.   However, so long as
the *Bunder Abbas* remained (or had ammunition),
and the nights were moonlit, this possibility did
not worry me.

Mr. Fisher kept on complaining of the few men
he had left—fifteen all told—which was a ridiculous
number to protect all three of the vulnerable sides;
but I implored him to arm the servants and any of
the labourers he could trust, and gradually convinced
him that this was safe.

As we came back to the front side I saw that thirty
or forty men were already shovelling the breastwork
back into the trench.   This pleased me.

Then he took me through the door—covered with
bullet marks and the dents of rifle butts—as I wanted
to see where best to make a defence should the wall
itself be captured.   I went all round the buildings,
and came to the conclusion that his own house would
be the most suitable.   It was strongly built; it had a
raised veranda running round it, and was almost overlooking the left-hand corner of the loopholed wall—
the corner nearest to the *Bunder Abbas*.   This was the
house on the roof of which the Maxim was already
mounted, and from the parapet there it would be easy

to pick off any Afghans who had gained a lodgment on the wall itself. Another point in its favour was that the well was close to it—in the rear.

I urged him to get sand-bags and pile them up round the veranda and in the open door-ways or windows. I also urged upon him the necessity of bringing in food from the telegraph stores and also all the reserve ammunition. All my arguments could not convince him that this was necessary, and he pointed out that, whatever happened, he could not abandon the telegraph instruments in the other building.

"We must keep them working at all costs," he said stubbornly.

He had not said this many seconds before up came a messenger, followed by an excited Eurasian "operator", to tell him that the overland wire to Karachi had been cut again some fifteen miles out.

"That solves part of the difficulty," I said, smiling. "You cannot pass on cable messages, so won't want so many of the staff at work."

He too seemed relieved, and told me that half his fellows had been lining the wall all last night and the other half working the instruments. "They can't keep awake twenty-four hours out of the twenty-four. Now they'll be able to get a little sleep.

"Oh, I forgot," he went on; "a dhow which came in last evening brought some passengers for Old Jask. They stayed here during the night, and are waiting to see me at my office, though how they think I can get them through I don't know. By the way, they brought a letter for your gunner. I've been carrying it about in my pocket. Here it is," and he handed me an envelope addressed in Arabic. "You might give it him."

I caught sight of Miss Borsen coming towards us and evidently wishing to speak to Mr. Fisher; so, as I did not want to worry her with my presence, and had done all I wanted to do, I took the letter and went down the slope to the dinghy and so back to the *Bunder Abbas*.

"Here's a letter for you," I told the gunner. "It's not Jassim's writing this time."

He grinned as he read it.

"It's from the governor of the Muscat fort. He says that Jassim's got out. I didn't imagine he'd keep him there long after my back was turned."

"Well, he won't bother us here," I said, much more amused to think how Mr. Scarlett's dread of him had disappeared than alarmed at any possible danger to myself.

For the rest of the morning and afternoon we kept a good look-out, in case the Afghans made any move; though, except for a few small foraging parties, they simply slumbered or smoked at the foot of the walls, shifting round with the shade as the sun travelled westwards.

It was a great temptation to stir them up with a few shells; though, if we had done so, we should only at the best have driven them out of range and out of sight, and once out of sight we should not have been able to observe their movements. There was another reason—a much more pressing one: we had none too much six-pounder ammunition.

An hour before sunset Mr. Fisher made a signal

that he wanted to see me again, and he came down to the beach to meet me. The Afghans had sent a messenger in to say that they would attack at dawn next morning with twice as many men as they had had yesterday, and he wanted my advice.

"Of course it's only bluff," he said nervously; "but I want you to persuade my wife and Miss Borsen to go aboard the *Bunder Abbas*."

On the way up to the door in the loophooled wall he took me along the trench to see how well his people had been working. They had filled in about a hundred yards of it, and were still busy. Those wretched huts, however, still stood there, right in the line of fire.

"Why the dickens don't you burn them?" I said, really angry, and he was muttering a half-apology when some noise behind me and a warning shout made me turn round.

Not ten yards from me stood Jassim. I knew him at once—how could I forget him?—his face flaming with hatred, the veins of his neck standing out; and in his hand he held a Mauser pistol levelled at me.

He fired, and instinctively I ducked, seized a spade which was lying at my feet, and dashed at him. Mr. Fisher drew a revolver from his pocket and I heard him fire. Then I felt something hit my chest on the right side. It tumbled me over like a rabbit; but I was up again on one knee in time to see Mr. Fisher fire a second shot and Jassim stagger back. He still had those awful eyes fixed on me, glaring death, and as he raised his pistol again I rolled into the trench to escape being hit a second time.

Something filled my throat, and I spat up a lot of bright blood, and felt dazed and foolish. I was trying to get to my feet again when Mr. Fisher came to me with a face as white as a sheet, jumped into the trench, and made me lie back.

"There!" I said, spitting up more blood; "he got me there," and I put my finger where the bullet had hit me.

I felt no pain whatsoever—only a peculiar half-drunk feeling—and tried to sit up again; but this only brought on more coughing, and Mr. Fisher pressed me down.

Then I knew that I should be no more use—only a burden to everyone.

I looked up at him apologetically.

"Get me aboard the '*B. A.*'; I shall be all right soon:" but the effort of speaking forced more blood into my mouth, and I had to stop.

With a frightened expression on his face he bade me stop talking and lie still.

"I'll have you carried down," he said; "wait till we can get a stretcher."

By this time there was a whole crowd of people round me, though I seemed hardly to notice them; someone put my topee over my eyes, to shield them from the slanting sun.

Presently, as if in a dream, I heard Mr. Fisher's voice.

"He's shot through the lung—the right side, thank God!" and someone touched my wrist very gently; and although I could not see her, on account of the topee over my face, I knew it was Miss Borsen's hand.

My mouth filled with blood again, and everything became quite dark and peaceful.

I opened my eyes, feeling most horribly weak, and not knowing what had happened or where I was.

Opposite me were two parallel streaks of white light, and these seemed to hypnotize me. I could not move my eyes from them for a long time; but gradually my brain pulled itself together, and my sense of surroundings came back. I was in a square room with shutter-closed windows all round it. Deep shadows on the whitewashed walls seemed to come from a lamp behind me, and I was lying on a little trestle-bed. Presently I realized that those two streaks of light were made by the moonlight forcing its way in through cracks in one of the shutters, and just below them I saw something white resting on a chest of drawers, and recognized my own topee.

I noticed that I could hardly breathe; something seemed to be squeezing my chest, and I put up one hand—very shakily—to find out what it was. As I did this there was a rustle behind my shoulder, and a very small white hand took hold of mine and put it back where it had lain, and Miss Borsen's voice, sounding ever so far away, told me to lie absolutely still and not attempt to speak.

I felt so extraordinarily weak—just as if I had lost all control of myself—that I obeyed without the slightest effort to resist. I did try to turn my head, but it seemed to be wedged on each side with pillows, and a finger she placed on my forehead stopped me immediately.

I lay quite still, staring at the ceiling and the round patch of light thrown on it by the lamp, until all that had happened came back to me. I looked at my topee to make sure, and the hard luck of being knocked over just when there was so much to be done made me so miserable that I could not help groaning.

"You must not make the least noise or speak; you must not move your hands or feet; it's your only chance," Miss Borsen said, speaking from the head of the bed: and her voice had such a soothing, hypnotizing effect that I closed my eyes and seemed to float away into space almost immediately.

When I woke again Mr. Fisher was sitting by my bedside. He turned quickly when my eyes opened, and he too said the same thing: "Lie absolutely still, and don't speak."

He saw by my face that I wanted to ask him something, and guessed what it was.

"Jassim is dead," he said. "I shot him."

"Poor devil!" I thought, and was sorry.

He then went on to tell me that Mr. Scarlett had been informed of all that had happened, and had come ashore to see me whilst I was asleep, and make all arrangements for the night in case the Afghans attacked.

"We are all ready. Your two men (the signal-man and the man you sent with the Maxim) and I are taking it in turn to keep watch down by the fence all through the night. The signal-man is there now, and half my fellows and twenty of the coolies are lining the wall, so they can't take us by surprise. The greater part of the trench is filled in, and there is nothing more to be done until daylight. I've wired to Muscat to tell the political agent about everything, and of you being wounded, and have asked him to inform the *Intrepid*, but she is not back yet.

"It's nearly midnight now, and my turn for the wire fence. Keep absolutely still, and try to go to sleep until I come back."

He rose—his shadow was thrown on the wall as he bent over to lower the lamp—and I heard him go out.

But sleep was now impossible; my chest was so tightly bandaged that I could hardly breathe, and though I counted all the cracks in the shutter through which the moonlight was showing, counted them time after time until it was almost maddening, sleep would not come.

It seemed ages before I heard a very soft footstep creeping towards me, and the lamp threw the shadow of a woman on the wall, and for a moment the silhouette of Miss Borsen's face.

For a second I had a great longing to ask her if she would forgive me, but I still seemed to be under the spell of her orders not to speak or move, and, fearful of seeing her, I closed my eyes.

She felt my pulse, lowered the lamp the slightest degree more, and I heard her go out as noiselessly as she had entered.

After that the night dragged on somehow. I seemed to be rather delirious, and fancied all sorts of strange things. At one time the shadows on the wall took on the shape of old Popple Opstein, and I thought we were sitting yarning on the little deck outside the cabin; and at another they turned to Jassim, and I thought he was "coming" for me again. Then I thought I was once more trying to carry Miss Borsen down to the dinghy, but my feet would not move, and Jassim was after us. It was horrid.

With the first streaks of daylight I came to my senses again, and waited and waited to hear the sound of firing and the yells of the Afghans charging up to the loopholed wall. I strained my ears to catch the noise of the six-pounder, but all was still. Gradually the light grew stronger, people began moving about in the house, and presently, when it was quite daylight—even though the shutters were closed—Mr. Fisher came in with a joyous expression on his face.

"They've thought better of it," he said. "They're still down there, but aren't making a move.

"Don't talk," he added as he saw I wanted to ask him something, and he brought me a block of note-paper and a pencil. He held the note-paper whilst I wrote in a very shaky way: "Thirsty", for I was most terribly dry.

He gave me some beef-tea of "sorts", holding the cup to my lips. My aunt, but it was good! I could have drunk a bucketful.

I pleaded with my eyes for more, but he shook his head. "Acting under orders—Miss Borsen's orders; can't," he said, and, thinking to relieve my mind, told me that his men were already at work on the trench.

He could only spare me a very few moments, but came in every now and then throughout the day.

Ellis and Hartley occasionally put their heads inside

the door to tell me that everything was quiet, and Mr. Scarlett paid me a visit during the afternoon. He was fearfully apologetic about my wound, and seemed to think it was his fault entirely. In case I wanted them he had brought me a clean uniform and my dispatch-box with all my letters.

"I've been down the slope, sir, to have a look for that chap, Jassim," he said, "but I'm hanged if I can find him."

I was too weak to worry about this.

Mrs. Fisher visited me once and tried to read to me, but the effort was too great for her nerves, so she did not stay very long. Miss Borsen never came near me, and it was the old butler or head boy who was my most constant visitor, bringing me beef-tea and jelly, feeding me, and trying to make me comfortable.

About sunset Hartley came in to tell me that several large bands of Afghans could be seen winding their way down from the mountains in our direction, and when Mr. Fisher came later to confirm this, I wrote on the note-paper block: "Send women to *B. A.*," because I fully expected that the great attack must come next morning.

With very great difficulty he at length persuaded his wife to go aboard the *Bunder Abbas*, but nothing would induce Miss Borsen to accompany her.

"She's got the idea into her head that she's responsible for the two Eurasians and yourself, and is not going to leave any of you till you're on your legs again," Mr. Fisher told me hopelessly.

That night was even more unpleasant than the first, but it did at length pass, and as the daylight crept through the shutters no attack was made—not a rifle was fired. It was very strange, and I could not understand it.

Perhaps an hour later Mr. Fisher came in, looking ghastly.

"We are isolated!" he cried. "They've crept round by the rocks during the night to the cable-house, cut the cable, and must have had a boat helping them, for we cannot find the sea end. I dare not send people out to look for it; they'd never pick it up."

I wrote: "Try. *B. A.* will help," and wrote a signal to Mr. Scarlett to get up steam and go round to the east bay.

Mr. Fisher promised to try, but did not see how they could succeed, as they had no proper grappling gear.

The cutting of the cable seemed to determine him to follow my advice about preparing his house for any emergency. All day I heard people lumbering in and out, and the old butler, looking scared, told me that they were putting sand-bags round the veranda and filling the upper rooms with stores, the most portable of the telegraph apparatus, and ammunition. They even carried sand-bags through my room and piled them up on the balcony outside.

Ellis and Hartley supervised these preparations and kept me informed of what the *Bunder Abbas* was doing; and when, later on, I heard a good deal of rifle firing and one or two rounds from her six-pounder, they told me that the Afghans were sniping at the boat whilst it was trying to grapple the end of the cable.

I could not help wondering whether this was very soothing to Mrs. Fisher's nerves, and I pictured her in the cabin with that six-pounder going off just below her, and wishing that she had remained on shore. At sunset they reported that the boat had returned, unsuccessful, and that the *Bunder Abbas* had steamed round to her former anchorage.

I now had not spoken for forty-eight hours, and had lain like a log all the time. I felt distinctly stronger, and no blood had come into my throat and mouth since the early morning.

I slept fairly well that third night, and was awakened from a nightmare by real shrieking and yelling, by the firing of hundreds of rifles beneath the windows, and the tut-tut-tut-tut of the Maxim on the roof above me. A moment later came the comforting sound of the six-pounder and the noise of the other Maxim aboard the "*B. A.*".

Not a soul could I hear stirring in the house, and the feeling of being left quite alone, without knowing what was happening and how things were going, was almost insupportable. A bullet, splintering a shutter, flattened itself against the wall over my bed and dropped with a thud on the floor, a shower of plaster following it, and some dropping on my face. Outside the wall of the room there was a sound as if men were hammering on the stonework, and I gradually realized that these were bullets, not hammers.

The horrid noises seemed to be drawing closer, and I thought that they were growing louder away to the right, where those huts stood.

CHAPTER XVIII

To the Rescue

As I lay there on my trestle-bed, groaning at my miserable position, more bullets came in through the shutters and brought down showers of plaster from the wall behind me.

At last I could stand the strain no longer, and was on the point of trying to reach the shutters and open them, so that at least I could see what was happening, when Miss Borsen, white as a sheet, came in, and, seeing me with one leg over·the side of the bed, bade me angrily to lie down and not move or speak.

I lay down, but had to speak to tell her to crouch on the floor, out of the way of the bullets, and the effort made more of that blood come into my mouth. Down I lay as flat as a pancake, and she huddled on the floor too, because, whilst she was bending over me to wipe the blood from my mouth, another bullet had smacked up against the wall and sprinkled her with plaster.

She crouched there, her face twitching as the Maxim overhead rattled, and the clamour and shrieking outside, coming from the direction of the slope and barbed-wire fence, seemed to grow nearer and louder.

At last the appalling uproar sounded as if it were

right under the loopholed wall itself—almost under the windows of the house.   Ellis's Maxim stopped—stopping, I realized, because the loopholed wall now screened the Afghans from its fire; but the Maxim aboard the "*B. A.*" fired more vigorously than ever, and six-pounder shells were bursting rapidly, one after the other, quite close beneath us.

Miss Borsen had buried her face in her hands.   Suddenly she raised herself, and, with open mouth and eyes, listened.   The character of the yells had altered; they were screams now, they were going away from us.   The attack was failing.

The Maxim on the roof opened again as the Afghans fell back from the cover of the loopholed wall.   I heard Ellis and Hartley shouting joyously, and knew they had got them on the run.

The second attack had been driven back.

Miss Borsen gave a great gulp and sprang to a shutter, opened it, and looked out.   In a moment she had recoiled, covering her eyes with her hands.

"They're flying down the slope; those awful white heaps are growing near the fence.   Oh God, it is awful!" she cried, and she burst into tears and ran away.

Ellis's Maxim ceased firing, and gradually all became quiet.

In perhaps half an hour Mr. Fisher ran in to see me—flushed and excited.   He stopped for a moment when he saw the blood-stain on my pillow, but then burst out with: "We've beaten them off! we've beaten them off!   Thank God!   Now they'll go!   I'm sure they'll go!   The Maxim from the *Bunder Abbas* got them whilst they were crowded under the wall and crumpled them up—crumpled them up—swept them down!"

Ellis came in too, grinning as he reported: "That little lot 'as gone 'ome—what was left of them, sir— 'oping as 'ow you're going on all right; but we ain't more'n 'arf a beltful of cartridges left, sir, that we ain't. If it 'adn't been for them blooming 'uts they'd never 'ave got near 'arfway."

Mr. Fisher jerked out: "It's no good burning the huts now. They'll go back to the mountains to-night! I'm certain they will! It's no use burning them now!"

He had been very enthusiastic about the slaughter and the terrible punishment the Afghans had received, but when he came to count the dead there were only thirty-two on the slope; and although that meant thirty-two fewer Afghans, it was more than counter-balanced by a very grave signal from Mr. Scarlett saying that he had fired forty-eight rounds of six-pounder ammunition and eight hundred rounds from the Maxim, leaving only thirty-five more six-pounder and three thousand rifle and Maxim rounds on board. This meant, as I knew only too well, that to repulse one more attack would leave the "B. A." practically helpless to assist again.

I kept this knowledge to myself, and sent a signal to Mr. Scarlett to come and see me and bring ashore with him another thousand rounds of ammunition for Ellis's Maxim.

A good deal of firing began again, as if to contradict Mr. Fisher's optimism, and I heard isolated shots, from a considerable distance, with occasionally the smack of a bullet on the outer wall of the house, though, as no one was with me, I did not know what was actually happening.

Presently the gunner arrived, with a very long face. "I was careful as I could be, sir, but you know what it is, and things looked so precious ugly at one time that we had to fire fast. It's my belief they simply did it a' purpose, just to make us waste ammunition. They haven't lost heart over it either, for they're skulking all over the place, down among the trees round the Old Fort, and along the beach. They potted at me all the way from the '*B. A.*', that they did. They are firing at everyone who shows his nose outside the wall, and none of these here people can go on with levelling the breastwork. They've given that up as a bad job and gone inside again.

"It's a nasty bit of work this, sir, and the sooner I have you safe and sound aboard the '*B. A.*', sir, the better I shall be pleased. And the little lady too; she ought to come and keep Mrs. Fisher company. Mrs. Fisher, sir," he added, lowering his voice and smiling grimly, "tried to come ashore again, but I locked her up in the cabin before I started, and told Percy to shove her breakfast through the port-hole."

I smiled too, for I could quite imagine him doing this, and not wasting any words over it either.

"It was the only thing I could do, for the cabin's made of good steel plate, and if she'd been left to wander round she might have been hit by some of them bullets," he explained.

"I'm certain we shall find them gone to-morrow morning," Mr. Fisher cried, coming abruptly into the room; "and if we don't, the Muscat people will know that the cable is interrupted and something wrong, so will tell the *Intrepid* as soon as she gets back from the coast. We shall have her here in no time."

" Do you know that we've only got enough ammunition for one more show like this morning? That's a fact," Mr. Scarlett growled, turning furiously on him. " This is going to be a regular siege; none of your rushing and firing, packing up and going home again. Them Afghans mean to get inside here, and if we can't stop them you can't. The sooner everyone comes aboard the '*B. A.*' safe and sound, and waits there for the *Intrepid*—well—the sooner the better. This isn't any darned tomfoolery business, I tell you —twenty times I'll tell you. If your chaps can't stand a few bullets smacking among 'em down by that trench," he went on savagely, " they'd better get along ramming sand into more sacks, bags, anything they can get hold of, and make this house shipshape."

I don't think that Mr. Fisher much cared about being spoken to like that.

" If you can get any work out of them you're welcome to try; I can't," he said sharply. " They've been awake and working, off and on, for the last thirty hours."

" Right you are, sir; you bet I will. If I can't do a bit of slave-driving there is no one in the British Navy who can," and, taking him at his word, Mr. Scarlett darted off.

He had hardly gone when Hartley ran in to say that a hundred or more Afghans had rushed up the slope from the Old Fort, and behind the sand-hills there.

"

" They've gone and 'idden among those blessed huts, sir."

Firing broke out again almost immediately, and bullets came thudding against the wall outside my room. Mr. Fisher darted away to line the loopholed wall with his men, and Hartley, singing out: "They're trying to knock out the Maxim; Ellis and me must get more sand-bags round it," disappeared too.

I knew that if one lucky bullet pierced the water-jacket the gun would be useless, and I lay there listening to Ellis and Hartley cursing, as they dragged heavy weights across the roof over my head, and to the patter-patter of bullets thudding against the outer wall and parapet.

Those chaps must not be allowed to stay down by the huts—that was imperative. If they got a firm footing there the others would join them during the night, and they would be within a stone's throw of the loopholed wall. Others could creep round at the foot of the rocks on the east of the building and attack the wall on that side; we could not stop them. Mr. Scarlett and Mr. Fisher both came to my room, and both were of the same opinion.

" I'll signal to the '*B. A.*' to plug in a few shells till they see us come out of the door, and Ellis and Hartley can work the Maxim, whilst we rush down and drive 'em out," Mr. Scarlett said, his eyes glowing with excitement. What a change had come over him!

"And we'll burn the huts whilst we're about it," Mr. Fisher added in a crest-fallen, disappointed, rather shamefaced manner.

The two of them went away to collect some men,

and I heard either Ellis or Hartley running down the stairs from the roof to join them. Firing went on vigorously from the direction of those huts. I heard the buzz of excited voices as people collected under the windows, somewhere near the door in the wall, and waited to hear it opened and the sortie commence. Presently "boom" came the report of the six-pounder from the "*B. A.*", and the Maxim overhead began rattling. Then the bolts of the door were thrown back, and I heard Mr. Scarlett's voice yelling hoarsely, "Come along," and the crush of people pressing out through the door-way after him with rather half-hearted cheers.

Miss Borsen entered the room and stood listening. "They've left me all alone," she said; "I am frightened," and the next moment, with a scared face, was at a window looking down the slope.

"They are rushing down," she cried. "Mr. Fisher and your gunner and the man ahead of the others. A shell has just burst in the huts. I can't see anyone firing at them. Oh, Mr. Fisher has tumbled down! He's up again. He's catching up your gunner." The Maxim overhead ceased firing. "Now they're right among the huts. The telegraph people are nearly there—yes, they've got there too. Some of them have cans with them—paraffin cans. There they go! there they go! The Afghans are bolting down the slope! Smoke's coming out of the huts. Why don't they come back?

"Now they're coming. Your gunner is helping Mr. Fisher. He's hurt; I know he is. I must go and see " and she ran away again.

The "*B. A.*" fired a few rounds of precious Maxim ammunition, and by the time all was quiet Mr. Scarlett had come to tell me, with a chuckle, that "That little business is all done correct, sir. Mr. Fisher got a bullet through his left shoulder, but it ain't done much damage."

Soon I heard the crackle of the flames and smelt the smoke from those huts, so knew they would not bother us any more.

That bullet through his shoulder muscles (I think it broke off a bit of bone there) seemed to alter Mr Fisher completely. When I saw him next—rather pale, and with his arm in a sling—he had given up all pretence of imagining that the Afghans would retire. In fact it was he now who suggested, feverishly, doing things to make the house ready to stand an assault. "But for goodness' sake," he told me, "don't let anyone suggest abandoning the telegraph buildings or going aboard the *Bunder Abbas*. I won't do so until the very last moment—I can't—I daren't. If the Afghans got inside for even half an hour they'd wreck the whole of the transmitting instruments, and it would be six months before the cable would work again."

With Mr. Scarlett, Ellis, and Hartley to help him, the four of them began to get things into order, divide the people into parties—those they could trust with rifles into batches, under Eurasians, to man the wall whilst the others rested; those for whom there were no rifles, or who couldn't be trusted with them, being set to work to complete the defence and provision the house.

All the rest of that day they laboured; the house was turned upside down and a litter of sand-bags filled up every aperture in the walls and along the verandas and balconies. Pillow-covers, blankets, sheets, everything that could be made to hold sand was requisitioned — and I could not help smiling when finally two burly nigger Zanzibaris dragged through my room one of Mrs. Fisher's dresses bulged out with sand and threw it on top of a wall of other sand-bags blocking a window. It was a jolly good thing that she was safely out of the way, and I wished most earnestly that Miss Borsen could be induced to go as well.

After the Afghans had been driven from the huts, and these had been burnt to the ground, they remained quiet for the rest of the day. Mr. Scarlett returned to the "*B. A.*", the sun set, there was a very unpleasant half-hour before the moon rose sufficiently to give light, and almost as soon as it did so distant firing began—a scattered occasional shot every now and again, quite sufficient, however, to keep everyone on the alert and nervous. The old head boy brought me some food and fed me. He also brought me a lamp, for which I was very grateful, as on account of the sand-bags in the windows the moonlight could not enter, and it was almost completely dark.

This was, I think, the worst night since my wound; for the atmosphere of the room was stuffy and smelly, hardly a breath of air came through the blocked windows, rifle bullets occasionally thudded up against the sand-bags, and with Mr. Fisher wounded I did not know who was carrying on in command in case the

Afghans attacked during the night. Why they didn't Heaven knows. If they had done so there was nothing to keep them out; but I suppose that they would not depart from their usual habits. At any rate they waited till dawn, when just the same awful din broke out, and they made just such another rush up the slope. The "*B. A.*" chipped in as she had done before, and eventually the attack recoiled; but I had counted twenty-three rounds of six-pounder, so knew that for all practical purposes she had none left—not half a dozen, anyway.

Mr. Scarlett almost immediately reported by signal —ammunition remaining—four six-pounder, twelve hundred Maxim and rifle. At the same time Mr. Fisher, haggard and drawn, staggered in to tell me that although the main body had been repulsed a large number had succeeded in reaching the fifteen-foot wall on the east side and could not be dislodged.

"They're there now," he said hopelessly. "We can't touch them; they're firing up through the loop-holes. They tried to climb the wall, but I got some of my men and your man Ellis to fire from the roof of an outbuilding close there, and they've cleared them off. What shall we do? Could the *Bunder Abbas* steam round and drive them away?" As this seemed reasonable I wrote out a signal telling Mr. Scarlett to raise steam at once and come round to the east bay. But the "*B. A.*" could not move for at least two hours, and meanwhile Ellis and his few natives remained on top of that outbuilding, lying down behind the parapet ready to pick off any Afghan who attempted to climb the wall. More ammunition and some sand-bags were sent across to him to make his position more secure. However, the Afghans were quite content to wait where they were—under the foot of the wall—and made no offensive movement.

If they had done so the time might have gone by more quickly. As it was, it seemed an eternity before Hartley reported that the *Bunder Abbas* was under way.

Perhaps half an hour afterwards I heard her Maxim firing—at a great distance seemingly—firing only a few of her precious rounds and then ceasing.

It turned out that she had driven the Afghans away from the rocks near the cable house, but owing to the contour of the ground she could not reach the fellows under the wall itself. She stayed there to prevent any reinforcements joining them, and then had to come back hastily again because more parties of enemy were taking advantage of her absence from the west bay to creep along the beach there—the beach where we always landed in the dinghy—to try to find a lodgment under the opposite wall of the telegraph-station.

However, the Maxim on the roof kept those in check, and directly the "*B. A.*" appeared round the end of the peninsula they all fled back to the New Fort.

One thing gave me much relief: we had not expended many rounds of ammunition.

The situation was now alarming, to say the least of it. If those fellows stayed where they were there was nothing to prevent them climbing the wall during the night, and Mr. Fisher explained (and I was perfectly convinced) that if they did this most of our natives would simply bolt. The Eurasians might put up some sort of a fight, but there were only eight of them now unwounded and they were almost exhausted.

We both realized that there were only two courses open: the first, to abandon the telegraph-station and take refuge aboard the *Bunder Abbas*; the second, practically to abandon the *Bunder Abbas* and bring her white crew on shore with their rifles and the few remaining rounds of ammunition.

As Mr. Fisher absolutely refused to consent to the first, the second plan was the only alternative. I decided to do this. First of all I took the block of note-paper and wrote: " Miss Borsen must be sent to *Bunder Abbas*"; but she, coming into the room at this moment, read what I had written and shook her head. She said there was work for her to do here and she wouldn't leave it; she stamped her foot angrily when Mr. Fisher implored her to go.

So I sent for Mr. Scarlett, and with my scribbled notes and Mr. Fisher's explanations we made him understand.

He was very furious, and "swung off" at Mr. Fisher for exposing everyone to such risks, doing his utmost to point out the horrible consequences which might happen if once the *Bunder Abbas* was abandoned and escape cut off, looking at me to back him up.

He felt that this second plan was more a disgrace to us than the abandoning of the station would be to Mr. Fisher; instead, he offered to bring ashore all the men he could spare, make a sortie, and drive the Afghans away from that side wall just as he and Mr. Fisher had driven them from the huts yesterday. He would bring his men ashore during the few minutes of dark after sunset (when they might hope to escape observation), lead them round the west wall and the wall towards the end of the peninsula, and then swoop along the eastern fifteen-foot wall from the top end. The Afghans would never expect an attack from that quarter, and whilst he was doing this he wanted Mr. Fisher (if his damaged shoulder let him), Ellis, and Hartley, with as many men as possible, to make a sortie through the door in the wall facing the slope, to creep along the face of that wall to the corner, and thus catch the enemy between two fires.

I, too, hated so much the idea of abandoning the "*B. A.*" that I nodded my head in consent, and, having made all the arrangements with Mr. Fisher, he went back to the dinghy, though not before Mr. Fisher had implored Miss Borsen again, unavailingly, to accompany him. Not long afterwards he made a signal that he had determined to bring all hands with him, and that until they returned the "*B. A.*" would be quite safe at her anchor.

I only hoped that she would, and I lay there dejected in the extreme, to think that now, of all times, I was helpless. It was no use pretending that I was not. Even without Miss Borsen to assure me that my only chance lay in remaining absolutely still, there was a funny feeling in my chest that the least exertion would finish me altogether. One or two drops of blood had come into my mouth during the day, and I instinctively knew that more was only waiting its chance. It was an extremely unhappy position to be in.

The remainder of the afternoon passed fairly quietly, and the dread of the coming night seemed to make the hours of daylight fly very quickly. Miss Borsen brought me some tea, and whilst she was in the room I remembered some signal I wanted to make to Mr. Scarlett. But the pencil had dropped off the bed and broken its point, so that it would not write, and I motioned to her that there was a knife in my dispatch-box. Whilst she was looking for it, jumbling among my letters and other papers, out slipped that little velvet bow, the one which had stuck to my button the night I had carried her over the swamp and made her so angry.

She picked it up, grew red, and I thought she was very angry at being reminded of the quarrel; because she shut up the box, said: "Bother the knife; it isn't here," and went away, sending in Hartley to help me with the signal.

This added to my worries.

As dark came on—very completely in the room, because of the sand-bags—I pictured the dinghy pulling to and fro to land Mr. Scarlett and the rest of the crew, and had a horrid feeling that they ought never to have left her. I feared, too, that they had not done this unobserved, because a good deal of firing broke out from the direction of the beach. However, there was no one to tell me what was happening, so I had to guess, listening anxiously to the murmur of voices outside, below the balcony, as Mr. Fisher and the others gathered near the door in the wall and prepared for their sortie.

I could hear them filling the magazines of their

rifles, occasionally dropping a cartridge on the ground, and my ears were straining to hear the bolts fly back and to hear them rushing out; but instead of this a tremendous fusillade broke out down the slope, and the same yelling which had always accompanied the previous attacks broke the silence. So fearfully excited was I that more blood came into my mouth, and thoroughly frightened I lay flat, hardly able to breathe. The noises seemed to grow until they became one awful roar, dinning into my ear-drums till they seemed to overpower my brain altogether, and I must have lost consciousness.

I had a dim recollection of men running through my room, of rifles going off, and then woke to the fact that rifles were being fired quite close to me, outside on the balcony, their flashes lighting up the room, and that from every quarter came the most fearful uproar. People were running backwards and forwards, up and down the stairs; Zanzibari niggers came dragging sand-bags back through my room; the old butler, without his turban, came and went without giving a glance at me; no one seemed to take the least notice of me, and for some time I thought it must be another of those nightmares and I should presently waken.

Then the uproar seemed to grow more distant; a red glow filled the room with weird shadows, and what finally brought me to a realization that I was actually awake was Miss Borsen's hand sliding down to my wrist to feel my pulse.

"Hush!" she whispered; "keep still; you're all right now. They've got inside the walls and have gone off to burn down the other buildings. Mr. Fisher is down below—most of the others too; we are safe for some time."

I remembered that Mr. Scarlett and all the rest of my men ought to be on the outside of the wall, and wondered what had become of them.

"Mr. Scarlett?" I muttered, but she put a finger on my lips. "Be quiet; be still."

The niggers and servants must have torn away some of the sand-bags to make better openings to fire through or to take them somewhere else, for the room now was filled with a red glare. The crackling noise of flames seemed to grow more furious and closer; but above everything I heard Hartley's voice down below shouting orders.

It was a comfort even to know that he was there.

Then men began to climb the stairs outside the room, panting heavily and running down again. Miss Borsen went out to see what they were doing. She crept back, terrified.

"They're carrying water up to the roof—the flames are so close. It's awful—awful!" and she crouched on the floor with her hands over her eyes. She pulled herself together when Hartley—bleeding from a wound on his head—rushed in to tell me that we were fairly safe for the present, but that Ellis and a few natives on the top of that outbuilding, where they had been all day, were cut off, and that no one knew what had become of Mr. Scarlett and his party. "What with the moonlight and these 'ere flames from the mess buildings," he said, "it's as light as day now, and the Afghans won't come out in the open. They're skulking in the shadows under the walls, and daren't run across the open spaces."

After this—for a time—there was but little rifle firing near us, and the glare from the burning building died down somewhat. Outside on the balcony I could see the Zanzibaris there moving about in the shadow behind the sand-bags and peering over them to look below. Presently one of them saw something to fire at, for he let off his rifle and called to the others. A regular fusillade broke out, and in the midst of it I heard, to my intense relief, Mr. Scarlett's stentorian voice roaring out: "Stop that firing," and then shouting something in Hindustani.

Before I realized what was the meaning of this Miss Borsen sprang to her feet and was out on the balcony in a moment, pulling the wretched servants and Zanzibaris away from the sand-bags and calling out: "Stop! stop!

"It's Mr. Scarlett and your men climbing over the loopholed wall," she cried. "They are crawling over the corner just below us."

In a very few minutes Mr. Scarlett was standing in the room.

"We got caught on the 'hop' that time, sir; they saw us coming ashore and we had a fight for it. Managed to get up the slope near the wall, but then had to fall back again. Couldn't make headway against them. Jones was wounded again—badly this time. Most of the chaps were knocked about, so we dragged him back among the rocks and kept the Afghans off till they cleared out up here to join in the loot. We found the dinghy on the rocks with her bottom stove in, so couldn't send Jones on board, and we've brought him along with us—dodged the Afghans and hoisted him in over the wall. He's down below—pretty comfortable; but Moore's missing. No one's seen him since we had the first 'scrap', poor devil. I hope he's killed outright.

" Don't you go fussing," he went on. " There's five of us, besides Hartley and me, and we'll pull you through—and the little lass too. We're just off to line the veranda and the sand-bags there till those devils come at us again at daybreak. They'll come sure enough then. I'm off now, sir."

He left me alone again, for Miss Borsen had slipped away directly she had heard that there was another wounded man below, and she did not come back.

To know that Mr. Scarlett and his men were safe and were on the veranda below put heart into me; but the position seemed so desperate that I wonder my brain didn't throb itself out of my skull that night. It seemed to be trying to do so. The noise of the flames had died down; but scattered rifle shots rang out in the compound below every few minutes hour after hour, and the room seemed to be so full of smoke that I could hardly breathe. The old butler, going out to the balcony with food for the people there, gave me some water once, and I was very grateful.

Towards dawn there was an almost complete lull, as if everyone was too tired to go on shooting. Mr. Scarlett took this opportunity to come in and tell me that, so far, the Afghans had not broken into the building where the transmitting instruments were.

They had to cross the concrete tennis-court to get to it, and Ellis and his people had kept them out so far. "We've done our little bit too, sir," he added, quite pleased with himself.

As dawn broke the Afghans first turned their attention to that outbuilding from the roof of which Ellis had punished them so heavily during the night. Of course I could not see this, but heard the uproar and the shooting, and in the middle of it Mr. Scarlett and Mr. Fisher came in (his left arm bound to his side) looking very anxious.

"We'll have to go along and bring Ellis out of it," the gunner said; "he and his chaps can't hold out much longer. Don't you worry, sir; we'll be back in a 'brace of shakes'." Stooping, before he left me, he placed a revolver on the chair at the head of the bed. "If you want it, sir," he said, and I understood.

They both went away, and I knew that they were going to lead another sortie across the compound and that open tennis-court. I heard them run down the stairs, heard the burst of cheering as they and others dropped down from the veranda, whilst the natives still on my balcony crowded away to the right of it and opened fire.

Almost immediately the noise of fierce hand-to-hand fighting came through the windows, and I waited, tremblingly, to hear the cheers which would tell me that Mr. Scarlett's people were coming back with Ellis; but, instead, the Afghans began yelling triumphantly, as if they were getting the upper hand. I turned my head and saw Miss Borsen stagger into the room, her face whiter than the dress she wore.

She stood still for a moment, listening, then saw the revolver, glided across and steadied herself to pick it up and to open it. She made sure it was loaded, and then, in a broken voice, told me that Mr. Fisher, Mr. Scarlett, and the rest had been cut off and forced back against the telegraph building.

"The Afghans are flocking down here now, and there is no one left in the house—only a few of the telegraph people down below, and they can't do it," she moaned. Then she stood at the side of my bed and handed me the revolver, saying, in a very low voice: "If the Afghans break in I want you to kill me."

She looked me through and through as I took it, as though she was not certain that she could rely on me; but then she seemed satisfied, for she knelt down close to the bed, with her head just above the edge of it, staring fixedly out to where the daylight grew and to where a surging wave of roaring, savage yells seemed to be beating round and against the whole house.

The Zanzibaris began coming back into the room from the balcony, grey with fright, running, throwing away their rifles and looking for somewhere to hide, taking not the slightest notice of us.

It was "all up" with us now, I felt sure, and I had to speak to her before the end did come.

"Will you forgive me?" I asked. "You know what for! I'm sorry."

She put out a hand and touched mine, the one which held the revolver, and said: "I have—for a long time." Then she turned her head away.

There we stayed—for how long I do not know—
and although every moment I expected to hear the
Afghans breaking into the rooms below us and charging up the stairs, and knew what I should have to do
then, I felt quite happy.

Suddenly, among all the furious tumult and clamour
below and all round us, I heard, we both heard,
another sound—the sound of cheering—cheering loud
and lusty.   All the noises seemed to die away before
it; it grew; nearer and nearer it came; it swelled
through the windows, across those sand-bags, in a
continued shout of victory; rifle firing died down as
though by magic, then burst out again; those shouts
of despair which we knew so well by this time
filled the whole of the compound, and Miss Borsen,
springing to the balcony, tore away a sand-bag, looked
down, and rushed back to me.

"The *Intrepid*!" she cried, fell on her knees, and
sobbed as if her heart would break.

CHAPTER XIX

The Grey-eyed Lady Decides

DEAR old Popple Opstein was the first to find us, rushing up the stairs two steps at a time, calling out my name, and bursting into the room, his yellow hair standing up from his forehead like a parrot's, and his eyes staring out of his violet face.

Miss Borsen flung herself at him, clinging to his great sunburnt hands, laughing and crying hysterically. She would not let him do more than grip my hand, taking him away very quickly for fear the excitement should start the bleeding again, although I imagined that if the agony of that last half-hour had not done so nothing else would.

Presently she brought Nicholson, who came lumbering into the room, fat and jolly as ever, felt my pulse, heard what she had to say about me, and told me the same old thing: "Just you lie still, absolutely still, and don't speak". He promised to come and overhaul me properly later on.

" I've a terrible lot of jobs on hand now," he said.

He must have given orders for no one to visit me, because I was left entirely alone, impatient to hear of all that had happened, and listening to the heavy booming of guns—the *Intrepid's* guns, out at sea—

shelling the retreating Afghans. At least I imagined that was what they were doing.

In about an hour's time the old head boy brought another trestle-bed into my room, and, whilst I was wondering who was going to use it, Mr. Scarlett was carried in, quite unconscious, his head swathed in bandages.

Nicholson followed, and told me that he had had "the devil's own whack" with the butt end of a rifle, and there was no knowing what would happen.

The reaction after the strain of the last four days was now very great, and there was no disguising the fact that I was as weak as a cat. I had had no real sleep for at least four nights, and listening to the long, slow, snoring noise coming from Mr. Scarlett's bed made me drop off to sleep too. When I woke it was night, but by the light of the lamp I saw Percy —a melancholy-looking figure in white—squatting on the floor at the side of the gunner's bed, with his eyes fixed on his hero's bandaged head. He turned and smiled at me when I moved, but only for a moment, turning again like some big faithful dog to watch the gunner.

For two whole days the only other people I saw were Nicholson, who doctored me, and the head boy —his yellow turban once more as smart as a new pin —who brought me food and fed me.

At the end of those two days Mr. Scarlett began to show signs of returning consciousness, and Percy, who had not left him day or night, wept tears of joy when his eyes opened and he asked where he was.

Popple Opstein was now allowed to come and talk to me.

From him I heard how the *Intrepid* had been called away from Muscat, on what turned out to be a wild-goose chase, after some dhow reported to be loading rifles down the coast; how she had heard on her return that Jask telegraph-station had been attacked in force and the telegraph cut; and how she had come across at full speed.

"I'm almost certain Jassim was the chap who brought the news which took us down the coast. We heard he'd shot you dangerously, and I put two and two together. My dear old chap, I was in the dickens of a funk. The skipper had the men all ready waiting to land; they were over the side and in the boats almost before the anchor dropped, and we were only just in time. Your fellows were all pushed up against the side of the building, with a crowd of chaps howling round them, and were getting the worst of it, half of them laid out already. Another half-hour and it would have been 'finish'."

He gave me a list of the casualties, and they were very severe. Jones had died of his wounds, and Moore's body had been found on the rocks close to the smashed dinghy, with three dead Afghans near him; so the poor, irritating chap had made a great fight for his life. There was not a single one of the "*B. A.*" 's who had not a wound of "sorts".

Mrs. Fisher had come ashore from the "*B. A.*", but her nerves were so completely shaken that she intended to go down to Karachi very shortly. Miss Borsen was to accompany her. Both of them visited

me occasionally, but always together, and I was longing for the day to come when Nicholson would give
me permission to talk, because I had much to tell the
little, sad, grey-eyed lady, and much, very much, to
ask her.   At last came the great day when I was
allowed to sit out on the veranda and talk—just a
little—as long as I did not raise my voice.   By this
time Mr. Scarlett was very nearly his old self, or,
rather, his new self, once more; and Percy was so
happy that we had to make the head boy kick him
—half a dozen times a day—to stop him singing to
himself.   We now had crowds of visitors, from Commander Duckworth, Mr. Fisher (his shoulder nearly
well), and Popple Opstein, down to Jaffa, clean and
white and as impenetrable as ever.   The one I wanted
most was Miss Borsen, but she seldom came, and
then only with Mrs. Fisher.   As I recovered, so she
seemed to shrink from coming near me, and I counted
the days before she was to sail for Karachi in fear lest
I should never have a chance of speaking to her alone.

One evening, as Mr. Scarlett and I were sitting on
the veranda, watching the last glow of the sunset
on the Baluchistan mountains, Popple' Opstein came
bounding up the stairs and out to us.

"We've just got the news!" he cried excitedly.
"There's going to be a great 'show' here.   The
Indian Government is sending a whole brigade from
Karachi, the Persian Government has ordered round
the old *Persepolis* with a lot of troops, the flagship's
on her way from Bombay, and we're going to land
a naval brigade—with guns.   There's to be a regular
expedition into the mountains to punish those Afghans,

and who d'you think is going in charge of the guns? Why, you, old chap, you! The skipper has just sent me along to tell you the great news. The Indian Government has asked for you. Just fancy that! It's a reward for collaring that caravan. 'Nick' says you'll be as fit as ever by the time everything's ready to start. I am so glad, old chap, and you bet I'll find some excuse for coming along as well, even if it's only to carry old Nick's 'first-aid' bag."

"What a ripping show!" I said, tremendously pleased, and Mr. Scarlett came over to congratulate me, as pleased as I was.

My chum fidgeted about, and although it was now too dark for me to see his face I knew that he had something else to tell me.

"Out with it! What is it?" I asked.

Smacking his knees, he burst out with: "I've done it! Old Martin, I've done it!"

"Done what?"

"Don't you know? Can't you guess? Little 'Grey-eyes' and I are engaged—engaged! What d'you think of that, old tongue-tied? I've felt it would come ever since we met her in the steamer coming out, and the last few days have done the trick. Isn't it glorious? She goes home to-morrow, worse luck! but I couldn't let her go without telling her, and we're to be spliced as soon as ever I get back to England. You'll have to do 'best man'. You will, won't you?"

It was dark. I stuttered out how pleased I was, and he, too excited to suspect anything, dashed downstairs again, singing lustily.

"D'you think you could manage to take me along with you, sir, when you land in charge of those guns?" Mr. Scarlett asked me diffidently.

"I will," I told him. "We'll land together, and have another smack at those Afghans—the treacherous brutes. We'll go back to the old '*B. A.*' to-morrow morning, doctor or no doctor. We can't stay loafing round here any longer. I'm sick of being a cripple."

The night air seemed to have turned cold, so we went back into our whitewashed room with its bullet marks on the wall behind my bed, and as Mr. Scarlett lighted the lamp we heard Popple Opstein whistling "Two Eyes of Grey" somewhere down the slope towards the beach.

"That used to be your tune," Mr. Scarlett said as he closed the shutters; "d'you remember, sir—a while back? It used to get on my nerves at times; that it did!"